Picture Her Dead

Also by Lin Anderson:

Driftnet
Torch
Deadly Code
Dark Flight
Easy Kill
Final Cut
The Reborn

Picture Her Dead

Lin Anderson

HODDER &
STOUGHTON

First published in Great Britain in 2011 by Hodder & Stoughton
An Hachette UK company

2

Copyright © Lin Anderson 2011

The right of Lin Anderson to be identified as the Author
of the Work has been asserted by her in accordance with the
Copyright, Designs and Patents Act 1988.

A CIP catalogue record for this title is available from the British Library

Hardback ISBN 978 0 340 99292 0
Trade Paperback ISBN 978 0 340 99293 7

Typeset in Sabon MT by Palimpsest Book Production Limited,
Falkirk, Stirlingshire

Printed and bound by Clays Ltd, St Ives plc

Hodder & Stoughton policy is to use papers that are natural,
renewable and recyclable products and made from wood grown in
sustainable forests. The logging and manufacturing processes are
expected to conform to the environmental regulations of the
country of origin.

Hodder & Stoughton Ltd
338 Euston Road
London NW1 3BH

www.hodder.co.uk

Acknowledgements

Thanks to Dr Jennifer Miller of GUARD, DCI Kenny Bailey (retired), Andy Rolph, R2S CRIME Forensic Services Manager, and in particular the staff at the British Heart Foundation Shop, Dumbarton Road, Partick (formerly The Rosevale Cinema), Christine Lindsay, playwright and old film reel aficionado.

I have taken some liberties with the Rosevale, restoring its beautiful foyer and wonderful Highland frieze and inserting a fictional basement. All the characters therein are entirely fictional.

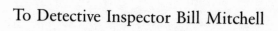

To Detective Inspector Bill Mitchell

Glasgow – Cinema City

Seventy years ago, Glasgow was home to over 130 'picture palaces' which could accommodate an astounding 175,000 film fans every day. With more cinemas per person than any other city outside America, Glasgow earned the title 'Cinema City'.

I

The manager slipped the key in the lock and turned it, and the click sent a shiver of anticipation through Jude. As the door swung open, light from behind her formed shadows in the darkness. She thought she could make out a ticket booth and a distant staircase.

'The switch is on your left just inside the partition door,' the woman told her. 'It only lights up the foyer, I'm afraid.'

'It's OK, I came prepared.' Jude showed her the large torch she'd brought with her.

'I can't leave the shop to go in with you.'

'I'll be fine on my own,' Jude assured her. 'I really appreciate you letting me take a look.'

'Rather you than me. I wouldn't go in there alone if you paid me.' The woman checked her watch. 'We close the shop at five. How long were you planning to be?'

Jude's heart sank. 'I was hoping for a little longer. I wanted to take some photographs.'

The woman thought for a minute. 'There's a fire exit off the balcony which takes you down to a back lane. I suppose you could leave that way. But you'd need to make sure you closed the door behind you.'

'That would be great. And I'll be sure to shut the door. I promise.'

The woman hesitated as though already regretting the

offer, but then gave a quick nod and headed back to the charity shop.

Jude waited until the clip of her heels had faded before locating the light switch and flicking it on. The shadows immediately dispersed, revealing a beautiful circular entrance foyer.

'Wow!' Jude breathed, gazing round in delight.

She knew from her research that the foyer's design was distinctive, but the reality was so much better. A terrazzo-patterned floor radiated from a central island paybox, still intact. Above this, the ceiling rose to form an intricately worked plaster dome, encircled by a painted mural of a Highland scene. In the centre was a ten-point Art Deco light fitment.

Jude extracted her precious camera and flash gun from the backpack. She would take a set of digital stills, followed by a 360-degree video recording. She began where she was, looking towards the ticket booth, with the wide carpeted staircase beyond.

This was what people would have seen when they entered the cinema in its heyday. Even in its present state, nothing could detract from the feeling of opulence; not the peeling paint, nor the scent of dust and misuse. Most of the other derelict cinemas she'd visited had been damp and mouldy, but in here the air was warm and dry.

Once she had a set of stills Jude switched to video and began recording with a voiceover. She set the place, date and time and gave a potted history of the Rosevale. Then she began a slow circular sweep of the foyer, recording her impressions as she went.

When she was satisfied she had enough material, she

checked her watch. She hated being late, but she definitely couldn't leave before seeing the balcony and the projection room. She pulled out her mobile and sent a text, then headed for the main staircase, still recording and narrating.

Halfway up, the route turned abruptly to the left and faded into darkness. Jude did an about-turn; she must have missed the balcony entrance. Running the beam over the walls, she picked out a narrow door on her right. The projection box was normally at the top of a cinema, but not always. In the nearby Tivoli, now demolished, the box had been at ground level.

The door swung back to reveal a corridor leading up to another door, this one marked 'No Smoking'.

Jude eased it open and shone her torch inside, illuminating a sign which read:

THE SOUND PROJECTOR APPARATUS
USED IN THIS THEATRE IS LEASED FROM
Western Electric Company Ltd,
Bush House, London

This was it. The projection room.

Seized by excitement, Jude looked round for an alternative light source. The manager had suggested there wasn't one beyond the foyer, but Jude knew from experience that some projection suites had their own power. Her beam finally found what she was looking for – a mains supply box.

She stepped down from the small metal platform and picked her way across the rubbish-strewn floor.

Fortune favours the brave, she thought, and threw the switch.

Two things happened simultaneously; the room was flooded with light, and the door shut with a bang.

Jude stood for a moment, her heart pounding.

'OK,' she said out loud to calm herself, 'I'd prefer the door open . . .'

As she retraced her steps something caught her eye; a pile of discarded bricks by the battery-room entrance. One of those could be used to prop the door open. As she bent to pick one up, she felt a cold draught brush her skin, prickling it, as though charged with electricity.

There were countless stories of supernatural presences in old cinemas, but Jude didn't believe in ghosts and had never felt strange in any of the abandoned cinemas she'd visited. Until now.

Her senses on high alert, she straightened up and stood listening. For what, she had no idea. Then she did hear something. The scratching went on for a few moments, then stopped before she could pinpoint where the sound had come from.

Mice, she thought, or rats. Neither of which she was afraid of.

As Jude resumed her path, brick in hand, she caught another sound, this time a heavier scuffling. Had the manager let someone in to view the cinema after her?

Reaching the door, she wedged it open with the brick and checked the corridor. It was empty.

Jude suddenly recalled the tale of a homeless man found burned to death in the old Bridgeton cinema. Could someone have found their way in via the fire escape and be squatting somewhere in the projection suite?

'Hello, is anyone there?'

Her voice echoed round the confined space. When it died down and silence returned, she had the weird but definite sensation that there *was* someone – or some*thing* – in there with her.

There were two openings off the box room. One led to the battery room, the other probably to the rewinding room. Jude went to check the battery room first. Save for three ranks of old batteries, the place was empty of anything but dust. As she had suspected, the smaller room next to it held the flat surface and mechanism for rewinding the reels. It, too, was empty.

OK, you're imagining things, she told herself.

It was time to get down to work, and she might as well start in here. As she set up her shot, a faint but nauseating scent made her wrinkle her nose. She ran her eye over the floor expecting to find the disintegrating mess of a rat, but there was nothing. She did notice now, though, that the far wall had been partially demolished, leaving a dark hole large enough for a person to climb through. Perhaps the smell was coming from there.

Jude approached and shone her torch in. The beam picked up a row of coat hooks, a narrow table, two wooden chairs and what looked like an ancient freezer.

'The usherettes' room,' she whispered, delighted.

Ignoring the smell, she eased her way through. The room was small, the table and chairs taking up all of one wall. Jude pictured the women getting changed into their uniforms in this cramped space, laughing and joking, drinking tea and smoking.

In the confined space the smell had definitely grown

more pungent. Jude glanced round. The smell had to come from something bigger than a rat. A dead cat maybe?

A sudden roaring sound filled the room, making her almost jump out of her skin. Then the roar settled to a steady hum, and she felt a wave of warm air brush her body. It had to be the heating system for the charity shop starting up. Jude relaxed, feeling foolish.

She began to photograph the room, aware that the smell had worsened further with the sudden increase in temperature. In the wall opposite the coat hooks was a bricked-up doorway. Most areas the public didn't see in cinemas consisted of bare brick, but this brickwork looked quite recent. Jude realised the smell seemed to be coming from a gap in the mortar halfway up.

Curiosity getting the better of her, she pressed an eye to the hole.

There was nothing but inky darkness.

She told herself firmly to get on with the job as she was already running late, but even as she thought this she was looking round for something to help her enlarge the hole between the bricks. She spotted a strip of metal with a jagged end, and began to scrape at the mortar.

A few minutes later she was able to prise the edge of the brick loose. The resulting rush of foetid air made her gag, but she focused her torch beam on the enlarged hole and peered inside.

Her eyes widened in horror.

2

Not many people got the chance to look into their own grave. Or indeed to see their own coffin after their funeral, but DS Michael McNab (deceased) was impressed with his. A very smart coffin it was, despite the damage to the lid where it had been forced open. Rich mahogany, the metal handles carved with the design of the Sacred Heart. Definitely not the bargain end of the market.

He wondered if someone had found the life-insurance policy he'd stuffed in his kitchen drawer, or had the Scottish Police Federation coughed up the cost of burying one of their own, killed in the line of duty? McNab tried briefly to remember what he'd estimated his life to be worth, but couldn't, although he was pretty sure he hadn't insured it for much. After all, he had no dependants. There would have been enough for a simple ceremony and a couple of rounds of drinks at the wake, if there was one. Probably not enough for a casket as fancy as this.

He examined the headstone. Carved in grey granite, with the inscription and the dates of his arrival and departure in gold.

Michael Joseph McNab
He died that others might live

It was enough to choke him up, if it was true.

No doubt the sentiment had been Chrissy's. Eight months pregnant, she had been with him at the Poker Club the night he had been gunned down on the orders of a Russian oligarch. McNab swallowed hard, tasting again the horror that had assailed him when he'd thought Chrissy might be in the line of fire.

He looked up from the gravestone and weighted coffin into the dawn sky, where layers of blood-red cloud heralded the day. It was time to leave. The cemetery was popular with the public, as evidenced by the well-tended graves and fresh flowers. It would only be a matter of time before the excavation was noted and reported.

The Serious Crime Squad wouldn't be able to bury this news as easily as they'd pretended to bury him. More to the point, his would-be assassins now knew he was available to appear as a witness in the upcoming trial of Nikolai Kalinin, head of a crime cartel that stretched from the Baltic via London to Glasgow.

McNab took a last look at his final resting place then turned on his heel and walked swiftly away, suddenly acutely aware that the men who'd desecrated his grave could be pointing a gun at his head right now. Sure he'd heard the explosion of gunfire, he ducked behind the nearest gravestone, fear clogging his lungs. Crouched and gasping, he furiously willed himself to breathe.

Eventually air rasped in through his clenched teeth. McNab cursed himself for succumbing to another of the all-too-frequent flashbacks. He couldn't afford to lose it, or he would end up in that coffin for real.

Brushing the dirt from his trousers, he rose and set off towards the gates.

3

Dr Rhona MacLeod exited Glasgow High Court and stood for a moment, listening to Chrissy's animated phone message.

'Someone dug up McNab's grave and the coffin was empty. Word is he's alive and SOCA are hiding him!'

Her assistant's joy at the news was only to be expected. Rhona had known for weeks, but hadn't been able to tell anyone apart from a select few, Chrissy not among them. She would take that pretty badly when she found out. Rhona read the text that had also arrived while she'd been in court: *Dead but not forgotten. Coffee?*

Speak of the devil. She didn't recognise the number, but it had to be him.

Rhona looked about her, but there was only a young hooded guy, leaning on a pillar and drawing on a cigarette as though it was his last. When he saw her checking him out, he was immediately on the case.

'Any chance of a pound for a cup of tea, missus? Ah swear on ma mother's ashes it's no for drugs.'

She shook her head. 'I've no cash.'

'Nae bother.' He shrugged and went back to his cigarette.

Rhona slipped her mobile into her bag. If the text was from McNab, he would be at the nearby Central Café waiting for her.

His cigarette finished, the guy by the pillar fiddled with

the drawstring on his hood and shoved his hands in his pockets, but didn't move on. Rhona had the feeling that he was waiting for her to leave first. She glanced at his feet, recognising an expensive brand of trainers. Perhaps he was waiting for a court appearance? Something about him told her to keep an eye on him.

As she was considering this, the man dipped his head decisively and set off in the direction of Glasgow Cross. Rhona gave him a few moments, then headed in the same direction.

The Saltmarket was busy with midday traffic and pedestrians. The normality of the scene didn't ease her concerns. If she was aware that the Central Café was a hang-out of McNab's, wouldn't others know it too? And what if she was the one being watched and she led them to him? Her stomach flipped at the thought. Then she told herself she was overreacting. If McNab imagined for a moment this place was being watched, he wouldn't be here.

When she opened the café door, a strong smell of fried food and vinegar met her head on. The queue at the shop counter was three deep. She could hear Rocco's Italian-accented Glasgow patter as he served up.

Rhona turned into the seating area. McNab wasn't at the usual window table. Very wise. She scanned the room and spotted a familiar figure in the far corner.

He gave her a wide smile as she slipped in opposite, while she examined the face that was both familiar and strikingly different. The auburn hair was cropped close to his skull, and he'd acquired glasses. But the wry look he threw her was all McNab.

'How are you?' she said.

'Not bad for a dead man. I was having a bit of bother keeping up with the new hair colour – the beard kept growing out ginger.' He studied her face. 'You know about the grave?'

'I picked up a message from Chrissy when I came out of court. How did *you* find out?'

'An early morning visit to the cemetery.'

Rhona wondered why he would visit his own grave; perhaps he'd suspected it might have been tampered with.

'Now they know for definite you're alive,' she said.

'They've known since they got to the soldier. No one Solonik tortures stays silent.' McNab looked pained, clearly remembering that only too well.

'If that's true, why bother digging up the coffin?'

He shrugged. 'To show me they know?'

A shudder of fear went through Rhona.

'Don't,' he said.

'Don't what?'

'Look so worried.'

'There's plenty to worry about.'

'Hey, I'm upright and I'm warm, that's more than you believed possible a few weeks ago.'

All the time she'd believed him dead and wished for the miracle of this moment. Now Rhona could only think of losing him again.

'I'm sorry.'

'You've got nothing to be sorry for, Dr MacLeod,' he said softly.

She drew her eyes from his. 'Why did you want to see me?'

'I need a reason?'

'You told me you wouldn't be in touch before the case came to court.'

'I changed my mind when I saw the grave.' He paused. 'I want you to contact Petersson.' Einar Petersson was the investigative journalist who had discovered McNab's resurrection and eventually persuaded Rhona of it. McNab pushed an envelope across the table. 'Give him this.'

'What is it?'

'Something that will help the case against Kalinin.'

'But why not give it to Bill?'

'The boss would have to go through the proper police channels. Chances are Kalinin's mole would pick up on it.'

Rhona slipped the envelope into her pocket just as her mobile rang. She didn't answer.

'I'd rather you let the Serious Crime Squad hide you,' she said.

'I tried that once, remember? This way I have no one to blame but myself if it all goes wrong.'

Rhona didn't want to think about that possibility. She avoided McNab's gaze and looked back over her shoulder at the counter. The lunchtime queue had dispersed and there was only one customer remaining – a young man in a hooded top and fancy trainers. She put her hand on McNab's arm and leaned in so he could hear her lowered voice. 'That guy at the counter. He was hanging around outside the court. I think he might have followed me here.'

McNab craned round her for a look. She saw him tense up when the man shoved his hand in his pocket, but then a small plastic bag was produced and emptied onto the counter. A pile of pound coins clattered out.

'Can you change these for notes, mate?'

Rocco muttered an expletive that held a note of admiration. 'A good morning's work, eh?'

Relief flooded Rhona and she laughed. 'He tried to beg a pound off me. Swore on his mother's ashes it wasn't for drugs.'

The guy was accepting his earnings in notes, about thirty quid's worth. He turned, sensing their interest, and met Rhona's accusing glance. A cheeky grin split his face when he realised who she was.

'You said you'd nae cash, so you were lying too,' he called over.

He reached for the sausage supper Rocco had wrapped in the interim and headed for the door.

In the silence that followed, Rhona's mobile rang again. She frowned and pushed the button to send the call to voicemail.

'You need to get back to work, Dr MacLeod,' said McNab.

She nodded and got to her feet.

He gave her an encouraging smile. 'I'll see you in court.'

Rhona wanted to embrace him and urge him to stay alive. Instead she left without looking back, her heart thumping, her mind in turmoil. When the mobile rang yet again on the way to the car, she answered.

'Didn't you get my message?' Chrissy's voice was shrill with excitement. 'McNab's not dead. The coffin they dug up was empty!'

The split second it took Rhona to respond was enough to alert Chrissy. 'You *knew*?' she said accusingly.

'We'll talk when I get to the lab.'

The strangled sound on the other end suggested Rhona's explanation would fall short of anything likely to placate Chrissy.

'I'll be there in fifteen minutes.'

Chrissy had already hung up.

Rhona took the route that ran parallel to the river. A low mist hung over the Clyde, obscuring the walkway that bordered it. She drove past the shadowed pillars where she and McNab had met with a young woman called Anya Grigorovitch; Anya's lover Alexsai had been murdered on Nikolai Kalinin's orders. Rhona recalled McNab's bristling anger that night, and his determination to bring the Russian gangster and his associates to justice.

And he had thought he'd succeeded. In fact, he and Chrissy had been invited to Paddy Brogan's Poker Club that night to celebrate. *On the house*, Paddy had said, as a thank you to McNab for getting the Russian contingent off his patch. Then DI Slater had released Kalinin and he'd headed straight to the Poker Club.

Rhona could still picture her frantic attempts to stem the unremitting flow of blood from McNab's body, and hear his last words as the life faded from his eyes. He had told her he loved her.

He's alive, she told herself. And he's going to stay that way.

Rhona could feel the icy atmosphere as soon as she entered the lab. She didn't blame Chrissy, who had been distraught at McNab's death – he had saved both her and her unborn child, and as far as she'd known he had given his own life to do so. That's why she'd named her baby boy Michael, and had insisted on giving Michael Joseph McNab a proper Roman Catholic funeral, just in case his soul needed saving.

Chrissy looked up from her work. 'How long?' she demanded.

'Not long.'

'This is what all these meetings with Petersson were about?'

'Yes.'

Rhona could see the distress on Chrissy's face.

'How could you not tell me?'

'I didn't believe Petersson at first. I didn't want to get your hopes up.'

'And?'

'Eventually the things he was saying turned out to be true.'

'Such as?'

'McNab was revived in the ambulance; but then, according to hospital records, he died on the operating table.'

'But he didn't die, did he?' said Chrissy.

Rhona shook her head. 'He was moved south, hidden in a safe house at the same time as Fergus Morrison.' She hesitated. 'Kalinin discovered where they were hiding Morrison. He had him tortured to find out if McNab was alive.'

'But I was the one who persuaded Fergus to hand himself in and testify against Kalinin,' Chrissy said, dismayed. 'I told him he would be safe.'

'It wasn't your fault. Someone on the inside is feeding

Kalinin information. That's why McNab left the safe house.'

'Have you seen him?'

'A few weeks ago,' Rhona lied.

'And you never *told* me?'

'I couldn't afford to take the chance.'

'Who else knows?'

'DI Wilson and Superintendent Sutherland.'

A look of hurt betrayal crossed Chrissy's face. 'You should have told me.'

'You would have wanted to tell Sam.' Rhona couldn't imagine Chrissy keeping a secret from her partner, especially one that involved the saviour of their son.

'Sam can keep a secret,' Chrissy said stoutly.

'It's not that easy,' said Rhona, with conviction.

'You managed well enough,' Chrissy fired back.

The truth was she'd been desperate to tell Chrissy, but the first meeting she'd had with McNab had convinced Rhona of the danger in telling anyone. To have found out about the safe house, Kalinin had to have an informant in the force, maybe even in the Serious Crime Squad. That meant anyone who knew that McNab was alive was in danger.

'Well, anyway, the whole world knows now,' Chrissy said. 'It's in the early edition of the evening paper.'

The banner headline said it all.

STAR WITNESS BACK FROM THE DEAD.

Below was a photograph of McNab, the way he looked before the makeover. 'It's from Bill's fiftieth birthday party at the jazz club. Look, you can see the stage in the background.'

'How the hell did a newspaper get hold of that picture?'

Rhona's immediate thought was that someone at the club had been responsible. Maybe even her ex, Sean Maguire, who partly owned the place.

'Now everyone knows what he looks like,' Chrissy pointed out.

'McNab doesn't really look like that any more. I hardly recognised him myself.' Chrissy was regarding her anxiously. 'His voice is the same, though. And his jokes.'

'Thank God for that!'

They lapsed into silent thought.

'What happens now?' Chrissy asked eventually.

'He stays in hiding until his court appearance.'

'With SOCA?'

Rhona shook her head. 'He's doing it on his own.'

Chrissy muttered an expletive. 'Who does he think he is, James Bond?'

'He doesn't trust anyone. Not after Morrison's death.'

'He trusts you,' Chrissy retorted. Her voice held a hint of accusation.

Rhona was reminded of the envelope – she needed to call Petersson. But not in front of Chrissy. She had already lied and said she hadn't seen McNab for weeks. She would have to keep up the pretence.

'I'd better get down to some work. Anything new come in?'

'An urgent request from DI Wilson to forensically examine an exhumation. Guess whose?'

Rhona tried Einar Petersson's number before starting up the car. It rang a couple of times then switched to voicemail, so she left a brief message asking him to call her back.

The drive to the cemetery gave her time to contemplate this latest development in the Kalinin saga. Having met the man and experienced both his charm and his cruelty, she didn't doubt he'd do everything in his power to find and kill McNab, just as he had Fergus Morrison. McNab thought he could hide out successfully on his home turf, but if Kalinin suspected he was here he would use all his resources to locate him.

She swung through the cemetery gates and drew up in the car park alongside an incident van and a couple of police vehicles. Retrieving her forensic case and suit from the boot, she locked up then set off towards the distant knot of people.

Despite the bunches of spring flowers adorning the graves, winter hadn't loosened its grip on Glasgow yet. The path was frosted underfoot and the surrounding grass was still patched with snow.

Rhona hadn't been back to the cemetery since the funeral. She remembered thinking, standing there in the full grip of winter, that McNab should have been cremated. Then they would have said goodbye to him inside, in the warmth, instead of gathering to freeze on this hillside.

Standing at his actual grave had been the most painful part of all. But Chrissy had insisted on the full works. A Roman Catholic service, a proper burial. At the time Rhona hadn't had the strength or the will to suggest an alternative. And the ceremony had helped in a way. The lowering of the coffin, Bill and five other colleagues holding the ropes. The words intoned as Bill scattered the first soil on the casket. Every action an acknowledgement of the man McNab had been.

The man he is, she reminded herself.

The tent was up, protecting the scene from the elements and any curious onlookers. The delights of a Glasgow cemetery on a raw day had brought a surprising number of visitors. Exhumations were rare, let alone ones that revealed there had been no body in the first place.

Bill had spotted her arriving and was on his way to intercept her. They hadn't spoken about McNab since that night in the pub when the team were celebrating catching the killer in their most recent case, the 'daisy chain' murders. The DI had told her then, against Superintendent Sutherland's strict orders, that McNab was alive. Rhona had already known, but hearing Bill say it had made it all the more real. Now it looked as though all their secrecy had been in vain.

'I tried to get in touch as soon as I found out about this,' he said, eyeing her worriedly.

Rhona hoped her expression didn't show just how concerned she was herself. 'I was in court all morning.' She began kitting up.

'Chrissy didn't come with you?'

'She found out I knew McNab was alive and didn't tell her.'

'And she's not well pleased?'

'The understatement of the year.'

'So I'm in for the cold shoulder too?'

'You have an excuse, you're a policeman.'

'Has McNab contacted you?'

Rhona hesitated. She ought to tell Chrissy and Bill the same story. 'Yes. I met up with him after you and I spoke in the pub.'

She didn't mention her initial shock at McNab's changed appearance, or the hours they'd spent together in a hotel room.

'SOCA are furious with him.'

'They failed to protect Fergus Morrison. What did they expect?' she snapped.

'If he gets in touch again, will you tell him I want to speak to him?'

'I tried that already. He said he would see us both in court.'

Bill shook his head. 'Let's hope he's right.'

Fully suited now, Rhona pulled up the hood and tucked in her hair.

'OK, let's take a look.'

Bill pulled aside the tent flap to let her enter.

She stood for a moment, breathing in the place. In normal circumstances she would be called out to examine a body, with all the accompanying scents of death and decomposition. In here she could smell only damp wood and freshly dug earth.

The coffin lay at the foot of the grave, the lid alongside and the interior exposed. Petersson had been right: the casket had been loaded with weights. It seemed strange to consider how often she'd pictured McNab's pale face and still body in this box, six feet underground.

The routine for examining an exhumation was straightforward. She would DNA-swab and fibre-tape the coffin *in situ*. Then it would be wrapped in clear plastic or tarpaulin to completely enclose it, belted top and bottom and lifted out with a Simon hoist or by six support officers. Because of the soil on the coffin surface, there was less likelihood of fingerprints, but she would use cyano-acrylate just in case.

As for the surrounding soil, there was tool mark analysis to consider, as well as footprints, tyre prints and soil sifting. The likelihood was that Kalinin had contracted out the work to members of a local gang, maybe someone already known to the police. And the average Glasgow criminal did love his expensive trainers. Rhona ran her gaze slowly round the open gravesite, spotting at least three sets of prints. They could belong to whoever discovered the open grave and reported it, or hopefully, to those who had dug it. Soon enough she would find out.

4

'Jude! Are you in there?' Liam pounded the door, knowing instinctively that she wasn't inside.

He pulled out his mobile and tried her number again, but it switched to voicemail almost immediately.

'Where the hell are you?'

Jude's OCD could be a pain at times, but at least it meant she was a stickler for punctuality and answering phone messages.

The next door along the corridor opened and a head popped out.

'You looking for Jude?' It was a girl wearing what looked like 3-D glasses.

'Have you seen her?'

'Not since yesterday. She was in photography class, but rushed off straight after.'

'Do you know where she was going?'

'Nope. But I don't know if she came back last night. I didn't see her in the kitchen or the common room.'

'Have you asked around?'

She put her head on one side, puzzled. 'No. Why would I?'

'When she comes back can you ask her to give Liam a call? Tell her it's urgent.'

She shrugged her shoulders, said 'Sure,' and disappeared inside.

Exasperated, Liam made for the lift. The elderly man on duty in the small office raised an eyebrow when he appeared. When he had let Liam in earlier he'd introduced himself as Charlie.

'Any luck?'

'No.'

'I know Jude. She'll turn up. She's one of the sensible ones.'

'What happens if she doesn't?' said Liam.

'The policy of the student residence is to call home after a couple of days. We explain to the parents that their son or daughter hasn't been seen for a while, then we leave it up to them.'

Liam didn't tell him that Jude had been brought up in care and had no family to call.

'OK, thanks for your help.'

'No problem, son.'

Back outside, Liam looked up at Jude's dark window. Could she have mentioned going somewhere specific last night, before they were due to meet in the pub? He had wracked his brains but couldn't remember anything. Since she'd begun recording Glasgow cinemas, she was always prattling on about derelict foyers and old projection rooms. The truth was he didn't listen most of the time.

He glanced at his watch. He would miss the last class of the day if he didn't hurry. As he headed for the main campus, he made up his mind to give it one more night. If Jude hadn't contacted him or shown up at the halls of residence by tomorrow, he would go to the police and report her missing.

Fifteen minutes into the tutorial, he received a text that

changed his mind. It looked as though Jude had tried to send it the previous evening from somewhere with no signal: Wll B l8 *Found gr8 cinema*

So she'd been visiting another cinema, but which one? And why hadn't she turned up after that? He'd sat in the pub until closing time. Even hung around outside for ten minutes afterwards.

Liam decided to risk the wrath of the lecturer and slip out early. The group was small enough to make it awkward, but he did it anyway. The caustic commentary that followed his departure was clearly audible as he closed the door behind him and headed down the corridor.

'So the young woman hasn't been seen since yesterday?'

'She was meant to meet me last night. She didn't turn up.'

Liam knew what the policeman was thinking. Someone isn't necessarily missing simply because they stood you up.

'You don't understand. Jude is very organised. She always turns up when she says she will, and she didn't sleep at the halls of residence last night.' Even as he said the words, Liam imagined the officer's interpretation of events. Jude had decided she didn't want to see Liam any more. Maybe she'd met someone she liked better. Someone she'd chosen to spend the night with.

He ploughed on regardless. 'And then I got this text. It didn't arrive until today, but it reads like it was sent last night. Jude photographs derelict cinemas. She said she'd found a great one and that she would be late.'

He showed the policeman the text.

'And you've tried calling her?'

'Loads of times. It just goes to voicemail.'

'What about her family? Could she have gone home?'

'Jude hasn't got a family. She was brought up in care.'

'So there's no one you could contact?'

Liam's exasperation and worry were growing. 'Something's happened to her. I know it has.'

The officer studied him intently. 'And what makes you say that?'

'Why else would she disappear?'

'We haven't established that she has disappeared.' The man's tone was firm. 'And we certainly haven't established that the young lady has been harmed. Now, this cinema she mentions. Have you checked there?'

'I don't know which one it is.'

'Is there any way to find out?'

Liam shook his head in despair.

The policeman sighed. 'When she visits these cinemas, does she go on her own?'

'Yes.'

'There's no one else involved with her on this project?'

'Jude prefers working alone.'

'And you two are an item?'

He shook his head. 'We're friends, that's all.'

'Did she have a boyfriend?'

'No.'

'You're certain of that?'

Jude had never mentioned one. In his heart Liam hoped something might happen one day, although Jude had never given him cause to believe it would. She'd just treated him like a mate, with no sexual undercurrent at all. He'd been satisfied with that, as long as she allowed him to spend some time in her company.

After a short silence the policeman said, 'My advice is to give it another twenty-four hours. Chances are she'll have turned up.'

'What if she hasn't?'

'They usually do.'

He was being dismissed. Liam stood for a moment, wondering whether he should argue, but the expression on the policeman's face suggested he would be wasting his time.

He left the building and slowly retraced his steps to the halls, trying to work out what to do next. He imagined what Jude would say if he did make a fuss and there turned out to be a perfectly logical explanation for her standing him up. It made him uncomfortable thinking about it, but it didn't stop the niggling worry that he should be doing *something*.

If he only knew which cinema she'd been visiting, he could find out who had let her in and ask if the same person had seen her leave. He could search the building, make sure she wasn't lying hurt inside.

But if she was, surely she would phone for help?

Liam started going through all the reasons why that might not be possible. Her phone had run of credit. Her battery had run down. She was somewhere with a poor signal. Well, that much was true – her message to him had come through very late. He immediately imagined her in the basement of some derelict cinema, hurt and alone. Hoping and praying that he would come looking for her.

Liam upped his pace, reaching the halls of residence

minutes later. The police officer who'd dealt with him in Strathclyde's Headquarters had given him one idea at least. If he could get access to Jude's computer, maybe he would be able to discover which of the cinemas she'd planned to visit last night. It was worth a try.

'Back again?' the warden said when he walked in the door.

'I've been to the police station – I tried to report Jude missing.'

'It's too early for that, son,' Charlie said sympathetically.

Liam took a deep breath. 'Look, Jude went alone to photograph a derelict cinema last night. I'm worried something might have happened to her there, so I need to find out which one. If I could check her laptop?'

'You want me to let you into her room?'

'You could come with me.'

'The man took a minute to decide. 'OK, let's take a look.'

As the warden was opening Jude's door 3-D Specs reappeared.

'Has something happened to Jude?'

'Not as far as we know,' the warden reassured her. He beckoned Liam to follow him and quickly shut the door, locking it behind them. 'We don't want the whole corridor in here with us.'

Liam glanced round the meticulously neat room. He'd only been here once before, and then only briefly. At the time he'd got the impression that Jude wasn't keen on people entering her private space, so he'd waited at the door.

Charlie seemed pretty impressed. 'I've never seen such a tidy room.'

'Jude was a bit obsessive. That's why I'm hoping she'll have a record of which cinemas she planned to visit and when.' Liam headed for the desk, where a laptop sat open. He powered on and was swiftly confronted with a log-in screen demanding a password.

Shit. He should have known Jude would be a stickler for security. He could be here all day trying out combinations and still get nowhere.

He checked out the desk drawers. The deepest one held a black metal box, which he slid out and placed on the desk. Opened, it revealed an old 16mm film reel. The other two drawers held neat bundles of pens and pencils, a sketchpad and a rule. Nothing specifically related to the cinema project.

'What about these?'

The warden indicated some photographs mounted on a wall board. 'That's the old Olympia in Bridgeton. I used to go there as a kid. Ninepence seats right down the front. You had to queue for hours to get in.'

There were seven labelled photographs in total, all depicting cinema façades – the Old Odeon Renfield Street, the Olympia Bridgeton, the Govan Lyceum, the Grand Central, the Parade in Dennistoun, the Riddrie and the Rosevale on Dumbarton Road.

'Maybe Jude was visiting one of these?' suggested Liam.

'Maybe, but Glasgow has scores of old cinemas, son. You'll have your work cut out if you plan to check them all.'

Without access to Jude's project diary, there was no way to pinpoint which one she'd planned to visit last night.

'This is a job for the police, son.'

'But they won't look.'

'They will, just not yet.'

'What if she's in trouble now?'

'She'd call you, wouldn't she?'

Liam wasn't so sure she'd be able to, but didn't say so. As if in response, the warden's mobile rang.

'Charlie here. OK, I'll be right down.' He turned back to Liam. 'Leave your number on the way out and I'll let you know as soon as Jude turns up. I have to get back to the desk. Can you pull the door shut behind you?'

Liam waited for him to leave then set about jotting down the names of the cinemas. None of them rang a bell.

When he'd finished, he took a last look round, his gaze resting on the laptop. If only he could take a proper look at that. If he gave it to his flatmate, Ben the hacker, he would gain access in no time. But he couldn't just remove it from the room, could he? As he dragged his eyes away, he spotted something he'd missed before – a memory stick, still plugged in.

Surely compulsive Jude would back up her data regularly? Liam hesitated before crossing to the desk, extracting the stick and slipping it in his pocket.

Thankfully Charlie was in full flow on the phone when Liam reached the lobby. He quickly scribbled down his mobile number and left it on the counter, before heading for the front door.

5

'So what have we got?'

'Some DNA swabs and fibre tapes, and maybe even a couple of partial fingerprints. Soil for sieving and a selection of footprint and tyre casts to run past the database. Unfortunately, I couldn't get the coffin in the back of the car.' Rhona's feeble attempt at a joke was rewarded with a withering look. Getting back into Chrissy's good books wasn't going to be easy.

'Einar Petersson's been trying to get hold of you.'

'He called here?' said Rhona, surprised.

'Why shouldn't he? There aren't any more secrets, are there?'

'I'll get back to him once I've logged what I have here.'

'I can do that.'

Rhona tried to sound innocent. 'OK. I fancy a coffee. What about you?'

A trip to the coffee machine would allow her to call Petersson out of earshot of Chrissy. But judging by the look on Chrissy's face now, her plan was pretty transparent.

Rhona made for a quiet spot in the corridor before pulling up Petersson's number. He picked up on the third ring.

'Rhona!' He sounded pleased.

'Why did you call the lab?'

'You didn't answer your mobile.'

'I was processing a grave.'

'McNab's?'

'Yes.'

'So the world knows our detective sergeant is alive,' he said.

'Seems that way.'

There was an expectant silence. Rhona knew it was her turn to speak; after all, she had been the one to contact him.

'I have something for you, from the recently deceased.'

'Really?' he said, clearly intrigued. 'May I ask what?'

'An envelope.'

'So you've met up with him?'

Rhona ignored the loaded question. 'When can you pick it up?'

'Tonight? I could also bring some food and wine.'

She hesitated. Would it be better to pass the envelope on in private or in public?

Petersson was reading her mind. 'Alternatively we could have dinner out and you can pass it across the table surreptitiously, wrapped in a napkin?'

'This isn't funny,' she said sharply.

'No, you're right. It isn't.'

Rhona was silent for a moment. 'Come round about eight.'

'OK. What do you fancy eating?'

'Surprise me.'

When she returned with two coffees, Chrissy was already at work sifting soil. She waved the coffee away impatiently,

34

but Rhona accepted the rejection with good grace. She had betrayed Chrissy, or at least that's how it must seem to her.

Rhona settled down to cast an eye over the photographic evidence she'd collected. There had been six distinct footwear impressions in the soft soil near the grave. She'd routinely sealed them with hairspray to prevent the casting material from damaging the finer details, before mixing dental stone and water to a thin pouring consistency. She'd been able to lift each of the casts after half an hour, but it would take a day of air drying before she could brush them clean and examine them properly.

She had also located a set of tyre marks a few yards from the open grave. The road through the cemetery was tarred, but the vehicle had drawn up partly on the muddy grass that bordered it. She'd used the same method of casting to record the three-dimensional negative print left in the soil. Tyre-tread designs were hugely variable and complex. They could be used to identify the tyre manufacturer and through this possibly the make and model of the vehicle. If they could link the vehicle in some way to Nikolai Kalinin, that would help the case against him.

It was a slender hope, thought Rhona; the Russian was far too well organised to leave such an obvious trail.

6

Liam plugged the memory stick into his laptop. The list of folders and files that appeared on the screen showed what an organised person Jude was. It was in direct contrast to the haphazard manner in which he stored his own files.

He chose the folder entitled 'Cinema Project'. It opened on a further set of files labelled 'City Centre', 'North', 'South', 'East' and 'West'. He opened the 'City Centre' folder first and saw sixteen further folders inside, each with the name of a cinema.

'West' offered a further eight folders; 'South', eight; 'East', nine; and finally 'North' had three. That made forty-four cinemas in total, and Jude could have been visiting any of them.

Liam gazed at the screen in dismay. Charlie was right, it would take forever to check them all. Even the police would be pushed to do that in a short space of time. The only chance he had of finding out where Jude was last night was a schedule of some sort. Surely Jude, of all people, would keep a diary, and keep it up to date? He knew she used every facility on her mobile whereas he had scarcely investigated half of them. Would she keep the project diary on her phone? The thought alarmed him.

To calm himself and feel as though he was making progress he opened the first of the 'City Centre' folders,

Britannia Panopticon. From the files inside he quickly realised that the Panopticon wasn't actually derelict, but was operating as an arts centre. He suddenly recalled Jude suggesting they go there to watch some Laurel and Hardy films. Free entry but no heating, she'd said. For some reason they hadn't gone, and he couldn't remember why. Liam tried another folder. The La Scala had been turned into a Waterstone's. Jude's text the previous evening had definitely not been sent from a bookshop.

He clicked his way through more of the folders. If a cinema had been converted and was in use in some other capacity he made the assumption Jude had already been there, since it was easy enough to get access. He suddenly realised that he should be checking for folders which had no photographic records inside – the ones yet to be visited.

It took him a while but eventually he had four possibilities, all of which had been included on the wall display. The old Odeon on Renfield Street in the city centre, the Olympia in Bridgeton, the Govan Lyceum, and the Rosevale on Dumbarton Road.

None of these had folders of images, save for one picture of each exterior. OK. He was down to four, which was a whole lot better than forty-four. The question was, which to try first? They were pretty well spread out across the city. Had he discovered this while at the Art School the sensible thing would have been to head for the Odeon first, then go east into Bridgeton. The Lyceum was across the Clyde on the south side, definitely out of the way. As his flat was in Gibson Street, he could either jump on the underground and head into town or go for the one in Dumbarton Road.

The room had gradually grown darker as the winter evening began to draw in. Whatever he decided, it had to be soon. Liam grabbed his jacket from the back of the sofa.

He made his decision at the front door. He would head for the Rosevale. The image had suggested the front of the cinema was now a charity shop, so surely someone in the shop could tell him if Jude had been around?

He began to walk briskly along Kelvinway. The street lights were already on, but here between the two halves of Kelvingrove Park and its encroaching trees it always seemed dark. A short while later he was turning right into Dumbarton Road. He had no idea where exactly on the street the cinema was, but he knew he was looking out for a sign for the British Heart Foundation.

He eventually found it, though at first glance he thought he'd got it wrong. How could a cinema have existed here? All the others he'd seen in Jude's photos had had impressive frontages, some even regal.

The building he stood outside now was a red sandstone tenement block with a shop at ground level, but according to Jude this had been the location of the Rosevale cinema.

Liam hesitated for a moment, then pushed open the door and stepped inside. The tinkling bell immediately brought a woman from a back room.

'Can I help you?'

'I'm looking for my friend Jude. She's a photographic student at the Art College and she's doing a project on old Glasgow cinemas, including the Rosevale?'

The woman smiled. 'Oh yes, that's right, but I'm afraid

you've missed her. She was here yesterday, taking photographs of the foyer and projection room.'

Liam's heart leapt. 'So she was definitely here?'

'I let her in myself, not long before closing time. Why? Is anything wrong?'

'Can you tell me when she left?'

'As a matter of fact, I can't. She arrived quite late, so I agreed she could leave by the back entrance when she'd finished her photographs.'

'You never actually saw her leave?'

The woman looked worried now. 'No, but she definitely shut the door behind her. I checked this morning. Can I ask why you're here?'

'Jude didn't meet me last night when she said she would.'

'You think something's happened to her?' gasped the woman, horrified.

'Is there a chance she could still be in there?'

'What, all night? I hope not.'

'Could we take a look?'

'I can't leave the shop, I'm afraid.'

'Can *I* take a look, then?'

The woman frowned, clearly unhappy with this idea. She had already allowed one person to wander about on their own, and she didn't seem keen to compound her error.

'She could have fallen and hurt herself,' Liam pleaded. 'Could I just check? It would put my mind at rest.'

'There's only light in the foyer,' she warned.

'That's OK. I'll manage.'

The woman gave in. 'I'll unlock the door for you.'

Minutes later Liam was standing alone in the well-lit foyer. Despite his unease, he could appreciate why Jude had decided to spend more time here even though it would make her late.

He glanced round the circular room, noting that there was nowhere here for someone to lie hidden, then approached the stairs. He paused at the bottom and shouted Jude's name, waiting for a moment in the answering silence before heading further up the stairs. Halfway up, the light faded to shadows as the staircase turned left, then disappeared entirely into impenetrable darkness. Liam stopped, nonplussed.

'Jude. Are you up there?'

The blackness seemed to muffle his shout like a blanket, in contrast to the echo effect in the foyer.

Liam was unsure what to do next. Should he carry on and hope that there was light, however faint, further up? He felt ashamed of his nervousness about stepping into the shadows.

I bet Jude brought a torch, he thought.

Thinking about Jude's preparedness and tenacity spurred him on. He edged nearer the wall and began to feel his way up. After a while the darkness seemed less dense and he could make out the edge of the steps. After a dozen stairs he reached a flat area and what looked like a set of double swing doors. Liam eased his way towards them and pushed open the right-hand one.

In here there was some light, albeit dim. He could make out descending rows of seats, some still upright, others dismantled. In the near-distance was the curve of a balcony rail and beyond, the hanging structures of a suspended ceiling, through which the light filtered.

'Jude!' he shouted again, knowing instinctively that there

was no one else on the balcony. He felt his way down the central aisle, glancing along the rows of seats. When he reached the rail he looked over.

The new ceiling cut across the upper section of the main auditorium. On the far side Liam could make out the curved arch of the main stage. All around him the grandeur and detail of the upper walls and roof were in direct contrast to the seventies-styled suspended ceiling. Suddenly he understood why there had been no palatial frontage. The Rosevale had been built in the back court of the surrounding tenements and accessible through a close entrance. No wonder Jude had been excited to find it.

Liam turned and headed back up the stairs. As far as he was aware, there was only the projection room left to search. If that was clear, he could stop fretting that she was lying hurt somewhere and simply wait for her to get in touch.

Outside the swing doors he stood for a moment re-adjusting to the darkness. The problem now was to locate the projection room. Was it above the balcony or below?

Liam realised he had no idea. He'd never even thought about it before. He tried to recall anything that Jude might have said about the cinemas she'd visited. Nothing came to mind. He decided that since he'd climbed this far, he might as well go to the top of the stairs, pitch black or not.

He turned right and began to climb. Half a dozen steps more and the stairwell opened out on to a landing. Maybe this was the location of the fire exit the woman had spoken about?

His eyes had adjusted enough to spot a Yale lock, and

he clicked it open and pushed. Cold night air flooded in along with light from the street lamps. Liam stepped out on to a fire escape. This is where Jude should have exited. He peered over on to a cobbled back alley below. He would check round there when he'd finished inside the cinema.

He pulled the door closed and made his way down the stairs. It was easier in this direction with the distant light of the foyer breaking the gloom. Probably that was the reason he spotted the narrow door on the left-hand side.

He pushed it open and called through it, waiting a few seconds before entering. The door opened on to a narrow corridor which ended in another door with a 'No Smoking' sign, suggesting this might indeed lead to the projection room. Liam tried the handle. It turned, but the door didn't budge. He banged on it.

'Jude, are you in there?'

Liam had a sudden image of Jude lying unconscious behind the door. He pushed harder. The door didn't move – it must be locked. Frustration filled him. Maybe he could ask the woman in the shop if she had a key. And if she didn't, what would he do then?

His frustration turned to annoyance. The place was derelict. What did it matter if he simply broke down the door? He was no rugby player, but he was strong enough to make some sort of impression on it.

He took a few steps back then launched himself at the door, slamming against it and driving the air from his lungs. The door shuddered in its frame but the lock stayed put.

Liam cursed loudly. If the door was locked when Jude was here, she didn't get in either, he told himself. Still, he decided to give it another try. This time the lock gave a little. 'Third time lucky,' he muttered. As his right shoulder struck, the lock broke and the door flew open.

Liam stepped inside, immediately conscious of a bad smell.

'Jude?'

He felt the wall for a light switch and flicked it on. He was on a metal platform and below him were the remnants of a projection room. He stepped down into it and took a slow look round. Small rectangular projection windows on the opposite wall, a sign about lighting. No big equipment but through an opening he could see what looked like ancient batteries. Apart from that, nothing but dust, a few bricks and the smell. Certainly nothing that suggested Jude had ever been there.

Liam turned and headed back up the steps. At the top he paused and turned for a last look. It was then he saw it. On the floor directly at the bottom of the steps was a clear footprint in the dust. A footprint he knew wasn't one of his own. Liam took a closer look. The print was around Jude's size, but it wasn't that that made his heart quicken. Jude had a thing about her belongings, including her clothes. Everything was marked with her initials – she'd even carved them into the soles of her shoes. He could see a J and an E on the heel of this print – Jude had been in this room.

Liam waited impatiently while the manager dealt with the current customer at the till. As soon as the elderly man had moved towards the door, Liam approached her.

'Your friend wasn't there?'

'No.'

'So nothing's happened to her?'

'I wouldn't say that.'

'What do you mean?'

'It's just that I found evidence that she'd been in the projection room, but the door had been locked afterwards.'

The woman looked bemused. 'Then how did you get in?'

'I thought it was just jammed.'

'You broke down the door?'

'I was worried that Jude had collapsed behind it.'

'Why would a healthy young woman just collapse? I hope she wasn't going in there to take drugs?'

'No, of course not.' Liam tried to get back on the subject. 'Who could have locked the door after Jude left?'

'If your friend isn't in there, what does it matter?'

He sighed impatiently. 'How do I get round to the alley at the back?'

'Why?'

'I just want to check . . .'

She interrupted him. 'I checked the door from the outside this morning. There was nothing there.'

Liam could tell by her increasingly irritable responses that he wasn't going to get any further. And the woman had a point. Jude might have been there, but she wasn't there now. He tried to thank her, but she had already caught sight of a customer and was headed towards her.

Liam stood outside the shop and checked his mobile just in case he'd missed a call or text from Jude, but there was nothing. Heavy hearted, he could think of nothing to do but return to his flat and wait. Going back to the police wasn't an option, not for another forty-eight hours.

Reluctantly, he set course for home.

As he walked past the Stravaigin on Gibson Street, he spotted his flatmate Ben inside and decided to join him. He had to tell someone about his dilemma.

Ben spotted him as he came in. 'What's up, mate? You look terrible.'

'I think Jude's gone missing.' Saying it out loud only made him more certain.

7

Rhona poured a glass of white wine and took it to the kitchen window. In the convent garden below, the spotlight illuminating the statue of the Virgin Mary had yet to come on, but dusk would see her bathed in a rosy glow.

Not for the first time Rhona felt blessed to look down on such an oasis of peace in the city. If the religious order ever sold the building and moved to somewhere more suited to the number of resident nuns, the place would likely be sold to a property developer. It was in a prime location and would convert to gracious flats. Rhona wondered if she could stay on here if such a thing happened. The garden had become such an important part of her life, even though she'd never set foot in it, merely waved at the gardener now and again.

She took a sip of wine and turned her attention to more immediate concerns. Einar Petersson would arrive soon and she would hand over the envelope that McNab had given her, but she was loathe to do this without knowing its contents. There was no guarantee that Petersson would share them with her, even if he opened the envelope in her presence.

She fetched it from her bag and placed it on the table. Why had McNab not simply told her what was in it? Because they were in a public place, or because she, like

Bill, might be compromised by the knowledge? There was a third explanation; McNab feared she might act on its contents herself.

The envelope was standard in size and not bulky. She held it up to the light, then examined the flap, which had been stuck down firmly. Rhona made a decision, fetched a knife from the stand and slit the envelope open. Inside was a single sheet of paper. She unfolded it and found, to her surprise, that it was blank. Rhona stared at it for a moment, bemused. Was this supposed to be a joke? Then annoyance began to take over from puzzlement. What did McNab think he was playing at? Arranging to meet her, passing on some 'important information' for Petersson which turned out to be a blank sheet of paper?

She held the paper up to the light. No secret writing, no markings of any sort. She placed it on the table. What was she to do now? Put the paper in another envelope and pass it off to Petersson as the original? What would he think? That she'd brought him here under false pretences?

Rhona glanced at her watch. Petersson could be here any minute. She went through to her study and checked in the desk for a similar envelope. She had none and had to settle for one from a Christmas card box. She would have to refold the sheet, which would be a bit of a give-away. The cloak and dagger nature of the whole business infuriated her. She took the paper back to the kitchen. She would simply tell Petersson she'd opened the envelope.

She drank the wine and refilled her glass, cursing McNab under her breath. Condensation from the cold glass had run on to the table, dampening the original envelope. It was this that drew her eyes to a dark mark. She picked up the envelope and looked inside. There was something written close to the bottom fold. Rhona took the knife, slit the seams and read the message.

She opened the door twenty minutes later to a smiling Petersson who was carrying a bag that emitted a delicious spicy smell.

'I hope you like curry?'

'You can't live in Glasgow and not like curry,' she assured him.

He followed her through to the kitchen and began unpacking the bag while she fetched plates and cutlery.

He spotted the wine glass. 'I brought a red, but I see you've already started on white.'

'Red on white, you're all right,' she quoted, and fetched two balloon glasses while he opened the bottle.

Her earlier irritation had passed now that she knew the contents of the envelope. She'd subsequently decided to use the new envelope to make a mock-up of the original one, complete with message – now written by her – and containing a new sheet of blank paper. It would be interesting to see how Petersson would react and whether he would decipher its contents.

They ate in companionable silence. The tall Icelander had an ability to exude calm, and she found herself unable to read his thoughts, unlike McNab, whose every passing thought and desire were often reflected in his eyes, even when he tried to disguise them.

Petersson topped up her glass.

'OK, let's see this message.'

He accepted it, turned it over in his hand, examined the outside, then pulled open the flap and extracted the sheet of paper. Unlike her, he didn't spend time puzzling over the blankness, but peered inside instead, then immediately parted the seams and read the message out loud. 'Brogan was in the car.' He studied her expression. 'You already knew what it said?'

'I opened it earlier.'

'He suspected you would, hence the blank paper.'

'McNab thinks he's a funny guy. He's not always right.'

'This is the first you've heard that Paddy Brogan was in the car that night?' Petersson said.

'His alibi placed him in the Poker Club.'

'So why didn't McNab reveal this before now?'

'Probably because it would prove he was still alive,' she suggested.

Petersson considered that.

'What does McNab expect you to do with this information?' asked Rhona.

'I'm not sure. Approach Brogan for him, I suspect.'

'And ask him to testify?'

'You said Brogan wanted the Russians off his patch?' said Petersson. 'Maybe this is a way for him to achieve that.'

'Have you had dealings with Paddy Brogan before?'

Petersson shook his head. 'But I can talk my way in, no problem.'

Rhona didn't doubt it. Einar Petersson had unmasked a number of criminals as an investigative journalist, and had the physical scars to prove it; she had seen them when she'd taken him into her bed. She had hoped he could help nail Nikolai Kalinin, if not for McNab's murder, then for something else. And he had done everything expected of him, both in and out of the bedroom.

'OK, I'll approach Brogan. See what he has to say.'

'He can turn on the charm, but he's ruthless,' she warned.

'As ruthless as Kalinin?'

She doubted that. As far as she was aware, Paddy Brogan didn't have a penchant for torture.

'To the world in general, Paddy looks like a bona fide Glasgow business man, who makes his money from gambling and bookies' shops,' she said. 'He had it pretty well sewn up here before Kalinin arrived.'

'So we could be doing him a favour if we can remove the Russian?'

'He might see it that way. Though the proposal would have to be carefully put.'

Petersson was eyeing her suspiciously. 'You weren't planning on approaching Brogan yourself?'

The thought had been crossing and re-crossing Rhona's mind since she'd opened the letter.

'Is that such a bad idea?'

He frowned. 'I shouldn't have shown you the message.'

'I knew already, remember?'

They were saved further discussion by the sound of the buzzer. Rhona rose and went to answer it. There was a short silence followed by a male voice she didn't recognise.

'Uh . . . Rhona?'

'Who is this?' she answered, sharply.

'It's Liam. May I come up? There's something I need to speak to you about.'

It had taken him ten minutes to work up the courage to press the buzzer. When he first heard her voice, he had been initially unable to find his own. Now she had released the door and he could enter, Liam questioned whether he shouldn't just turn and go. It had been Ben's idea to come here, and after a couple of pints it had sounded like a good one.

'People go missing all the time. You only have to buy the *Big Issue* to see that,' Ben had said. 'And let's face it, Jude's not a wee kid. They won't spend a lot of resources looking for her. What about that guy that went missing up Aberdeenshire way six years ago? A bloke's just confessed to his murder. He'd buried him in a field not far from the village they both lived in.'

'You're not helping.'

'Hey, mate, you've got contacts. Use them.'

Liam had blanched. He'd forgotten he'd recently spilled the beans on his adoptive status and the identity of his birth mother. He'd had too much to drink, and Dr Rhona MacLeod had hit the headlines in the foetal-theft case in Kelvingrove Park.

'I don't know,' he'd muttered into his beer.

'Look, mate, if you're worried about this Jude chick, you've got to do something about it.'

By the time he'd drained his second pint, Liam had agreed.

Now he took his time climbing the stairs, trying to work out what he would say. He hadn't contacted or been to see Rhona for over six months. Back then, she'd been living with an Irishman called Sean Maguire, a jazz saxophonist. Liam had arrived at the flat unexpectedly and Sean had invited him in, given him a drink and they'd got to talking. Liam had liked the guy.

When Rhona had eventually arrived to discover him

sitting at her kitchen table she'd been taken aback, but it had all worked out all right in the end, mainly because of Sean. When Liam had eventually left he'd promised to keep in touch. A promise he hadn't kept.

When he reached the landing, the door to the flat stood open and Rhona was waiting for him. As an adopted child, he still found it unsettling to gaze upon his birth mother. Rhona was essentially a stranger and yet Liam could see himself in her, particularly the quizzical expression she wore at this moment.

His other features – the height, the hair colour – he attributed to his father, whom he had never met. Rhona had told Liam a bit about him and the circumstances that had led her to give her son up for adoption. He was aware that his real father was married with two grown-up children, and that he didn't want Liam to know his identity. That had hurt at the time, but he could understand why. His adoptive parents had also been hurt when he'd set his heart on finding Rhona, although they had tried to hide it from him. He would always think of James and Elizabeth Hope as his real parents. So what did that make the woman who stood before him?

'Liam. It's good to see you.'

He stuttered a reply. 'I'm sorry I haven't been in touch before now.'

She stood to one side. 'Come on in. We're in the kitchen.'

She had visitors. Liam stopped short. 'I'm sorry, I could come back at another time.'

'Einar and I had some business to discuss, but we're finished now. You timed your visit well.'

Liam hesitated at the kitchen door until Rhona urged

him inside. The smell of curry hung in the air and the table held the remnants of a meal. The man seated there stood up as Liam came in. He was tall and blond with a well-toned physique. Liam worked out himself and was a member of the Glasgow University judo team, but he didn't think he could hold his own against Rhona's visitor.

'Einar Petersson,' the man held out his hand. The look on his face was friendly but intrigued. He obviously had no idea who Liam was.

Rhona cleared that up immediately.

'Einar, this is my son, Liam Hope.'

'Pleased to meet you, Liam.'

If Einar had been unaware that Rhona had a son, he didn't show it. Nor did he ask why his name was Hope. After the introduction, Rhona seemed unsure what to do next. It was Einar who saved them. 'I'm afraid we've finished the wine, but there's still some curry if you're hungry?'

Liam was very hungry, having forgotten to eat, but he wasn't about to say so.

'Seems a shame to waste it. What if I heat a plate up for you?'

Liam nodded gratefully. It seemed the thing to do.

Rhona was clearing the table of their debris and setting him a place. Liam sat down at it. He was already imagining the scenario where he would eat in silence. Petersson would leave and Liam would then explain to Rhona why he was here. But what if this Einar was a permanent fixture at the flat, and not a visiting colleague? What if he had replaced the jazz musician? He was certainly moving around the kitchen as though at home there, fetching a plate from the cupboard and opening the right drawer first time to get cutlery.

'How's Sean?' Liam blurted out.

Rhona gave him a cool look. 'Sean and I aren't together any more.'

'Oh, I'm sorry,' he muttered, red with embarrassment. 'I didn't know.' How could he, when he hadn't been near the place since last summer?

Luckily at that moment the microwave pinged. Einar retrieved the plate of curry and placed it down in front of him. The sight and smell of it made Liam realise just how ravenous he was. He set about the curry with a will. At least while he was eating he didn't have to speak.

Contrary to what Liam had hoped, Einar didn't look as if he was about to leave. In fact he went to a nearby cupboard and extracted a bottle of whisky. Liam saw Rhona's eyebrows rise as he poured a couple of drams and added a little water to each.

'I thought you'd have to get back,' she said.

'I'm not in any hurry.'

Liam, watching this exchange, tried to work out what it meant. It appeared that Einar didn't live in the flat, although he seemed to know his way about. The thought crossed Liam's mind that this may have been a sexual tryst and he'd interrupted their romantic meal. He choked a little on this and covered his confusion by waving his hand in front of his mouth as though the curry was hot. Rhona smiled and poured him a glass of water.

They sat in silence as he finished eating, although Liam had the impression that Rhona was thinking about something other than his visit.

His plate cleared and two thirds of the jug of water drunk, Liam decided it was time to say his piece. Einar showed no sign of leaving and perhaps his presence might make things easier. Liam turned to face Rhona.

'I came to ask your advice.'

'Go ahead,' she said with a smile.

Liam cleared his throat. 'A friend of mine, Jude Evans, is a student at the School of Art. She's doing a photographic project on old Glasgow cinemas.' He paused. 'She went to visit the old Rosevale on Dumbarton Road yesterday evening and . . . disappeared.'

Rhona had been listening carefully, waiting to hear how this might pertain to her. And now she knew.

'Disappeared?'

Liam rushed on. 'She arranged to meet me after the visit but didn't turn up. I checked the halls of residence but she didn't go back there either. So I visited the Rosevale today, and the manager of the shop downstairs had let her through to view the old foyer and projection room. She didn't see her leave.' He stopped to catch his breath. 'I asked to go inside, and the projection room was locked. I broke down the door,' he said sheepishly. 'Jude's footprint was there in the dust, and the manager of the shop had no idea who could have locked the door.'

He stopped and searched her face. Rhona didn't look disbelieving, just puzzled.

'What happens when you try to call her?'

'There's no answer. I got a text telling me she was going to be late but it didn't arrive until the next day, as though she'd been out of range. I went to the police, but they say it's too soon and she'll turn up.'

'What about her family?'

'She doesn't have one. She was brought up in care in Sunderland.'

'Have you tried the hospitals? Accident and Emergency?'

Liam felt his face flush hotly. 'I never thought to do that.'

'They didn't suggest it to you at the police station?'

'I don't think so.' He'd been so agitated and desperate for them to take him seriously, Liam wasn't sure he'd really listened to what was being said.

'Well, that's our first port of call.' Rhona paused, thoughtfully. 'She was last seen in Dumbarton Road, you say?'

'She went into the British Heart Foundation shop just before five o'clock.'

'OK, we'll start with the Western Infirmary.'

Half an hour later, they'd established that no Jude Evans had been admitted to the hospital. Even though it didn't help find her, Liam felt they'd achieved something.

'There's no chance that Jude has a boyfriend she's staying with?'

'Jude is,' Liam hesitated, looking for a description that didn't sound critical, 'very organised. She likes routine. If she says she'll do something, she does it.'

'So not turning up is out of character?'

'Very much so.'

Einar had made a pot of coffee and he set it on the table. His interest awakened by Liam's story, he was showing no desire to leave.

Rhona seemed to come to a decision. 'I think I should take a look at the Rosevale. Particularly the room you say was locked after Jude left it.' She looked steadily at

Liam. 'You're sure there was no sign of a struggle? No blood?'

'No, just the footprint.'

'How do you know it was hers?'

'Jude has a thing about her belongings. She doesn't like anyone to touch them. She carves her initials on the soles of her shoes.'

Rhona nodded. 'OK, meet me at the shop tomorrow morning at eleven. If Jude gets in touch before then, text me and let me know.' She handed him her business card.

Liam let the outside door close behind him and stood for a moment. It was pouring. He zipped his jacket shut and flipped up his hood before stepping out into the rain. He was glad he'd come and asked for help. Rhona had been great about it and hadn't offered him the same platitudes he'd been given at the police station, but the respite from the worry and concern that had brought him here was brief.

He checked his mobile just in case, but there was nothing and it was too late now to call the halls of residence and check in with Charlie. He could only hope that wherever Jude was she was warm and dry, and, more importantly, safe.

8

With the arrival of British Summer Time and lighter mornings, Rhona invariably woke before she needed to. She'd got into the habit of getting up anyway, but today she lay on, letting her mind roam over the events of the previous day.

When she'd believed DS Michael McNab to be dead, she'd begun referring to him as Michael in her mind and her speech. Now that he was alive again, she found herself reverting to his surname. Chrissy had once called McNab our 'urban warrior', and it felt wrong to call a resurrected warrior by his first name when that name was as prosaic as Michael.

Rhona recalled the look on McNab's face as he'd handed her the envelope and felt her irritation rise again. Did he hide the words just to annoy or thwart her, knowing she wouldn't be able to stop herself from opening the envelope? Or, more charitably, had he simply not wanted her to know, for fear of what she might do? If so, he'd been right. The moment she'd seen Brogan's name, she'd wanted to confront him.

By the time Petersson had left the previous evening, they'd reached a compromise. Rhona would accompany the journalist to the Poker Club, ostensibly as his date. During their time there, Petersson would ask to meet with Brogan. It had taken a fair amount of persuasion to get Petersson to agree to her going with him. He was only swayed by his fear of the alternative; that she would go and speak to Brogan herself.

'As long as you're sure Brogan won't recognise you,' he'd said.

'How could he? I've never met him.'

'What about that night?'

'Brogan's alibi puts him inside the club at the time of the shooting. He knew better than to show his face outside afterwards. He never saw me, and I never saw him.'

Finally Petersson had given in. They'd parted, agreeing that he would collect her the following night at nine o'clock.

Rhona threw back the duvet and headed for the shower. Once under the pounding water she allowed herself to recall the pleasure she'd felt when she'd realised who was on the intercom. Her eagerness, mixed with anxiety, as she'd heard Liam climb the stairs. Then the first view of her son's face in six months.

He looked so like her. How could she have forgotten?

Rhona raised her face to the spray, letting it beat against her closed eyes and mouth. Liam had sought her out and asked for her help, and the idea pleased her. She could never hope to be his mother – someone else had done that job too well to be replaced – but she could do this for him.

From what Liam had said about Jude, it did sound out of character for her not to turn up as arranged. And, in Rhona's world, people who were 'unlikely' to disappear were just as likely to turn up dead. It was a morbid thought, but one that had to be considered.

Once dried and dressed, she logged in and set about

checking that no one matching Jude's description had turned up dead in Scotland in the last twenty-four hours.

Liam was waiting for her outside the shop, his face pinched with cold. The switch to British Summer Time had brought a sudden drop in temperature and an inch of snow. It was melting quickly, turning to slush under the constant passing of feet and cars, but a bitter easterly wind had taken its place.

As she approached, Rhona saw Liam glance down at her forensic bag, before greeting her with a nod.

'I take it there's been no word from Jude?' she asked.

Liam shook his head.

'OK, let's take a look.'

A bell tinkled as she pushed open the door, causing the woman behind the counter to look up. She spotted Liam and a worried look crossed her face.

Rhona approached the woman with a smile and offered her card.

'Forensic services? Is that the same as the police?'

'Not quite.' Rhona held out her hand. 'Dr Rhona MacLeod.'

The woman shook her hand reluctantly. 'Carol Miller.'

'I'm sorry to bother you, Carol, but we're growing increasingly concerned about a missing girl who I understand visited the old cinema a couple of days ago.'

Carol nodded at Liam. 'He's already looked. She's not in there.'

'I know. I just wanted to check for myself. Could you let me through, please?'

The other woman gazed uncertainly at Rhona. Her

previous experience of letting people visit the remains of the Rosevale hadn't gone well.

Finally she shrugged and said, 'Well, I suppose if it's police business.'

Rhona let that small misconception pass. 'I'm very grateful.'

Somewhat mollified, Carol indicated they should follow her through. She unlocked the interconnecting door, stepped inside and switched on the light.

'It's at your own risk, you know that?'

'I understand. Thank you.'

Carol bustled away fretfully, obviously not fully happy with her decision.

Rhona stepped inside the illuminated foyer and stood mesmerised for a moment. The immediate smells were of dust and disuse, yet others filtered through, the scent of wood, the plaster of the mouldings, the thick carpet on the stairs. The space was palatial, from the circular ticket booth and parquet floor to the frieze that circled the wall.

Rhona remembered her parents talking about cinemas such as this one, but by the time she was old enough to go to the pictures – as the Scots said – most of these stunningly designed buildings had been converted into bingo halls.

'This way.' Liam interrupted her thoughts, urging her towards the stairs.

Rhona took a last look round the impressive room, then followed him. If this turned out to be the locus of a crime she would have to cover every inch of this space, but for now the projection room was her priority.

The light dwindled as they climbed. Rhona fished in her

bag for her torch, but Liam had one ready and flicked it on. He pointed ahead.

'The balcony and fire exit are up there. The projection room's this way.' He swung the beam round to the right, illuminating a narrow set of steps.

Rhona followed as he pushed open a door and held it back for her to enter. The old carpet odour faded here, replaced by a musty concrete smell. At the end of a narrow corridor was a second door.

'This is the one that was locked.' Liam indicated the broken catch and splintered wood. He pushed open the heavy door, reached inside and found a light switch.

Rhona stepped on to the small platform beyond the door and looked down on the projection room.

Liam pointed. 'Jude's footprint is at the bottom of the steps.'

'OK. Can you stay up here for now?'

'Why?'

'It's better if we don't both walk about disturbing things. Did you touch anything when you were here before?'

Liam shook his head. 'Apart from breaking down the door.' He gave her a brief smile.

'Good.'

Rhona stepped back into the corridor and pulled on a forensic boiler suit.

'Is that really necessary?' Liam looked worried.

Rhona ignored the question, lifted her bag and made her way down the steps. She didn't glance back but could sense the boy's intent gaze following her. If Jude was found harmed, then the last place she was known to visit was significant to any investigation; if she turned up safe and well, their visit here didn't count. Rhona prayed for the latter.

She located the footprint Liam had indicated and crouched for a closer look. He'd been correct about the initials. Rhona could clearly make out *JE* imprinted in the layer of grime and dust. She took some photographs, then stepped carefully across to continue her examination of the room. Apart from a few fixtures and fittings and scattered lengths of metal, there appeared to be nothing of note.

She moved on to the side rooms. One wall of the second room had an aperture at the back, and as Rhona went over for a closer look she caught the trace of a scent she knew only too well.

The smell of a body in the initial stages of decomposition was unforgettable. Whatever was rotting in this building was well past the first stage, which meant it couldn't be Jude.

Rhona's initial concern subsided into curiosity as she squeezed through the hole into a small cloakroom. A quick look round revealed nothing that could be giving off that smell. She closed her eyes and stood for a moment, breathing in, trying to pinpoint its source. When she re-opened her eyes she was staring at a brick wall with a hole halfway up. The smell was coming from there.

The mortar was loose and fell away with ease, as did a large chunk of the brick bordering the hole. Now Rhona had a space big enough to take a proper look through. She aimed her torch directly in.

The small hope that there might have been a dead animal behind the wall was quashed when the beam hit what looked like a pair of mummified human eyeballs partly covered by scraps of light-coloured hair. Rhona yelped in shock, despite herself.

'What is it?' Liam called down, his voice high with fright.

'It's OK. It's not Jude,' she shouted back. Jude had disappeared forty-eight hours ago, and this body had been walled up here for a lot longer than that.

Rhona retraced her path to the stairs where Liam was peering down at her, terrified. 'What did you find?'

There was little point in lying.

'There's a body behind a wall. It's been there for some time.'

'Jesus!'

Rhona expected a barrage of questions as they made their way back through the foyer, but Liam seemed to have been struck dumb. When they reached the shop, Rhona called the manager across. Carol's default expression of exasperation melted into concern when she saw Liam's white, frightened face.

'What's happened? Did you find the girl?' she asked Rhona.

'No, but we found someone else.'

9

The crime-scene manager had made the decision to use the fire exit as their main entry point. That way, access could be restricted and a mobile incident unit parked at the rear of the building instead of on Dumbarton Road.

The occupants of the neighbouring flats were having a field day, their windows offering them a bird's-eye view of the proceedings. No doubt the comings and goings of crime scene personnel would end up on YouTube. The decision had suited Carol Miller too; she'd been spared the need to shut up shop while the body was forensically examined and removed.

A shaken Liam had gone home, promising to let Rhona know if he had any word from Jude. In return, Rhona had said that under the circumstances she would officially report Jude missing, since the last place she'd been seen had turned out to be a crime scene.

'There's still a chance Jude will turn up unharmed,' she'd assured Liam as he'd left. 'Don't give up hope on that.' When he hadn't looked convinced, she'd gone on: 'She left the building. Someone will have seen her. With the degree of interest this case will generate, people will come forward. And the police will be reviewing all security-camera footage from the surrounding area.'

Liam had left, shoulders hunched in worry.

When Chrissy arrived, Rhona had given her a brief resumé of how the body had been discovered, including the presence at the scene of Jude's footprint. Normally Chrissy would have been intrigued at Liam's reappearance and eager for more information, especially since the story now involved a missing girlfriend and a dead body. However, she'd clearly not yet forgiven Rhona. Rhona watched as Chrissy struggled with this dilemma, eventually settling for a straight question.

'And there's no sign of this Jude yet?'

'No.'

'OK.' Chrissy finished pulling on her boiler suit. 'Let's take a look.'

The staircase leading from the fire exit was no longer in shadow, and below them arc lights now revealed the foyer in all its glory. Despite the dust and decay it was still an impressive sight, and Chrissy momentarily forgot her huff.

'Wow! My mum's always going on about how amazing the Olympia in Bridgeton was. Now I know what she means.'

The double doors to the balcony stood open. Beyond, a team of SOCOs were working their way through the rows of seats. Rhona led Chrissy to the projection suite, which had been cordoned off and was guarded by a uniformed officer. Rhona asked if R2S had been requested to map and photograph the locus, and was told that Roy Hunter was expected at any time.

As they picked their way across the metal treads and into the spool room, the foetid smell grew stronger. Chrissy raised her mask before following Rhona into the cloakroom.

The arc light in here was trained on the brick wall, and Rhona indicated the cavity halfway up.

'There was no sucking noise when I removed the brick, and no sudden rush of stronger odour.'

'So the brick was already loose?'

Rhona pointed at a small pile of broken mortar. 'I would say someone had scraped at it fairly recently.'

'Jude?'

'Maybe.'

Chrissy crouched on one of the metal treads already in place and put her eye to the hole. 'The smell's not fresh. It's been in there a while.'

In the early stages of human decomposition the smell of putrefaction would be overwhelming, sometimes even for a seasoned professional. It began at around 10 degrees centigrade but favoured a range of 21 to 38 degrees. Any higher a temperature tended to retard the process, drying out the body fluids.

This body had been held in a confined and airless space, the atmosphere warm and dry, which explained the mummified eyes.

By the time Roy arrived, they'd numbered the bricks ready for removal. He took his time, surveying the wall with interest and not a little pleasure. It wasn't every day he was called to a scene like this and it was obvious he relished the prospect.

'How do you want to play this?' Rhona said, finally.

'I suggest I put a probe through and we capture as much as we can before we remove any more bricks. That way you can view the interior without disturbing anything. With the HDR camera you'll get up to thirty different exposures.

We can start in darkness and then gradually bring all the detail on screen.'

'Sounds good to me.'

Roy set up the camera on its tripod, attached it to his laptop then eased a probe through the aperture. The first exposures began in darkness, gradually lifting to light.

They began to make out a narrow alcove. Against the lower half of this were the collapsed remains of a naked body. As the exposures lightened, they saw a mesh of silvery spider webs. The light from the lens provoked a flurry of activity amid the inhabitants and a long-legged spider took flight, escaping through the aperture to fall on to Rhona's hand. She shook it lightly to the floor, where it scuttled off at great speed, and focused back on the screen.

'Looks like the deceased was male,' said Chrissy. 'What's that across his chest?'

'Some kind of harness?' replied Rhona. The camera moved slowly upwards to glint off a semicircle of silver spikes. 'And a studded collar.'

'OK, I'm beginning to get the picture,' said Chrissy.

The scalp and hair had detached from the skull and slid forward to partially cover the eyes, as Rhona had seen when she'd first peered through the hole. Now she could also make out the exposed cranium. It looked intact, with no obvious evidence of trauma. The human skull varies in thickness, with a thicker frontal area and the temporal region thinner and therefore more vulnerable to fracture.

'No obvious evidence of a fractured skull. Can you come down a little lower to the mouth?'

Roy did so.

'The tongue's still attached, and it's protrusive,' she noted. 'Can you focus on the neck?'

This was more difficult due to the collar. Roy moved the camera about.

'I can't see a ligature.'

'Unless the collar acted as one.'

'OK, let's take another look at the torso.'

The collapsing body had slumped at the waist, the legs folded sideways, the abdomen obscured by the bent legs. There were no obvious puncture holes from bullets or sharp implements in the brown-black leathery skin.

As they reached the lower half, the left hand came into view. It had broken free of the wrist, and now lay across the remains of the left knee.

'Hold it there.'

Rhona studied the image closely. The hand was shrivelled and dried out. Hanging loose on the forefinger was a chunky tarnished silver ring, but what interested her was the mangled state of the fingernails.

'Can you find the right hand?'

The camera scanned slowly across the torso.

'Stop there.'

The right hand was visible now, propped against the back wall.

'Give me a close-up on the fingernails, please.'

Roy zoomed in. Those that had not detached were also badly broken, several of them to half their normal length.

'So, what d'you think?' Chrissy said.

'No blunt-force wounds to the head. No obvious ligature, no weapon holes visible. A protruding tongue and damaged nails and fingers.' Rhona paused. 'I'd hazard a guess and say he suffocated trying to claw his way out. Which might account for the loosened brick.'

'You mean the poor bastard was walled up alive?'

'It's a strong possibility.'

'What is?' a disembodied voice called from the next room. The suited figure of DI Bill Wilson eased through the aperture. Rhona watched his reaction as the smell hit him.

'Minging, isn't it?' Chrissy offered helpfully.

'Not as minging as that burned body in the skip, or the remains we fished out of the sewage farm.' Bill came for a closer look. 'Any ideas on how long it's been in there?'

'We're working on it. Rhona thinks he might have been walled in alive.'

'So not an accident or suicide?'

'Not unless he laid the bricks himself from the inside. The body's shrunk and collapsed as it decomposed, but it must have been upright when it was put in there, otherwise the space is too narrow to accommodate it. Can you magnify the left hand again?'

They waited as the shape of the hand became more defined.

'That looks like a metal nail head between the lunate and scaphoid bones of the palm.' Rhona turned to Roy. 'Can we take a look at the wall behind, say two thirds of the way up?'

The camera tracked as requested, then moved horizontally across the wall.

'There,' Rhona stopped Roy. There was a mark in the

plywood that looked like a nail-hole, surrounded by a circular stain.

'I think he was nailed to the wall.'

Chrissy and Rhona adjourned to the projection room. The next stage would be for Roy to remove a few bricks at a time, repeating the process of 360-degree spherical high definition video capture using different lights to highlight the presence of various substances, including blood and semen. He would also video the back of the bricks before they were removed. All of this took time, which meant they could take a break.

'I spotted a café across the road. You coming?' Chrissy offered.

Rhona quickly nodded, hoping the invitation meant she had at least started on the road to forgiveness.

They emerged on to a sunlit Dumbarton Road, busy with shoppers. Chrissy led the way across the street to the café. It proved a bit of a find, serving fresh baked goods.

Rhona ordered a giant cherry scone with her latte and Chrissy went for something even more substantial, a roll which appeared to have every possible filling in it. Silence reigned while Chrissy demolished it.

'OK,' she said finally. 'I haven't forgiven or forgotten. So don't think I have.'

Rhona remained silent, which seemed the safest option.

'But from now on, I want to know if you're plotting anything.'

'I'm going to the Poker Club tonight.'

'What?' Chrissy looked astonished. 'But why?'

'Petersson wants to speak to Brogan.'

'About the shooting?'

Rhona nodded. It was as much as she was prepared to reveal, forgiveness or not.

'Why are *you* going?' Chrissy said suspiciously.

'He asked me to,' Rhona lied.

'What if Brogan recognises you?'

'How could he? He's never seen me.'

Chrissy mulled this over, all the while scrutinising Rhona through narrowed eyes.

'Petersson didn't ask you. This was your idea, wasn't it?' Chrissy knew her too well.

'Let's say we came to a mutual understanding.'

Chrissy made an indignant sound that was identifiably Scottish. Their gazes locked, and Rhona wondered which of them might be classed as the more stubborn. It was a close call.

'OK.' Chrissy drew herself up. 'I *won't* tell Bill about this excursion, *if* you promise to tell me what happens.'

Rhona couldn't help but be impressed. Chrissy was an expert at going for the jugular.

'OK,' she conceded.

Chrissy nodded, well pleased.

Rhona quickly changed the subject, before any further compromises were extracted.

'Once Roy's finished, I'd like you to go over the projection suite while I process the body.'

Chrissy wrinkled her nose in disgust. 'Fine by me.'

She might be vocal about smells, but she wasn't squeamish. At eight months pregnant she'd been in the burned-out skip Bill had mentioned, scraping the remains of an arson victim from its walls. Rhona's forensic assistant was formidable in more ways than one.

They paid the bill and headed back. Judging by the number of customers, either the charity shop was doing a roaring trade or there were a lot of rubberneckers looking for an update on the dead body found on the premises.

Roy Hunter met them by the mobile unit.

'All finished in the box. I'll start on the foyer and balcony.'

Rhona nodded her agreement.

'I spotted a footprint in the projection suite. It had the initials JE on the sole,' Roy added.

'Thanks. Chrissy will deal with that.' Rhona chose not to fill him in on Jude's visit for the moment.

Leaving the outer rooms in Chrissy's capable hands, she went into the cloakroom, pulled up a chair and sat down with her notebook, intent on recording her initial reaction and observations.

The collapsed remains had been fully exposed now, and the bricks removed and taken to the laboratory for further study. In the brightness of the arc lamp, the patches of mummification were more identifiable. The hands in particular had survived well. To retrieve fingerprints, she could attempt to cut off the upper level of skin. Alternatively, she could remove the fingers entirely and soak them overnight in a Photoflow solution to help her achieve a print.

She decided on the second method, but elected to leave the removal until the post mortem. She didn't want to introduce any contamination, and if she bagged the hands before transportation they should survive unharmed.

Before she disturbed the body any further, Rhona began

taking her own photographs to study later, building up a picture of the victim as she did so. Slim and of average height. Most likely male by the width of the shoulders and hand size.

Having recorded and photographed all the details to her satisfaction, she set about testing the stain on the back wall. She folded a small circular piece of card in half then half again to form a point, using it to scrape a little of the substance. Presumptive tests were based on the ability of haemoglobin present in blood cells to catalyse the oxidation of certain reagents. In this case the resultant pink indicated the presence of blood, backing up her suggestion that the victim had been nailed to the wall, later breaking free in an attempt to claw his way out.

When she'd processed the torso, Rhona turned her attention to the hands. She dealt with the detached left hand first, as it was more easily bagged for transportation. The right hand was trickier. She feared at one point her attempts might result in the whole body collapsing further. The head she processed last, carefully swabbing the remains of the mouth. Satisfied, Rhona finally sat back on her haunches.

There was no good way to die, but this end struck her as particularly ghoulish. If given a choice, being buried alive would have been her worst option. The idea of coming to, in a confined space, knowing there was little air, little time and even less hope of rescue fed into her own claustrophobia. As a murder method it suggested a particularly sadistic killer. Or was it a sex game that had gone one step too far?

The shop manager had said that her staff never came

up here; in fact, most people didn't realise there was anything left of the old cinema. Jude had been the first person to ask for access since Carol Miller had been working there.

There were only two ways to get in here as far as Rhona was aware; through the shop using Carol's key, or via the fire exit which had to be opened from the inside. Rhona was also puzzled by the layout of the cloakroom itself. She'd entered via a hole in the wall of the spool room. Usherettes wouldn't have had to go through the projection suite to reach their cloakroom. So how had they got in here normally?

The most likely explanation was that the alcove had been the original entrance, boarded up some time later. Roy's recording and the resulting floor plan would hopefully show if that were the case.

Which led to the issue of the body's removal. Transporting it undamaged through the hole to the spool room wasn't a possibility. The better option would be to remove it intact from behind, if they could work out how to get round there.

She stood up to stretch her legs, conscious that she was both thirsty and hungry. The warmth in the room, topped up periodically as the heating for the charity shop roared into action, had left her feeling dehydrated, much like the body she was studying.

'I thought you were going out tonight?' Chrissy squeezed through the hole.

'What time is it?'

'Eight o'clock.'

'Eight!'

'Time flies when you're having fun.' Chrissy looked as though she meant it. 'I found three footprints besides the "JE" one. I've taken casts.'

'Anything else?'

This was the question Chrissy had been waiting for. She held up a bagged silver object, the size and shape of a small mobile phone. Rhona waited for her to explain.

'A digital voice recorder,' Chrissy said triumphantly. 'And I'd take a wild guess and say it's Jude's, because there's a sticker on the back with her initials.'

Bill had taken up residence in the mobile unit and was currently engaged in drinking a mug of tea. A triumphant Chrissy handed him her prize on entry, before demanding to know if there were any decent biscuits. While her assistant raided a box of Jaffa Cakes, Rhona explained to Bill why she'd come to the cinema in the first place.

'And this Jude disappeared how long ago?'

'Forty-eight hours now.'

'Liam reported this?'

'He tried yesterday, but was told it was too early and to come back later.'

'And she definitely hasn't turned up?'

'Liam hasn't called or texted, so I assume not. There's something else odd about Jude's visit here. When Liam came looking for her, the door to the projection suite was locked. He broke it down, worried she might be stuck inside. The manager can't explain who might have done that after Jude left, or why.'

'That's Jude's recorder,' Chrissy piped up through a mouthful of biscuit. 'See the initials?'

'Liam said she initials everything, even the soles of her shoes.'

Bill pulled on a pair of latex gloves, extracted the recorder from the bag and pressed the play button. Nothing happened.

'The battery's probably flat,' sighed Chrissy, disappointed.

'Could this Jude have been aware of the body?' Bill said.

'She might have smelt it. Also there was a loose brick which may have been taken out before.' Rhona glanced at her watch. 'I'm sorry, I have to go.'

'She's off out tonight,' Chrissy said sweetly.

Rhona threw her a warning glance.

Chrissy countered it with a glare of her own, silently reminding Rhona of their deal.

'I'd like a word with Liam tomorrow,' Bill said as she made her exit.

'I'll text you his number,' Rhona promised.

As she made for the car, she thought how odd the situation was. Having her son back in touch was good, the circumstances leading to it not so positive. If Jude didn't turn up soon, then Liam would have to be involved in an investigation into her disappearance. Rhona wondered how he would cope with that. If she was honest, she wondered how *she* would cope.

10

Liam found himself shivering uncontrollably. It had started on the way to the flat. Thankfully Ben wasn't in, so he didn't have to explain what had happened at the cinema. He knew the shivering meant he was in shock, but since he'd not actually seen a dead body, only heard that there was one, Liam felt a wimp.

After fifteen minutes, he managed to get himself together enough to head for the pub. His only concern was he might not be able to lift the pint to his mouth. He solved this by taking a seat at one of the dining tables. He had no appetite, but he'd rather order food than stand at the bar.

Hidden in the furthest corner, his body turned from the door, Liam ran over what had happened at the cinema. The terrible moment when he'd heard Rhona cry out and thought she'd found Jude. Rhona had changed after that, her interest in Jude gone, swept away by what she'd found behind that brick wall.

She'd been kind enough in her dismissal, mouthing encouraging words about reporting Jude missing, telling him she was sure to turn up soon, but the discovery of the body had become Rhona's primary concern.

Liam couldn't shake a nagging feeling that Jude's disappearance had something to do with the dead body. Jude was curious, obsessively so. He couldn't help thinking that if Rhona had been drawn to the body by the smell, then Jude would also have discovered it.

He suspected she'd texted him from inside the cinema, excited by what she'd seen. His own mobile had had no signal in there, which explained why Jude's text hadn't arrived until later. But how had it taken until the next day? Had Jude been in the Rosevale all that time? And if so, where was she now?

He had a sick feeling in his stomach. He'd never thought about someone going missing before. He bought the *Big Issue* fairly regularly and had seen the adverts for missing people, but they'd barely registered with him.

What if Jude never got in touch, like those people in the adverts? Would he just give up and forget her? Liam raised his pint with a trembling hand and took a gulp as an even worse scenario presented itself. Jude would be found, but she would be dead, like that body behind the wall.

He would have to do something constructive or he would go mad. Liam reached in his pocket for the memory stick. There were other files stored on it he hadn't looked at yet, including sound files from Jude's interviews. He would listen to those, maybe get in contact with the people she'd spoken to. He eyed the stick, thinking he should have handed it over to Rhona.

If she'd reported Jude missing, would the police search Jude's room and take away her computer? Should he hand over the stick to them? Liam decided that wouldn't be necessary. Anything on the memory stick would be on the computer. He tucked it back in his pocket.

He was glad Ben still wasn't at the flat when he got back. It meant he could avoid bringing him up to date on his meeting with Rhona. Ben, having suggested he get in touch with her, now regarded the whole thing as his business.

Liam made himself a coffee then settled down in front of his computer. He inserted the memory stick, then copied all the folders on to his hard drive before checking out the sound files. There were three of them in a single folder, WMA files numbered VN550001, 0002, and 0003. He played the 0001 file and was startled to suddenly hear Jude's voice.

This is a test using my new digital sound recorder. I've set up an interview with a former projectionist at the Olympia Bridgeton. I plan to record this.

The message ended there.

Liam selected the 0002 file and double clicked. There was a whooshing noise he didn't at first recognise, then some background chatter and the chink of what he suddenly realised was crockery. She was in a café somewhere and the whooshing sound was the coffee machine in the background. Jude spoke first.

So, the batteries would have been in a separate room?

A man's voice answered.

Yes, the battery room. Of course they needed to be topped up with distilled water. Each one was about one and a half volts, and you needed about a hundred and ten volts to feed the emergency lighting in the cinema. That's why you had big banks of them.

There was a pause as some crockery was placed on the table. Liam heard a rattle of spoons then Jude encouraged her interviewee to just chat about what life was like in the projection room. The man began to talk about how the reels were sequenced and the projectors maintained.

There was a lot about arc flames and negative and positive carbon rods, mirrors and tending your light. Even how the curtain was managed, because apparently the projectionist was responsible for that too. Much of the talk was quite technical, especially something about a mercury box Liam couldn't understand. Jude said very little, just an encouraging word here and there, but he could tell by her tone that she was genuinely interested.

He listened through to the end. The interviewee had started as a projectionist in 1953 and had worked in lots of cinemas in Glasgow; many of the names, including the Rosevale, were familiar to Liam from looking through Jude's folders.

The excitement he'd felt as he began playing the recording had dissipated into disappointment by the end. It had been good to hear Jude's voice but the content of the recording didn't help him find her. She hadn't even said the name of the man she was interviewing, so he couldn't try to find him and ask if he might know anything.

Liam sat back in a fog of despair. He was no investigator. He would just have to leave it up to the police to find Jude.

His mobile drilled and he grabbed for it, hoping to see Jude's name on the screen. It took a moment to register that it was Charlie calling from the halls of residence.

'Is that you, son?'

'Charlie, what's happened?'

'She's back.'

'Jude's there?'

'She came back last night, according to the girl in the next room. She says she heard her banging around.'

'I'll be right there.'

He was already grabbing his coat and making for the door. Joy bubbled up inside him as he sprinted along Gibson Street. He imagined Jude's face as he told her of his fears. She would look at him with those penetratingly clear eyes as if he'd lost his wits. How often had she told him in no uncertain terms that she could look after herself? She'd been doing it her entire life. Liam didn't care if she was cross with him, he would hug her anyway, whether she liked it or not.

He negotiated the multiple routes at Charing Cross without waiting for a green man and continued his run along Sauchiehall Street. By the time he panted up the steep brae to the halls his heart was pounding so hard he couldn't hear anything else.

Charles emerged from his kiosk when he saw him.

'Can I go up?'

'Go ahead, son.'

'Have you seen her?'

'No. I just phoned you when that lassie came in and told me she'd heard Jude come back. I wasn't on last night.'

Liam sprinted up the stairs and knocked on Jude's door. 'Jude, are you in there?' He waited for what seemed an age before trying again. 'Jude, it's me, Liam.' As he said this he leaned against the door. With a dull click it eased open. Liam stood, hesitant. Should he go in? Maybe she was in the loo or taking a shower?

'Jude, can I come in?' He waited. When nothing happened he slowly pushed the door open. The greeting he'd been preparing suddenly stuck in his throat. The scene before him was so incongruous, so absolutely wrong, that the breath left his chest.

The room he looked on could not possibly be Jude's. She would never countenance such disorder, not even momentarily. It was as though a bomb had hit the place. The wardrobe lay open, clothes, shoes and books flung about.

'My God. What happened here?' It was Jude's neighbour, the one with the weird glasses. Her eyes, now that he could see them for the first time, were wide with surprise.

'Did you see Jude last night?' Liam demanded.

'Not exactly. I told Charlie I just heard someone moving about the room.'

'So you don't know it was Jude?'

She shook her head, frowning. 'You don't think something's happened to her?'

That was exactly what he did think but didn't want to admit it. Liam began to register other things besides the mess. The laptop was no longer on the desk, and the contents of both drawers had been emptied on the floor. He spotted the black metal box open and upside down, surrounded by pencils and pens.

'Go get Charlie,' he told the girl.

She turned and went immediately. Liam retreated to the doorway and had a closer look at the lock. To his eyes it seemed intact, with no marks on the wood to suggest it had been jemmied open, which meant whoever entered had had a key.

Charlie came puffing along the corridor behind the girl, his face red with the effort. 'What's up?'

Liam stood aside to let Charlie take in the devastation. 'What the hell happened here?'

'The laptop's gone,' Liam told him.

'So it's a break in?'

'I don't think the lock's been forced.'

Charlie turned to the girl. 'Did you see anybody go into this room?'

She shook her head. 'I just heard noises.'

'OK. I'm going to call the police.' Charlie ushered them clear of the door. 'You didn't touch anything?' he asked Liam.

'Only the door handle.'

Now in the lobby, Liam waited while Charlie made the call from his small office. After a few moments' discussion which Liam couldn't hear, he replaced the receiver and came out.

'The police want to talk to you about Jude. Can you hang about until they get here?'

Liam nodded. It was what he'd wanted all along. Now that it was happening, he didn't feel so sure.

11

He was digging his own grave. At least, that's what Rhona would accuse him of. But McNab didn't care – he'd spent too much time in a hotel room, staring out of the window. Relying on Petersson to do his job for him was no longer an option.

The girl behind the desk smiled pleasantly as he crossed the foyer. She had almond eyes and coffee-coloured skin. When she smiled she dipped her head a little and her curtain of black hair swung forward and back again. McNab was almost tempted to linger. He was a free agent, he reminded himself, and it had been some time since he'd been close enough to a woman to smell her hair.

The last occasion had been with Rhona, upstairs in this hotel. It had been the first time they'd seen one another since she'd found out he was alive. When Rhona had asked him, 'What next?', he'd chose to interpret the question in his own way, suggesting they go upstairs. Making love to Rhona was the moment he'd really returned from the grave.

McNab gave the receptionist one of his best smiles as he exited through the double glass doors on to Bath Street. There was no point in writing Rhona into his future, if he had a future. The old McNab always kept his options open, and he fully intended to become the old McNab again.

He set off towards the city centre. Had he turned in the opposite direction he would have been in sight of police headquarters on Pitt Street within minutes. He toyed with the idea of turning up there, pretending to be Joe Public complaining about kerb-crawling or litter. He relished the thought, but resisted the temptation to turn round. He knew that if he got close or spoke to them his colleagues would recognise him; the changes in his appearance, although dramatic, were fairly superficial. Now wasn't the time. Maybe after the court appearance, when he'd seen Kalinin leave the dock in handcuffs.

He turned right on Renfield Street and made his way steadily downhill towards the river. Since he'd been 'hiding out' in Glasgow he'd taken to walking everywhere. He certainly couldn't use his car which must have been towed from outside his flat by now. He'd been there briefly on his return to Glasgow, choosing to go late at night so the neighbours, who hadn't shown any interest in him when he was alive, wouldn't see a dead man opening the front door.

He'd stood in the hall, smelt the cold and dust and disuse. Considering how little time he'd spent there when alive, he had been surprised how unnerved he was by the abandoned atmosphere of the place.

The sitting room had looked too tidy and there had been no dirty dishes in the kitchen for the first time since he'd moved in. Someone had cleaned up. Chrissy immediately sprang to mind. She was no more domesticated than Rhona and he'd heard terrible rumours about the state of her own flat, but he sensed that it was something she might do, like organising his funeral. The thought was an oddly pleasant one.

The main problem he'd had since leaving the safe house had been access to ready money. He had funds in his old account, but withdrawing it would put him on the map. Kalinin was no fool. You didn't run a financial enterprise that stretched from Russia to Glasgow via the South of France and London without having some pretty efficient people on your books, including IT professionals who would track him down if he gave them half a chance. Holed up in the safe house, money hadn't mattered, except to use in the poker games with the soldier.

His new persona under the witness protection scheme was one William McCartney, an Ulster protestant born in County Antrim. The thought amused McNab even now, although God knows what his late mother, a devout Catholic, would have had to say. He had McCartney's documents, even a bank account with his police salary going in every month and his outgoings, no doubt, being monitored by SOCA, if only to make sure he was still alive. McNab didn't begrudge them the information; he just liked to keep them guessing as to his whereabouts.

So he'd returned to the flat for the money he had hidden there, the cash from his mum's savings. A single parent, she'd always feared poverty, even as she'd lived in it. So she'd saved something from nothing, and left it for him when she died.

He'd approached the hiding place with some trepidation. If Chrissy had tidied up she'd probably gone through his things, if only to look for his life insurance policy. Chrissy was like a ferret, which is why she was so good at her job – she discovered things that other people thought were well hidden.

The meagre selection of books that had occupied his

shelves consisted of novels by male crime writers. He'd bought each one on a whim and never got past the first couple of chapters. Ignored as reading material, they'd provided a cover for what had lain behind.

The tin box was long and narrow, an idealised snowy Christmas scene painted on the lid. Inside were spools of thread and a selection of rusty sewing needles, buttons and pins. A pair of scissors had brought back memories of having his fringe cut, his eyes screwed up and the hair tickling his nose.

He'd scooped everything out. Fitted in the bottom was a folded piece of brown paper, which he'd prised away from the edges of the box to expose a wad of twenties, a bank card and a small piece of paper with a number on it.

He'd never used the card. Had no idea how much was in the account. She hadn't wanted to be a burden on her son, so had left him no debts and more than enough money to bury her. McNab had never considered using the remainder until now.

He'd flicked through the wad and counted £500, committed the PIN to memory and scrunched up the paper.

'Good on you, Mum.'

He'd headed for the kitchen then and opened the cupboard above the sink. His heart had risen when he'd seen the bottle of Grouse, two-thirds full, still in its place. He'd poured himself a substantial shot and toasted the woman who was still looking out for him, even after death.

He was passing Central Station now. A newspaper vendor was selling early editions of the evening paper, although, if you weren't Glaswegian, you would have been hard pressed to work out what he was shouting. McNab contemplated buying one then decided against it. He would have no time to read it where he was going.

When he reached Argyle Street, he headed east. The fancy designer shops in Buchanan Street and the Merchant City were conspicuously absent here; this area served a different Glasgow population. One that still liked to dress in style, but wasn't able to pay exorbitant prices for it.

The nearer he got to Glasgow Cross the more at home McNab felt, and not just because he was in the vicinity of the High Court. His mother had come from even further east in the city. As a kid he'd spent lots of time at his granny's in Bridgeton. The tenement on Broad Street where she'd lived was demolished now, as he'd discovered when he'd gone looking for it on one of his frequent walks through the city. Funny how a brush with death made you remember your youth. He had been seized by a rush of memories focusing mainly on playing football in the cobbled street and treats that his granny, despite her meagre income, had provided for him. Empire biscuits and bottles of ginger beer always sprang to mind.

The Commercial Bar was festooned outside with Union Jacks, just as he remembered. McNab smiled as he pushed open the door. This time he was entering a Rangers supporters' pub as an Ulster Protestant, William McCartney from Ballymena, County Antrim. He wondered if he should adopt an accent to reflect his new identity but decided against it. A phoney accent would immediately arouse suspicions. Besides he suspected the man he had hopefully come to see would know him, regardless of the shaven head and glasses.

Entering the pub, he was struck by how weird it was to be in a room stained brown by nicotine yet free from smoke. The ceiling still sported the extractor fan, now blissfully silent, as a reminder. Even as he considered this, two men pushed past, unlit cigarettes in hand, headed outside to feed the craving.

McNab surveyed the room discreetly. Three shortish middle-aged men stood at the bar in a familiar stance, bellies out. One was speaking in an irritated, finger-jabbing manner, growling guttural sounds, obviously complaining about something. The others nodded intermittently, jowls set. Round the corner to the right, an elderly man was sitting on a barstool. There was a recently poured pint of lager in front of him, still glistening with condensation. He continued to eye its foamy surface although McNab was pretty sure he had been seen and noted. He made his way to the bar.

'What are you for, big yin?'

'A pint of lager.' He wasn't asked to specify a particular type or to study a menu of imported varieties which might be served with slices of lime stuffed in the neck of the bottle. A pint of Tennents was placed in front of him. McNab handed over a modest sum in comparison to Merchant City prices, then took a long, slow mouthful.

He took a place to the right of the seated man, who didn't acknowledge him, but went on contemplating his pint. The nearby trio were pontificating on the dire state of Scottish football, using language that would have made his mother turn in her grave. Fifteen minutes later the lone man lifted his glass and made for a table near the toilets. Five minutes later, McNab followed. He took a seat with his back to the room. The other man had pulled out a *Daily Record* from his pocket and was studying the sports pages. Without looking up he said under his breath, 'You look like shite.'

'It's nice to see you too.'

'You're supposed to be dead.'

'Some people wouldn't let me rest in peace. They dug up my grave.'

'You should have been cremated. It would have been safer.'

Niceties over, McNab allowed himself a proper look at the man across from him. Jaundiced skin hung loosely on his skull as though it might slide off at any moment. The nose had been broken so many times it sat at an angle. There was a vicious scar above the right eyebrow and both ears had the appearance of having been pummelled often and for long periods. Kev 'Boxer' MacMillan might have had the body of a fighter twenty years ago, but not any more, although the big knuckled hands looked fit to throttle someone if required to do so.

'You're chancing your luck showing your face round here.'

'Anything to see an old mate.'

There was a deep throated chuckle like a drain emptying. 'Who dug me up?'

'Nae fuckin idea. But from what I hear the plan is to bury you again. Alive, this time.'

Boxer said this with such conviction it made the hairs stand up on McNab's neck.

'I need a name,' he insisted quietly.

'You need your head looked at.'

A tense silence fell between them, the background chink of glasses and murmur of voices only serving to heighten it. Eventually Boxer relented. 'From what I hear, Paddy Brogan did the hiring.'

McNab felt the heat of anger rise in his chest. He'd assumed Brogan had stayed well clear of this and left the search for him to Kalinin. How stupid was he?

'Bastard!'

'Never trust the Irish, especially the Fenians.' Boxer threw him a pointed look.

McNab slipped a twenty into the folds of the newspaper, now lying on the table. The movement was acknowledged with a brief nod.

'I'll use it to drink to your short-lived resurrection.' Boxer slipped the note deftly into his pocket and turned his attention back to the football pages.

McNab drank down the rest of his pint and headed for the door. Outside, he passed the same two men, apparently on another fag break. As he eased past them, one took out his mobile and made a call. McNab crossed the road, seeing a bus into town approaching. He flagged it down and jumped on, forgetting he needed the right change for his fare. After a brief contretemps in which he wished he could flash his police badge again, he paid over the odds and took a seat. From the window he saw the guy outside the pub end his call and watch the rear of the bus as it headed west.

So all roads led to the Poker Club. In his nightmares he was never away from the place. Dashing down corridors looking for a way out, dragging a pregnant and terrified Chrissy with him. Every corner they turned, a smiling

Solonik stood waiting, blocking their way. McNab would grind to a halt, his eyes fixed on the huge ham-like fists, watching them rise and flex. Then one of them would slam into Chrissy's swollen stomach, smashing the tiny body within. Whatever the scenario, and there were many, the nightmare always ended in the same way. The oncoming car, the screech of tyres, Solonik's grinning face above the gun.

Despite his best efforts, the shot rang out again in his head, just as it had done in the graveyard. This time he couldn't dive for cover, although his body still reacted, jerking as the imagined bullet slammed into his back. He looked round into the alarmed face of the young woman seated next to him. McNab opened his mouth to offer some jokey explanation but nothing emerged, so he rose and made for the front, pressing the bell. When the bus drew to a halt he sprang off and began walking quickly away down the nearest side street, adrenaline still pumping a desire to run.

After a few hundred yards, his mind began to calm and the twitching in his limbs lessened. He forced himself to consider the situation more methodically. So Brogan had organised the gravediggers. No doubt some wee punks looking for drug money. He had no quarrel with them, and didn't give a shite who they were. It was Brogan he wanted to see. And the angrier he grew, the stronger his need to confront Brogan became. He'd given the job to Petersson, but McNab knew he could do it better. He knew Brogan and what it would take to persuade the bastard on to the witness stand. But did he have the nerve to do it?

Glancing round, he realised he was back near Glasgow Cross. If he headed across the river he could be at the Poker Club in fifteen minutes. He checked his watch. Wouldn't it be better to arrive in the evening, with the rest of the punters? Dressed in a penguin suit he might merge with the crowd better. He could suss out the situation before making a move.

He patted his pocket. He also had the ready cash for a few games. Despite the circumstances McNab felt his spirits rise at the prospect of playing poker again. The best outcome would be if he met with Brogan and managed to persuade him to shop Kalinin and thereby avoid being implicated in McNab's attempted murder. The worst scenario? Brogan handed him over to the Russian. The thought made McNab's blood momentarily run cold, before the fear this induced restored his anger. If Brogan saw him alive and strong he just might consider his position. Using a third party like Petersson, although the safer option, held less chance of success.

McNab found himself warming to the whole idea. But a visit to the Poker Club as a punter would require a tuxedo, his previous suit having been ruined by his untimely death. He gave this some consideration. He was in a part of town that boasted a large number of charity shops, but he doubted they sported many tuxedos on their racks.

Alternatively he could hire a suit for the night. There was a hire shop in Howard Street down near the river. He'd used it before. He immediately reminded himself that if he were to go there he would need to use his alias, William McCartney. Dead men weren't a likely source of repeat business.

Energised by the prospect of confronting Brogan, he quickened his pace towards Howard Street. He smiled to himself as he imagined taking some of the bastard's money into the bargain.

12

She had exactly fifteen minutes to shower and change.

The smell of dust and decay permeated her nostrils, skin and hair. Despite the forensic suit, the dead always left their scent on you, whether fresh and bloody or, like today, old and mummified.

She shampooed twice, and would have gladly stood there for another hour, letting the warm water take the ache and smell from her body, but she didn't want to be in the shower when Petersson arrived.

She turned off the water and wrapped herself in a towel. The dress she'd chosen lay spread out on the bed. Black, sexy without being too obvious, it seemed to her to fit the bill. The Poker Club clientele were not the same men who frequented Brogan's housing scheme betting shops, but the moneyed of Glasgow and its surrounds. The ones with homes in the West End, or expensive new riverside apartments, or the even wealthier owners of larger houses equipped with stables and paddocks in the lush Renfrewshire countryside.

She dressed, applied make up and dried her hair, all without an interruption from the door buzzer. Then she headed for the kitchen, opened a bottle of white wine and poured herself a glass.

It was all so reminiscent of the night this had begun,

when McNab had arrived in his tuxedo to pick up Chrissy. Rhona recalled how happy they'd both been. How keyed up by Kalinin's arrest and by the successful resolution to the case they'd been working on.

McNab had tried to persuade Rhona to go with them, but she'd declined, a decision that had seemed insignificant at the time. How life can change in a moment, she mused. Turn left, instead of right, say yes instead of no. The randomness of it seemed out of place in her scientific world.

She thought about Jude, Liam's friend. What decision had she made, or what random act had changed her path? Everything pointed to her being in the vicinity of the body before she disappeared. Was that significant?

The buzzer interrupted her thoughts and she went to answer.

'Come on up, I'm ready.'

She left the front door open for him and went to fetch a jacket. When she re-entered the hallway he was there at the open door. The sight of him dressed in the tuxedo made her stomach flip, and not in a pleasant way. He didn't really resemble McNab, but the height and build were the same.

'Changing your mind?' Petersson said.

'Not at all. I was just admiring the outfit.'

'And I, yours.'

Rhona looked quickly away. 'This is strictly business,' she said.

'If you say so.'

'What about money?'

'I never charge for the pleasure of my company.'

The sincerity in his voice made her laugh.

'I'll deal with our float, and claim it back on expenses,' he said. 'Can you play poker?'

'Chrissy tried to teach me, but she says I'm no good. My face gives me away.'

'Then you can stand behind, with your hand on my shoulder, but don't look at my cards.'

Rhona found her spirits lifting. Maybe this outing would prove useful, although she was still of the mind that she could have done it alone.

'Have you heard any more from McNab?' Petersson said.

She shook her head. 'He'll be waiting for you to speak to Brogan.'

'No doubt.'

'Then let's get on with it.'

She alighted from the taxi at the exact spot outside the Poker Club where she and Chrissy had scoured the gutter looking for a bullet casing. The pool of blood that had stained the tarmac was long gone, but Rhona could have drawn its outline, so clear was the memory.

Petersson paid the driver and took her by the arm.

'OK?'

She nodded and he led her towards the pillared entrance. A set of glass doors slid open to accept them. As Rhona stepped across the threshold, she was momentarily blinded by the light, and thought of the spider escaping from the hole in the brickwork on to her hand. Only in this instance, it was she who was entering the spider's parlour.

'Funny how dirty money can be washed so clean,' Petersson said as he surveyed the marble foyer. He gestured towards the chink of glasses and the sound of laughter emerging from nearby double doors. 'A drink?' When she nodded, he led her in that direction. 'I think champagne is in order, don't you?'

Rhona watched Petersson weave his way through the crowd towards the bar, his tall blond figure causing a ripple of interest from both women and men. The place and its clientele exuded wealth and a few expensive perfumes. You obviously didn't gamble here unless you could afford to lose.

She spotted a discreet sign for the Ladies and gestured to Petersson she was headed there.

She washed her hands and dried them on an individual snow-white hand towel, before dropping it in the basket provided. No one had come in while she was there, so there were no interesting conversations to listen in on. She emerged and checked the corridor. Now she was here, she might as well take a quick look round. The door at the far end said 'Private' which seemed a good start.

Rhona pushed it open and found a set of stairs. She followed it to the first level, where through a glass door she could see the sweep of the main staircase in the distance. The corridor leading there had at least three doors, all of them closed. Rhona stood for a moment outside the first. From within came the murmur of voices, no doubt a poker game in action. Suddenly the neighbouring door opened and a man appeared. Dressed in the mandatory evening suit, he looked surprised and a little annoyed to discover her there. Rhona smiled innocently.

'I was looking for the Ladies.'

He muttered something in a language that could have come from anywhere in Eastern Europe and steered her pointedly towards the staircase.

Petersson was waiting near the door when she reappeared. He handed her a glass.

'Anything interesting happening in the Ladies?'

'For once, no. Heard anything in here?'

'Brogan's on the premises.'

'How did you find that out?'

'I just asked.' Petersson smiled. 'I'm seeing him in ten minutes.'

'How did you wangle that? Don't tell me, you "just asked"?'

'I gave the go-between my card. Well, Henrik Erlendson's card.'

'Who does Brogan think you are?' Rhona said, aghast.

'He knows I'm from Iceland and that I have some money I want to spring clean.'

'You would make a very good criminal.'

'Some people already think I am.'

The exchange was cut short as Rhona spotted a couple entering by the double doors from the foyer. The man was tall and fair haired, with just a touch of grey at his temples. The woman on his arm was groomed to perfection. As they surveyed the room, Rhona stepped behind Petersson.

'What's up?'

'Someone I know.'

'An old boyfriend?'

'Liam's father.'

'Really?' Petersson sounded intrigued. He eased round, still shielding her from view.

'It's probably better if he doesn't see me.'

'I agree. Shall we head for the foyer?'

He tucked her arm in his and, completely obscuring her

from view, walked them towards the exit. They were almost there when a voice rang out.

'Mr Erlendson?'

Petersson turned, still keeping Rhona behind him.

'You asked to see me?' A pair of cool eyes examined the Icelander.

Petersson assumed his new identity swiftly, and when he spoke his voice was strongly accented. 'Mr Brogan?'

They shook hands. Brogan's eyes flitted to Rhona. 'And this is?'

When Petersson hesitated, Rhona jumped in, hoping that Edward was sufficiently far away not to hear, and sufficiently engaged in his own conversation not to pay attention.

'Eve.'

Brogan gave her a shrewd look. She imagined what he was thinking. Was she worth any effort or was she merely arm candy? While Rhona wondered which she should be aiming for, Petersson made the decision for her.

'Will you wait here for me, sweetheart?' he smiled down at her.

Rhona considered saying she'd rather tag along, then decided to give Petersson his chance. If it didn't work out, she would take hers. Brogan was eyeing them with interest, having registered their unspoken conversation. To compensate, Rhona gave Petersson's arm an affectionate squeeze.

'Of course,' she said.

Rhona watched them exit, her back still turned to where she believed Edward to be. In this crowd, surely it would be possible to remain unobserved? She could seek a seat in the corner, nurse her champagne and await developments. The hope was short-lived.

'Rhona?' The voice and its tone had that quality she knew so well, containing notes of both affectation and surprise. Rhona turned and took in the full view.

'Edward.'

'How strange to meet you here.'

'Really? Why?' She heard the irritation in her voice.

He arched an eyebrow. 'You aren't a gambler, as I recall?'

'And you are?'

'I enjoy an odd game of poker. Sharpens the mind.' He sounded pleased with himself, as always. 'Although we're here in another capacity tonight.'

Rhona waited in silence, because he was bound to tell her what it was.

'Lord Dalrymple invited us.'

The name was familiar, but not in a pleasant way. Back then he had been simply Sir James. Rhona could see that Edward was waiting for a comment on Dalrymple's elevated status, but she had no intention of obliging him. She remained silent.

'You remember Sir James?' Edward pressed her.

'The man who was involved in the rent-boy case?'

Anger suffused Edward's face. 'You know perfectly well that's not true.'

'Do I? Wasn't there a porn video shot in his gatehouse? A rent boy being tortured, I seem to remember?'

'That had nothing to do with Lord James.'

'DI Wilson seemed to think it did.'

Edward threw her a warning look. 'You're on dangerous ground, Rhona.'

'Is that the lawyer in you talking, Edward?'

They were saved a further deterioration in the exchange

by Fiona's arrival. Rhona had to admit that Edward had chosen the perfect mate for himself; confident and cultured, with exactly the same outlook on life. If Fiona had her way Edward would, in time, don an ermine-trimmed robe just like Lord James.

'Rhona. How nice to see you.' No one could lie as sincerely as Fiona. She glanced about. 'Alone?'

'Henrik is in a business meeting with Mr Brogan.' Rhona watched Edward absorbing this and knew he would dearly love to know who Henrik was. Fiona did the job for him.

'Henrik?' she questioned, teasingly.

'A banker from Iceland,' Rhona obliged. 'Who still has money.' She made to move away, but before she did so, Rhona fired one last shot. 'I saw Liam yesterday. You'll be pleased to know he's doing very well. He's at Glasgow University studying Physics.' On that, she turned and strode away. Rather than heading for a corner of the bar, she made for the foyer where she downed her glass of champagne in one.

Conversations with Edward always played out the same way. If she was honest with herself, she instigated most of the drama, but Edward was so self-satisfied and superior that she needed to see him bleed, if only momentarily. The trauma, she knew, would swiftly abate, smoothed over by Fiona. The only difficulty with the recent episode was that she now found herself outside the bar and in need of another drink.

She hovered uncertainly as people moved past, some headed for the bar, others up the wide staircase. Then she felt a hand on her shoulder, and a voice she recognised as McNab's hissed in her ear.

'Upstairs. Now.'

Rhona did what she was told, her heart racing. What the hell was McNab doing here? At the first landing he propelled her left through a door marked 'Staff'. On the other side she could hear the distant clanging sounds of a kitchen in action. McNab caught her wrist and swung her round to face him.

'What are you doing here?'

'I was about to ask you the same thing,' she retorted.

They eyeballed one another for a moment, then McNab let go of her wrist and stood back. 'What *am* I going to do with you, Dr MacLeod?'

'Telling me the truth might be a start.'

He regarded her with equanimity. 'The blank sheet of paper pissed you off?'

'This isn't a game.'

'Too fucking right it isn't. What if Brogan had seen you?'

'He did.'

'What?'

'He thinks I'm Petersson's arm candy.'

That didn't amuse McNab, then he seemed to realise what that meant. 'Petersson's in with Brogan? Now?'

'Yes.'

McNab clenched his fists and hissed an expletive.

'You gave him the lead,' she reminded him sharply. 'What did you expect him to do with it?'

McNab contemplated this, then seemed to come to a decision. One, Rhona suspected, she wouldn't like.

'I want you out of here.'

'I'm waiting for Petersson. That was the arrangement.'

'The game has changed.'

'Why? What are you going to do?'

'What I came here for.' He took her arm, more gently this time, then slid his hand down to take hers. 'Go back to the flat, Rhona. Please. Wait for us there.'

13

Bill studied the young man opposite. Liam resembled Rhona, especially around the mouth and in his gestures. Even in the tone of his voice. Bill was rather pleased that he didn't sound like his father. He remembered how irritating he'd found Edward Stewart. Still, the man had been devastated when his other son had gone missing during the rent-boy case a few years back. There had been no doubting Edward Stewart's sincerity then.

They were sitting in a tiny office, more of a cubicle. Charlie the warden had made them mugs of coffee, both of which sat untouched on a nearby table as Liam repeated his story of Jude's disappearance.

Bill was intrigued and not a little alarmed by it. In his experience, true runaways had a reason for going. It might be brought on by depression, or some other mental health condition; difficult family circumstances, or debts they couldn't deal with. Jude, according to Liam, was a reliable and extremely organised person who loved her studies. At first glance, there was simply no reason for Jude to run away, but then first glances rarely provided the entire picture.

There was another oddity about this conversation. Bill had the impression Liam wasn't telling him the entire story. That was another feature he shared with Rhona, an open countenance that made it difficult to lie. He might be withholding something trivial or something embarrassing. Honest people were often discomfited by small untruths just as much as larger lies.

'And Jude doesn't have a boyfriend?' Bill asked again.

'No. Or not that I know of,' he corrected himself.

'Would you be able to give me a list of her friends or acquaintances?'

'I don't think she has other friends. She never mentioned anyone.'

'Didn't you find that odd?'

'Jude is a bit of a loner.' Liam hesitated. 'The truth is I think she might be a bit autistic or maybe has Aspergers.' He shrugged awkwardly. 'I'm afraid I don't know the exact difference between the two conditions.'

'What makes you say that?'

Liam struggled to put his thoughts into words. 'She's obsessed with order and routine. And she completely misreads people sometimes.'

'She misread you?'

'At the beginning, maybe, but it's OK now. We got on – get on well, but we're not an item.' He looked at Bill to emphasise the fact. 'Jude wasn't keen on parties or on being in a big crowd. She didn't like physical contact. You know, the way people hug one another nowadays, and kiss on the cheek. Jude wouldn't have any of that.'

Bill was a bit suspicious of all that himself. Fortunately the habit hadn't yet infiltrated the police station, and as far as he was concerned it wouldn't.

'Did Jude have any special support from the Art School because of her condition?'

'She didn't mention any support apart from a bursary. It's the only reason she was able to come here.'

'And she has no family contact?'

'She said she was brought up in care in the north of England. She never mentioned anything about a family.'

The next step would be student support. They should be able to fill him in on Jude's background. Liam was shifting in his seat. He looked weary and not a little stressed.

'Is there anything else you can tell me that might help find her?'

Liam shook his head, looking embarrassed.

Bill waited as Liam struggled with himself. Eventually the words burst out. 'I took a memory stick from Jude's desk the first time Charlie and I were in the room. I needed to know which cinema she'd gone to. I thought she might keep an electronic diary. I couldn't get on the computer, so I took the back-up.' He waited for the axe to fall.

'And?' Bill prompted, more interested in the memory stick than its removal.

'That's how I figured out she'd gone to the Rosevale, but there are sound files she recorded on there too. She interviewed someone, a man, a former projectionist.'

'Where is this stick?'

With a sheepish look Liam took it from his pocket and laid it on the table. 'I thought if you did start to look for her, you had the laptop.'

Bill watched as Liam visibly wilted under his penetrating look. Had he been too easy on this young man up to now, because he was Rhona's son?

'Is that the real reason you took the memory stick? You

weren't worried there was something on it? Something awkward or embarrassing?'

Liam looked shocked. 'No!'

'Did you delete anything?'

'No!'

Bill tried to read the boy's reaction. Had he been told the whole truth? He decided he had enough, for the moment. He stood up.

'Can I go now?' said Liam eagerly.

'If you think of anything else . . .'

'Do I tell Rhona or call you?'

Bill gave him a card. 'Call me.'

Bill watched Liam leave the building before he went to check on the SOCO working upstairs in Jude's room. He'd already had a chat with Charlie Murdoch who'd proved to be a solid source of information. He'd confirmed most of what Liam had said, although there had been no mention of the memory stick. However, Charlie had intimated that he'd left Liam alone in the room for a short period, while he dealt with a call at the desk. Long enough to remove something.

He took the stairs to the first floor. The building was brick built, the same yellow bricks that now peppered a city that had once been only blond and red sandstone. Regardless of that, it seemed to fit into the line of older, grander buildings, halfway down Garnethill. Through a landing window he looked on to Buccleuch Street and the smooth-faced three-storey houses opposite, now split into flats, a few with 'To rent' signs in their windows. A suited man with a briefcase waited patiently at a communal front door. He'd been there since Bill's arrival.

It looked as if someone hadn't been keeping up with the rent.

In the corridor all was quiet. Studious, even. No loud music, no frantic student life. Bill imagined his daughter Lisa living in a place like this, when she headed for Edinburgh University in the autumn to study medicine. For a moment it looked safe, safe enough even for his precious daughter. But when he reached Jude's door and saw the police tape, he knew it wasn't. Nowhere was.

He opened the door. There was only one white suit working the room. Bill didn't recognise the wearer until she looked up and he saw the distinctive eyes above the mask. One blue, one brown.

'Sadie?'

The mask creased as Sadie Martin attempted a smile behind it. 'Sadie, all alone.'

'Anything I should know about?'

'I've picked up a couple of prints,' she indicated a desk drawer, 'but the place is spotless, apart from the scattered clothes. No evidence of a forcible entry. What about the occupant?'

'No one's seen her for the last forty-eight hours so the warden checked the room yesterday. There was a laptop on the desk and no mess.'

'If she ran off, she didn't take much with her. Lots of clothes still here. Usual toiletries in the bathroom.'

'So nothing obviously missing?'

She shook her head. 'Except maybe that.' She indicated two parts of a flat metal circular tin. 'It's an old sixteen millimeter reel tin. It was lying open on the floor, but there's no sign of any film. There's a label.' She showed him with gloved hands. The neatly written label said, 'Olympia Bridgeton' and was dated a week before.

Liam could hear Ben's voice and that of a girl. He quietly closed the main door and tiptoed along the hall to his own room. Once inside he locked the door, leaving the light off. The street lamp would give him enough light to move about. If Ben was to check he would hopefully think he'd gone to bed.

He went straight to the computer and brought up the folders he'd copied from the memory stick. The deep discomfort Liam had felt when talking to the policeman had metamorphosed into a grinding apprehension. Something bad had happened to Jude. He was convinced of it.

He checked the sound files again, putting on the earphones, listening repeatedly to each section of the interview. Apart from the pleasure he got from hearing Jude's voice, he could recognise nothing of significance.

He then opened the folder called 'Olympia Bridgeton reel'. That had been the name on the label of the old reel tin he'd seen in the desk drawer. He recalled standing in the ransacked room. The desk drawers had been emptied on the floor. He'd spotted the tin there too, but couldn't recall if it had been open or not.

He went back to the folder. Inside were dozens of jpg files, numerically named Frame1, Frame2, up to fifty of them. Liam clicked on the first and it opened to reveal a black and white image of poor quality. He could barely make out what looked like two male figures. He opened Frame2. It looked much the same, as did Frame3 and Frame4. All the surfaces were speckled white.

Liam sat back. They looked like individual frames from the reel of film, judging from the slight differences between each shot. Curiosity awakened, he recalled a time when Ben had run together a series of photos from a party into a film clip. He tried to remember what software Ben had used and whether he could get access to it. The other possibility was to engage Ben in the exercise, which at any other time, Ben would gladly welcome. But just now?

Liam rose and went quietly into the hall, then made a point of opening and shutting the front door, loud enough for Ben to be in no doubt he was back.

'Ben! Mate, are you here? You'll never believe it. We found a dead body walled up in that cinema Jude visited.'

It was a smart move. Liam heard some frantic whispering then Ben's voice shouted, 'Cool. I'll be right out, mate.'

Liam retreated to the kitchen, pulled a beer from the fridge and opened it. Moments later a dishevelled Ben appeared, slowly followed by a pretty girl with brightly coloured dreadlocks, who didn't look too happy.

'You found a body?' Ben eyeballed him.

'Rhona did. It was walled up in the projection room.'

'Fuckin' hell!' Ben was impressed. Then he remembered. 'What about Jude?'

'She'd been there. We found a footprint, but still no sign of her.'

Ben was swithering between his need to know more about the body and his concern about Jude. 'You think Jude saw this body?'

'I don't know. There was only a small hole in some brickwork. There was a weird smell coming out of it.'

The story was getting ever more intriguing for Ben. Liam decided to take advantage of this.

'Jude's room in halls has been ransacked and her laptop's gone.'

Ben's eyes opened even wider. 'Jeeez.'

'I've got a back-up of some of her stuff. Want to take a look?'

Did he ever? Sexual encounter forgotten, Ben headed swiftly for Liam's room. Liam threw an apologetic look at the forsaken girlfriend. 'D'you want to come?'

'I'll leave it, thanks.'

Ben didn't even register the slam of the front door. He was already sifting through the folders on the screen.

'There's something in particular I wanted you to take a look at.'

'Yeah, what?' Ben gazed up eagerly.

Liam indicated the frame images. 'Can you run these together like you did with those party photos?'

Fifteen minutes later they were seated in front of Ben's impressive computer system.

'OK, I'd take a guess and say Jude photographed individual frames from some old film reel she'd found, probably because it was too fragile to run on a sixteen millemeter projector, even if she had access to one.' Ben began selecting and dragging each image, explaining as he went along. 'I grab each of the images and insert them.' He chose 'Insert frame' from the drop menu and located Frame 1 on his hard drive. 'Normally when an image changes, say in place or people, we would insert it as a key frame, indicating the next sequence, but since we don't know what any of these contain, we'll give each image the same time and just run them together. We can play about with the timing later if need be.'

Liam nodded, just wanting him to get on with it. Ben set it running. Along the top a vertical red marker began moving through a horizontal line of frames while below a 550 by 400mm window opened on the screen. Now that the images were blown up larger it was much easier to see the figures.

As the movie reached the end of its frames and came abruptly to a halt, Ben gave a long low whistle. 'Wow. I never thought your Jude would be into old-time gay porn.'

14

Rhona woke with a start and stood up, still fully dressed. She had fallen asleep waiting for the buzzer to sound.

She remembered pacing up and down the sitting room until 2 a.m., before finally dozing off in front of an old black and white movie, filled with people in evening dresses and tuxedos, bizarrely like the Poker Club.

As her head began to clear she registered it was still pitch black outside. She checked her watch. Three thirty. So there was still time for Petersson and McNab to appear. But what was taking them so long?

She looked about for her mobile then remembered she'd been holding it in her hand, willing it to ring, before she'd fallen asleep. She eventually located it partway under the couch, and eagerly scanned the screen for a missed call or text. Nothing.

She cursed under her breath. She'd only agreed to leave the Poker Club because McNab had promised to come here with Petersson. She should never have listened to him. And what of Petersson? Had McNab even told him why she'd left?

A second thought occurred. What if the two men had been in on this together from the start? Petersson had definitely not wanted her to go with him and McNab had been furious to find her there. The thought ran on, growing bigger, gaining momentum like a snowball running down a hill.

Petersson hadn't managed to persuade her, finally agreeing that she tag along. Rhona recalled that exchange, Petersson's closed expression, the tone of his voice. Had he known McNab would be there? She'd never been sure about Petersson. Even now she didn't completely trust him. And did she even trust McNab?

She went to the kitchen, made a pot of extra strong coffee and took a mug of it back to the lounge. Sipping it, she considered what her next move would be in the event that the two men didn't appear by dawn.

She considered calling Bill, telling him of her visit to the Poker Club. She'd done nothing wrong in going there, she reminded herself, but Bill would seriously question her judgement in revisiting the scene of the attempted murder, especially now that McNab's apparent resurrection was the subject of speculation. The second issue was Petersson; she'd never revealed her connection to the investigative journalist even when Bill had brought her the news that McNab was alive. And finally, how would Bill react to the news that McNab had also been on the premises? All things considered, Rhona decided she would wait a little longer. And hope.

She flicked from the movie channel to BBC News 24, where a newsreader with a grave expression was reciting the world's ills. Rhona finished her coffee and went for a refill. When she returned a breaking news banner was running across the bottom of the screen.

'Gun attack in Glasgow Club.'

The words swept past and disappeared, to return seconds later. Rhona grabbed the remote from the coffee table and turned up the sound.

'A shooting at a well-known Glasgow nightclub has left one man dead. The incident happened in the early hours of this morning. The popular club was in the news just two months ago, when a police officer was gunned down outside the building. Detective Sergeant Michael McNab's killer has not yet been brought to justice. More recently the same police officer's grave was exhumed by person or persons unknown. Speculation is that his remains have been removed. It is not yet known if this new attack is connected to DS McNab's murder.'

Rhona froze. *Please, God, no.*

The remote clattered to the floor as she grabbed for her mobile. All concerns about calling Bill had dissolved in the panic of the moment. She brought up his number and dialled, only to be immediately forwarded to voicemail. She didn't wait to leave a message, so pulled up Petersson's number next, then McNab's most recent number.

They too went to voicemail. Frantically, she tried to focus her thoughts. Just because there had been a shooting didn't mean it had anything to do with McNab, but instinct and intuition were telling her the opposite. There was no other choice, she would have to go down there.

The Poker Club, a beacon of light, was surrounded by vehicles, with a cordon already set up. Rhona abandoned her car beside a line of no-parking cones. Retrieving her forensic bag from the boot, she pulled on a suit before approaching a uniform on guard duty.

'Dr Rhona MacLeod. Forensic.'

The fresh-faced uniformed policeman gave her a quizzical look. 'You're here fast.' He checked her ID then lifted the tape for her to slip under.

'Where is it?'

'Up the main staircase, on the left.'

Crossing the marble lobby, Rhona registered that it all looked the same, from the glittering chandeliers to the thick carpet that hugged the elegant staircase. From the bar came a hum of conversation, although the clinking of glasses had ceased.

Her distant self surmised that those present at the time of the shooting were in there, their details being recorded, their statements taken down. She wondered if Edward was one of them, and momentarily imagined his reaction to that, then remembered that Dalrymple was a golfing partner of Superintendent Sutherland, therefore unlikely to have been kept hanging around.

She hesitated at the top of the stairs. On her left was the glass door to the corridor she'd visited earlier. It was closed, with a uniformed policeman standing outside. He nodded at her and indicated ahead without speaking. She walked on. Already she could smell it. A thick aroma of gunshot residue and fresh blood.

Rhona approached the open door, the death smell pervading her senses and stopping her heart. It took every grain of strength she had to step across that threshold. Even more to lift her gaze.

Patrick Brogan was seated at a magnificent mahogany desk. Across the red leather surface, his arms, stretched out, palms facing upward, suggested a supplicant's pose. The bullet's impact had thrown his head backwards so that his startled gaze was directed at the ornate ceiling.

Relief flooded Rhona, followed immediately by foreboding as she recalled the last words she and McNab had exchanged.

What are you going to do?

What I came here for.

Had he come here to kill Brogan? All the time making her believe he'd come to persuade Brogan to testify against Kalinin?

She remembered McNab's sweating anger when he'd discovered her in the foyer. The strong grip of his hand on her arm as he'd propelled her up the stairs then pinned her against the wall. He hadn't wanted her there. Why? To keep her safe or to make sure she wasn't present when a murder took place? The thought sickened her even more than the death smells in that room.

Another thought flickered through her mind. What of Petersson? What role had he played in all of this?

She turned, hearing footsteps, then Bill appeared in the doorway. He looked surprised when he recognised her eyes above the mask.

'I saw it on the twenty-four hour news,' she said before he could ask and turned her attention back to the body, unable to meet Bill's gaze. Would he ask why she was up at that hour of the morning?

Keeping her voice steady, she said, 'What happened? Do

we know?' and said a silent thank you when she heard his voice emerge sounding normal.

'Someone found him like this around two-thirty. No sound of a gunshot reported.'

Petersson went to see him after eleven. I went home just before midnight.

'So no witnesses?'

'Everyone in the place is deaf and dumb with the memory of an Alzheimer's sufferer.'

She wanted to say, 'I was here. Petersson was here. So was McNab.' She heard the words in her head but they wouldn't pass her lips. Rhona opened her mouth to try again, but was prevented by the arrival of another suited figure whose cool ice-blue eyes regarded her over his own mask.

'You were quick getting here,' Dr Sissons remarked.

'News travels fast,' Bill said, saving her from an explanation.

Rhona stepped aside to allow Sissons a view of the body. Despite her distress, she'd already noted the stellate nature of the entrance wound, suggesting Brogan had been shot at point-blank range.

Sissons confirmed her thoughts.

'No other injuries apparent.' He looked to Rhona for affirmation and she nodded. 'You have a time frame?'

'He had a meeting with someone around ten, then went for a walk round the gaming tables. Seen in a poker game on the upper level at one o'clock or thereabouts. Retired to his office after that. Found at two-thirty like this.'

'Two shootings in as many months. Not a place I'd choose to spend an evening,' Sissons remarked dryly.

Rhona waited for Sissons to depart, then got in quickly before anyone else should appear.

'I need to speak to you. In private.'

Noting the tone of her voice, Bill threw her a sharp look. 'What about?'

She nodded towards the corpse. 'This.'

Bill crossed to the open door and disappeared outside for a moment. She heard him call over the officer by the stairs and order him to let no one else up. Then Bill closed the door.

'OK,' he said, waiting.

Rhona took a deep breath. 'I was here earlier tonight.' Before he could respond, she rushed on, 'I came with Einar Petersson.'

'The journalist?'

'Yes.'

Suspicion began to dawn. 'I take it you two weren't on a date?'

'McNab told Petersson that Brogan was in the car the night he was shot.'

'What!'

'He asked Petersson to try to persuade Brogan to come forward as a witness.'

'And?'

'Petersson made an appointment to see Brogan, ostensibly as an Icelandic banker who still had money to invest.'

'Money laundering?'

'It was his way in, that's all.'

'Go on,' he said sternly.

'McNab was here too.'

'For Chrissakes!'

'He just turned up,' she said, hoping it was true but still suspecting the two men had been in it together.

'The stupid bastard. The stupid bloody bastard . . .'

She quickly intervened. 'When he found me here, he was very angry and insisted I leave. I agreed when he promised he and Petersson would come by my place after he saw Brogan.'

'But they didn't turn up?'

'No.'

'And that's why you were awake and watching the news in the middle of the night?'

She nodded. The seriousness of the situation rendered them both silent for a moment.

'What time did you leave?'

'Around midnight.'

Bill made an exasperated noise in his throat. 'Why didn't he come to me?'

'He wanted to keep his moves quiet. He thinks Kalinin's got someone working on the inside.'

Bill didn't look surprised.

'Anyone else know you were here?'

'Chrissy.'

'She's in on this too?'

'She doesn't know Brogan was in the car. Only that Petersson wanted to speak to him about the shooting.'

Bill took a minute to digest this then said, 'Is there anything else you want to tell me?'

Rhona could sense his unease and, far worse, his disappointment in her. She shook her head. 'No, that's it.'

'You can't officially process this scene. You know that, don't you?'

Rhona wasn't going to argue. She'd come because she'd feared that McNab was the victim. Now she feared he might be the killer.

15

The centre of town was devoid of traffic. Caught between late-night revellers and the morning rush hour, the grid-like layout resembled an empty film set, doubling for New York or Chicago. A lone hooker leaning against a lamppost sprang to attention when she saw the car, then lost interest when she realised the driver was a woman.

Rhona drew up on a double yellow line outside the hotel on Bath Street. She had no idea if McNab was still staying here, but there was one way to find out. She should have told Bill about this place and her earlier assignation here with McNab. She hadn't lied, merely omitted a few details. That had been the pattern for a while now and with every conversation she felt herself dig a deeper hole.

She locked the car and climbed the steps, to find the glass door locked. She could see no one in reception so she rang the bell for the night porter. Eventually a figure appeared from the shadows. A young man with his dark hair in a ponytail approached the door, his eyes bleary from sleep. He'd no doubt been kipping in some back room somewhere. Rhona realised she had no idea how she planned to handle this. As he unlocked the door, she made up her mind not to play the official card.

'Room 803. I forgot my key,' she said in a breathless, worried manner.

He eyed her warily.

'Mrs McCartney, Room 803,' she said brightly. 'My husband's up there now.'

The guy looked her up and down in a pointed fashion. Rhona was suddenly aware she was still wearing the outfit she'd visited the Poker Club in. And that he didn't believe her story.

'Got some ID, *Mrs McCartney*?'

Rhona decided to play him at his own game. She smiled knowingly. 'OK. Discerning Escorts. Ordered on company expenses.'

She let her coat part so he could see the dress. Now *he* smiled and stood aside to let her enter. 'Wish I worked for his company.'

Rhona slipped past and walked swiftly to the elevator. He called after her, 'Shall I warn him?'

'No thanks. He knows I'm coming.'

She stepped into the tiny lift and selected the button for the top floor. Now she was in, what next? If McNab was there, what would she say? If he wasn't, what would she do?

The lift doors pinged open as a soft female voice informed her she was on the eighth floor. Rhona got her bearings then headed right. She found herself muttering, 'Be there', as she approached the door. She stood for a moment, composing herself, then knocked.

When there was no answer, she tried the handle. The door moved under her slight pressure, swinging open. Inside all was dark and silent.

'McNab,' she called softly. When there was no response she reached for the light switch and flicked it on. Waited, then called again, knowing it was of little use, but hoping just the same. Maybe he was upstairs, asleep, drunk, exhausted?

The narrow staircase that wound to mezzanine level was in shadow, her footfall swallowed by the deep carpet. She hesitated before turning at the top. Moonlight through the upper section of window lit up an empty bed.

She felt her heart stop, then start again.

McNab wasn't here but he had been and not that long ago. His dinner jacket was over a chair by the bed, and the sharp scent of his aftershave was still in the room. Rhona found a row of switches near the headboard and pressed them all on. In the dazzling brightness she studied the room.

McNab hadn't checked out. There were clothes hanging in the wardrobe space, a pair of shoes below. A holdall sat on the luggage rack. So where was he, and why was the door unlocked? She was seized by the thought that McNab had left swiftly and suddenly. But why? There was no disorder. No evidence of a struggle. No blood.

She had an image of McNab being frog-marched out, a gun pressed to his back. But why not just kill him here? Because Kalinin wanted him alive? To do what?

The theories were coming thick and fast. Kalinin had dispensed with Brogan and taken McNab; McNab had shot Brogan and gone on the run.

But where did Petersson fit into any of these scenarios? Rhona tried his number and got voicemail again. She would go round to Petersson's flat, she decided. That was the obvious next move.

Halfway down the stairs, she heard the room door open

and close again. She stood in the shadows, waiting. A second click told her the door was now locked. She peered gingerly around the corner and breathed out when she saw the night porter waiting by the door.

He gave her a sly smile. 'No one in?'

'Yeah, too bad,' she answered nonchalantly as she descended the rest of the stairs. 'So I can head home.'

'So soon?'

She observed his stance, the look in his eye. God, she didn't have time for what was about to happen. He confirmed her fears almost immediately.

'Seems a shame, since it's already been paid for.'

'For Mr McCartney only.' Rhona attempted to pass him, but he blocked her.

'Come on,' he wheedled. 'It's no skin off your nose. I get laid, you get paid.'

Enough was enough. 'Fuck off, or—'

'Or what? You'll make a scene? Then I'll call the cops. Tell them I have a hooker on the premises rifling through a customer's room.'

Rhona met his eager gaze and decided there was no alternative. She reached into her coat pocket, extracted her ID and thrust it in his face.

'I *am* the police.' She watched with pleasure as he read the card, his face contorting in surprise, shock, then anger.

'You bitch,' he finally muttered under his breath.

'The door,' she commanded.

He turned the key. The look he gave her as she pushed past suggested he could have cheerfully throttled her. They had reached the wider space in front of the elevator.

'Did Mr McCartney leave alone?'

He blanked her.

'The police will be here soon. DI Wilson won't be pleased when I tell him you didn't co-operate.'

He considered the veiled threat.

'Especially if I mention the sexual harassment of his forensic officer.'

His eyes clouded with fury. Rhona thought for a moment she had pushed him too far.

'Was McCartney alone?' she repeated.

He regarded her for a moment, then seemed to come to a decision. 'He left with this massive guy. Big ugly bastard.' He watched as this news took effect, registering that he had scored a hit. He decided to embellish and watch her squirm. 'The big guy didn't look happy, and your Mr McCartney was sweating like a fucking pig.'

The lift had arrived. 'I'll go first,' she snapped, 'and alone.'

Rhona stepped inside and didn't turn as the doors closed, not wanting the porter to see her face. The news that McNab had left with someone who looked like Solonik frightened her more than the assault she had narrowly escaped.

As she pulled away in the car, the porter was watching from the door and making a mobile call. Who the hell was he phoning? Not the police. Kalinin? Solonik?

It suddenly struck her that as soon as Kalinin believed McNab was alive, she would have been on the Russian's radar. He knew she and McNab were close. He would have suspected McNab might get in touch with her, if only to let her know he wasn't dead.

Rhona glanced in the rear-view mirror. Maybe she'd had

someone on her tail all along? Maybe that's how they'd discovered where McNab was hiding out in Glasgow? Maybe this was all her fault?

The drive from Bath Street to the West End took no time at all. Byres Road was still slumbering, even the normally busy traffic lights at University Avenue were clear to cross. As she entered Petersson's road, she spotted a light on in his flat and her heart leapt. *Please let him be there*. Rhona left the car double-parked and headed for the door and pressed the buzzer. Moments later someone picked up.

'Yes?'

'It's me, Rhona.'

He let her in. She climbed the stairs two at a time to find the door to his flat standing open.

'Einar?' she called on entry. When there was no reply, she checked in the kitchen, the sitting room and finally the bedroom where a light shone from the en suite bathroom.

'Einar, are you in there?'

There was a horrible retching sound.

'Einar, are you OK?'

Another long and distressing retch, then an expletive. Rhona tried the door. It was locked.

'Open the door.'

A rush of water hit the sink as a tap was turned on full force. She heard splashing and groaning, then eventually the snib on the door was pulled back and the door slowly opened.

Petersson stood before her, his face as pale as his white blond hair. The tuxedo jacket was stained with mucus, the shirt and tie awry. He swayed a little and Rhona grabbed him to prevent him falling.

'You need to lie down.'

He nodded and she helped him across to the bed. He groaned as she eased him on to it. Apart from his ghastly pallor, she could see nothing obviously wrong. No bruising or bloodstains.

'What happened?'

Petersson drew himself up against the pillows and the movement made him wince in pain. 'I took a kicking.' He unbuttoned his shirt to expose a mass of red bruising and the imprint of at least three shoes.

The sight horrified Rhona. 'You need to get checked out at Accident and Emergency. There could be internal injuries.'

'There's nothing broken.' He observed her worried expression. 'Believe me, I know what I'm talking about.'

'How did it happen?'

He laid his head back wearily.

'I was escorted from the premises for trying to involve its owner in money laundering, and taught a lesson. I never got a chance to say why I was really there.' He paused for a moment. 'Brogan was all smiles at first. Offered me a Cuban cigar, a brandy. Asked about the money. I played along for a while, then requested we talk in private, hoping he'd remove the bouncer from the room. The bouncer did leave but he took me with him. Next thing I know I'm round the back and three guys are scoring goals in my stomach. I passed out. Came to on my doorstep.'

'So they know who you are?'

'And where I live.'

'And why you were there?'

'That I don't know. It may be that Brogan did suspect

I was looking for a money-laundering story and decided to warn me off.' He caught her worried eye and pulled himself up. 'What is it?'

'Brogan's dead. Shot at point blank range through the head.'

'What?'

'I've just come from the crime scene.'

She watched as he processed this information, trying to figure out if it was a surprise to him. 'I told Bill we were at the club.' He was waiting, anticipating more. Rhona paused, afraid to voice what would come next. 'McNab was at the club. I saw him just after you went with Brogan. He was very angry to find me there and insisted I left. He said you would both come to my flat after he'd spoken to Brogan.'

'I had no idea he was there.'

Rhona studied him closely. He'd lied before or, in his own words, omitted to tell her the whole truth. Was he lying now?

'I take it McNab never turned up at your place?'

She shook her head. 'I went round to his hotel. He's not there. The night porter said he left with a big guy who sounded like Solonik.'

'*Dj' fulsins Helviti!*'

'They've got him, haven't they?'

Petersson wouldn't answer. He didn't have to.

16

'OK, so what are we looking for?'

Ben sounded eager, as though he was playing one of his online computer games.

'I don't know. The porno said 'Olympia Bridgeton' on the label. Jude must have been here.'

Liam looked up at the red sandstone building. The impressive curved and porticoed entrance had weeds growing from its cracked stones, the windows and doors boarded up.

'How do we get in?'

'You mean you don't have a sonic screwdriver?' Liam said sarcastically.

Ben observed him grandly. 'Word of advice, mate. You don't diss the Doctor. You never know when he might come in handy.'

Liam shook his head. Ben might be a computer genius but at times Liam wondered if he was actually living on this planet.

'How did Jude get in?' Ben said.

'I don't know. Talked to the council or something.'

'We could try that?'

'And how long would that take?'

Ben must have been able to see Liam was worried. 'We'll find a way in. Let's take a look round the back.'

The right wall of the building faced the main road and was plastered with fly posters. Hard on its end was a white building containing offices, followed by another sandstone one. Neither offered any obvious access to the rear of the Olympia.

The other side street looked more promising. There were two doors, both obviously former exits from the cinema. Both were padlocked. At the end of the building was a concreted back court, surrounded by a high barbed-wire fence.

They stood in silence, neither wanting to voice the opinion that it was hopeless.

'OK. What if I pick a padlock with my sonic screwdriver?' Ben offered.

'Fuck off.' Liam was in no mood for joking.

Ben, unmoved by the expletive, pulled out what looked like a mini-screwdriver. 'I told you, don't diss the Doctor.'

He took himself back to a padlocked door. 'OK, stand in front of me and act casual.' He glanced up at the tenement and corner pub opposite. 'Anyone taking an interest in us, we move off. Right?'

'Right.' Liam assumed what he hoped was a casual stance, glancing about occasionally as though waiting for someone.

'Take my advice, bro. Don't audition for the RSAMD,' muttered Ben from behind him. 'You can't act for shite.'

Liam heard a click, then a rattle as the chain was pulled free. Seconds later they were in, the door shut firmly behind them. They stood in the dark, panting and smothering laughter.

Liam switched on the torch. 'Holy shit, you're good.'

Ben grinned. 'So now *we've* done the breaking and entering bit, what next?'

'We find the projection room.' Liam shone the beam up a set of concrete steps. 'Follow me.'

They climbed up either side of a metal railing. The beam bounced off glossy red walls. When they reached a landing they paused.

'Which way?'

'Give us a chance.' Liam surveyed the landing walls searching for the 'No Smoking' sign he knew would indicate the location of the projection suite. Here the ceiling plaster had partially collapsed. The smell of damp was overwhelming, nothing like the warm stuffy dryness of the Rosevale.

'Well?' Ben urged, just as the beam caught a double door. 'What's in there?'

'Probably the balcony.'

'Let's take a look.' Ben pushed open the door.

They moved from pitch darkness to a diffused light. It *was* the balcony, still full of rows of plush red seats. Below was a full view of the old auditorium, the light coming from a cupola on the top right-hand side of the exposed roof.

'Wow!' Ben said, gazing round.

The ceiling was badly damaged and various broken items were scattered about the auditorium floor, but the proscenium arch was still spectacular, despite the cheap hand-painted banner that hung limply across it: *Glasgow Suite Centre Open 7 days.*

'It must have ended up as a furniture store before it finally closed,' Liam said.

'Shame. I could imagine watching a cool movie in here.'

Liam swivelled round to look at the back wall, spotting the telltale portholes. 'The projection room's up there. Come on.'

The higher they climbed the more apparent the damage became. Blackened and burned in places, the roof was obviously letting in the rain big time.

'God, this place stinks,' Ben said.

'Not as badly as the Rosevale.'

'It smelled like this?'

'Believe me, dead bodies have a smell all their own.'

'You think we'll find another body?' Ben said, half eager, half afraid.

Liam stopped suddenly and Ben bumped into his back.

'The projection suite.' Liam directed the torch at a wooden door with a heavy brass closer. Above it the sign emphasised 'No Smoking!'.

'The holy of holies. Cool.'

The door had a heavy bolt which slid back easily.

'Weird. It's the only thing not rusting round here.'

Liam pulled the door open and they stepped inside. The brass closer immediately swung the door shut behind them.

'Shit!'

The beam picked out Ben's startled face.

'It's OK, we're not locked in,' Liam assured him.

'If you say so.' Ben made big eyes at him.

Liam ran the torch round the room. It looked much the same as the one at the Rosevale. The only difference was the existence of two empty projector stands and the fact that the space was cleaner. Much cleaner.

'Someone's tidied up in here,' Ben remarked. 'It doesn't smell so bad either.'

'Bone dry,' Liam looked up at the ceiling. 'No leaks.'

'No nothing,' said Ben, swivelling round to check the entire space.

'So where did Jude find the reel of film?'

The torch lit on a metal cabinet, doors standing open. Liam went for a closer look. Three shelves, all empty. On the floor in front was a half-smoked cigarette.

'Jude doesn't smoke, does she?' Ben bent to pick it up.

'Don't!'

'Why not?'

'DNA?'

Ben liked that. 'Cool. Ultra cool. So what do we do? Bag it and deliver it to your mum?'

But Liam's attention had settled on the cabinet. The lock looked as though it had been oiled, the interior was dust free. He eyed the width of a shelf. The reel would have fitted it easily.

Ben was following his thoughts. 'You think Jude found the reel in there?'

'Maybe.'

'So what? Gay pornos aren't illegal.'

'Back when that one was made, they were.' Liam shook his head. Nothing made sense. Jude visited this place and took home an old porno film, then she went to the Rosevale and disappeared.

'Are you going to tell Rhona about this?'

'She's got her hands full with the body,' Liam said sharply. 'Unless Jude turns up dead, I don't think she'll be interested.'

'That's a bit harsh.'

Liam stood up. 'Let's go.'

'What about the cigarette?'

'Leave it.'

They made their way down the stairs. Once outside, Ben re-padlocked the door.

Liam watched, deflated and depressed. He had no idea what he'd hoped to find at the Olympia; he'd just wanted to prove to himself that he was doing something, when the truth was he was running around like a headless chicken.

Jude's intense little face came into his mind. How he longed to see it again.

'You're not giving up, are you, mate?' said Ben.

When Liam didn't answer, Ben slipped an arm round his shoulder. 'OK, I suggest we go for a pint and plan our next move.'

'What next move?' Liam said, moodily.

'Jude was on Facebook.'

'Was she? How d'you know that?'

'Because I'm one of her cinema friends.' Ben grinned. 'Don't look so freaked. We have a mutual passion for sci-fi films, that's all.' He paused. 'I take it you're not on Facebook?'

'No.'

Ben looked askance and shook his head. 'It's time you entered this century, bro. I vote we use Facebook to try and find her.'

'Use Facebook?' Liam was still trying to process this new aspect of Jude. The sci-fi fanatic. He was beginning to suspect he didn't know anything about her. Or at least, he only knew what she'd chosen to tell him.

'Watch and learn, bro. Watch and learn.'

17

Bill stood in the Super's office, sure that he must look as though he had a bad smell under his nose. He did, and it was generated by Detective Inspector Geoffrey Slater.

Slater hadn't improved in looks since his departure. If anything he'd put on more weight, and grown meaner looking. Or maybe he was trying to project a tough-guy image to give himself more authority. It wasn't working on Bill, who hated everything about the man. It was, in his opinion, Slater's fault that McNab had been shot in the first place. If Slater hadn't released Kalinin that night, or had at least warned McNab, Bill doubted they would be standing here now with another murder on their hands.

'Sit down, gentlemen.'

Bill would have preferred to stand, but the look on the Super's face suggested that wasn't an option.

Sutherland waved the stranger in the room to a seat first. He'd been introduced as Harry Black, and was a fresh-faced, smart-suited DI from SOCA.

'I know you understand how important it is that we co-operate with SOCA on this?' The remark was directed at Bill.

'The shooting occurred on our territory, Sir.'

'I am well aware of that, Detective Inspector,' Superintendent Sutherland said smoothly.

The argument over jurisdiction in McNab's case had rubbed salt in the wound for his team, after the shock of the murder itself. In retrospect, Bill could appreciate SOCA's motives. The Serious Organised Crime Agency needed McNab as a witness in their high-profile case against Nikolai Kalinin. That gave them precedence over their Scottish equivalent, the Scottish Crime and Drug Agency. So SOCA had spirited the seriously injured McNab away, nursed him back to health, then hidden him. It was a neat trick, or would have been if it had worked.

They all took their seats. The Super's room, for all its airy size, was hardly big enough for the combined force of adrenaline and testosterone present. Bill thought to himself that if McNab had walked in at this moment the place would have ignited.

As he observed in silence, Bill wondered who was really in charge of the investigation into Brogan's shooting: Slater or Black? Slater had made mistakes the first time round, but then SOCA had lost the soldier Fergus Morrison even when they had him in a safe house.

The truth was, Kalinin and his gang were running rings round all of them. Only recently the Metropolitan Police Commissioner had publicly stated that some of Britain's wealthiest and most dangerous criminals were operating with complete impunity, and that policing had a meaningful impact on just ten per cent of the 6,000 crime gangs operating across Britain. Intelligence had identified 68 criminal organisations that each held assets of £10 million or more; Kalinin, Bill suspected, had a bigger bank balance than even they could imagine.

And now with Brogan, yet another witness was conveniently dead. Which left only McNab.

'Tell them what you told me,' said Sutherland.

Bill cleared his throat. 'Dr MacLeod arrived at the Poker Club with Einar Petersson at around nine o'clock yesterday evening. Their intention was that Petersson would approach Brogan and ask him to testify against Kalinin.'

Black got in first. 'In what capacity?'

'McNab had been in touch with Rhona . . . with Dr MacLeod, and revealed that Paddy Brogan had been in the car the night he was shot. He thought if Brogan was made aware that he was alive and would testify, Brogan himself might be brought onside. The other sweetener was that Kalinin's conviction would get him off Brogan's back.'

Black was sitting forward in his seat, his interest and excitement obvious. Slater was more wary, circling the revelations with suspicion.

'Einar Petersson has a history of messing in things that don't concern him,' Slater said.

'Others might say he has a better track record than the authorities at bringing crime-lords to book.'

Sutherland darted Bill a warning look which he chose not to acknowledge before dropping his bombshell. 'When Petersson went to speak to Brogan on the pretext that he was an Icelandic banker with money to launder, Dr MacLeod discovered DS McNab was in the building.'

There was an audible intake of breath from the other two men. Bill had waited until this morning to tell the Superintendent, hoping they might locate McNab first, but Rhona's phone call had put an end to that.

He weighed up their reactions. Slater, he deduced from his smile, either already knew this or was delighted by it. Black's response was harder to decipher. He went on: 'DS McNab insisted Rhona go home, where he and Petersson would meet her later. He never turned up, and is still missing. Brogan pretended offence at being asked to launder money and Petersson was violently ejected from the premises. Petersson maintains he neither saw McNab nor had any idea that he was there.'

Bill stopped there, seeing no need to reveal Rhona's mad dash to the Poker Club or her concern that McNab could have been either the victim or the perpetrator.

Silence descended. It was a lot to take in. Bill suspected Slater would stick his oar in first, which he did with barely suppressed glee.

'I take it McNab has a firearm?'

'No, not unless SOCA issued him with one.'

Black looked momentarily uncomfortable. 'One gun was unaccounted for after DS McNab's disappearance from the safe house.'

From Slater's expression he was already writing McNab into a firearm's charge, perhaps even a murder charge. But Bill hadn't finished yet.

'In the early hours of this morning DS McNab was witnessed leaving a hotel in Bath Street, where he'd been staying. He was in the company of a man who might have been Ivan Solonik, Kalinin's right-hand man.'

That was news even for the Super.

'You're sure about this?'

'We've brought the night porter in for further questioning, but it's fairly conclusive.'

A heavy silence followed. Nobody said McNab could already be dead, but they were all thinking it. Bill's chest was so tight at the thought that he could barely draw air into his lungs.

'Thank you, Detective Inspector Wilson,' Black said formally. 'Myself and DI Slater will take over from here.'

Bill had been anticipating this moment, but it didn't make it any easier. He opened his mouth to protest, however useless that might be, but the Super stalled him.

'How are things progressing on the body found in the cinema?'

'It was transferred to the mortuary this morning, Sir. The PM's this afternoon.'

'Good. Let me know what happens.' Sutherland stood up pointedly, followed by the others. Bill was being summarily dismissed. The idiots who'd endangered his DS first time round were intent on finishing the job.

He walked stiffly to the door.

The incident room fell silent as he passed through. Everyone knew something was up. DS Clark followed him into his office.

'I have to ask, Sir. Rumour has it the Russians have picked up McNab. Is it true?'

Looking at her strained face, Bill thought it would have been better for them all to go on believing McNab was dead. Burying a colleague and friend once was more than enough.

'We don't deal in rumour here, Sergeant.'

Janice nodded. 'Yes, Sir,' she said, and retreated.

Bill waited until the door closed, then swivelled his chair to face the window. Who was he kidding? There weren't many men who could fit Solonik's description, although there was something about that weasel of a night porter that had made him uneasy.

He'd got the impression when he went to the hotel after Rhona's phone call that the guy wasn't telling him the whole story. That's why he'd brought him in. Although an opportunity to question him further had gone now that Slater was involved. Bill wondered how soon Slater and Black would pick up Petersson, and whether he could have a word with him first.

He glanced at his watch. A couple of hours until the post mortem on the Rosevale remains. Like him, Rhona had had little sleep, but he knew she would be there. Maybe they'd get a chance to talk afterwards.

He gazed sadly out of his window.

A few years ago, he would have had a clear line of sight to the railway line that ran west out of Glasgow. The new-look city had put paid to that with its explosion of glossy high rises. He might not be able to take in the old view, but he remembered it well enough.

Bill had fond memories of visiting Eglinton signal box as a boy. Set high, it had been the only box you had to cross tracks to get to, and he'd climbed what seemed like hundreds of steps to reach it. Up there he had felt like king of the tracks.

Glasgow was changing. Where once the great railways had ruled, now the new roads were cutting across old streets and railway lines – including the main west coast line he'd looked down on as a boy.

The last decade had brought other changes, changes Bill neither liked nor understood. The Glasgow hard men he had known were being replaced by something much worse, whose new activities brought in money and misery on a scale Bill could hardly have imagined ten years ago: identity fraud; online paedophilia; human trafficking; prostitution, and – as always – drugs.

Glasgow bastards were bad enough, but at least Bill knew how their minds worked because most of them had come from similar backgrounds to his. Paddy Brogan's father would never have countenanced the shooting of a policeman outside his club. That would have been a sacrilege, endangering a lifetime's work. The elder Patrick Brogan had respected the police enough to make sure he never crossed them on purpose. And he would never have exposed his family and business the way his son had done.

And that was why Paddy Brogan junior was dead.

'You could press charges,' said Bill.

When he had called Petersson, the Icelander had suggested he come over to talk face to face. His voice on the phone had made it clear he was in a great deal of pain, and in person he looked terrible.

'I could, but I won't.' Petersson shifted uncomfortably in his seat. 'My main concern at the moment is McNab, as, no doubt, is yours. You spoke to the night porter?'

Bill nodded. 'His description of the man he said left with McNab was fairly minimal. A massive, ugly, muscled guy, he said.'

'That's it?'

'I think he was lying or not telling the whole truth.'

Petersson frowned. 'You know Rhona pretended to be an escort to get in to see McNab?'

Bill raised a quizzical eyebrow. 'And?'

'And the porter made a play for her. She turned him down, then revealed who she really was.'

'And that pissed him off?'

Petersson nodded.

'So he could have made it all up to get back at her?' Bill said.

Petersson looked serious. 'Could be, but I don't think so. It'd be quite a coincidence that his description fitted Solonik. My gut feeling is there's more. Maybe someone did come looking for McNab and the night porter let him in? Rhona says the porter made a phone call as she was driving away.'

'So we check out his mobile.'

'If he still has it.'

Bill was silent for a moment before he said what was on his mind. 'You should have told me what was going on.'

'I work alone.'

'Then why involve Rhona?'

'Come on, Bill. You know Rhona MacLeod better than I do. I'd say she chose me as much as I chose her.'

That, Bill didn't doubt. He changed the subject.

'DI Slater's in charge of Brogan's killing. He has a London SOCA man with him, DI Black.'

Petersson straightened up, wincing. 'Harry Black? Short hair, sharp dresser, looks about twelve years old?'

Bill nodded. 'That's him.'

'He was in charge of the safety detail on McNab and

Morrison. When he lost them both, he made a fool of himself.'

'Can he be trusted?'

'Whatever he does will be in his own interest,' Petersson replied. 'He needs to redeem himself. Get his career back on track.'

Bill said nothing for a moment, taking stock of the situation. He was on the outside now, like Petersson. True, he would have access to some information on the Brogan killing and the search for McNab. SOCA would have to rely on local back-up who would be keen to keep him up to date, if only to spite Slater. But it would do no harm to be in Petersson's confidence too. Bill had no doubt of the journalist's capabilities, injured or not. After all, he was the one who'd discovered McNab was still alive. And it would be better to keep an eye on him.

'What d'you say we work together on this? In an unofficial capacity, of course.'

'That wouldn't put you on the spot?'

'Let's just say you've joined my list of informants.'

'And Rhona?'

'I'll tell her we've talked when I see her at the post mortem.' Bill paused, before asking the question he really came here for. 'OK, you probably know the way Nikolai Kalinin operates better than anyone. If he did abduct McNab, what next?'

'I don't think he'd necessarily kill him immediately. McNab has a lot of information he's interested in. And as long as he has him, McNab can't turn up in court.' Petersson looked grave. 'My guess is Kalinin will make this last as long as possible in order to derive the most pleasure he can from it.'

'He'll torture him?'

'Without a doubt.'

18

'Bloody hell!'

Chrissy was wild eyed. Rhona had just finished filling her in on Brogan's shooting.

'We won't be processing the scene.'

'*You* won't, but who says I can't?' Chrissy retorted.

'I don't think that's a good idea.'

Chrissy pulled out her mobile and made a quick call. Rhona only heard her half of the conversation, but it was obvious what was going on. Chrissy rang off.

'Pull over. I get out here.'

'What about the PM?'

Chrissy glared at her. 'We need someone at the Poker Club. What if that stupid bastard McNab did have something to do with Brogan's death?'

'You can't cover for him.'

'I have no intention of doing that. I just want to know what the hell's going on. I'll pick up a taxi. Call you later.' Chrissy was already out of the vehicle. Rhona watched her turn the corner on to the main road and disappear.

McNab, once Chrissy's nemesis, had become her champion. He had that effect on people. Difficult to be with, but difficult to shake off. Chrissy was right, though; if they didn't have someone on the ground at the Poker Club, they wouldn't get the full picture.

Rhona still had a gnawing feeling that McNab had done something terrible. But why would he kill Brogan now? It didn't make sense. McNab had been in hiding, believed dead, for months, and could have targeted Brogan at any point during that time. The thought comforted her somewhat. McNab wanted his job and his life back. He had made that plain enough when they last met. He wouldn't jeopardise that. Would he?

What did any of this matter if Kalinin had him?

That was a thought she couldn't deal with. She tried to focus on the road instead. Today's journey through the city centre was nothing like the previous night's. No longer an empty film set, it was now jam-packed with vehicles snaking round the one-way system.

After phoning Bill from Petersson's, she'd finally driven home to try to snatch a few hours' sleep. The Rosevale remains had been scheduled for removal to the mortuary first thing this morning. Supervising the proceedings had kept her mind occupied, although she'd still tried McNab's mobile every half hour.

When the body was finally on its way, Rhona had encased the backboard in a plastic bag and seen it safely to the lab before writing up her notes. There had been little opportunity to speak to Chrissy in private during the proceedings, so she'd skipped over her questions about the trip to the Poker Club, promising the full story on their way to the PM.

She'd eventually given Chrissy a potted version of the previous night's events, omitting her visit to the hotel and her conversation with the night porter, deciding to wait until Bill had interviewed the man.

She was aware she was nursing a forlorn hope that the night porter's account of McNab's departure had been designed to get back at her. She'd run the conversation over in her mind a thousand times, wondering if she'd assumed he'd been describing Solonik, because that was her greatest fear.

Bill appeared in the changing room at the mortuary as she was suiting up. He looked as weary as she felt.

'Fancy a coffee after this?' he asked.

'If you still have the stomach for it.'

He looked as if he wanted a heart to heart. Rhona's own heart sank at the prospect.

The body was laid out, the curled limbs straightened. The harness had been removed, as had the collar and studs from the nose and tongue. These were set out on a table nearby like a display of medieval torture implements, waiting for forensic examination.

Now that the pubic region was fully exposed, it was clear that they were dealing with a male: the pathologist was in the process of removing a metal testicle cuff from the dried and ragged remains of the scrotum.

An hour later, much of what Rhona had already surmised had been confirmed. The victim had not been stabbed, shot or bludgeoned to death. Judging by the intact hyoid bone and no evidence of broken cervical vertebrae, he was unlikely to have been strangled either. All of which brought them back to Rhona's initial theory that he may have been walled in alive and asphyxiated.

At this point Rhona asked if she might remove the fingers and take them to the lab for fingerprinting. Dr Sissons greeted her request with wry humour, not something he was normally known for, and declared he would take a short break while she cut them off. The rest of the audience went with him.

Cutting off the fingers was the worst bit. After that the process of preparing them for fingerprinting was routine. Rhona set to it, glad that she had been left alone to carry out the procedure. The fingers safely stored for removal to the lab, Rhona decided not to stay for the rest of the procedure; her part was done. She told Sissons the corpse was all his, and went looking for Bill. He was waiting in the changing room, stripped of his white suit and talking on his mobile. Rhona changed and washed her hands thoroughly. The lingering scent of the mortuary would have to stay with her until after she'd processed the fingers, then she would have a shower.

Bill finished his phone call. 'OK, let's find a decent cup of coffee. We've a lot to talk about,' he said, ominously.

The City Mortuary and the High Court being neighbours, it seemed fitting that they should head for McNab's favourite café. They walked in silence. Whatever Bill was thinking, it wasn't happy thoughts. Rhona sensed his gloom and anger and immediately assumed the worst. Had he learned more about McNab's abduction? She glanced round at him as they walked, hoping Bill might put her out of her misery, but he continued to stare straight ahead.

When they reached the Central Café he urged her into a booth next to the one she'd sat in with McNab.

'Coffee?'

'Black and strong. A mug, please,' she said.

He nodded and headed for the counter, returning empty handed. 'They'll bring them over.' He sat down opposite, catching her enquiring look. 'Let's wait. I don't want to be interrupted or overheard.'

They sat in heavy silence, surrounded by the hum of other conversations. Eventually the coffees arrived, served by a wee woman with a distracted air whom Rhona didn't recognise. She bumped the two mugs down unceremoniously and swiftly departed.

Rhona blew on hers and took a mouthful, needing the caffeine hit to face whatever was coming next. Bill studied his own coffee for a few minutes before looking up.

'I went to see Petersson.'

'Oh.'

'I wanted to speak to him before Slater got there.'

'Slater?'

'He's taking over the Brogan shooting. Him and a guy from SOCA, DI Black.'

So she wasn't the only one forbidden to have anything to do with the case. 'If it wasn't for Slater—' she began angrily.

'I know.' Bill stopped her. 'I don't trust him either. That's why I asked Petersson to work with me on this. Unofficially, of course.' His next words were tentative. 'We also discussed Kalinin, and the possibility that McNab was abducted.'

'We don't know that for certain,' she said, swiftly.

'That's true,' he assured her. 'And I'm not sure I believe everything your night porter says.'

'Petersson told you about the escort thing?' she guessed.

He smiled. 'Good undercover work, Dr MacLeod. I could get you a part-time job.'

'I thought I just signed up for one?'

The moment of levity over, Rhona waited with trepidation for what was to follow.

'Petersson knows Kalinin's ways better than anyone.' Bill was choosing his words carefully. '*If*, and I stress *if* Kalinin has McNab, Petersson believes he won't kill him straight away.'

Rhona's initial rush of relief gave way to dread. 'Why?'

Bill looked down at his coffee again.

'He'll . . . hurt him?' She couldn't bring herself to say *torture*.

'The longer Kalinin keeps McNab alive, the better our chances of finding him.'

'But you're not sure he has him?' she repeated.

'We have no definite proof, either way.' Bill met her worried look. 'McNab's tough. He's survived whatever they've thrown at him up to now.'

Rhona wasn't sure if Bill was saying that to boost her spirits, or his own. She tried to focus on doing something positive.

'So what's our next move?'

'I'm going to run a check on Matthew Sinclair, our night porter. See if he has any previous, find out who he mixes with. Maybe even threaten him with a sexual-assault charge against an officer in the line of duty. Petersson has his own contacts, and he thinks he can find out if Kalinin has picked up McNab.'

'Petersson can hardly walk.'

'He can sit at his computer. Apparently that's enough.' Bill was silent for a moment. 'Before we leave this, is there anything else about that night you need to tell me, before Slater comes asking?'

Rhona realised she would probably be interviewed by Slater. God, it would take all her resolve not to spit in his eye. She took a moment to think. She'd been keeping secrets from Bill and Chrissy for months. Even now she hadn't told Chrissy the whole truth. But had she told Bill everything that had happened that night?

There was something. She didn't think it had any relevance to McNab but she would say it all the same.

'When Petersson went off with Brogan and left me in the bar, I saw Edward and Fiona Stewart. I tried to avoid them but Edward spotted me and came over.' She grimaced at the memory. 'He made a big thing about telling me he was there with *Lord* Dalrymple.'

Bill gave a low whistle. 'So it's *Lord* Dalrymple now. Funny how scum always rises to the top.' He thought for a moment. 'I don't recall any mention of Edward Stewart or *Lord* Dalrymple having been on the premises when I arrived. I think I'll check up on that. Maybe, with friends in high places, Dalrymple managed to wheedle his way out, again.'

Superintendent Sutherland and Lord Dalrymple were old acquaintances. Moving in the upper echelons of society, as the senior officer did, it would be hard to avoid knowing Dalrymple. But Rhona understood Bill's disquiet. A lodge house on Dalrymple's country estate had featured in a murder enquiry. The fact that the evidence for this came from a rent boy, Neil MacGregor, had made it, in Sutherland's eyes, inadmissible. Neil MacGregor had almost died because of what he knew.

And two other young men *had* died; garrotted, their bodies bitten and mutilated. They had caught the guy organising the supply of vulnerable young males and discovered he'd groomed many of the teenagers online, one of them Edward and Fiona's son Jonathan. Jonathan, one of the lucky ones, had escaped with his life. Of course Dalrymple had insisted he'd had no knowledge of what his lodge house had been used for, and the police had found nothing.

'According to Black, McNab took a gun from the safe house,' said Bill. 'We need to know if that gun was the one used to kill Brogan.'

'Chrissy's inveigled her way on to the forensic team. She's at the Poker Club now, and she'll have access to details on the murder weapon.'

Bill's face broke into a grin. 'Bloody hell. I love that lassie. As long as Slater doesn't recognise her,' he added.

'Chrissy knows the score. She'll be careful.' Rhona glanced at her watch. 'I have to get those fingers to the lab if I want to lift prints tomorrow.'

'Before you go, I need a quick word about Liam.'

'Oh?' she said warily.

'Jude's neighbour in the Hall of Residence thought she heard Jude come back. The warden called Liam. When they took a look, they found the room had been ransacked and Jude's laptop taken.'

'My God!'

'Liam gave me a memory stick he'd removed from Jude's computer. I had its contents checked. Mostly photos of old cinemas, a sound file of an interview with a former projectionist . . . and something else.'

Rhona waited.

'There were about fifty still shots. The tech guy who studied them thought they were digital photographs of individual frames of an old film reel. They ran them together in movie software and it *was* a film. Two men involved in S and M, shot in black and white. Amidst the debris in Jude's room we found an empty film canister, labelled 'Olympia Bridgeton' and dated a week ago. Whoever ransacked her room took her laptop and possibly the reel of film she was photographing.'

Rhona felt terrible. All this had been going on in Liam's life, and she hadn't contacted him as promised.

'You think the reel's in some way linked to our body?'

'I have no idea, but I'm beginning to think Jude might.' Bill chewed his lip, suddenly awkward. 'Rhona, how well do you know Liam?'

'What?' Rhona was unsure how to answer. How could she admit to having had only three conversations with her son, all of them difficult? 'Not well,' she conceded. 'Why?'

Bill regarded her sympathetically. 'It's just that I wasn't sure he was telling me the whole story when he handed over the memory stick. It might be that he was just embarrassed about removing it without permission, or maybe he'd seen the images.'

Rhona found herself immediately jumping to Liam's defence. 'If Liam had anything to do with Jude's disappearance, why would he report her missing? And why get in touch and ask for my help?' Even as she said it, Rhona knew the guilty sometimes did that, believing it would make them look innocent. The thought distressed her.

'I'm not accusing Liam of anything, except perhaps omitting part of the story,' Bill said. 'Or maybe he's just being loyal and not telling a secret Jude asked him to keep.'

'I'll speak to him.' Rhona stood up. 'And now, I really must go. You'll get in touch as soon as you hear anything about McNab?'

She knew she had left abruptly, but the conversation had made her uneasy. Did Liam know something more about Jude's disappearance?

19

The Glasgow School Of Art, Charles Rennie Mackintosh's most famous architectural contribution to the city. Even to Bill's artistically untrained eye it looked good, although his own favourite Mackintosh building was the less-well-known Queen's Cross Church in Maryhill.

He stood for a moment on the other side of the street, drinking in the façade as small groups of students drifted in and out.

Student support had been helpful, but unwilling to discuss one of their own over the telephone. Already aware of Jude's missing status, they were anxious to assist with his enquiries, but only in person.

Five minutes later he found himself sitting in a tiny office, with a mug of tea and a ginger biscuit. Angela Wakefield, the woman behind the desk, looked like a former art student herself; stylish, and definitely not conservative in dress.

'Jude did have special support in her studies here,' she confirmed. 'She was diagnosed as having high-functioning Asperger's syndrome while in the care of Sunderland Social Services.'

'And this means?'

'In Jude's case, it means she's gifted artistically, but lacks non-verbal communication skills and displays a limited empathy with her peers.' She smiled. 'Jude works hard, but plays little.'

'Some would say a perfect student.'

'For her to succeed at her chosen profession, she will have to engage with the world, not just a tiny part of it. We try to help her make that happen.'

'She was happy here?'

'Jude was obsessed with her studies.'

'Is that the same thing?'

'It is to her.'

'What about friends?'

'If you mean close friends rather than just people in her class, I don't think there were any.'

'The boy who reported her missing. Liam Hope. She never mentioned him?'

'No.'

'What about family?'

'We believed, initially, that she had none. But just recently there has been some correspondence from an uncle in Sunderland wanting to know how to get in touch with her.'

'You told her this?'

'I gave her the contact details.'

'Do you know if she did anything with them?'

'She never said.'

'Do you still have these?'

She checked her file. 'I believe I just handed over the piece of paper with the name and number to Jude.'

'Can you remember the name?'

She thought for a moment. 'It wasn't the same surname as Jude's, I remember that.' She gestured her regret. 'I'm sorry. That's not much help, is it?'

'If you remember the name, or he calls again, you'll let me know?'

'You think if Jude did make contact with this uncle, she might have returned to Sunderland?'

Bill wished he did think that. 'It's a possibility,' he said.

She didn't look convinced. 'Jude wasn't the kind of person to act spontaneously, Detective Inspector. Everything she did was planned, down to the smallest detail.'

Bill's next port of call was the halls of residence. Maybe Charlie had heard something about Jude's mystery uncle. When he arrived the older man was in his cubicle, having words with a young man about the noise level coming from his room. Bill was impressed with his non-confrontational style – Charlie would have made a good policeman.

'You're back. Any luck finding Jude?'

'We're working on it.'

'So how can I help?'

'Student Support said an uncle of Jude's called them trying to get in touch with her. I wondered if he came here, or if she mentioned him.'

Charlie must have seen hundreds of visitors coming through these doors, so asking him to remember one in particular was a long shot.

'It's funny you turning up now. I was going to call you. I've been thinking a lot about the lassie since she dis-appeared. Especially after someone got in her room and stole her computer.' He sounded personally affronted by this. 'She didn't like people much. Preferred her own company. Liam, the lad that came by looking for her. He was the exception. Then I remembered the phone call.'

Bill's ears pricked up.

'A man called, asked if he could speak to Jude Evans. I told him we don't bring students to the phone and that he should call her mobile. He said she'd contacted him about an interview for a photographic project on old cinemas and he'd misplaced her mobile number.'

'And?'

'I told him I didn't have it, which isn't strictly true, because we keep a contact number for each resident. But I don't hand them out willy-nilly. I told him I would pass on the message and Jude could get back in touch with him.'

'He left his name and number?'

'He said Jude had his number already. Wouldn't even say his name.'

'And you passed on the message?'

'Yes.' He sighed. 'The lassie usually never showed any emotion. I tried to make her laugh once or twice, and she blanked me as though she had no idea what I was on about. That time was different. I thought she looked, well, a bit worried. I asked if everything was OK. She never answered me, just headed out with her backpack.'

'When was this?'

'A week, maybe ten days ago.'

'And nothing since?'

Charlie shook his head.

'Thanks, Charlie.'

'No bother. You will let me know about the wee lassie?'

'I will.'

As Bill left the building, he wondered if Charlie had been the nearest thing to a father figure Jude had had in Glasgow.

He doubted an uncle had turned up from nowhere, and surely if one had their contact would have been Sunderland Social Services. That was something he could check up on. As to the second caller, Jude had definitely met a man and recorded him. Had he been the one to phone the Hall of Residence? If so, why not leave his name? And why had the call worried Jude?

Bill didn't like the way this was going. A girl disappears after visiting a crime scene, having previously found and restored some old porn film. Mind you, who would worry about that? What it showed wasn't considered a crime nowadays.

His mind kept working at it during his drive to the station. Ask the right question and you got the answer you were looking for. But the right question wasn't always the obvious one. No matter which path his brain took, it ended up at Liam. The boy was the only person who apparently knew Jude at all. As such, he was the one who might have the answers – whether he realised it or not.

He recalled Rhona's speed in jumping to her son's defence. It had been a natural reaction, something he would have done himself. It was also clear that she hadn't had the opportunity to get to know Liam and felt guilty about it. She shouldn't. He had two teenage children of his own and after almost twenty years probably didn't really know them either. People let you see what they wanted you to see. As a detective he knew that only too well.

Liam had retreated to his own room. Ben had tried to give him a lecture on Facebook, and his plan to set up a *Find Jude* page. Viewing Jude's own page, her wall messages

and the photos of the cinemas she'd visited had disturbed
Liam. Here he was thinking she had nobody but him, when
she actually had all these cinema and sci-fi 'friends'. He
was beginning to realise that he had no idea who Jude
really was. She'd let him into a very small part of her life,
and he'd believed that was all there was. Jude was a private
person. Very private. He was lucky to have got as close to
her as he had.

Ben had been gobsmacked by Liam's lack of interest in,
or knowledge of, the workings of Facebook.

'What planet have you been on?'

'The Physics lab planet.'

'You don't have computers in there?'

'To calculate, not to indulge in cyber babble.'

'Don't diss the cyber talk. Remember the sonic screwdriver,' Ben had replied.

Liam had left Ben to it, feeling gloomy once again. If
Ben could enlist help in finding Jude, that was great. It
was something he had singularly failed to do himself.

He lay on the bed. There was an assignment due in soon,
but for once particle physics didn't exert its appeal. He
thought about calling Rhona. Did she know about the
ransacked room, the stolen laptop? If she did, surely she
would have got in touch with him by now?

His despair grew deeper. Why did he think she should
care enough to call? Just because he'd turned up on her
doorstep asking for help. The long-lost son she'd given
away at birth. Why should she suddenly give a shit now?

He hated himself for his neediness. He should never
have approached her. He'd vowed not to make contact
again and just get on with his own life. How do you form

a relationship with someone who was your mother, but who gave you away? The concept nagged at him like toothache. Finding his birth mother had been an obsession for years. He'd imagined the moment all the time. When it finally happened he'd been elated. Seeing Rhona was like finding a missing piece of himself. But the reality hadn't matched the fantasy; he'd never imagined the awkwardness that would lie between them, or the guilt. He could taste it whenever Rhona looked at him.

Liam shut his eyes, trying not to remember his visit to her flat and the subsequent journey to the Rosevale. He squirmed at the memory of his reaction to the news of the dead body. She must have thought him a complete idiot. He recalled how her intensity and excitement at the discovery of the remains had unnerved him. Rhona had gone into a different mode then, rendering him as invisible and unimportant to her as he'd always been.

He wondered if that's why he'd gone to her with the story about Jude's disappearance. To try to enter her world. It was true that Ben had urged him to, but only because he'd got drunk and bragged about his relationship to Rhona.

This was going nowhere. Liam dragged himself off the bed and went back through to check on Ben, taking two bottles of beer from the fridge on the way.

'How's it going?'

'Good, bro. Very good.' Ben accepted an opened bottle and took a slug. 'I figured Jude made contact with plenty of people about her project. That's our starter. Then there's the puzzle. People like a puzzle. Sci-fi friend goes to visit an old cinema and disappears. We'll get the weirdo stuff like she was abducted by aliens, but hey, maybe she was.' He grinned at Liam. 'We're going to find her, mate. Dead or alive.' He stopped short, realising what he'd just said. 'Sorry, I didn't mean . . .' Ben rushed on to cover his discomfort. 'Then there's the porn film. I posted that online too. If someone stole it from her room, then that someone doesn't want it out there. I thought it might be good to piss them off.'

'I don't think that was a good idea,' said Liam, suddenly alarmed. 'What if the person who stole it has something to do with Jude's disappearance?'

Ben hadn't thought of that. 'Shit!' He eyed Liam in horror. 'You think Jude met some weirdo through this cinema thing and he's, like, kidnapped her?'

Liam realised that's what he'd been fearing all along.

20

Rhona leaned over her work-bench. The various bondage items and metal piercings had been logged and stored for study tomorrow, and now she immersed the blackened and wizened fingers in Photoflow, a soapy liquid normally used for developing photographs. They would soak overnight and tomorrow morning she would dry them, photograph them to scale, then print them using black powder and low-adhesion white tape. If the victim had had any police contact in the past, his prints would be on the database. If he was a missing person, they might be able to match his DNA with a family member and identify him that way.

Job done, she cleared up and changed, anxious now to get home and take a long hot shower. There was still no sign of Chrissy and her mobile went unanswered. Rhona suspected she was still at the Poker Club, and fought off a desire to go down there herself. If Slater was about she would get short shrift, and it might also alert him to Chrissy's presence. She would have to be patient and wait for Chrissy to contact her, difficult though that might be.

When Rhona opened the front door Tom came bounding towards her, flicking his tail in welcome. He hung around just long enough to be fed, then miaowed to be let out of the kitchen window and disappeared up on to the roof. Rhona had given up worrying about him falling off and tried instead to be pleased that he had so much flat rooftop to roam on.

Before she headed for the shower, she phoned the local pizza place. Gone were the days of coming home to the delicious smell of cooking and the sight of Sean in the kitchen opening a bottle of wine.

Rhona felt a pang of regret before reminding herself how much she preferred her own space. And God knew she had enough guilt and emotional baggage on her plate right now, without the complications of living with Sean. She toyed with the idea of phoning Liam, which she knew would be an awkward call. She should have called before now, and the longer she put it off the more difficult it would be. She brought up his number and pressed the call button before she could change her mind, but it rang for a bit then went to voicemail. His voice on the recorded message sounded young and serious.

'Hi, it's Rhona. Can you give me a call?' She almost added 'about Jude' but stopped short, worrying that he might think it was bad news, or even good news, when it was neither. She thought again of the look on Liam's face when she'd emerged from finding the body. He'd been truly frightened, and immersed as she'd been in the discovery, she hadn't registered just how much. She was used to death in all its horrible forms; not immune to the tragedy of it, but without a thick skin she couldn't survive. Her coping mechanisms, she realised, must have made her look offhand to Liam. She'd followed this by getting rid of him as quickly as possible, just as she would have done with any member of the public at a crime scene. Except Liam wasn't any member of the public. He was her son.

Rhona heard her mobile ring while in the shower and sprinted naked for it, leaving a trail of water in her wake.

It was Petersson. 'Can you come over?'

'I've just got in. I've ordered a pizza.'

'Bring it with you.' He rang off before she could question him further.

Irritated, she almost called back to demand an explanation, but decided it must be something important from the tone of his voice. She dried and dressed quickly, and the pizza arrived as she was putting on her coat.

As she left, cardboard box in hand, she remembered she'd left the kitchen window open. She should close and lock it, but Tom hadn't returned from his nocturnal ramble yet.

When she buzzed Petersson, he let her in immediately. Rhona wondered as she climbed the stairs, how he had managed to get to the intercom so quickly in his present state.

He was waiting for her at the open door. 'I was at the window,' he said, answering her unspoken question. He glanced down at the box. 'That smells very good.'

Rhona followed him through to the kitchen. There was an open bottle of red and a couple of glasses on the table. It seemed her earlier fantasy featuring Sean had come true, although she was the one supplying the food.

The suite of computers in the corner was shining brightly. Petersson resumed his seat there. 'I'll show you first, then we'll eat,' he said, motioning her across to stand behind him. There was a map of central Glasgow on the screen, McNab's hotel at centre stage. To the right was a grid of black and white grainy images, which Rhona presumed came from security cameras.

Petersson selected one and brought it forward. The clock below indicated the image had been taken the night of the shooting at 01.04. It was a picture of two men on the front steps of the hotel.

'McNab did leave with a man,' said Petersson.

'But who?' She peered at the screen. The image was so grainy, she could barely recognise McNab from it.

'That's not Solonik?' asked Petersson.

Rhona recalled the bulk of the man, his huge arms and gigantic fists. She'd met him in person only once, when he'd been preventing her from leaving Kalinin's flat. The fear she'd experienced then was every bit as real now. 'He's of a similar build, but it isn't Solonik,' she confirmed.

'They got in a car. It's too far to see the licence plate clearly, but I'm working on it.' Petersson paused. 'What I don't get is this. If McNab went of his own free will, then why hasn't he been in contact? He promised you he'd come by. He never made contact with me at the Poker Club. What the hell happened between speaking to you and this point?' He brought forward the first image again. 'And who the fuck is he with?'

Rhona couldn't answer any of the questions, but just seeing McNab alive with someone who wasn't Solonik had made her feel better.

Petersson pulled himself up. 'Let's eat. You must be starving.'

He poured them each a large glass of wine and they settled to devouring the pizza. Rhona was glad of the chance to think, because she had questions of her own.

Petersson appeared to anticipate what she planned to ask. As they slowed on the last slice of pizza, he said, 'Bill hasn't seen these yet. And if you don't ask how I came by them, I won't have to lie.' He met her eye as he topped up her glass. 'McNab definitely hasn't got in touch with you?'

'No.'

'You're sure?'

'Of course I'm sure. I would tell you if he had.' Even as she said it, Rhona wondered if that were true. What if McNab asked her not to?

Petersson was studying her closely. They had played this cat and mouse game before. Neither trusting the other. He suddenly smiled in that disarming way of his. 'Let's finish the wine, then have a whisky to celebrate.'

'Celebrate what?'

'The fact that he's still alive.'

'We don't know that for certain.'

'If McNab were dead, Kalinin would have made sure we knew it by now. And there's something else. If McNab was back at the hotel by one o'clock, then it's unlikely he shot Brogan.'

She'd already worked that one out. Bill must have filled Petersson in on the time frame, otherwise how did he know when Brogan was shot? Rhona pushed the refilled wine glass to one side.

'I need to go home and get some sleep.'

Petersson tried to hide his disappointment. 'I'll see you out.'

'No need. I'll pull the door behind me.'

'I like to double lock it.'

He followed her to the door. He was walking more

freely now. Rhona wondered if his discomfort had been exaggerated for her benefit. But why would Petersson pretend to be more injured than he really was?

Once outside, Rhona walked swiftly to the car, and when she got inside she locked the door and switched on the radio for company. It was late, and she was home in minutes. She slipped her key in the lock, her eyes heavy with fatigue.

Her first impression was that the flat was very cold. The central heating, set on a timer, would have switched off by now, but the cold felt sharper than that. Then she remembered the kitchen window.

Rhona called softly for Tom. When no cat appeared she headed for the kitchen. The window sat open, Tom's basket empty. Rhona swore under her breath. She was damned if she was leaving the window open all night. She leaned out and called the cat again. When no answering miaow came she pulled the window closed. The night was getting shorter by the moment and she desperately needed some sleep.

Shivering, she shut the kitchen door and headed for the bedroom where she stripped quickly and slipped under the duvet. Her mind was racing, but Rhona tried to focus on one thought and one thought only. McNab was alive.

But for how much longer?

21

Petersson. It was the only way they could have known he was at the hotel.

Bastard, thought McNab.

Anger quickened his heart, its pounding so rapid it pained his chest. He took a deep breath and tried to slow it down. His eyes blindfolded, feeling a crushing sense of airlessness, he tried to imagine space around him, a room, high ceilinged with a window that opened on to countryside. Acres of open fields and an endless sky.

Christ, he hated the countryside.

He yelped as vomit swelled into his throat, then coughed the hot liquid out into the darkness.

Fucking bastard.

Kalinin must have got to him. But how? Did it matter now? It mattered because the Icelander was still out there, pretending to be something he wasn't. Manipulating Rhona. Maybe even fucking her. The last thought made the anger swell again. A huge wave of it slamming his heart, vibrating it like stones on a beach. Maybe that was how it would end. His heart would beat at twice its normal speed until it finally gave out. For a moment he wanted it to happen. That would piss the Russian off. No more fun. No more games. No more pain.

He wondered what it was like to enjoy inflicting so

much pain. It was like a sexual turn-on for Kalinin, he could tell. When McNab imagined turning the tables, he pictured a room with three seats. One for Kalinin. One for Solonik. And a special one for Petersson.

22

Liam played the message again. Rhona's voice sounded different on the phone. Was it guilt that she hadn't called before now? Or was she just pissed off at having to phone at all?

He'd chosen not to pick up when he saw the caller's name the previous night. He'd struggled a bit, in case it had been news about Jude, then reminded himself that DI Wilson had promised to get in touch if they had any luck tracing her. To put his mind at ease, he decided to call the Detective Inspector and check.

'DI Wilson?' Liam said.

'Yes.' A pause. 'Who is this?'

'Liam Hope.'

There was a sound like a door banging and someone said, 'Sir?' in a questioning voice. Liam heard a muffled answer before DI Wilson came back on.

'I'm glad you called, Liam. I was going to suggest we talk.'

'You've found something?' he asked eagerly.

'Maybe. Can you come down to the station?'

'Sure.'

'In about an hour? Just ask for me at the desk.'

Liam's hand was trembling as he slipped the mobile in

his pocket. They'd found something. That's what he'd said. They'd found something.

Slater had commandeered an office all to himself and his sidekick, Flash Harry. That's what the team were calling the smart-suited SOCA detective, who was absent for the moment. As for Slater, he was non-affectionately known as The Louse. Bill felt sorry for Slater's namesake, the poor wee woodlouse, who had definitely got the rough end of the deal.

Slater was regarding him now with some impatience. The more irritated Slater looked, the more patient Bill became.

'Remind me again why Dr MacLeod went to the hotel,' Slater said.

'McNab was staying there.'

'You knew this?'

'No.'

'Then how did she?'

'You'll have to ask her.'

Slater pursed his lips. 'If Dr MacLeod was withholding information as to DS McNab's whereabouts while aware that SOCA sought him . . .'

'DS McNab was not obliged to stay with SOCA. He is not a fugitive; not from them, anyway.' He threw Slater a hostile look. 'You did run a check on the night porter's mobile before you let him go?'

'Why would we do that?'

'He made a call as Dr MacLeod left the hotel. He also threatened her while she was there.'

'He thought she was a hooker.'

'And that makes a threat of sexual assault OK?'

Slater decided to let that one drop. He never fought a battle he didn't expect to win. 'CCTV picked up McNab leaving the building with another man around one a.m.'

That was the first Bill had heard of it. 'Who?'

'No idea.'

'I'd like to see that footage.'

'You will, in due course.'

'After McNab's dead?' Bill said, sharply.

'He left of his own free will.'

'How the hell do you know that?'

'It was obvious.'

'I'll tell you what's bloody *obvious*. First, Fergus Morrison is shot while in SOCA's care. McNab gets out of the safe house by the skin of his teeth. McNab knows Brogan was in the car. So guess what, Brogan's next on the shooter's list. And finally, they pick up McNab.'

Slater studied him for a moment. 'We have no evidence to suggest Kalinin has McNab.'

'And you couldn't care less.'

'Just what are you insinuating?'

'That the mess you made when you released Kalinin that night is about to be cleared up.'

Bill knew he had overstepped the mark.

Slater's face flushed a deep, ugly red but he came back fighting. 'You might be interested to know that I expect a result on the gun used in Brogan's murder shortly.'

'And I'm sure you *expect* it to conveniently turn out to be the one taken from the safe house.'

'Perhaps your view of McNab is a little clouded. I was his partner once, remember?'

'And I am his commanding officer. As such I expect to be kept fully informed about this enquiry.'

'Didn't I just do that?'

Bill took a deep breath. So that was what this was all about. Slater had been ordered to keep Bill informed and had just fulfilled his obligation as minimally as possible.

Bill could depart now or fire another shot. He decided on the latter. After talking to Rhona, he'd done a little investigating of his own. He might not be in charge of the case, but that didn't mean he was completely off it.

'I meant to tell you something about the list of customers at the Poker Club,' he said nonchalantly. 'It isn't complete.'

Slater had looked down in attempted dismissal, but at this his head snapped up again. Now that he had Slater's attention, Bill continued.

'There was a private party that night, all of whom seem to be missing from the list. Lord James Dalrymple, Edward Stewart, the esteemed advocate, and his wife Fiona . . .'

Slater's face was a picture, and it told a story. Slater had known about Dalrymple's presence there, but hadn't realised anyone else did.

'Dr MacLeod knows the Stewarts. Edward chatted to her in the bar and told her that's why they were there. He seemed pretty pleased about it.'

Slater was rallying. 'We are aware of that. Lord Dalrymple and his guests left early.'

'They were in the building at the same time as Dr MacLeod and DS McNab. I take it you'll be questioning them too?'

Then something happened that Bill didn't expect. Slater seemed to muster himself. The anger faded from his face. When he spoke, his voice was low and measured, almost persuasive.

'I know we don't see eye to eye, but I'm going to have to ask you to trust me on this.' He was watching Bill intently. 'I want McNab brought in alive, just like you do. I need him to testify. I've spent the last two years trying to nail Kalinin. I intend to do just that.'

Bill felt utterly perplexed when he left Slater's office. A sneering, two-faced Slater he could handle. A Slater who asked to be trusted, in a voice verging on actual sincerity, was another matter. It had been his mention of Dalrymple that had changed the tone of the exchange.

He could of course ask Superintendent Sutherland if he was aware that Dalrymple was there that night. Bill wasn't up for that, not yet anyway. There might come a time when he really needed to rock the boat.

And what if it hadn't been Sutherland? If he hadn't been instrumental in omitting Dalrymple's name, maybe Slater had – but why? The boss had his golf outings to think about, but Bill couldn't recall if Slater's name had ever been officially linked to Dalrymple's. A DC at the time of the rent-boy murders, he hadn't been directly involved in the investigation.

Despite the fact that, on parting, Slater had reiterated his plea for Bill to trust him and promised to keep him informed, Bill opted for one of his alternative sources of information.

Chrissy answered on the third ring.

'Hey, you took your time. You and Rhona both.'

'She hasn't been in touch?'

'She called. I couldn't answer. I called her back, she was engaged.'

'Can we meet?'

'Good idea.'

'Where?'

'The Jazz Club. Sam's playing tonight and Mum's babysitting. You can buy me a drink. As an undercover agent I deserve one.'

'Will you let Rhona know, or will I?'

'She's been avoiding the Jazz Club. Sean, remember?'

'I'll speak to her. Shall we meet there at eight? And listen, I've got Petersson working on this – unofficially. Would you object if I asked him along?'

Chrissy agreed immediately. 'It'll make a change to know what Rhona and him are up to,' she finished, dryly.

When reception called, Bill went straight down. Liam was waiting for him, looking guilty as hell. Being summoned to a police station tended to do that to people. Bill considered taking him to an interview room, but opted for a nearby coffee shop instead.

The café they chose was more upmarket than the Central. The majority of customers were 'to go', so they had no difficulty finding a seat. They carried their coffees to an empty table at the window.

Liam's eagerness was obvious. They were barely seated when he asked, 'You said on the phone that you'd found something?'

Bill stirred the froth into his coffee before answering.

'I spoke to Student Support. They confirmed that Jude had been diagnosed as having Asperger's.'

'Oh.' Liam looked disappointed. He was expecting more.

'They also confirmed she'd been brought up in care, but that a man professing to be an uncle had contacted them wanting to get in touch with her. Did Jude ever mention an uncle?'

Liam looked puzzled. 'No, she didn't.'

'Also, Charlie says someone phoned the halls of residence looking for Jude before she disappeared. The caller said he was helping her with her project.'

'She never mentioned that either, although it could've been the guy she interviewed and recorded.'

Liam looked apprehensive, and Bill asked, 'Is there something you're not telling me?'

Liam shook his head vigorously, then caught Bill's eye and seemed to think the better of it. 'Me and Ben, my flatmate. We went looking in the old Olympia Bridgeton.'

So that was the secret. Liam had been doing some sleuthing of his own.

'When?'

'Yesterday. The whole place is a mess, except the projection room. Someone had cleaned up in there. There was an empty metal cabinet. It looked like a place you would store film reels.' Liam rushed on, his anxiety gaining momentum. 'Jude found that film in there, then she visited the Rosevale and found the body.'

'What are you suggesting?'

'I don't know.' Liam was struggling to put his thoughts into words. 'Maybe someone saw her take the film. Maybe someone saw her in the room where the body was hidden.'

'We don't know for certain that Jude did discover the body. And as for the film, none of what's on that is illegal nowadays.'

'But we only saw the start, the few frames that Jude had photographed. What if someone was killed in that film, like the body in the Rosevale? That would be a reason to get it back, wouldn't it?'

23

A person's fingerprints were unique, and once the ridges and patterns were formed in the womb they stayed that way for life.

Not even identical twins had the same patterns. If superficial damage occurred the skin grew back in exactly the same way as it was at birth. Plus, fingerprints were one of the last features to decompose after death. So even a mummified body could render up the pattern for study, if treated properly.

As this mummy had done.

Rhona was pleased with the results. Now the fingers would have to be returned to the corpse and re-attached. Not her job, she was glad to say.

Fingerprint impressions from all those convicted of a criminal offence in Scotland were held in the National Fingerprint Collection. In excess of 350,000 records. If Spike, as she was calling the corpse, was in there, they could give him back his real name.

She updated R2S's software with her results. The details of the crime scene were already in there. Maps of the locality, architectural plans of the building, videos they'd taken through the wall before they'd dismantled it.

Roy had also created a body map, a blank-faced computer-generated version of the body, accurate in all dimensions.

Alongside, Roy had displayed photographs he'd taken of the various items found on the body: the harness and jewellery, the nails from the hands, the cuff.

Rhona selected each hand on the body map and attached an electronic copy of the fingerprints, before scanning the results of the post mortem again. After her departure, Dr Sissons had added more details about the condition of the body. On careful removal of the testicle cuff, the dried remains of the scrotum showed evidence of tearing or cutting. It was the only obvious wound apart from the nail holes in the hands.

The pathologist had estimated the victim's age as early twenties, based on the fusing of the bones and evidence of wisdom teeth. As to how long he had been imprisoned there, that was up for conjecture. Ageing mummified remains would require the expertise of a forensic anthropologist, unless they could identify the victim and try to pinpoint when he had disappeared.

Rhona spent the rest of the morning working on the samples she'd collected at the scene. Bill's call came in around midday. She'd taken a break with coffee and a sandwich and was missing Chrissy's usual lunchtime chatter. The phone calls between them had continued to cross, so Rhona was delighted to hear that they were all meeting up – until she heard where.

'I'm not sure about the Jazz Club.'

'I thought you and Sean parted on good terms?'

Rhona decided to be honest. It was Bill, after all. 'Sean has a new girlfriend. According to Chrissy she hangs about the club a lot.'

'So?'

Bill was right. Why should she care? 'OK, what time?'

'Eight. I intend asking Petersson along.' It was a statement, not a question.

'Have you spoken to him this morning?'

'No. Should I have?'

'He has CCTV images of McNab leaving the hotel with someone who isn't Solonik. He said you hadn't seen them yet.'

'Slater only informed me of their existence this morning, and I didn't know we'd ruled out Solonik. How did Petersson get a hold of them?'

'He said not to ask.'

Bill went silent for a moment. 'How did you do with the fingers?'

'Good. A ten-print form. I sent it to AFR and entered it on the software.'

'Excellent. Listen, I had coffee with Liam this morning.'

'Oh?'

'He and a mate visited the Olympia Bridgeton. He said the projection room has been used recently. He's also convinced the missing film and the body are in some way connected to Jude's disappearance.'

'It's a possibility,' she said.

'He also mentioned something I should have thought of.'

'What?'

'We've only seen the first few frames of the film. What if it recorded something worse than bondage and that's why someone wanted it back?'

'Whatever's on it happened a long time ago. Black and white film started to go out in the sixties, even among amateur film-makers,' she reminded him.

'If someone was killed in that film, it doesn't matter when it happened,' Bill replied. 'I think we should take a look at the Olympia.'

'OK. What about the other cinemas she visited?'

'I'll get a team to check them over, but it'll take a while.'

When Bill rang off, Rhona tried Liam's number again. The phone rang several times before finally switching to voicemail. Rhona imagined Liam seeing her name on the screen and choosing not to answer. It looked as though he was willing to talk to a policeman, but not to her.

The idea took root and soon became the only explanation for the unanswered call. She considered how much effort it had taken Liam to come round that night to ask for her help, only to find Petersson looking as though he had his feet under her table. She recalled Liam's enquiry after Sean, and his disappointment and embarrassment when she'd revealed that they were no longer together. Rhona could well imagine the conclusion he'd come to – that he had a mother who was incapable of sustaining any relationship, with a lover or a son.

The thought depressed her.

She discarded the remains of her coffee and went back into the lab. Skirting the evidence from the Rosevale, she made instead for McNab's coffin.

A team had winched it out of the grave and delivered it to the lab. She'd managed to retrieve a couple of prints from the surface and had a good idea of the shape of tool used to prise open the lid. Her work round the grave area had also produced the clear sole pattern of a trainer, which unfortunately was not on the shoe database. She was still waiting to find out from AFR if they'd found a fingerprint match.

Chrissy had made a big scene when the coffin arrived, raving on about how long it had taken her to choose and how much it had cost. Eventually Rhona had said, 'Would you rather McNab was still in there?'

Chrissy had shut up then, temporarily, at least.

Rhona ran a hand along the still glossy surface, wondering why people bought such solid expensive wooden coffins. Did they think that sealed in one of these, the body of their loved one would remain intact for ever? That no insects, or bacteria, or worms could get to it?

For her, the coffin brought other memories, of waking from sleep only to find herself buried alive. When she'd begun to believe McNab might not be dead, her recurring nightmare had been of him desperately trying to tear his way out of this coffin.

Just like the Rosevale victim.

The broken fingernails had been packed with brick and cement fragments, evidence that the victim had tried to claw his way out from behind the wall. Rhona had dreamed the horror; the man behind the wall had lived it.

There was no easy way to die. When asked, people often said they wanted to die peacefully in their sleep. That didn't work for Rhona either. It made her think of either being too fearful ever to go to sleep or waking up to find someone you love lying dead beside you.

She knew her dance with death was her way of avoiding thinking about McNab. She didn't want to run the various scenarios over in her head any more. Her brain was like some old cine film flickering its way through imagined horror, the soundtrack even worse than the pictures.

24

'What did the cop want?'

Ben had really got into this. Fancied himself as some sort of Sherlock Holmes. Which put Liam in the role of the nice but not-so-bright Watson.

'I told him about the Olympia.' At Ben's panicked look, Liam added, 'Not how we got inside.'

'Phew.'

'Your prints aren't on a database somewhere, are they?' Liam asked, half joking.

'Maybe.'

'What?'

'A juvenile indiscretion. Nothing more.'

'Shit, Ben.'

'No worries. Well, what did the cop say?'

'He's going to take a look at the Olympia. In fact they're going to check all the old cinemas.'

Ben nodded. 'That's good. So we don't have to.'

'You want out of the Govanhill trip?'

'I didn't say that. But what if the cops turn up?'

'There are forty-four cinemas on Jude's list.'

'I take it you didn't mention the Facebook stuff?'

'There wasn't anything to mention.'

'But there is now,' Ben reminded him.

Ben had set up a 'Find Jude' page as promised. It had

attracted a few responses, most of them for entirely the wrong Jude. Even Ben had been deflated. Then a contact that sounded promising. Someone claimed to have seen a girl who looked like Jude with a man, photographing the exterior of the old Govanhill Picture House in Bankhall Street.

They'd gone online and checked out the cinema. Liam recognised the crumbling white Egyptian-style façade as one of the images on the memory stick.

'Maybe we should head there now? Before the police pick up on it,' Ben suggested.

Liam nodded his agreement. Doing something felt better than hanging around waiting for a call, from Jude or from the police.

Govanhill wasn't on the underground line, and without a car it wasn't that easy to get to. From an online map they located the nearest railway station as Crosshill and settled on heading into town and catching a train there from Central Station.

The carriage was half empty. They sat near an Asian woman with four young girls, aged from a baby on her knee up to a serious-looking girl of about thirteen. The only one not wearing a headscarf was the baby. The woman and her brood alighted with them at Crosshill, along with two Eastern European men who were speaking in a language Liam thought might be Polish, and a black couple who were smartly dressed and carried bibles.

This was a part of Glasgow neither Liam nor Ben was familiar with. During the day it all looked fine, but after dark Govanhill's reputation wasn't so good. Immigrant gangs, particularly Eastern European and Romas, were said to run various rackets from there, including prostitution, drug dealing and human trafficking. Liam's knowledge of this had come from news reports focusing mainly on two recent high-profile cases, the rape of a middle-aged woman and the murder of another, whose body had been discovered in Queen's Park.

Liam imagined Jude coming here to meet someone she didn't know. It wouldn't have bothered her. When she'd set her mind on something, Jude didn't let fear stand in her way.

'OK. Which way?' Ben had come to a halt where two roads crossed.

Liam had no idea. 'Right?' he ventured.

It wasn't hard to find. The Olympia, though built in red sandstone like the surrounding tenements, had stood out because of its grandeur; the Govanhill Picture House stood out because it was completely weird.

Ben whistled his admiration. They'd viewed the images online, but the photos hadn't prepared them for the reality of the building. 'It looks like the fucking Taj Mahal.'

'It's Egyptian not Indian. Look.' Liam pointed above the entrance. 'That's a scarab.'

Ben whistled again. 'Egyptian, eh? Hope we don't find any more mummies.'

'That's not funny,' Liam said sharply.

'No, sorry, bro.'

'How do we get in?'

'Let's do a recce.'

This cinema wasn't a tall building, nowhere near the height of the Rosevale or the Olympia, but the frontage was the most architecturally complex they'd seen. The white and grey marble-tiled entrance was pillared, the moulded scarab set between two domed copper-topped towers. The open-work balcony running the length of the building was lined with windows, all of them heavily barred.

Ben had a quick look at the main doorway. It had a blue-painted metal shutter which looked pretty secure, a peeling gang slogan suggesting how long it had been there. The portico entrance jutted outward. In the right angle between it and the main building was a small barred window and a door, also shuttered.

'No chance,' Ben pronounced.

They walked on, turning nonchalantly into the side street. Here was a two-storey wall, peppered with small barred windows. There were also two exit doors, both heavily shuttered.

'Take out your mobile. Pretend to be photographing the place,' Ben said. 'If someone asks, we'll say we're cinema buffs.'

Liam did as he was told.

Ben swore under his breath as he checked both doors. This place wasn't going to be as easy as the Olympia to get into. They'd reached the end of the building. An eight-foot wire gate, firmly padlocked and partially screened by a clump of low trees, blocked the way into a derelict concreted yard.

Ben glanced at the row of tenements that faced this side of the building. There was at least one inhabitant watching them with interest from a second-floor window. A middle-aged man, balding, with a paunch.

'Maybe that's the guy who contacted you on Facebook?' Liam suggested.

'I can't tell, he had no photo. Maybe we should find out,' Ben said, giving the guy a wave.

Liam wasn't impressed. 'What if he thinks you're taking the mickey?'

'Then in good Glasgow style he'll come looking for a fight and we'll run.'

The man had deserted his post at the window. Minutes later, the entrance door opened and he emerged. At close quarters, he wasn't at all scary. Shorter than both of them, his weight might be put to good use in a fight, but only if they stayed around for one.

'You two looking for that lassie? The one on Facebook?'

'Yes. Did you see her?' Liam said.

'Like I said. She came here about a week ago with a man. She took pictures with a fancy camera, not a mobile like you.'

'What day was that?'

He shrugged. 'I don't remember exactly.'

'She disappeared last Tuesday.'

He thought about it. 'It was before that, I think.'

'What did the man look like?'

'About my height. An old guy, grey hair where there was any. Wore glasses.'

A description that could fit half of the male population of Glasgow.

'Did they go inside?' Ben said.

'I don't know. I went to answer the phone, when I came back to the window, they weren't there.' He eyed them with interest. 'Are you planning going in?'

Liam looked at Ben, not sure how to answer.

'We'd like to,' said Ben.

'If you can get over the fence, there's a door at the back that's not shuttered.' He watched as they considered his proposition. 'I haven't told the polis I saw her. If you check she's not in there, I don't have to.' His expression suggested he had no desire to make himself known to the police.

'OK,' Ben said. 'Let's take a look.'

Liam wasn't so sure. 'It's still daylight. What if someone sees?'

'That won't be a problem,' the man told them. 'Folks round here mind their own business. You just go ahead.'

Ben was the first to try. He took a running jump at the gate and caught a good hold on the top. Then he was up and over with ease.

Liam hesitated, not anxious to make a fool of himself in front of the paunchy guy or Ben. Once Ben was out of sight, Liam made his move. It wasn't as graceful a leap as Ben's but he managed to catch a grip, and though winded he scrambled his way over, landing with a thump on the other side, his knees creaking in protest.

He shouldn't have worried what it looked like. Ben wasn't interested in his ungainly arrival, so intent was he on picking the lock. It was taking longer than the Olympia, but close on the back wall and shielded by the trees, they were less exposed than they'd been there.

Eventually Ben made a pleased noise that suggested success.

'Let's go,' he said, easing the door open.

Liam followed him inside. The choking smell of damp had been bad in the Olympia, but it was much worse in here. The plaster walls were slick and green with mould.

Ben led the way along a doorless corridor, the barred windows filtering enough light to see by.

A door at the end opened into what must have been the auditorium. Stripped of fitments and seating, the large space had obviously ended its life as a warehouse of sorts. The stage was still there, although possessing none of its former glory. At the rear, the balcony sloped down to meet the stalls, separated by a wooden partition. The place was in an even sorrier state than the Olympia.

Liam pointed at the portholes above the balcony.

'The projection room.'

They made their way across the floor, skirting the rubbish and broken boxes. Ben stopped suddenly and held up his hand.

'Did you hear something?'

'What?' Liam asked, heart pounding.

The three pigeons seemed to appear from nowhere. Liam ducked to avoid the flapping wings as they came in to land. Ben, startled, reacted by flinging his hands in the air and shouting, 'Fuck off!'

The pigeons did as directed, disappearing up into the roof space.

'Holy shit!' Ben looked at Liam and they broke into semi-hysterical laughter. 'Must be a way out up there, otherwise those pigeons would be dead meat by now.'

It was an uncomfortable choice of words, but Liam didn't bother remonstrating. 'Come on.' He headed for a set of double doors to the right of the balcony.

Back at the rear of the building again, they realised they'd travelled in a full circle. It took the torch to finally locate the door with the telltale 'No Smoking' sign.

Liam came to a halt outside it, a terrible sense of dread assailing him, although he had no idea why. There was nothing to suggest that Jude had got in here. Without a key or Ben's breaking and entering skills, it didn't look possible.

'OK, mate?' Ben said impatiently.

'Sure.'

Liam said a silent prayer and opened the door to the projection room.

25

Bill's conversation with Liam had unnerved him.

It had crossed Bill's mind that Jude's disappearance might be linked with the older crime, but it was often too easy to jump to dramatic conclusions. In all likelihood, there was a more mundane explanation.

She'd had a fight with Liam and stayed away to punish him.

She'd met her uncle and was spending time with him.

A fellow resident at the Hall, knowing her room was empty, had taken her laptop.

There were other, less comfortable explanations, but still nothing to do with the walled-in corpse.

She was hiding from someone she feared. Perhaps the caller, or the supposed uncle.

She had been abducted by that person.

She had been killed by that person.

As soon as she'd been officially reported missing, they'd done the usual media calls, alerting the public to their concerns about Jude's welfare. Response had been minimal. One unlucky Detective Constable was currently trawling her way through CCTV footage from Dumbarton Road. Nothing so far, although the quality was poor, and they had no idea what Jude had been

wearing, so it was doubtful she would be able to recognise the girl anyway.

Now Bill was on his way to the charity shop with the
intention of talking to the backroom staff, the men who
dealt with the shop's furniture donations. Carol Miller
had sent him through a staff list; the five workers all
lived within walking distance of the shop. One was a
teenager, three in their early fifties and one an older
man.

The tinkling bell that sounded on his entry brought Carol
Miller from the office. She looked as worried as she had
the last time he'd seen her – selling furniture for a charity
hardly equipped you to deal with turning up at work to
find a dead body hidden behind a wall.

'You're here to talk to the boys?'

'If I may, yes.'

'They're on a tea break. I'll take you through.'

They skirted a polished dining table, six chairs and an
upended black leather settee, all waiting to be placed on
display. Behind was a red door marked *Staff Only*. When
Carol pushed it open the sound of friendly banter drifted
out, only to be silenced when the men saw who was with
their boss.

'This is Detective Inspector Wilson. I told you he was
coming in to talk to you.'

All immediately fastened their eyes on Bill, except for
the teenager who studied his can of Irn Bru instead. The
older man, Angus Robertson, was easy to spot, although
he looked pretty fit for 69. The teenager Bill remembered

as being called Jason Donald. The other three, all in their fifties, he couldn't put individual names to.

'I'd like to see you one at a time.' He looked to Carol. 'If I could use your office?'

'Of course,' Carol said, flustered. 'It's through here.'

Bill decided to start with the oldest, because he looked the least concerned.

'Angus?' he offered. 'You want to make a start?'

'No, problem, son. Lead the way.'

Carol's office was cupboard sized with a small desk, a half-height filing cabinet and only one chair. Carol apologised and said she would get one of the men to bring in another seat. When she disappeared, Angus said, 'The lassie feels terrible about this. Like it's her fault some bampot got himself killed here.'

Bill said nothing. It was almost impossible to keep crime-scene details a secret. Police personnel talked to one another, and this scene had given them plenty to discuss.

'I used to come here as a kid,' Angus continued. 'Cowboy films on a Saturday morning.'

'I used to go to The Seamore.'

'A Maryhill boy, eh? Not any more, I'll bet?'

The chair arrived then, so Bill didn't have to answer the barbed question.

'Who's got a key for this place?' Bill asked as soon as Angus was settled.

'Carol and me.'

'That's it?'

Angus nodded.

'How long have you worked here?'

'Since I was made redundant from the yard. Nine years this Christmas.'

'You knew the previous manager?'

Angus snorted. 'Admiral Nelson? I knew him all right. Used to filch the best stuff for himself.'

'I take it he had a key?'

'And used it when no one was around. We had this painting handed in, from some old dead wifie up Crow Road. I collected it. Sailing ships. Very nice. Even I could see that. The Admiral spotted it. Next day it was gone. When I asked he said the canvas got torn and he'd had to dump it. Like hell he had. My bet is he sold it on, or it's hanging on his wall.'

'You know where he lives?'

'Sure I do, if he's still there. Unless he's away on his yacht.'

'He has a yacht?'

'So he said. Used to go off weekends up the west coast.'

'What's his address?'

'Observatory Road.'

'Number?'

Angus shook his head. 'No idea.'

'Is Nelson his real name?'

'It's what he called himself. How long's the body been in there, then?' Angus asked.

'We don't know, yet.'

'Ten years?'

'Why d'you say that?'

'I've been here nine.'

'And you think you would have known if there was anything going on in the old cinema?'

'Not much gets past me.'

Bill had a feeling that was true. 'What about the girl who visited? Did you see her?'

'I saw her go in with Carol. I didn't see her come out.'

'You'd left by then?'

'I leave five on the dot.' He sat back in the chair and folded his arms. 'But I did see her later that night.'

'Why didn't you say anything before?'

Angus shrugged, seemingly unconcerned by Bill's re-action. 'I never saw the lassie's face when she went in with Carol. Just the big backpack she was wearing. Then her picture was on the telly last night and I realised who it was. Carol said you were coming down today, so I waited and told you.'

It was a reasonable enough explanation.

'Where and when did you see her?'

'Like I said. The same night. About seven. I was having a pint on the corner. I went outside for a fag and I saw them. She was with a young guy. Tall with fair hair. They were arguing. I don't know what about.'

'What happened?'

'I went back inside.'

'That's it?'

'Aye. That's it.'

'Would you recognise the man again?'

'Maybe.'

'What was he wearing?'

Angus thought for a minute. 'Jeans, a green jacket. With a hood, but he didn't have it up even though it was raining. It's a bugger having to stand in the rain to have a smoke. I made it quick.'

It was a minimal description, but Bill couldn't dismiss the fact that it could match Liam. Maybe he *had* seen Jude that night. Maybe they'd had a fight and she'd stormed off. Maybe he was scared to tell Bill that. A lot of maybes.

'OK, Angus. Thanks for that.'

Angus rose to his feet. 'Happy to help. If you need me to look at photos?'

Bill nodded. 'I'll be in touch. Could you send in the lad?'

Angus hesitated. 'Go easy on Jason. He's been in trouble in the past, but he's clean now and works hard.'

Jason appeared moments later, still clasping the can of Irn Bru. He stood, avoiding Bill's eye and awaiting instructions. Bill motioned him to sit down. For a moment he looked as though he would bolt, then he perched himself on the edge of the seat.

'How long have you been working here, Jason?'

'Six months.'

'Angus says you're a grafter.'

His head rose a little. 'I like it here.'

Bill saw the boy's face clearly for the first time. One of his eyes was bruised. Fairly recent, judging by the colour.

'What happened to your face?'

Jason's hand lifted, then dropped back to finger the can. 'I was shifting a wardrobe and ma hand slipped.'

'I bet working here keeps you fit.'

He nodded. 'I like it. It's a laugh wi the lads.'

'They're good to you?'

'They joke about, but aye they are.' Jason eased himself into the seat, relaxing a little.

'You're full time?'

'Nine to five, five days a week,' he said proudly.

'So you were here when Jude came to photograph the old cinema?'

'I never seen her,' he said, quickly. 'I was in the back.'

'But she went through there to get to the door.'

'I never seen her.'

'When you left work that night, did you go straight home?'

'I went for a drink.'

'Where?'

'I'm eighteen,' he said defiantly.

'Where?'

'The pub on the corner.'

'With Angus?'

Jason nodded.

'You a smoker?'

'Naw.'

'So you didn't go outside for a smoke with Angus?'

'Naw.'

The fingers that clasped the can of Irn Bru didn't look nicotine stained, but it would be easy enough to find out if Jason was a smoker.

'So, you didn't see Jude in or outside the building that night?'

'That's right.'

Lies weren't as easy to pull off as most folk believed. The real liars tended to give you more than you needed, tell you details, thinking that made their story more plausible. In fact most people didn't register a high level of detail when asked to recall an incident they'd witnessed. That was the problem.

Jason's head was back down, his fingers worrying at the can. His left hand jerked and a spray of orange liquid marked his jeans. He swore under his breath and drank what was left.

There was nothing more to ask, but Jason didn't stand up or make any sign that he was anxious to be off. The lad had something else to say. Maybe nothing important, but something all the same. Eventually it came out.

'I seen the lassie's photo on Facebook. Somebody's running a page trying to find her.'

This was news to Bill.

'Who?'

'They call themselves Sherlock and Watson. They're getting replies. Someone said he seen her with a guy outside the Govanhill Picture House.'

'Did they say when?'

'Naw.'

'And the other replies?'

'Newcastle and London.'

The incident room had received news of sightings after the media announcement. Newcastle and London had both figured in them.

'Thanks, Jason. I appreciate you telling me about the Facebook campaign.'

Bill let him go then and took in the other men one at a time. Jimmy Dixon, Robert Hennessey and Graeme MacLaren all told the same story. They'd been out together on a pick-up when Jude arrived. They'd collected the furniture, parked the van in the side street overnight, went home and unloaded it the next morning. Carol confirmed their story. She also confirmed that the former manager's name was Albert Nelson and that she had no idea if he'd handed in his key when he'd left.

So Bill now had two possible leads. One placing Jude alive outside the cinema on the night she'd disappeared. Another involving Facebook. Bill wondered, as he headed for Mr Nelson's flat, if the Tech guys had come across this Facebook page. And if so, why the hell he hadn't been told about it.

Before he'd driven off he'd contacted Janice and got her to look for an Albert Nelson in Observatory Road. His luck was in. The Admiral was still registered as living in the street. Bill scribbled down the address, thanked her and rang off.

Observatory Road was dominated by a magnificent church at its eastern end, and consisted of a row of handsome blond two-storey terraced houses overlooking a well-kept central garden.

Bill found the right house and gave the buzzer a try. When there was no answer, he waited a bit then tried again. These were big flats. It could take a while to get to the intercom, he reasoned. He was eventually rewarded by the sound of a gruff but modulated voice. 'Who is it?'

Bill explained who he was and that he'd like to come up. There was a moment of silence before the voice said, 'You have ID?'

He confirmed that he had and the front door sprung its lock. On reaching the first level he stood outside the door, took out his warrant card and held it up to the spy-hole. A few moments later the door was opened, but only as far as the thick door chain would allow. Bill held the card in full view of the elderly face peeking round the door. At last Mr Nelson seemed satisfied. 'Can't be too careful,' he said as he unfastened the chain.

'I agree,' Bill said.

Now the door was open, Bill could see the man Angus had so scornfully called The Admiral. He was smartly dressed in a shirt, tie, fine-knit lemon sweater and smart trousers. He was straight backed and balding with glasses and a sour expression. Bill got the impression just from looking at him that Admiral Nelson had a grievance or two and liked voicing them. Bill had a certain sympathy for that.

'May I come in?'

'What's it about?'

'The British Heart Foundation shop in Dumbarton Road.'

'I haven't worked in that shop for nearly seven years.'

'I know, but I'd still like to talk to you.'

Eventually Mr Nelson opened the door wide and motioned Bill inside to a smell of polish and the distant drone of a Hoover.

'My cleaning woman is here,' Mr Nelson said as he led the way into a sitting room where the scent of lavender was overwhelming. 'She's a bit heavy on the polish,' he apologised. 'I open the window once she's gone.' It was a kind remark, swiftly tempered by, 'Cleaners who don't steal from you are hard to find.' He closed the door firmly behind them and urged Bill to a seat before settling himself. 'Now, what's this all about?'

Bill spotted the painting as he sat down. Two sailing frigates on a choppy sea, framed in gold. It was very nice, as Angus had said. Probably a collector's item. Mr Nelson caught his interested gaze.

'It's lovely, isn't it? Found it rummaging one day in a junk shop. A British Frigate and a Spanish frigate in combat, by Thomas Butterworth,' he added, proudly.

Bill had no idea who Thomas Butterworth was but he guessed he was worth collecting.

'I expect you discovered the odd treasure among the charity donations to the shop?' he said.

Nelson gave him a swift, penetrating glance. 'I don't steal from charity, Inspector. I bought that painting fair and square.'

'The seller knew its worth, then?'

'I paid what they asked.' Mr Nelson's mouth set in a thin line. 'I discovered later that it was a Butterworth.' He paused. 'But you're not here to quiz me on my painting.'

Bill began to wonder if Nelson knew about the grim discovery in his previous place of employment.

'I assume you've heard on the news about the discovery of a body in the old Rosevale cinema?'

'What? No. I've been away on the west coast, sailing. A body in the old cinema? Dear God!' His distress seemed genuine. 'Who? A vagrant dossing down there?'

'We haven't identified the victim yet, but it was a young man. He had been walled up in the projection room.'

'Walled up?' He looked suitably horrified by the revelation. 'How do you mean?'

'The body was discovered behind a bricked-in alcove.'

Mr Nelson's eyes seemed to glaze over as he tried to assimilate this information.

'Were you ever in the old cinema?' Bill asked.

'Only glanced in the door at the Highland Frieze.'

'So you had a key to the place?'

'Of course. As manager I had a full set of keys for the building.'

'Did you hand them back when you left?'

Nelson looked insulted by the question. 'Naturally.' His

expression moved to suspicion. 'Who says I didn't? I bet it was Angus Robertson. That old bugger was a thorn in my flesh. Thought he was the one running the place. Calling me Admiral Nelson behind my back.'

'You're certain you gave back the key?'

'I did, no matter what Robertson said.' Despite his best efforts, his glance strayed momentarily to the painting. He pulled himself together. 'How long had the poor chap been there?'

'We haven't confirmed the date of death yet.'

'So it wasn't recently?' he said, astutely.

Bill ignored the question and continued. 'Did anyone ever ask to see the old cinema while you were manager?'

'Of course. They're like train spotters, these old cinema buffs. Want to take photos "for posterity". As if anyone in their right mind wants to view some broken balcony chairs and a disused projection box.'

'Or a handsome wall frieze?' Bill had a sudden image of Nelson sizing up the frieze, wondering if there was any way he could remove it and sell it on.

Nelson gave him a dirty look.

Bill ignored it and continued. 'So you let them in?'

'I did, although I warned them it was at their own risk.'

'And you didn't go with them?'

'Of course not. I had to supervise the shop floor and the back room.'

To watch out for bargains, no doubt.

'Can you recall any of the people who visited?'

'I left seven years ago, for goodness sake. And they all look the same. Anoraks and cameras.' He paused. 'I do remember the twins, however. Who wouldn't?'

'The twins?'

'Former projectionists at the Rosevale. Like two peas in a pod. Even spoke the same way. *They* didn't wear anoraks. They wore proper overcoats, old-fashioned but smart. I remember they reminded me of a second world war movie.'

'Their name?'

'Mulligan. Jim and John, I think.'

'When did they visit?'

'Shortly before I left.'

'The body was bricked up. Have you any idea how the bricks got in there?'

He thought for a moment. 'Maybe when they put the new central heating in the shop?'

'And when was that?'

'The first year I was there. What a mess. Dust everywhere.'

Bill hesitated before posing the next question. The state of the body was already being hinted at in the press. It wouldn't be a secret much longer and he was interested to see Mr Nelson's reaction.

'The body was naked apart from various bondage gear. It may be the old cinema was being used as a meeting place for S and M enthusiasts.'

'Good God.'

'For that to happen, those involved must have had access to a key.'

'As I have said already, I do not have one.' Mr Nelson checked his watch, then rose. 'Now if you'll excuse me, Detective Inspector, I did promise a friend a round of golf.'

Bill handed him his card. 'Thank you for your co-operation, Mr Nelson. If you think of anything, please get in touch.'

'Naturally, although I believe I've told you everything I know.'

As Bill headed downstairs, he heard the door open again and Mr Nelson and a woman exchange goodbyes. The honest but over-zealous cleaner was muttering under her breath as the door was firmly shut behind her, and Bill thought he detected a curse in there somewhere.

Mrs MacDougall, he discovered after introducing himself at the foot of the stairs, didn't like her employer much. She examined the warrant card and observed Bill with interest.

'What's his nibs been up to then?' she said.

'Nothing that I know of.'

She looked disappointed. 'I had to leave because he's off to play golf,' she snorted. 'Football, golf. What is it about men and balls?'

Bill tried to look sympathetic. 'You don't have a key to his flat?'

'Not likely. He doesn't allow me in unless he's there. He thinks I'm out to steal his priceless antiques.'

'They're priceless?'

'The way he goes on about those paintings and bits of old furniture and crockery, you'd think so. Personally I wouldn't give them house room. So why did you want to see him?'

'He used to work at the British Heart Foundation Shop in Dumbarton Road.'

'Where they found the body?' She shook her head. 'I live near there. Been watching the comings and goings.' She eyed Bill. 'You don't think *he's* got anything to do with it?'

'We've no reason to. I just wanted to ask him if he still had keys for the shop.'

'He used to take stuff from there, you know, before it went on display. Thinks I don't know, but I do.'

'You've been with him that long?'

'Three years, but my sister Moira cleaned for him before me. Couldn't stand his whining any longer so I took over. He's mean, but it's only twice a week.' She gave Bill a long hard look. 'You think he still has keys for the place?'

'Do you?'

'Did you ask him?'

'He said no.'

She shrugged. 'He's a good liar. Just told me he's off to play golf with a Lord! Aye, that'll be right.'

They parted at the car, but not before she gave Bill her sister's mobile number.

'I'll tell Moira you'll be giving her a ring,' she said with relish.

He was on his way back to the station when the call came through from Janice. Bill pulled into the side and answered.

'Sir, someone's reported what looks like a body in the water near Harbour Place, south of Rosevale Street.'

Bill swore under his breath. 'Male or female?'

'No word, yet.'

'I'll meet you there.'

Bill waited for a break in the traffic then did a U-turn and headed for the Clydeside Expressway.

26

'You need to phone Rhona. Tell her what we found.'

'It might not be Jude's.'

'You said you recognised it.'

'I said it looked like Jude's jacket, but I don't know for certain.' Liam lapsed into silence, staring into his pint.

They'd abandoned the cinema and after considerable difficulty on Liam's part, climbed back over the fence. Their lookout had been waiting for them. Liam had got in before Ben, revealing they'd found nothing, just some old clothes.

'No sign of the lassie?'

'No sign,' Liam said.

'So you don't think she got inside?'

Liam eyed the fence. 'She's too wee to get over that. Unless whoever she was with had a key for one of the front doors, I don't see how she could have.'

Their new friend looked pretty disappointed. 'Sorry to get your hopes up,' he told Liam, with sincerity.

Liam felt equally sorry.

'Well, good luck, pal. I hope the lassie turns up soon.'

After the exchange they'd taken refuge in a nearby pub, ordered a couple of pints and taken them into a corner. There was no one to overhear anyway. The place was empty apart from two old guys sitting silently studying their drinks at the bar.

'But you said . . .' Ben began again.

'It looked like her size and Jude did have one that colour, but there was nothing in the pockets to say it belonged to Jude.'

'Then why did you take it?'

Liam wasn't sure himself. When he'd opened the door to the projection room he'd been terrified of what he might find there. Then he'd seen the coat on the floor and for a moment he thought Jude was wearing it. He'd rushed over, shouting her name like a maniac, before realising the coat was empty.

'You need to give that coat to your mum. Maybe she can DNA it or something. See if it is Jude's.'

'First of all, she's not my mum.'

'You said . . .'

'My mum's name is Elizabeth Hope. Rhona is the woman who gave me up for adoption as soon as I was born,' he said sharply.

Ben stared at him. 'Who the fuck cares about that? It was years ago. It's now that matters. It's Jude that matters. Not the *I'm fucked up because my mother gave me away routine.*'

Liam winced as the words hit home. Ben, perhaps registering just how harsh he'd been, fell silent. The silence was painful. After Ben had managed to keep his mouth shut for longer than ever before, he opened it again. Before he could start, Liam cut in.

'I'll call her.'

Ben looked taken aback, then said, 'Good on you, mate,' and took a long slug of his lager.

Liam pulled out his phone. There were two messages

waiting, both from Rhona. He didn't bother listening, just did a call back. The mobile rang long enough for him to think it would go to voicemail, but then she answered. Liam realised immediately he had no idea what he was planning to say.

'Liam, I'm glad you called. I've been trying to get a hold of you.'

'Oh?' he said, stupidly, as though he didn't know.

'Where are you?'

Liam hesitated. 'Govanhill.'

There was a moment's silence. 'Near the Picture House?'

How did she know that?

'Inspector Wilson told me about the Olympia.'

So she'd discussed him with the policeman? And no doubt with the journalist, too. The son she hadn't wanted, come back to haunt her.

'We broke in,' he said.

'And?' Her calm reaction demolished his attempt to shock.

'We found a coat, it looks like Jude's.'

Rhona had never known him as a child, so had never had to chastise him, but Liam could imagine that look on her face now.

There was a moment's pause.

'Did you leave it where you found it?' By her tone, she wanted him to say yes.

'No.'

Another pause.

'Where is it?'

'In my backpack.'

'OK. Don't handle it any more. Was there anything

else in the cinema that suggested Jude might have been there?'

'No.'

The moments of strained silence that followed gave Liam a really bad feeling.

'What is it? What's wrong?'

'I've just had a call-out, so I can't come and pick you up.'

He knew she meant pick the coat up. Then it struck Liam what she was really saying. A call-out for Forensics surely meant that someone had found a body. Whose body?

'You've found her, haven't you?'

The second's hesitation was enough to make his stomach rise. He forced back the nausea. 'Haven't you?' he repeated, hearing a tremor in his voice.

'No. That is, I don't know. A body's been reported in the river behind the Rosevale. I'm headed down there now.'

'No!' he shouted. Ben was staring at him, alarmed. Liam was already on his feet. 'I'm coming.'

'Don't.' Rhona's voice was firm. 'They won't let you through.'

'I'm coming,' he shouted, even though he'd already shut the phone.

Liam slung the backpack on his shoulder and made for the door, Ben following. Once outside, he was unsure what to do next. How the hell did he get to Dumbarton Road from here?

'The station,' Ben suggested.

Liam nodded and looked round, trying to get his bearings. Were they on Cathcart Road? If so, which direction was the station? His head felt unnaturally light, as though his feet weren't anchored on the ground.

'This way.' Ben took his arm, swinging him to face the opposite direction.

Liam took off, the torch in the bag slamming against his back. Shallow breathing soon brought a stitch like a knife in his side. Ben overtook him then slowed enough to let him catch up. They panted into the station. The half-hourly service was due in four minutes. Liam bent double, sucking in air.

Ben didn't ask what had been said on the phone until they were seated on the train.

'They've found a body in the Clyde, down behind the Rosevale.'

Ben's face drained of colour.

'She didn't say it was Jude,' Liam said, to convince himself as much as Ben.

'Shit.' Ben was shaking his head as though doing so would make the whole thing go away. 'We're going down there?'

Liam nodded.

Ben took refuge in the practicalities. 'OK, we'll get the train into Central then pick up the underground to Partick. We can walk from there.'

The rest of the journey seemed agonisingly slow and complicated as they hurried through the thicker pedestrian crowds of the city centre to the packed underground plat-form, caught a train to Partick Cross, then set off on foot towards the Rosevale.

The charity shop was locked up and in darkness when they walked past. They used a pedestrian crossing to cut through the rush-hour traffic and made their way over towards the new harbour development. In the distance a group of police vehicles was parked near the river's edge, a cordon already up and manned. As they approached, it became obvious that there was little chance of getting any closer than the half dozen residents who'd abandoned their balcony view to try to discover what was going on below.

Liam, desperation and fear giving him courage, headed for the uniformed officer standing guard at the tape.

'Sorry, police personnel only beyond the barrier.'

'My name's, uh, Liam MacLeod. I'm Dr Rhona MacLeod's son. She asked me to meet her here.'

The uniform digested this.

'I'm sorry, son, you still can't come on site.'

'Is my mum here?'

The uniform looked taken aback by the use of the word 'mum'.

'I'm not sure.'

'If she is, can you tell her I'm here? It's *very* important.'

His request was considered. 'I can't leave my post, but if you stand back from the barrier, I'll see if I can send her a message.'

Liam retreated, Ben in tow. They climbed a small bank of mown grass and stood at the top. Liam was tall, but he still couldn't see over the vehicles to the activity near the water's edge.

'Well done, mate.' Ben slapped him on the back.

'I want to know if it's Jude. Rhona owes me that, at least.'

27

The body was partially wrapped in black plastic. It bobbed face down in a corner, trapped between the smoothness of the newly built walkway and a jutting peninsular of waste ground. A portion of the boarding erected to hide the wasteland from expensive waterfront apartments had been dismantled, offering access.

Rhona picked her way across the weed-strewn rubble. No doubt the intention had been to continue building waterfront apartments here, perhaps as far as the gleaming silver mound of the new Museum of Transport. Whether that would happen in the current recession remained to be seen.

For now, the body floated somewhere between Glasgow's industrial past and its yet-to-be-decided future. Rhona stood for a moment surveying the scene, noting the relative ease of access for a vehicle. The low metal railing of the walkway, simple to climb, fall or be pushed over.

SOCO photographers were recording the scene before an attempt was made to retrieve the body. A police diver floated near by, awaiting instructions. Rhona recognised the figures of Bill and Janice standing halfway down the stony bank. Bill spotted her arrival and waved her over.

'Male or female?' she asked, as soon as she was within earshot.

'We're just about to find out.'

Bill gave the signal. The diver approached the plastic mound and, catching a hold, attempted to roll it. It took a couple of attempts before the corpse flopped on to its back, long dark hair obscuring the face. The diver pushed the hair to one side. The exposed face was that of a man, and one Rhona knew. In the middle of his forehead was a neat, dark hole.

'It's the porter from the hotel,' she said, in a rush of relief.

Liam was standing with another boy on a small incline behind the other onlookers. Rhona passed under the tape and walked swiftly towards him. Taking his arm she led him to one side.

'It's not Jude,' she said quietly and felt the tenseness in his body dissipate.

'Who . . .' he began.

'I can't tell you that.'

'You know?'

'Yes, but believe me, the body has nothing to do with Jude or her disappearance.' She met his eye.

'OK.' He nodded.

'I have to go back now.'

'But I need to talk to you about Jude.'

'This isn't a good time.'

'Can I come round tonight, then?'

Rhona was about to agree then remembered the meeting scheduled for the Jazz Club. That had to take priority. Rhona shook her head. 'I'm sorry. That's not possible either.' She watched as Liam's face fell. 'What if I call you tomorrow? Arrange something?'

'You've given up on her, haven't you?' he said accusingly.

'No. Inspector Wilson . . .' she began.

'Is he there? Can I speak to *him*?'

'He is, but believe me, now isn't the time.'

'What about the coat we found?' Liam swung a bag from his shoulder and began to unzip it.

Rhona stopped him. 'Leave it in the bag.' She held out her hand.

'But my torch is in there!'

'Liam,' she said firmly. 'It's better if you leave the cinema searches to the police from now on.'

He stepped back as though she'd punched him. 'I'm sorry. I know how worried you must be . . .'

'No, you don't,' he said sharply.

'I'll call you tomorrow. We'll talk about it then.'

The look he gave her was bordering on dislike.

'Don't bother.' He turned on his heel and walked away.

Rhona made to go after him, then stopped herself. Nothing she could say at this moment would make things any better. She couldn't tell him that the body was the night porter, and he'd been shot in the head just like Paddy Brogan. The discovery meant that any hope they'd had that McNab might have left the hotel of his own free will had just evaporated.

Dipping back under the tape, she was struck by the thought that this was what it must be like if you had a family. Bill spoke to Margaret, she knew that. But he didn't tell her everything, or she wouldn't sleep at night. Most people never encountered true evil. And that's how it should be. Liam would just have to think badly of her, for the moment at least.

An incident tent had been erected in her absence and the body placed inside. Now that it was fully exposed, it was obvious an attempt had been made to weight it down. A length of barbed wire had been wound round the black plastic sheet. Whatever had anchored the wire to the bottom had broken free, maybe with the power of the incoming tide, or simply the flow of the river. This meant that it hadn't necessarily been dumped at the place it had been discovered.

Initially a body dumped in water would sink, resurfacing once decay began and the gases it generated made it buoyant. According to Bill the night porter had been interviewed by Slater only yesterday, which made the time frame for his murder short. Whoever killed him hadn't intended he be found this quickly, if at all.

While she took her set of photographs, Rhona decided that when she met Bill this evening she would explain about Liam's search of the Govanhill Picture House, tell him about the coat which might be Jude's and reassure him that her son wouldn't be entering any more deserted cinemas. Rhona hoped Liam would actually heed her on that; she recalled his surly reaction to what had been more of an order than a suggestion, and suspected ordering him not to do something might just make him all the more determined.

Her visual recording complete, she began an examination of the head. The man's long hair, caught back in a ponytail when she'd first met the porter, had given the initial impression that they were dealing with a female; that and his slender build, noticeable even through layers of plastic sheeting.

She swabbed the various orifices then checked the sides and back of the head. There was an exit hole at the rear and another opening on the left-hand side of the skull. Rhona cut away some hair for a closer look, realising she'd seen such a wound before, after a gangland attack over drug territories. A power drill had been used to torture a rival gang member, piercing the skull and entering the brain to devastating effect.

This wound hadn't penetrated as deeply but it bore the same hallmarks. It seemed whoever killed the porter had had fun with him first, or had set about extracting information.

Rhona recalled leaving the hotel and seeing the porter make a mobile call. Had he endangered himself by telling her about McNab and the mystery man he'd left the hotel with?

Bill had said he'd check out if the porter had form, or possibly Glasgow underworld connections. Maybe his death had nothing to do with the Russian. Maybe he, like the previous power-drill victim, had just crossed into enemy territory.

It sounded plausible enough, but in her heart she didn't believe it. It would have been too much of a coincidence; the bullet wound in his forehead linked his murder to Brogan's, and therefore to Kalinin and McNab.

Her examination complete, she called in an officer and told him the body could be taken to the mortuary. When she emerged from the tent Bill was nowhere to be seen, but a text on her mobile reminded her of their meeting later at the Jazz Club. She would have to keep her emerging theories to herself until then.

28

McNab never forgot a face.

Despite his half-shut eyes, the hazy outline of the one currently inches from his own was instantly recognisable. They said the brain automatically recalled certain faces because the owners had brought you either pain or pleasure.

McNab remembered this one because it was hideous.

'Sergeant McNab. Long time no see.'

The face came closer and McNab caught a blast of rotten breath. With all the money Johnny Lang made dealing, you'd think he could afford a dentist. But that would put him on the other end of a drill for a change, which was something Lang obviously didn't fancy.

'Hi, Johnny, How's it going?' he slurred thickly.

Johnny smiled, or at least twisted the corners of his mouth upwards. Another foetid blast hit McNab's face. What the hell did Johnny need a power drill for, when he could kill by breath alone? The semi-delirious thought brought a cackle of laughter from McNab's split lips.

Johnny didn't appreciate the joke.

'You laughing at me, Mikey boy?'

'What d'you think?'

McNab wanted his fearless alter ego to shut up, but he just kept on. Maybe the pain had become like a drug?

Or maybe pissing the bastards off gave him such a shot of pleasure that it diluted what followed.

Johnny hung there so that they were nose to nose for a bit, then withdrew and eyed McNab from a more fragrant distance.

Then he moved behind the chair. Fear slithered like a snake up McNab's back, tightening its hold on his spine. He preferred to see what was coming and pre-empt it, if not with his fists then with words. This way he felt exposed.

McNab heard a faint click then the whine of a motor. The whine became a shriek as it approached his left ear.

'I like a thick skull like yours. Lasts longer.'

'Fuck off!' McNab spat. Anger flooded his veins with adrenaline.

'OK, pal. Let's start with the woman who's screwing Petersson.'

McNab twisted furiously in his chair.

'Settle down, now. What do you think, Mikey? Does she know he's the one that handed you over?'

29

Rhona hesitated at the top of the steps leading to the Jazz Club. She was early – should she go down anyway and hope she wasn't the first to get there?

The truth was she didn't fancy arriving to find Sean with her replacement. She'd spent too much time imagining that when they were still together. Her suspicions were never proved, of course, and Sean had always strongly denied it; with the benefit of hindsight, she had come to believe she may have falsely accused him. Certainly Chrissy had told her so often enough.

Rhona headed downstairs, and was relieved to see Chrissy already sitting at the bar, with her partner Sam behind it. They'd met here when Rhona and Chrissy were investigating a case involving child trafficking and Sam, a Nigerian, had helped them solve the abduction of a little boy.

The pair were an unlikely coupling, and not just in looks. Sam, of Fulani extraction, was a committed Christian; Chrissy, a lapsed Catholic with a drunken father and a gaggle of brothers who, according to her, should all *be* committed. Love against the odds.

Chrissy looked round and waved her over. As she skirted the tables, Rhona became aware that she was being observed.

Sitting at a corner table was the woman she'd seen in Sean's car when he'd come to pick up the rest of his things from her apartment.

'*She*'s here,' Chrissy said as an opening.

'So I see.'

'Even though they're not together any more.'

'Oh, really? That didn't last long.' Rhona felt oddly pleased about that.

'I knew it wouldn't,' Chrissy told her smugly.

Sam gave her a welcoming smile. 'Good to see you again, Rhona. The usual?'

'Yes, make it a large glass, please.'

'Sean knows you're coming,' whispered Chrissy conspiratorially.

'Thanks a bunch.'

'Did you want me to lie?' Chrissy widened her eyes in mock innocence.

Rhona shrugged. 'I don't care either way.'

Chrissy and Sam exchanged a look.

'Are we talking in here?' She glanced around. The place wasn't full but the noise level was fairly high even before the music had started. She also didn't much fancy watching Sean play. She would have to see him sometime tonight, but rather later than sooner.

'Sean suggested we use his office.'

'He's in on this?'

'He knows about McNab's grave being dug up, but then who doesn't? And he's aware that McNab's in hiding until the trial.'

'That's it?' Rhona said.

225

Chrissy nodded.

Sam had moved off to serve a group of customers further down the bar.

'What about Sam?' asked Rhona.

'Sam doesn't ask, because that way he thinks I won't have to tell lies. He doesn't want me to stain my soul.' Chrissy smiled indulgently. 'My own personal priest.'

'You look happy enough.'

'I am. And so will you be when I tell you what I've found out so far.'

'The gun used to kill Brogan . . . ?'

'. . . was not the one taken from the safe house,' Chrissy finished.

'Thank God for that.' It didn't take McNab out of the picture altogether for Brogan's murder, but it did improve his chances, especially after the latest discovery. 'I take it you've heard about the body in the river near Harbour Place?'

The smile slipped from Chrissy's lips. 'What body?'

'The night porter from the hotel. Matthew Sinclair. Shot through the head, just like Brogan.'

'Well, well, well.'

Their discussion was interrupted by the arrival of Bill and Petersson. Petersson was walking better, but even the discreet lighting couldn't hide his colourful facial bruising.

'What the hell happened to your face?' asked Chrissy.

'It's a long story.'

'Shall we head for the back room and bring everyone up to date?' Bill suggested.

'The gun used to kill Brogan wasn't the one taken from the safe house? You're sure?' Bill asked.

'We're sure,' replied Chrissy.

'So, McNab is in the clear?'

'Not exactly. His prints were found in Brogan's room. Yours,' she pointed at Petersson, 'were not.'

All eyes turned to the Icelander.

'I thought you said you were in there?' said Rhona.

'I was. I just made certain I didn't leave any prints.'

That made sense. The question was, why would McNab leave his?

'Where were McNab's prints?' Rhona asked Chrissy.

'On both the door handles of the en suite toilet.'

'What was he doing in there?'

Chrissy shrugged. 'Taking a piss?'

'That's the only place he left prints?'

'Yes.'

Rhona said what they were all thinking. 'If McNab was OK about leaving his prints, then he can't have gone there to kill Brogan.'

'I agree,' said Bill. 'And the fact that the night porter was dispensed with in the same way—'

'What the hell are you talking about?' interrupted Petersson.

'The man who let Rhona into the hotel, and who said that McNab had left with someone resembling Solonik, turned up dead in the Clyde with a bullet through his head. Just like Brogan.'

Petersson paled under his bruising.

'I ran a check on him,' Bill continued. 'He had a few minor infringements, mostly by association with a character called Johnny Lang. Lang is involved in serious organised crime. Drugs, girls and guns. He's not at the top of the ladder, more of a fixer. His calling card seems to be his predilection for power drills. He finds applying them to skulls can be very persuasive.'

Rhona nodded. 'The night porter's skull had a wound above the left ear which could have been made by a drill.'

'Well then, it looks like the Russian employed a local to do his dirty work. So we bring in Johnny Lang,' said Bill.

'That's not a good idea,' Petersson said quickly.

'Why?'

'The copy of the CCTV footage I showed Rhona came indirectly from Sinclair.'

'And now Sinclair's dead.'

'If the body was weighted down then they didn't intend for you to find it, at least not so soon,' Petersson said. 'Now that you have, anyone linked with Sinclair may be in danger.'

'You?'

Petersson conceded this with a nod. 'But I'm primarily thinking of McNab. If Kalinin believes there's the slightest chance we've found a trail leading to him, then he will execute McNab sooner rather than later.'

'Assuming he hasn't already done so,' Bill said grimly.

'I believe Kalinin is holding McNab alive.'

'You have evidence to prove that?'

'No. Just an intimate knowledge of Kalinin's methods.'

'If what Rhona suggests is confirmed at post mortem, Lang will be on top of the list of suspects. He has to be brought in,' insisted Bill.

Petersson looked in danger of further argument, then seemed to master his emotions.

'OK, but in the interim there might be another way of

getting to Kalinin. I've been working on the CCTV footage and I have a possible number plate for the car McNab left in. If I'm right about the number it belongs to a fleet car-hire company, based here in Glasgow, called "Way to Go". They appear to be bona fide. One of the directors is Stan Brown.'

Bill looked surprised. 'Stan Brown is a long-term friend of the Brogan family,' he said.

'That's right. He also has money invested in the Poker Club,' Petersson told him. 'And he owns a construction company involved in the new flyover.'

'Stan Brown and Paddy's father were like brothers.' Bill shook his head. 'I can't see him having anything to do with Paddy's death.'

'Times change.' Petersson sounded exasperated. 'As do the rules. Who knows what Kalinin has on Brown? What he has on any of us?'

'What are you trying to say?'

'That you are still underestimating the man. He is clever, brilliantly so. And ruthless. We are his enemies, so he knows our weak points. McNab barged in, that's why he was caught. You, Bill, he'll try to bring down professionally. Maybe he's already using Slater to do this. And as for Dr MacLeod, you have already thwarted him and he won't like that.'

A stunned silence followed his impassioned outburst.

'What about you?' Rhona asked.

He didn't answer at first, then seemed to make up his mind. 'I too have my Achilles heel. Someone very dear to me. I shield her to keep her safe. Because of this we are never seen together in public. Does Kalinin know about her? I hope not.'

Maybe it was the way Petersson steadily held her gaze, but Rhona believed him. Petersson was frightened for the woman he was talking about. Very frightened.

'So what *do* you suggest?' Bill said.

'Let me check out the hired car. If it was the car on the CCTV then we have a lead, but the longer we keep that a secret, the better for McNab.'

'You don't want me to check the number plate officially?'

'McNab suspects there's a mole working against him in the police force. I'd rather we didn't take the chance that he's right.'

Rhona could tell Bill was struggling over this.

'We did say we'd keep it between the three of us,' she reminded him.

'Hey, what about me?' Chrissy protested.

Her indignant expression broke the stalemate.

'OK,' Bill conceded. 'But if the post mortem links Lang to the Sinclair murder, I'll have no choice but to bring him in. You have until then.'

Rhona would have liked a moment alone with the Icelander, but never got the chance. As soon as the meeting broke up, Bill cornered her.

'Can you hang around for a bit? We need to talk.'

'The cinema case?'

Bill nodded. 'Will I get us both a drink?'

'I could use one.'

'Wait here.'

With Bill gone, Rhona stood alone and suddenly awkward in what was definitely Sean's domain. She'd been in here many times, but always with Sean. Now she felt like an interloper.

When the door opened, she was taken aback to see Sean rather than Bill.

He looked equally surprised. 'Sorry, I thought you'd finished. I saw Bill at the bar.'

'He went to get us both a stiff drink.'

'That bad?'

'Well, it wasn't good.'

Sean broke the uncomfortable silence that followed. 'You planning on sticking around to hear Sam's set?'

Rhona's first instinct was to decline, then she thought better of it. 'I might just do that.'

He looked surprised and pleased. 'Great. I'll see you later in the bar.'

What was she doing, Rhona thought as the door closed behind Sean. She could imagine the grin on Chrissy's face when she heard Rhona was planning on sticking around for a while. Chrissy would take it as a personal triumph.

Well, Rhona consoled herself, it was either stay here with Chrissy and Sam for company, or else go home alone and spend the night worrying.

'I've told Liam to leave the cinema searches to the police from now on.'

'He's a determined young man. I'll give him that. Can't think where he gets it from.'

Rhona ignored him. 'I'll take a look at the coat he found.'

'He's sure it's Jude's?'

She shook her head. 'He only said it looks like one she's got.'

'I interviewed the men in charge of the furniture for the

charity shop. One of them, Angus Robertson, maintains he saw Jude the night she disappeared outside the corner pub next to the shop, arguing with a young man. He described the man as in his twenties, tall, blond, wearing a green jacket with a hood.' He let the description sink in.

'It does sound like Liam,' she said anxiously.

'Even down to the clothes.'

'So Liam's lying about meeting Jude?'

'Just hear me out. If we assume Liam is telling the truth, then two possibilities present themselves. Either Angus saw Jude with someone who looks like Liam, or Angus is lying.'

'Why would he lie?'

'Maybe he saw Jude with someone, but he doesn't want us to know who that person was.'

'But why describe Liam?'

'He may want to deflect attention from someone else, maybe even from himself. If he saw Liam in the shop asking about Jude, he had a description to use.'

'Or he's telling the truth and Liam is involved in Jude's disappearance?'

Rhona recalled Liam's constant anxiety, his determination to find Jude. She was reminded of an English case some years before, where a student had reported his girlfriend missing. The police had eventually discovered her body under the floorboards of his flat.

'I have no idea who my son really is,' she said.

'From what I know of him, he has a lot of you in his character. Genetics don't disappear just because you weren't there when he was growing up.'

'What about the half that comes from Edward?' Rhona countered. 'Liam's father is one of the most inveterate liars

I've ever met. He could persuade himself of anything if it suited his purpose.'

Bill, sensing the extent of her worry, said, 'OK, let's leave Liam for the moment. I made contact with the former manager of the charity shop. "Admiral" Nelson.' He raised an eyebrow. 'According to Angus, the Admiral wasn't above helping himself to items which had value before they reached the shop floor. Mr Nelson was helpful enough, but didn't want to admit to having a key, or discuss whether people might have had access to the cinema while he was managing the premises.'

'You think he knew something was going on in the projection room?'

'I think he's reticent with the truth. However, I have the mobile number of a woman who used to be his cleaner, Moira. I have the feeling she might have quite a lot to say about the Admiral. When are you seeing Liam?'

'I'm not.'

'What do you mean?'

'He told me not to call.'

'He's just upset.'

Rhona shrugged. 'I don't think I'm cut out to be a parent.'

'Join the club.'

'What are you talking about? You're a great dad.'

'I'm an absent one. It's Margaret who does all the work.' He glanced at his watch. 'Which reminds me, it's time I went home.'

It was strange sitting in the Jazz Club again, listening to Sean play his saxophone. Rhona had thought it would disturb her, but it didn't. Initially Chrissy had shared her table, but when Sam went back behind the bar, she'd asked if Rhona minded if she went to sit with him.

And Rhona hadn't. Maybe it was the copious amounts of wine she'd drunk. Maybe it was the music, or the fact that the 'other' woman had left, but she felt all right about being there. Eventually she realised the true reason for Chrissy's departure when Sean appeared at the break to sit with her.

'Do you mind?' He grinned.

'It's your club.'

'I'll go if you want me to,' he said, serious now.

'Sit down,' she ordered.

Sean placed a bottle of red and two glasses on the table and eyed her glass of white pointedly. 'I never did refine that palate of yours, did I?'

'Nor did you get me to like jazz.'

'But you enjoyed the set tonight?'

'You were playing tunes I recognised.'

'That was my intention. Would you like to taste the red?'

'Why not?'

He poured two glasses.

'I may be a little drunk,' she said, as she took a mouthful.

'A state I have rarely seen you in.'

'You always could drink more than me.'

'I'm a man. And Irish. My bones soak up the alcohol.'

Rhona heard herself say, 'Chrissy tells me the romance is over.'

'It is. And yours?'

'It wasn't a romance. It was sex.'

'Then we have that in common.'

'I hope you made it plain to the person in question,' Rhona said, glancing towards the other woman's now-empty seat.

'I hope you did too,' Sean replied.

'I've found with men it's always about sex.'

'It wasn't, not with you and me.'

His declaration silenced Rhona for a moment. 'We screwed up,' she said, as though she'd just discovered the fact.

'*I* screwed up,' he said, quietly.

'With me or with her?'

'Both.'

'It takes a man to admit his mistakes.'

'It takes a woman to remind him of them.'

'Touché.' She tried to smile.

He studied her. 'What's really wrong? Is it McNab?'

'Yes.' She could have stopped there, but didn't. 'But it's not just that. Liam doesn't want anything more to do with me.'

'What happened?'

She shrugged. 'I had no time for him. I was working. I wasn't there when he needed me. Just the usual.'

'That can be mended.'

'You think so? Like *we* can be mended?'

Sean gave her a long hard look. 'Do you mean that or are you *actually* drunk?'

'Maybe I needed to be drunk to say it.'

'Have you eaten?'

'No. Probably why the wine has gone to my head.'

'Let's go.'

'What about your second set?'

'Sam can fill in for me.'

* * *

They walked together through the cold night air. Rhona felt able to talk to Sean about Liam; he'd been there when she'd begun her search for her son, and when Liam had come looking for her. He had kept him in the flat until she'd come home and held together what could have been a disastrous evening. He'd saved her relationship with Liam once. Maybe he could do it again?

'Where are we going?' she asked him.

'It's late for a restaurant. I can feed you at my new place. If that's OK with you?'

'I'm not sure that's such a good idea.'

'All right,' he said, 'if you prefer a carry-out kebab to my home-made spaghetti . . .'

Sean was right. She was being stupid.

'OK.'

'Good, because we're here.' He indicated the next door along and produced a key.

'You're only round the corner from the club!' she said.

'Close enough to stagger home.'

'*I'm* not staggering – yet.'

'No, you're not.'

The flat was two floors up, facing south. Open plan, airy, with a good view of the city.

'Very nice,' she said.

'I like it. Take a seat. I'll bring a starter.'

In moments Rhona had a plate of olives, feta cheese and bread placed before her.

'Main course in ten minutes. D'you want any more wine?'

'Definitely.'

Rhona ate a good portion of the olives and bread before

sipping cautiously at the wine. She watched Sean move about the kitchen, engrossed as he always was when cooking. Maybe it was the wine or the smell of the food, but she found she didn't mind being on such dangerous ground.

'OK. We're ready.' He ushered her to the table.

'I haven't eaten a proper meal at my kitchen table since . . .' She came to a halt, suddenly realising what she was about to say.

'Since I left?' Sean suggested.

'Einar can cook,' she said defensively.

'I'm not getting into a cooking competition with your Icelander.'

'He's not *my* Icelander.'

'Good.'

Sean placed a plate of spaghetti in front of her and sat down with his own. 'Tomatoes, black olives, basil and anchovies.'

It smelt like heaven. Rhona attacked the food with gusto, realising just how long it had been since her last meal. When they'd cleared their plates, she sat back with a contented sigh. 'That was delicious.'

'Good. Coffee?'

She nodded.

'Take a seat. I'll bring it over.'

She carried her replenished wine glass with her. The food had restored her equilibrium, although she was well aware how weird this evening had turned out to be. Her plan tonight had been to avoid Sean at all costs, not to let him cook for her. Yet she felt OK about it. Maybe even better than OK.

Sean re-introduced the subject of Liam over coffee and listened in silence as she revealed her fears.

'I don't believe it. There's not an ounce of violence in the boy.'

'How can you possibly know that?' Rhona protested.

'When you've had a father like mine, you recognise the signs, however well hidden. You're not really serious about suspecting him, are you?'

'Some things don't add up. I can't really say what they are.'

'Have you spoken to him about it?'

'Professionally, I can't.'

Sean thought for a moment. 'What about Bill?'

'He's asking all the right questions.'

'But what does he think?'

'He's a detective. He knows something's not right.'

'But does he believe Liam's involved?' he persisted.

'Not really.'

'Well, there you go.'

'That's not all. Liam thinks I'm not taking Jude's disappearance seriously, so he's been breaking into disused cinemas looking for her himself.'

Sean looked impressed. 'It's obvious who his mother is.'

'That's not funny.'

'I didn't say it was funny, just that it was obvious. I take it you told him to stop?'

She nodded. 'And he told me not to contact him again.'

'He didn't really mean that.'

'I think he did.' Rhona took refuge in her glass of wine. 'I think he's disappointed in me. In more ways than one. When he came round to ask for my help in finding Jude, Petersson was there.'

'That happened to me once,' Sean said dryly.

'It wasn't like that. We were discussing McNab's situation.' She hesitated. 'It's just, Liam asked after you as though he expected us still to be together.'

'But you put him straight?'

'I did.'

'So. Let me read this correctly. You're worried that Liam thinks his mother can't hold down a relationship, and that he might have applied that logic to how you feel about him?'

Rhona said nothing.

'That *was* what you were thinking?' he insisted.

She conceded. 'More or less.'

'And if we add in a prick for a father?'

'A lying one, who'll say anything to cover his mistakes.'

'Let's face it. The boy's doomed.'

There was a moment's silence as they eyed one another, then the absurdity of it hit Rhona and she started to laugh.

'You can't outdo the Irish when it comes to making a drama out of a crisis,' he said.

She knew that she still wanted him, but now was not the time. For now, she was glad to have him back in her life.

30

Bill arrived at work early next morning.

He'd risen and left home before breakfast, trying not to rouse the sleeping household. The previous night, after a restless couple of hours, he'd eventually moved to the spare room to give Margaret peace. He was aware they hadn't had a proper conversation in days and felt guilty about it, but when he arrived home and saw she'd gone to bed, he'd been relieved to have the time to himself. He'd slipped the meal she'd left for him into the microwave. The truth was, he'd done enough talking and listening for one day and had found himself none the wiser for it.

What Petersson had said troubled him, mainly because the journalist had only reinforced what he already knew; anyone who messed with Nikolai Kalinin had their card marked. But he was also unsettled by Petersson's manner and the sudden revelation that he had a partner, hidden from view. Bill couldn't shake off the feeling that he'd been issuing them with a different warning, more subtle and therefore more worrying.

His talk with Rhona hadn't gone well either. He'd found himself defending Liam, giving the impression he believed the boy, though he wasn't sure he did, not entirely. And Rhona was shrewd enough to pick up on that.

All in all, it was a mess. And they still had no idea who the cinema victim was, nor any sightings of Jude.

Now Bill headed to the canteen and bought himself tea and a filled roll, carrying them up to his office. He was surprised to find DS Clark already in the incident room.

'You're early,' he said.

'So are you, Sir.'

'Something on your mind, Sergeant?'

'A lot of things. Can I show you?'

He waved her into his office and they both took a seat.

'The Tech boys have been examining the audio recording from Jude's computer,' she told him. 'They say the voice in the interview isn't one man, but two – but the voices are virtually identical. It wasn't until they started studying them in detail that they discovered the differences.'

Bill sat up in his chair. 'The former manager of the charity shop said a set of twins came to view the old cinema when he was in charge. Apparently they'd worked there as projectionists. Their name was Mulligan, Jim and John. See what you can find out about them.'

'We also have a sighting of someone we think is Jude outside the Rosevale pub about seven.'

'Show me.'

She led him through to the small room where junior officers were put to work watching endless CCTV in an attempt to put them off the job for life, found the required section and set it running. The clock on the footage said 19.10 and it was dated the day Jude disappeared.

A couple of men stood smoking outside the pub. Neither

of them was Angus. A figure appeared from the side road, wearing a blue coat. She was slightly built with shoulder-length dark hair, and carried a backpack.

'That's Jude,' Bill said.

A figure came into view beside her. Male, not tall and blond, but medium height and also dark haired.

'Stop there.' Bill stared at the screen.

'You recognise him, Sir?' Janice said.

'His name is Jason Donald. He works in the charity shop, shifting furniture. Any more?'

Janice set the tape running again. After a short but animated conversation with Jason, Jude walked east past the Rosevale and Jason entered the pub, just as Angus emerged for his smoke.

'No sign of a tall fair-haired man in the vicinity?'

Janice shook her head. 'Jude must have turned off Dumbarton Road shortly after that. We've checked all CCTV in either direction, but there's no other sighting.'

'So she came out of the old cinema by the fire exit, possibly with Jason. They parted at the Rosevale and she left Dumbarton Road?'

'That's what it looks like, Sir.'

'OK, Sergeant. Well done on that. Anything on the cinema body?'

'We have a match based on the fingerprints retrieved by Dr MacLeod.'

Now this was good news. 'And?'

'Well. The victim doesn't appear to be dead, Sir.'

'What?'

'His name is Dominic McGeehan. He was charged in connection with a drugs offence ten years ago and his prints taken then. According to our enquiries the same man is currently living in Dennistoun.'

'No two sets of prints are the same, Sergeant, even twins.'

'I know that, Sir.' Janice looked offended.

'Is this McGeehan aware we're interested in him?'

'Not yet, Sir.'

'Good.'

They were getting somewhere at last. A dead man pretending to be alive. And a girl who still might be.

'Get me McGeehan's address. And bring in Jason Donald. I'd like a word with him away from Angus Robertson.' He halted Janice on her way out. 'And find out what you can about Johnny Lang's current activities. Keep your enquiries low-key, for the moment. I don't want Lang alerted to any interest we might have in him.'

She looked puzzled. 'You think he's involved in the cinema case?'

'It's always good to know what Johnny's up to,' Bill said.

He had promised Petersson he'd wait until after the post mortem before he launched a full-scale search for Lang. He would keep his word on that.

When Janice had gone, Bill checked his watch, then rang the number the Admiral's cleaning lady had given him for her predecessor. Moira Cochrane sounded delighted to hear from him, and Bill got the impression she was more than a little anxious to dish the dirt on her former employer. He made arrangements to meet her later that day and sat back to enjoy his filled roll and mug of tea, cold now, just the way he liked it. Things were moving at last on the cinema murder and he would be able to tell Rhona that they had CCTV footage to prove the man Jude met outside the pub wasn't Liam.

McGeehan's flat wasn't far from Glasgow Green, within sight of the colourful tiles and decorative glasswork of the famous Templeton's Carpet Factory, said to be modelled on the Doge's Palace in Venice. There was nothing else like it in Glasgow.

The area surrounding the unique building had seen peaks and troughs, but was currently on its way up again. Plenty of new flats were being built, one of which turned out to be the living dead McGeehan's.

Bill located the number and buzzed. It was ten o'clock so he didn't really expect an answer, not if McGeehan was a nine-to-five man.

'Yes?'

'Dominic McGeehan?'

'Who wants to know?'

'Detective Inspector Wilson.'

There was a pregnant silence. 'With regard to what, exactly?'

'Just a general enquiry.'

A thoughtful moment, then the click sounded. 'Come on up.'

McGeehan might be dead but he wasn't stupid; and better still, he was curious. Almost a decade was a long time to be living undiscovered as someone else, especially if the real McGeehan was walled into a building and unlikely to be revealed in your lifetime. Might make a man confident. Possibly over-confident.

The door on the first landing was open, the flat's owner

standing there. Bill did a quick calculation. Ten years ago the man in front of him must have been in his teens or early twenties. The real Dominic had had a drugs conviction, never repeated according to his paperwork. A teenage indiscretion. There were plenty of people who had those, including current MPs and MSPs.

The man smiled. He was tall with blond hair, cut in a contemporary style. Dressed in a striped open-necked shirt and smart suit, he looked like a Merchant City banker. Cool, modern and not short of a bob or two. So why was he wearing a dead man's shoes?

Bill held out his warrant card.

'This is official, then?'

'I'm obliged to show you my ID.'

Dominic led him through to a designer sitting room. All black leather and shining glass. A TV big enough for cinema showings, and no doubt excellent surround sound from the hi-fi system. A man of means.

'How can I help you, Detective Inspector?'

Bill wasn't sure how he wanted to play this. He'd assumed Mr McGeehan would probably not be at home, and planned to take a look around, speak to a couple of neighbours and find out who the dead man was, or at least something about his impersonator. Finding him at home had been a bit of a surprise.

Bill decided to go for gold.

'Have you ever had your fingerprints taken?'

Dominic looked taken aback, then recovered. 'Not that I remember,' he joked.

Bill smiled, because that was what was expected of him. He wondered if Mr McGeehan, or whatever his real name was, had heard about the body in the Rosevale cinema; was he aware that the dead man whose identity he'd stolen had been discovered?

'We have a set of prints on the database that have your name on them.'

The man looked puzzled. 'There must be more than one Dominic McGeehan in Glasgow.'

'What were you doing ten years ago?'

'That's easy. I was at Glasgow University studying Astronomy.' He indicated his get-up. 'As you can see, I did not become an astronomer. I changed my course and became an accountant. More reward in managing money than in studying the stars.'

He had an answer for everything.

'Would you be willing to have your fingerprints taken, then?'

'Since I've done nothing wrong, I'd be happy to.' He eyed Bill with some concern. 'What exactly is this about, Detective Inspector?'

'The remains of a man bearing the fingerprints registered as belonging to Dominic McGeehan have been found in the old Rosevale cinema on Dumbarton Road.'

His reaction was not what Bill expected; McGeehan's legs seemed to give way under him. Bill caught him as he crumpled, and eased him on to the fancy leather couch.

'Jesus. Dominic.'

'Would you like me to fetch you some water?'

He shook his head. 'I'd rather have a whisky. From the cabinet over there.'

Bill went to fetch him one. McGeehan took the double in both hands and swallowed it in one go. If he was pretending to be in shock, he was doing a hell of a job. Bill waited until some colour came back in his cheeks.

'Want to tell me who you are?'

The man looked up at Bill for a long moment, then shrugged resignedly. 'What the hell. If you have the fingerprints, you're going to find out anyway. I'm Tony, Dominic's younger brother.'

'Why are you using his name?'

'Because he was in America and I had some debts I couldn't pay.'

'You had no idea your brother was dead?'

'Last time I saw Dominic was at Mum's funeral, nine years ago. With Mum gone we had no other family. He told me he was planning on emigrating to Canada or America.'

'And you've never heard from him since?'

'I got a card when he arrived. One five years later. He was doing well. Married with kids.'

'You never went to visit?'

'He never sent an address. I figured he didn't want to be reminded of the old life.'

'Which was?'

'Scotland. Glasgow.' He paused. 'You said you found his body. How did he die?'

'Asphyxiation.'

'How did that happen?'

Bill decided to spell it out for him. That way he might get some answers. 'Someone buried him alive behind a brick wall.'

'Jesus Christ. What kind of maniac would do a thing like that?'

'I was hoping you would tell me.'

McGeehan looked at him in horror. 'You can't believe I would harm my own brother?'

'You didn't mind stealing his identity?'

'He'd left the country, I told you. When he went he said he had no intention of coming back here.'

'He knew what you planned to do?'

'We didn't discuss it.'

'You waited until he left?'

McGeehan nodded.

Bill tried another tack. 'Was your brother into bondage?'

McGeeghan looked nonplussed. 'He dressed a bit punky for a while, wore chains and had his ears pierced, if that's what you mean. It was a phase. Everyone goes through phases.'

'What about sado-masochism?'

'What are you saying?'

'Was your brother involved in S and M?'

'Jesus. I don't know.' Tony McGeeghan collapsed against the back of the seat. 'Look, I feel sick. I've not eaten yet and the whisky's not doing my stomach any good.'

Bill let him be for a moment. His distress seemed genuine, although Bill supposed it might have been brought on by simply being found out. The next question supported that theory.

'Will my employer have to be told?'

'If you used your brother's National Insurance Number, yes.'

A thin film of sweat was breaking out on McGeehan's brow. 'God. I'm up shit creek.'

'At least *you're* alive.'

The remark seemed to bring him back to his senses. 'Look, I thought my brother was in the States and happy. He sent me postcards, for fuck's sake.'

'Do you still have them?'

Tony regarded Bill in disbelief. 'You're kidding me, right? Who the hell keeps old postcards?'

'Pity.'

McGeehan sighed as though the whole world had just landed on his shoulders. 'What happens now?'

'You come down with me to the station and we take your prints. On the way you try to remember everything you can concerning your brother in the run-up to the time you thought he was leaving the country.'

'I'll have to phone into work. Tell them I'm sick or something.'

'You do that.'

'How long before I have to tell them the truth?'

'The sooner the better, and certainly before the newspapers get a hold of it.'

'You're going to tell the press?'

'Believe me, I won't need to.'

McGeehan looked defeated in every way possible.

'Can I go to the toilet?'

Bill nodded his agreement. As he listened to the water running in the bathroom he mulled over McGeehan's story. He'd said he'd assumed his older brother's identity to avoid debts. Bill wondered if the younger McGeehan had form too, and if so, for what?

The tap was still in full flow. What was McGeehan doing in there?

Bill went to check on him. The bathroom door was

closed and the light on. Bill knocked, and when there was no answer, he called out, 'Mr McGeehan, are you all right?'

Still no answer.

Realisation hit Bill like a sledgehammer as he threw open the door on an empty bathroom. McGeehan was gone, probably since shortly after he'd left the sitting room. He'd turned on the tap loudly enough for Bill to hear and simply sneaked out the front door.

He'd been played for a sucker. Thirty years on the force and he'd bought into McGeehan's sob story, even fetched the bastard a whisky. If he hadn't been so angry, Bill would have laughed. McGeehan was a professional, no doubt about that, but he doubted if he was an accountant.

'You lost him, Sir?' DS Clark couldn't disguise her surprise.

Bill ignored the question. 'I need a SOCO team round here pronto. I want his fingerprints checked and the place gone over.'

'You think he had something to do with the Rosevale victim?'

'He says he's his brother, name of Tony – find out if that's true. Check "Anthony", both spellings, too. I want as much as you can get on this guy by the time I get back from the post mortem.' A tall order, especially since he was the one who had lost the suspect.

'Yes, Sir.'

Bill knew he was being unfair, but being pissed on was infectious. He rang off before he could annoy himself further and checked his watch. While he waited for the SOCO team to arrive, he would take a look round. He slipped on a pair of latex gloves and started where he was now, in the fancy sitting room.

Plenty of glass. Even though it was well polished, there were bound to be prints. He opened the cupboards and checked out the DVD collection. Nothing of particular interest. A desk in the corner had a few papers in the drawer. He was suddenly struck by the lack of computer equipment. If McGeehan was working in finance, surely he would have a PC, and at least a laptop? Bill tried to recall if he'd seen one when he came in. He went to the front door and retraced his steps.

There *had* been a laptop case next to the coat stand. McGeehan had been about to leave for work when Bill arrived. And he'd taken the laptop with him when he did a runner.

31

'What do we do now?'

'Nothing.'

Ben rolled his eyes at Liam, exasperated. 'We've got to keep trying.'

'*She* says we've not to break into any more cinemas. *She* told me to leave it to the police. So that's what I'm doing.' Liam turned his attention back to his coursework.

Ben stood for a moment, undecided. Liam heard him mutter a word under his breath, which might have been 'wanker', then he marched out.

Liam slammed the Physics textbook shut. He couldn't solve anything. Not the physics problem he'd been set earlier by his tutor, and not what had happened to Jude. Let's face it, he *was* a wanker.

No wonder Rhona wanted him off her back.

He pushed the book and notepad away. He should go and apologise to Ben, who was a good mate; suggest they go for a pint together. But Ben would only see this as an opportunity to discuss Jude again. Liam couldn't face that.

He swallowed, tasting again the fear he'd experienced when he'd heard they'd found a body in the river. What if that body *had* been Jude? The truth was he'd begun to believe she *was* dead and that it was only a matter of time before her body was discovered. He realised he'd stopped searching, not because of Rhona, but because he didn't want to be the one to find her. Seeing the coat lying on the floor of the Govanhill projection room had been bad enough.

He shook his head, dispelling the image, and stood up. Agitated, he knew that studying wasn't an option. He would take a walk. He could hear music from Ben's room, playing even louder than usual. Liam hesitated outside the door then decided not to go in. He would try to walk off his frustration, then text Ben to meet up later for a drink.

He set off on foot in the direction of Sauchiehall Street, with the vague idea of calling into the halls of residence and speaking to Charlie.

When he got there Charlie wasn't in his office, so Liam went upstairs to check on Jude's room. The door was closed and a length of police tape was still strung across it. The sight of the tape just reinforced his feelings of failure.

The girl from the neighbouring room emerged, no longer wearing the 3-D glasses. She observed him with concern.

'No sign of Jude yet?'

Liam shook his head.

'D'you want to come in for a coffee?'

Liam nodded. Why not?

'I'm Aurora, by the way. And you're Liam. Jude told me about you.'

Liam was slightly taken aback. He'd never imagined Jude talking to anyone about him. As he entered the room it struck him that the name Aurora seemed appropriate for its occupant. The walls were festooned with bizarre luminescent pictures – a psychedelic wonderland. On a large computer screen in the corner was a similar image which she appeared to have been working on.

Aurora registered his startled gaze. 'My project. Three dimensional computer-generated worlds. That's why I wear the funny glasses.' She switched on a small kettle and spooned coffee into two mugs. 'No milk, I'm afraid.' She gestured for Liam to take the one easy chair. 'Jude's project on old cinemas was going really well. She'd used light to give the impression that ghostlike people were sitting in the rows of empty seats. Really spooky. And sort of profound.' She looked to Liam for confirmation of this.

He nodded as though he'd understood and appreciated Jude's work, but inside he felt he'd let her down. He hadn't shown any interest in it at all.

'She wanted to capture the magic of the places. Show what they meant to the people who went there,' Aurora said. She handed him his mug of coffee and sat on the bed. 'Jude didn't do small talk. That's why she never went to parties. She only talked about things she was passionate about. Like her photographs. And no one was allowed in her room. That's what was so odd about that night.'

'What do you mean?'

'I thought I heard a man's voice from her room. I assumed it was Charlie. He often takes a walk round the corridors to check everything's OK.'

'But you said you just heard noises.'

'I'd been at a party. When you're drunk you don't remember half of what happens. It's just recently bits and pieces have started coming back.'

'Did you tell the police this?'

'I only just remembered. I'm not even sure it's true.'

Liam tried to imagine what that might mean. Had Jude stood him up because she was meeting someone else? Had she brought the guy back here? He didn't like to think what the noises might have been if that was the case. But why was the room trashed? And where was Jude now? God, even though the idea of it burned him he half hoped she was holed up with this guy somewhere, unaware of the search for her.

No, that wasn't a possibility. Jude never did things spontaneously, and she would never have left her room looking like that. And what about the missing laptop and the film reel?

'Did Jude say anything to you about the old film reel she had in her room?'

'The porno flick?'

'You knew about it?'

'She said she found it in an old cinema. She thought it was too damaged to run on a projector so she was digitally photographing the frames. How weird is that? An old black and white gay porn movie.'

'You know it went missing from her room?'

Aurora looked surprised. 'No. Is that significant?'

'Did Jude talk to anyone else about the film?'

The girl thought for a moment. 'She *was* in contact with old cinema internet sites, I know that. Wait a minute, there *was* a guy who got in touch with her. She said he collected old reel-to-reel films. She was quite excited about that.'

'Did she meet him?'

Aurora shrugged.

'Did you tell the police about this guy?'

'It wasn't until you mentioned the film going missing

that I remembered him.' She looked worried. 'Maybe I should phone that policeman.'

'No. It's OK. I'll tell him.' Liam drank down the remainder of his coffee and stood up. 'I have to go.'

She nodded, scribbling a number on a Post-it. 'If you hear anything?'

'I'll call you.'

Ben was still in his room with the music turned up. Liam knocked on the door.

'Ben?'

If Ben did hear, he was choosing to ignore him.

'Fancy a pint?' Liam called through the door.

Seconds later, the door opened and his flatmate eyed him warily.

'Sorry,' said Liam.

'Forget it, mate. Pub?'

Liam nodded.

He kept his news to himself until they were settled in the pub and nursing their pints. Ben listened with interest.

'Well, well, well. That changes things a bit,' he said thoughtfully when Liam had finished.

'What d'you think?'

'I'd say Jude's been abducted by someone who knew about the film.'

'Isn't that jumping to conclusions?'

'Were you ever invited into her room?'

'No. She made me wait outside the door.'

Ben raised an eyebrow. 'There you go then. In your version, Jude brought this guy home, had noisy sex with him – trashing her room in the process – then left with her laptop and the film to hole up at his place and have more of the same?'

Liam didn't reply. He didn't have to.

'Way off, bro.' Ben shook his head. 'OK, so we have to find this guy. The one who collects the films, or at least says he does.'

'How do we do that?'

Ben thought for a moment. 'There might be a way, if you're lucky enough to have a computer genius for a mate.'

32

'So?' Chrissy said.

'So, what?'

Chrissy grinned. 'You've got the glow.'

'Rubbish.'

'It was *rubbish*?' Chrissy said in disbelief.

'Can we change the subject?'

'Sure, now that I *know*, we can.'

'Chrissy . . .'

'Right. What's up for examination this morning? Bodily fluids?'

Rhona ignored that one. Any encouragement and Chrissy could keep the innuendoes going on for ever.

'Where are you with the Brogan case?'

Chrissy got the message. She gave Rhona a look that said *You're not off the hook yet*, then assumed a more serious expression. 'I've put a copy of the bullet report on your desk. Just as I said. It's not a match for the gun taken from the safe house. So, what d'you want me to do now?'

'Can you take a look at a coat for me? It might belong to Jude. Liam found it in the Govanhill cinema.'

Chrissy raised an eyebrow. 'He's still breaking into cinemas?'

'Not any more.' Rhona didn't want to revisit that story.

'See if it's a match for her DNA. And anything else you can find on it.'

'OK.'

'I'm going to take a look at the samples I took from Matthew Sinclair before the post mortem.'

They parted company, sparing Rhona from any further discussion of Liam or of Sean, which suited her very well. She didn't want to think about either of them right now.

She decided to take a look at the ballistics report before she started on the Sinclair evidence. The matching of bullets to guns was one of the simplest principles in forensic science. The grooves around the insides of the barrel, there to increase speed and force, caused matchable 'rifling' marks on the bullet. That's how they knew the bullet that killed Brogan hadn't come from the SOCA gun. It was a relief to see it in print, although it did nothing to alleviate her concern about McNab's current well-being.

Rhona put the report to one side and gowned up. The only thing she could do for McNab at the moment was to find a route to his abductor. The night porter's death might just help with that.

As it was, she had very little to go on before the post mortem: the swabs taken from Sinclair's head; the water debris caught in his hair, and a hair sample. Toxicology tests would show if Sinclair had been a drug user, which would explain how he'd got involved with someone like Lang.

Before she began, she checked the R2S cinema crime scene. There were a couple of new postings. It seemed a match had come up on the fingerprints of the victim; his name was Dominic McGeehan, and he had an old drugs conviction. There was also a group of new overhead shots of the streets surrounding the Rosevale. Viewing them, it struck her how close the old cinema was to the crime scene at the river. No wonder they'd thought the body might be Jude.

Rhona buried herself in work until the time came to head for the mortuary. Chrissy was nowhere to be seen when she went to get changed, which meant she was still working somewhere in the lab. Rhona decided not to look for her. Chrissy knew where she was headed, anyway.

Bill was gowning up when Rhona arrived.

'I see you got a match on the mummy's prints?' Rhona said as she joined him.

'Dominic McGeehan. I went to visit him this morning. Alive and well.'

'*What?*'

'Or at least I went to visit the man who stole McGeehan's identity. He maintains he's Dominic's brother. According to him, Dominic moved to the States. The brother, Tony, had debts he couldn't pay here, so he became Dominic.'

'Is he in custody?'

'He got away from me. Played the oldest trick in the book – the "can I use the bathroom" one – and I fell for it.'

'You can't win them all,' said Rhona sympathetically.

'I'll try to remember that. As should you. Now, listen. I've seen CCTV footage from outside the Rosevale. Liam wasn't with Jude. That was Jason, the boy who works in the charity shop. They emerged from Rosevale Street together, parted outside the pub. Angus was lying. He'd hinted Jason had been in trouble before but was clean now. Probably the reason he spun me a tale.'

Rhona couldn't disguise her relief. 'Thank you.'

'Don't thank me. Thank DS Clark and the poor sod who watched a lifetime of CCTV footage.'

'You think this Jason might be involved in Jude's disappearance?'

'I've ordered for him to be brought in. We'll see what he has to say.'

'Any word from Petersson on the car?'

Bill shook his head. 'Let's hope there's something soon.'

The barbed wire had been removed, as had the plastic sheet. Rhona was keen to take a closer look at both of them. Most perpetrators had no idea the forensic tale a plastic sheet could tell.

Sinclair's clothing had been bagged for transfer to the forensic lab. Various items from his pockets were laid out nearby: a wallet and its contents; a mobile phone; a comb and a hairband, no doubt a spare for the ponytail he'd favoured.

The naked body lying on the slab looked gaunt, the exposed arms showing evidence of old needle tracks. Rhona recalled her meeting with the porter, his obvious agitation, the brassy glint of his eye. She'd assumed it had been just his reaction to the possibility of a freebie from someone he assumed was an escort. But now that she replayed the scene in her head it did seem possible Sinclair had been high on something. Hopefully the Tech department could find out who he'd called that night.

Bill, apparently thinking along the same lines, lifted the mobile with gloved hands and waggled it at Rhona.

'I'll see if the Tech guys can get us anything from this. Give me a ring when Sissons delivers his verdict,' he said.

Rhona didn't have long to wait.

Sissons had completed the preliminaries and was concentrating on the head wounds. The bullet's entrance and exit points had already been noted and discussed. The pathologist had made a point of noting the similarity between Brogan's gunshot wound and Sinclair's, indicating that both had been at point-blank range. The second wound above the left ear was now under scrutiny.

'I've seen one of these before. Made, I believe, by an electric drill.' Sissons had come to the same conclusion as Rhona. 'The last time it punctured the skull and damaged the brain. In this case, the drill hasn't perforated the bone, although it's been applied more than once.' He indicated two smaller marks close by. 'As a means of persuasion, perhaps?'

As Sissons set about measuring the indentations, Rhona excused herself and went to call Bill. When his mobile went to voicemail she left a brief message confirming the existence of three electric drill injuries to Sinclair's skull.

Chances were she would find trace evidence on the plastic sheeting of those responsible for preparing Sinclair for his watery grave, but based on the drill attack alone Bill would very soon be bringing Lang in for questioning.

Rhona tried Petersson next, anxious to know if he had made any progress on the car, but there was no answer from him. She had a choice; she could wait for the completion of the PM and transport the items and trace samples to the lab herself, or she could head back there now and call in on Petersson on the way.

Rhona decided on the latter.

On reaching Petersson's apartment block she pulled over on a yellow line and tried his number again. When the mobile went to voicemail she decided to park anyway, aware that when Petersson was engrossed online he didn't always pick up. She eventually found a space way past the bridge to the west of the Botanic Gardens and had to walk back. Ten minutes later she arrived at his main door to find someone had wedged it open with a door stop. Noises in the stairwell confirmed that a resident was either moving in or moving out.

Rhona ignored the buzzer and headed upstairs, passing a young man on his way down carrying a large box. He gave her a long-suffering look.

'Coming or going?' she said.

'Wish I knew.'

Rhona pulled the old-fashioned brass bell and waited, hearing its loud jangle echo through the flat. Nobody could miss that, she thought, even if they have earphones on.

After the second pull she decided to take a look through the letterbox. The hall was in semi-darkness. What little light there was filtered through to the hall from the south-facing bay window of the sitting room. At first Rhona could see nothing, then as her eyes became accustomed to the dimness, she thought she saw a movement near the kitchen door.

'Petersson,' she called out. 'Are you in there? It's me, Rhona.'

The shadow flickered then steadied.

'Petersson. Open this door,' she shouted, convinced now that someone was definitely in the flat.

A tall figure slowly emerged from the shadows and approached the door. Rhona stepped back, letting the letterbox snap shut. She watched as the door opened, at least as far as the door chain would allow.

'For God's sake, Petersson, it's me, Rhona,' she said exasperated.

'Dr Rhona MacLeod?' a clear female voice asked.

'Yes.'

The chain was disengaged and the door opened wide. In the doorway stood a young blond woman with very blue eyes. Her voice when she spoke had a distinctively Icelandic accent.

'I'm sorry. I had to be sure. Einar made me promise not to open the door to anyone but you.'

33

Everything came with a time frame. It was understandable, but enough to drive Bill mad.

'How soon?'

'It depends how damaged the mobile is.'

'What if I said someone's life depended on it?'

Sandy looked him in the eye. 'Is this anything to do with DS McNab?'

'It could be,' Bill lowered his voice, 'but it's not common knowledge.'

'I can make it first in the queue, although DI Slater won't be pleased. But then I trust you to find McNab more than I trust him.'

'You'll get back to me?'

'As soon as,' Sandy assured him. 'You got my message about the two voices on the recorder found in the cinema?'

'I did. Thanks.'

'Weird. I always knew twins sounded alike. I just never guessed how much. There's other stuff too. I found the Facebook page your private investigators set up. It looks like they made contact with someone who'd seen the girl at the Govanhill Picture House.'

'I know. They broke in and found a coat which might be the missing girl's.'

'Hey, they're way ahead of you. And me!'

'They've been told to stop.'

'And give the professionals a chance?' Sandy laughed. 'Maybe we should recruit them into the Force.'

Bill headed for his office. The incident room was quiet but the occupants looked as though they were working hard, or else they'd got the word that he was on his way. A sea of faces looked up on his entry. Bill knew they wanted to know if there was anything new on their missing colleague. He shook his head.

'Coffee, Sir?'

'I thought it wasn't your job to bring me coffee, Janice.'

'You look as though you could do with one, Sir.'

'Bring one for yourself. We need to talk.'

They sat down together, Bill leaving the coffee to one side to cool to its optimum temperature.

'A woman called,' DS Clark told him. 'Moira Cochrane?'

Bill slapped his forehead. 'I was supposed to meet her. I forgot all about it. I'll call her back.'

'And Jason Donald is in interview room six. I ran a check on him as requested.' She handed Bill a folder.

'Give me a quick précis, Detective Sergeant.'

'He was accused of sexual assault on a sixteen-year-old girl a year ago. The girl withdrew the charges before it reached court.'

Assuming Angus knew the boy's history, and he'd given the impression that he had, it wasn't surprising he didn't want Jason's name in the same sentence as Jude's. But if he was aware that there might be CCTV footage, why mention the girl's appearance outside the pub at all?

'Anything else I should know before I see him?'

'He appeared in front of the children's panel half a dozen times before he was sixteen.'

'Anything in the last year?'

'No. Clean as a whistle. His probation worker thinks he's turned a corner.'

'He turned a corner all right, walking right alongside our missing girl. How are the cinema searches going?'

'We have SOCO teams in the Olympia Bridgeton and the Govanhill Picture House.'

'That's it?'

'Three more tomorrow, Sir.'

'And what do we have on Dominic McGeehan?'

'He was an only child. Father's dead. His mother lives in Partick, not far from where he was found. Someone's been round there already to tell her. Mrs McGeehan suffers from Alzheimer's and has a daily carer. We're not sure if she understood the news.'

'But there definitely isn't a brother?'

'According to a neighbour who's known the family for years, Dominic was an only child. And a difficult one. He lived at home sporadically and gave his mother a lot of grief when he did.'

'We need to build up a picture of what Dominic was up to before he disappeared. His friends, work . . .' He was telling her things she already knew, so he changed tack. 'Was there anything in this man's flat that related to his real identity?'

'Everything was in Dominic McGeehan's name.'

'What about work?'

'Nothing.'

'What did the neighbours have to say?'

'Only knew him to nod to on the stairs.'

'Whatever happened to the old Glasgow, where the entire stair knew your business and was willing to talk about it?'

Janice couldn't answer that one.

'Women? Girlfriends?'

'Female visitors. Often and varied, apparently.' Janice raised an eyebrow. 'According to Ms Webster on the floor below.'

'Thank God for one nosy parker. Check out the city escort services. High class only.' Bill tried his coffee and found it cool enough to drink. 'He isn't a man who likes to rough it. He'll be spending, wherever he is. So we follow his cards, and hopefully his phone. Also he has a laptop, he took it with him when he went. So he's logging on from somewhere. What about prints?'

'They picked up some in the flat.'

'Let's hope he's on file, then.'

Jason looked younger than the last time Bill had seen him. Fear and worry usually aged people, but in some cases it made a suspect appear younger and more vulnerable.

When DS Clark set the tape running, Bill sat in silence. Jason's head was down, but with no Irn Bru can to fiddle with his hands were lost for something to do. Eventually he folded his arms.

'Tell me about Jude.'

'I never met her. I told you that already.'

'We both know that's not true, Jason.'

Perhaps it was the certainty in Bill's voice that caused Jason's head to rise a fraction. He peered at Bill through the hair.

'I never met her.'

Bill sighed and waited as though Jason would change his mind. When he didn't, Bill said, 'So how come you were caught on CCTV walking side by side from the back of the cinema?'

The head shot all the way up this time. 'Angus said—' Jason began, then stopped himself.

'Angus said what? To keep your mouth shut about that?' When Jason didn't answer, Bill continued, 'I take it Angus knows about Helen Craig?'

Jason blanched.

'I didn't do that,' he said, his voice choked.

'Do what?'

'What she said.'

'And what was that exactly?'

'I didn't rape her. She lied. She was drunk. She told the police later she'd made a mistake.'

'But you did have sex with her?'

'She wanted to. I didn't force her.'

Jason had retreated as far back in the seat as was possible.

'What about Jude?'

'What about her?'

'What did you do to her?'

'Nothing! I met her coming down the fire escape and asked her how she got on. She said she had some good photos. That's it.'

'That's not what it sounded like on CCTV.'

Jason looked stunned. 'There's no sound on those things.'

'Who says?' Bill watched his words sink in. The interchange between Jason and Jude had looked more than just casual, that much had been clear on the tape.

Jason seemed to be wrestling with something.

'OK,' he conceded. 'It was me that told her about the Rosevale. That's why she came.'

This was a bombshell Bill hadn't expected, although he tried not to let it show.

'So how did you two meet?'

'She contacted a website about old Glasgow cinemas. I answered her. Most people don't know about the Rosevale because it's got no frontage. I told her she should contact Carol and get in to see it.'

'You've been inside?'

'Lots of times, but don't tell Carol. I'll lose my job.'

'What about the body?'

Jason shook his head. 'I never knew about that.'

'Did Jude see it?'

'She said there was a bad smell in the projection room. She thought there might be a dead animal behind the wall.'

'That's all?'

Jason nodded.

'How come you have a key?'

'I made a copy of Carol's. Look, I wasn't doing anything bad. I just went up there sometimes.'

'Alone.'

Jason thought for a bit before he answered. 'Not always.'

'Who with?'

'A couple of girls. I showed them the foyer. Scared them a bit with ghost stories. We sat in the balcony in those—'

'Loveseats?'

'Yeah. Loveseats.'

'Did you take Jude to the loveseats?'

He shook his head. 'No way. She was weird.'

'Because she turned you down?'

'I never asked,' Jason protested.

'You spoke to her when she was in the projection room?'

'No, I waited for her round the side.'

'Where was she going when she left you?'

'A text came in when we were talking. She said she had to meet someone.'

'Did she say who?'

'Something to do with an old film. She seemed pretty excited about it.'

'Did she mention any other cinemas she'd visited?'

Jason shrugged. 'She'd photographed a few by the time she came here. She said this was her first back-court one.'

Bill let him go after that. He had nothing to hold him on, as in the last sighting of Jude she'd been walking away from Jason.

Bill took himself back to his office to mull over the interview. On paper Jason could be a prime suspect in Jude's disappearance. He'd already been accused of sexual assault and he had a key to the Rosevale. He'd taken girls there, and not to watch films. He'd parted company with Jude outside the pub, but that's not to say he hadn't met up with her later.

Then again, Jason had been the one to bring up the subject of reel-to-reel films, which weren't common knowledge. Maybe Jason was telling the truth and Jude had been going to meet a collector.

Bill realised he was going round in circles, and not just with Jude. Finding a live Dominic McGeehan had seemed like a breakthrough until he'd been stupid enough to let him walk away. And no matter which way he looked at it,

Bill couldn't shake off the feeling that the real Dominic's death and Jude's disappearance were somehow linked.

He checked his mobile and found Rhona's voicemail, the message she'd left coming as no great surprise. As soon as Rhona had mentioned the drill mark on Sinclair's skull, Bill had suspected Johnny Lang was mixed up in the night porter's death. Maybe in the Brogan killing too. Dispensing with irritants was the way Lang earned his money.

The post mortem would be over by now and no word yet from Petersson, which probably meant the Icelander had nothing to offer. He gave the number one last try. When it rang unanswered, Bill picked up the internal phone.

'I want Johnny Lang located and brought in, as quietly as possible.'

34

They'd left him alone for what seemed like hours. How many, he had no idea. In the constant dark and muffled silence all his attempts at measuring the passing of time had failed.

When he'd been picked up there had been just over a week to go to the court case. He'd been on the point of heading south before his crazy decision to visit Brogan to try to persuade the bastard to come onside.

What a fucking disaster that had turned out to be.

McNab shifted in the seat in an effort to ease the griping cramp in his legs and arms.

Maybe it was already too late. But then why was he still alive? To prolong the agony? To wring every last drop of pleasure from his torture, before he finally gave up the ghost? Or did it simply please Kalinin to know he was holding the chief prosecution witness, when he took to the stand himself?

McNab's ears picked up a sound and magnified it in the stillness. A mouse or a rat? He'd grown used to the skittering movements of their constant search for food. No doubt he would provide their main course soon enough.

For all he knew there might have been a dim light, but the swelling round his eyes following Solonik's last attack had rendered him almost blind.

I ought to be grateful to the bastard, he thought. At least he didn't scoop out my eyeballs and shove them down my throat, like he threatened to.

McNab shifted again, this time sending a searing pain up his spine to clamp his head. Fatigue had lessened the flow of adrenaline through his veins, which made the pain more intense. He drew himself upright and tried to focus on his anger. When Lang was in the room it was easy, as he had someone to direct his hatred at. When he was left alone for hours, despite his best efforts, the fire died down and despair began to creep in.

Even his loathing of Petersson had diminished, replaced by a need to work out why and when the journalist had betrayed him.

McNab was sure it had been from the very beginning. The moment the bullet had been pumped into his chest, Kalinin had wanted to know for sure that he was dead. Maybe Petersson had had no idea who he was working for when he set out to find out the truth. Or maybe he'd known all along.

And I made it easy for them.

He remembered Brogan that night, wanting so badly to come onside but so fearful of doing so. 'You don't fucking mess with the Russians,' Paddy had said, forgetting it was he who'd started that ball rolling. Poor Paddy had thought he was safe in Kalinin's arms. How wrong he was.

And so was Petersson.

An investigative journalist in the pay of a Russian magnate. Ingenious. He would take a bet that the authorities would need to take a very close look at Petersson's work before they discovered it all benefited Kalinin one way or another.

And what about Slater? Where did he fit in? Was he the mole that fed Petersson his inside information, or was he in direct contact with the Russian? If Slater hadn't released Kalinin that night, if he'd even called to warn McNab . . .

I would never have been at the Poker Club. I would never have been shot. None of this would have happened.

Suddenly the rodents skittered away, denied their meal, scared off by the clang of a door and the clip of footsteps on the concrete floor.

'Hello, DS McNab,' said a voice he recognised.

Petersson.

35

'OK, I've checked and re-checked her Facebook page. No sign of a reel-to-reel contact there so he must have got in touch some other way, probably by email. Jude has a Hotmail account, but I need to know her password to access it.' Ben looked expectantly at Liam.

'I don't know. It could be anything.'

'True, but we might be able to figure it out.'

'How?'

'Most people use a word they'll remember easily. I bet yours is something to do with physics.'

Liam's mouth fell open.

'Knew it,' Ben said triumphantly. 'Einstein?'

Unnerved, Liam shook his head.

'But close?'

He couldn't deny it.

'Right. Jude likes films, photography, sci-fi. What d'you think?' Ben said.

'You're her sci-fi friend.'

His accusing tone was lost on Ben. 'Her favourite sci-fi movie is *Blade Runner*. She might have used one of the main character names.' Ben tried typing in a few one after the other – *Deckard, Pris, Rachael, Tyrell, Kowalski, Zhora* – with no luck. 'I would have chosen . . .' He typed in *Skin-job*. It didn't work either.

'This is hopeless,' Liam said.

Ben ignored him. 'You're advised to stick a number in there somewhere. Most people tag it on at the end. The simplest is a one.'

The small sound of surprise from Liam brought his head round. 'Einstein 1, is it?'

'Not exactly.'

'If I get it will you buy me a pint?'

'We're supposed to be finding Jude's password.'

'If I find hers will you buy me a pint?'

'I'll buy you two.'

'You're on.' Ben gave him a pointed look. 'I'll give you a shout when I have something.'

Dismissed, Liam retreated to his room. Ben was better left alone to get on with it. When he was about, Ben spent half his time explaining what he was doing.

Liam considered his next move. He should really call DI Wilson and tell him what Aurora had said. He pulled out his mobile, then hesitated. He'd been told to stay out of it. If he called, it would be obvious he wasn't doing that. Besides, the police were the investigators, not him, and they had an entire IT department to figure out what Ben was doing on his own.

He decided to call Aurora instead.

She answered right away. 'Liam? Has something happened?'

'We might be able to access Jude's emails.'

'That's great. D'you want to meet up?'

'I could come by the halls.'

'No. Let's meet at the Driftwood at Charing Cross in half an hour? There's something I'd like to run past you too.'

Liam rang off feeling a little guilty. Jude was missing and he was practically going on a date with her friend. It shouldn't feel like that, he told himself. Jude had never shown any interest in him other than as a friend, and she didn't even do friendship all that well. It had taken a lot of effort on his part to reach that status.

Liam knocked on his housemate's door and told him he was headed out and to text him if anything came up. There was a muttered affirmative from an obviously engrossed Ben.

It was raining. Heavily persistent, it had penetrated his jacket before he reached Charing Cross. The Driftwood was a café-bar, popular with students, serving coffee, drinks and mostly Mexican food. He'd been before but only once or twice.

Aurora had got there before him although it was difficult to see her in the low lighting. She spotted him first. As he walked towards her, he saw the anxious expression on her face.

'What's up?'

'Sit down. They'll come over. Then we'll talk.'

Once they had their coffees, Aurora said, 'Look, I'm just going to say it. Sally Murphy, a girl that used to be in halls with us, has just told me Charlie tried it on with her more than once. Well, more than tried it on – he scared her quite badly. She moved out of the halls after he started visiting at odd hours, using his pass key to get into her room.'

Liam's mouth dropped open.

'But . . . he seems so nice.'

'Yes, I couldn't believe it either.'

'She must have been mistaken?'

'She swore it was true. She left the halls because of it.'

'But wardens are vetted, aren't they?'

'It's not a school. Everyone living there's an adult.'

'It never happened to you?' asked Liam.

She shook her head.

'What if we tell the police and it turns out to be a lie?'

'And what if it's true and I *did* hear his voice that night?' Aurora replied.

'But that was after Jude disappeared, and we know now she was going to meet the reel-to-reel guy.'

Aurora put her head in her hands. Clearly she was struggling with this as much as he was. Charlie, a sexual predator?

'Why didn't she say something before now? Why did she just leave?'

'She didn't think anyone would believe her. Look at us – we keep saying maybe it's a lie. But then she heard about Jude and started to worry.'

'Even if Charlie did harass this Sally, that doesn't mean he had anything to do with Jude disappearing.'

'You're sure about that?' Aurora said.

Liam didn't feel sure of anything.

He walked Aurora back to the halls. The rain continued to fall, making the pavements slick and greasy. His mind went once more to Jude, imagining her lying somewhere in the rain, somewhere they would never find her. The thought made him feel sick.

'I'm going to talk to Charlie,' he said.

'Is that wise?'

'He doesn't know that we know about Sally, so he won't be suspicious.'

Aurora gave him a long hard look. 'I'm not sure you're a good enough liar. Your face might give something away.'

'I can lie if I have to,' he protested.

'Or I could speak to him,' she offered. 'Maybe mention I heard a man's voice that night, see what he says.'

'No.' Liam didn't want that. He still couldn't imagine Charlie in his new role, but just in case. 'Is he on duty?'

'Yes, that's why I came out to meet you,' she said.

They parted before they reached the building. Aurora went in first, agreeing that it was better if Charlie didn't know there had been any communication between them.

Despite his insistence that he do it himself Liam felt awkward as he approached the old man, but the welcome he got was as cheery as ever.

'Any news, lad?'

'Not really.'

Charlie cocked his head on one side. 'What d'you mean, not really?'

Liam tried to look worried, which wasn't hard. 'I think Jude might have gone to meet someone that night. Someone who collected old films.'

'Really?' Charlie looked interested. 'After she left the cinema?'

Liam nodded, not looking him in the eye.

'You think that might have been the bastard that broke into the lassie's room and took the laptop and the film?'

Liam shrugged. 'Maybe.'

He found himself reading something into every intonation in Charlie's voice and every twitch of his facial muscles.

If Charlie had harmed Jude, wouldn't it suit him down to the ground if the police were chasing after some reel-to-reel collector?

'D'you know who this guy is?' Charlie said.

'I didn't say it was a guy.'

Charlie gave him a sharp look. 'No, but it's usually men who spend their time collecting stuff like that, isn't it? I just assumed.'

Liam nodded. 'I wondered if Jude mentioned anything to you about him?'

'Can't say she did. Have you told the police about this?'

'Not yet,' Liam said, sheepishly. 'They said not to interfere any more.'

Charlie frowned sympathetically. 'They don't appreciate how worried you are, son. So, what now?'

'We're trying to trace him.'

Charlie seemed impressed. 'Really? Any luck so far?'

'My friend Ben's a computer geek,' Liam said, as if that answered the question.

'Well, good on you, son. You'll let me know if you find out anything?'

'Sure, Charlie.'

Liam felt the man's eyes follow him to the door, or imagined he did. During their conversation a frightening thought had occurred: the police gave nothing away, Rhona was testament to that, but he himself had shared everything with Charlie from the very beginning, every little detail of his search for Jude.

Liam waited until he was well out of sight of the building before calling Aurora.

'I told him about the reel-to-reel guy.'

'And?'

'He was really interested. Wished me good luck.'

'But did he behave oddly?'

'I'm beginning to think everyone's behaving oddly. I'm not cut out for this game. I think we should call that detective and tell him everything.' As he said this a message arrived from Ben. 'Wait a minute.' Hoping he wouldn't cut her off, Liam took his phone away from his ear to open it, quickly scanned it and returned to the call. 'Ben says he's found him. He's found the reel-to-reel collector.'

36

The young woman shut the door quickly and ushered Rhona through to the kitchen.

'Would you like some coffee?'

Rhona nodded distractedly. This must be who Petersson had referred to at their meeting. The person he hoped Kalinin didn't know about. Rhona had assumed he'd been talking about a lover, but not one in her early twenties.

The woman filled two mugs. 'Milk?'

'No, just black, thanks.'

She brought the coffee to the table and gestured that Rhona should sit down. She was glad to. Her legs felt like water. She'd primed herself to interrogate Petersson, never an easy task. Now she had to deal with his lover.

'I think you didn't expect me to be here,' said the girl.

'I'm sorry. Who are you exactly?' The question had to be asked.

'Einar hasn't told you?'

'He said there was someone he loved and was worried about.'

A small smile played on the girl's lips. 'Pabbi fusses a lot.'

'Pabbi?'

'My father.'

'Einar's your father? I thought . . .'

'That I was his girlfriend?' The girl laughed wryly. 'I'd be a bit young for him! Don't worry, you're not the first woman to think he was cheating on her with me.'

'Einar and I aren't in a relationship,' Rhona said firmly.

'Really? That's a pity. He obviously likes you a great deal or he wouldn't have allowed you to meet me.'

'Have you been here long?'

'I arrived unexpectedly yesterday. My father wasn't pleased.'

Which helped explain Petersson's uncharacteristic emotional state that morning.

'He's working on a difficult case.'

'My father is *always* working on a difficult case. And these cases mean that we can't be seen together. In Iceland, in Scotland, in London, wherever. So I stay indoors and I wait for him to return.' She observed Rhona. 'The interesting thing this time is that he has allowed me to meet you.' She held out her hand, 'My name is Brynja.'

'And I'm Rhona, but you know that already.' They smiled at each other.

'I know much more than your name,' she continued, more serious now. 'I know that you are a forensic expert. That you have a teenage son called Liam. That a friend and colleague of yours is missing and my pabbi believes that the Russian he investigates is involved in his kidnap.'

Rhona wasn't sure she was comfortable with Petersson sharing so much information with his daughter.

Brynja, perhaps sensing this, said, 'He tells me this to make sure I heed his warnings and stay inside.'

'He talks to you about Nikolai Kalinin?'

'So that's his name.' The girl looked thoughtful. 'I know he has been following this man for a long time.'

'You said your father suspected I might come here?'

'He did, and he left you a message.' Brynja composed herself as though reciting something she'd learned by heart.

'William McCartney is alive and will be home soon.'

Rhona's heart leapt. 'You're sure of that?'

'Yes.'

'Did he say anything about a man called Johnny Lang?'

Brynja shook her head. 'No. That's all.'

It always had to be cloak and dagger with Petersson. Why not phone her and tell her himself? Because he knew she would ask questions. And he obviously didn't want to have to answer them. Petersson might pretend to be working in a team but he never had been, and never would. That much was obvious.

'You're annoyed with him?'

'It would have saved time and worry if he'd just called me.'

'Maybe he was afraid the call might be intercepted?' Rhona rolled her eyes, and Brynja must have caught her, because she continued: 'Since my mother was killed he has become even more paranoid and secretive about his work.'

'What happened to your mother?'

'A car accident two years ago. We were living in Prague at the time. The road was icy. The police told us a lorry skidded and hit her car. My mother sustained multiple injuries and died before she reached hospital.' She said the words as though they too had been repeated many times.

'I'm sorry to hear that.' Rhona waited a moment before asking, 'Did Einar say when he would be back?'

'Not before I leave.'

'You're leaving tonight?'

'I'm booked on the last flight to London. I stay overnight there before flying to Switzerland tomorrow. Pabbi made the arrangements.'

Petersson definitely didn't want his daughter around.

They said their goodbyes in the hall.

'It was very nice to meet you. I hope we meet again soon.' Brynja seemed to mean it.

'I hope so too.'

The girl opened the front door just wide enough for Rhona to slip through, then she heard the chain and lock being fastened behind her. Brynja might scoff at her father's fears, but she was taking them seriously.

The street door was still wedged open, but there was no sign of the young man she'd seen earlier. Rhona freed the door and closed it firmly behind her.

On her way back to the car she thought about Petersson, man of secrets. Hiding not a lover, but a daughter. Using Brynja to signal two things to her: that his warnings about Kalinin should be taken seriously and, more importantly, that a man who would trust Rhona with his daughter was a man to be trusted himself.

Rhona tried Bill before driving back to the lab to fill Chrissy in on what she'd learned. When it went to voicemail, she decided not to leave a message. This was something better said in person.

37

'He's not a nice man. I told my sister that, but there you go, she needs the money.' Moira topped up both their cups from the teapot.

Behind Bill a budgie chirped in its cage. The sound reminded him of his childhood. Back then everyone had a budgie and most of them were called Joey, regardless of their sex.

'You don't mind Bluey?' Moira said.

Not a Joey this time, then. 'Not at all. I had a budgie when I was a boy.'

She nodded approvingly.

'You were saying about Mr Nelson,' Bill prompted her.

'There's a room he keeps locked. I thought at first it was full of stuff he'd nicked from the charity shop. Like that painting of the sailing ships.'

'But it wasn't?' Bill urged her on.

'No. I wasn't allowed to clean in there. Neither is Peggy. But he left it unlocked one day, so I had a look inside.'

'And?'

'It was full of books and old films.'

'Films?'

'Stacks of them. Sixteen millimetre and eight millimetre like the ones we had for the first movie camera we bought. A couple of old-fashioned projectors too. One of them big and professional looking. I bet he took that one from the Rosevale,' she finished, triumphantly.

Bill felt a flash of hope he didn't dare acknowledge. 'You didn't happen to notice what kind of films?'

Just the question Moira had been waiting for. 'I never saw one running, mind, but some of the titles suggested they were, you know, sexual. And I did take a look at a couple of the books. Photographs of men mostly, with *things* being done to them.' Moira emphasised the word 'things' and gave Bill a knowing look. 'I'm no prude, Inspector. Live and let live is what I say, but sex is one thing, violence another.'

'The photos depicted sexual violence?'

She nodded. 'Maybe those men wanted those things done to them, but I can't believe the man in that cinema asked to be walled up, do you?'

'No, I don't.'

'If you're planning on taking a look, the room's off his bedroom. Peggy says he keeps a laptop locked in there when he hasn't got it away with him on the yacht.'

'Have you any idea where he moors the yacht?'

'When I was cleaning for him, he kept it at Helensburgh. Peggy thinks it's still there. It's called "The Saucy Sailor".'

'You've been very helpful, Mrs Cochrane.'

'Moira. Everyone calls me Moira, except his Lordship.'

The word 'Lordship' reminded Bill of something else he wanted to ask. 'Peggy said Mr Nelson plays golf with a Lord sometimes. You don't happen to know who that is?'

'He used to mention a "Sir" now and again. As if I'd be impressed.'

'Can you recall the name?'

She thought for a minute. 'I've never been very good at names and it's getting worse the older I get. If it comes back to me, I'll give you a call.'

Moira escorted him into the hall, the budgie's loud chirps following them.

'Bluey doesn't like being left on his own,' she said. 'I usually leave the television on for him when I go out.'

When they parted, she wished Bill good luck. 'I never liked the uppity old bugger, but I hope he didn't have anything to do with that body.'

As he left, Bill considered his next move. His first instinct was to use the element of surprise, head for Nelson's flat and ask to see the room Moira had spoken about.

Nelson could of course refuse if he arrived without a search warrant. And getting one would take time.

Another possibility had occurred by the time he'd reached the car. What if Nelson had already taken fright and emptied the flat of anything incriminating? After all, it had been twenty-four hours since Bill had first interviewed the man.

Bill made a quick phone call, then started the engine. He wanted to hear what his Lordship had to say.

Nelson's flat was in darkness. It looked as though the front rooms, at least, were unoccupied. Bill tried the buzzer anyway, and was surprised when it was answered.

'Mr Nelson? It's Detective Inspector Wilson. May I come up?'

'It's a little late for visitors.'

'I was on my way home and took a chance you might be available. If you are, that would be very helpful.'

A studied silence followed, before Nelson decided to play the role of obliging citizen.

'Of course, come on up.' He released the door.

When Bill reached the landing he found Mr Nelson waiting for him there.

'I was shut away in my study. You're lucky I heard the buzzer.'

'Working on something nautical?'

'No, my other hobby. Old film. I run a website for enthusiasts. I picked up a box of sixteen millimetre reels at a car-boot sale last Saturday. No titles, so I've been checking them out.'

'Anything interesting?'

'A fascinating home video of a family in Germany in the lead-up to the war. It looks like they're having a garden party, then suddenly they all line up and give a Nazi salute. Quite unnerving.'

'What sort of projector do you use?'

'I've a couple of makes. You're interested in these things yourself, Detective Inspector?'

'My father was an enthusiast,' Bill lied.

'Well, come through and take a look. My study's a former dressing room, so I'm afraid you have to go through my bedroom to get to it.'

The room was compact and well organised, with two shelved walls. One held books, the other was carefully stacked with film reels and cassettes. The remaining wall, facing the door, provided the screen. The projector was still running, throwing out a grainy image of an extended family in a garden in summer, at least four generations gathered together.

'They must have been wealthy for the time – there's a swimming pool in the background,' said Nelson. 'By their looks and colouring I think this might be a Jewish family, and in saluting they were mocking the Fascists. Sadly, they had no idea what was in store for them.' He threw a switch and the crackling reel came to a halt. 'Now, what did you want to talk to me about?'

For the second time in a couple of hours, Bill was surprised. He'd expected Nelson to be evasive at least, at worst downright hostile, yet here he was being invited into the secret room and shown its hoard.

'I came because I wanted to ask you about this.' He gestured at the film cans.

'Really? How did you know I was a collector?'

'Your former cleaner mentioned it.'

'You've spoken to Mrs Cochrane?' Nelson looked slightly unnerved for a second. 'I had to ask that woman to leave my employment, I'm afraid. I had reason to believe she was pilfering.'

'But you employ her sister now?'

'Yes. But I don't give her a key, so I'm always in the house when she's here.' He scrutinised Bill. 'But what have old films to do with your murder case?'

Bill didn't answer. He had stepped over to study the spines of Nelson's books. At first glance there were various tomes on films and film making, nothing along the lines of Moira's discovery.

'Are you looking for anything in particular?' Nelson enquired.

The exaggerated nonchalance in his tone was unmistakable. In an instant Bill could tell there was a charade being played out here; Nelson had removed everything incriminating from this room, probably immediately after Bill had been shown the door on his previous visit. No wonder Peggy had been swiftly ejected shortly after him on the excuse that Nelson was off to play golf with a Lord.

'Did a Jude Evans ever get in touch with you online, in your capacity as a film collector?' he asked.

'Jude. Is that a girl's name?'

'Yes, it is.'

'And you think this Jude may have contacted me about what, exactly?' His voice sounded plausibly concerned.

'Reel-to-reel films.'

'I get a great many enquiries. I certainly don't remember the name.'

'We ran several televised requests for information about her. She's been missing since she visited the Rosevale a week ago.' *As well you know*, Bill thought.

'I must have missed those. I don't watch the TV much.'

'Jude had in her possession a sixteen millimetre film which she found in the Olympia Bridgeton. She'd taken photo shots of the frames.' Bill stopped at that point, awaiting Nelson's reaction.

The other man affected puzzlement. 'And what has this film to do with her disappearance?'

'The digital images show the film depicted violent sexual acts.'

'Really?'

'Have you ever come across any films of that nature?'

Nelson arched an eyebrow. 'Pornography, violent or

otherwise, isn't a new invention, Detective Inspector. It's been depicted in art and film since the beginning of time.'

Bill didn't like being lectured by someone he'd decided was a sanctimonious git, and a seasoned liar to boot. He decided he'd been nice long enough.

'Have you any such films in your possession?'

'No, I do not.'

'And have you ever met or talked with Jude Evans?'

'Not to my knowledge, no, and I object to being inter-rogated in this manner about someone I've never met.'

'I'd like to take a proper look through your collection.'

'Help yourself,' Nelson said, almost triumphantly. 'I have nothing to hide.'

Bill's mobile rang and he answered it.

'Nice timing, DS Clark.' Bill spoke loud enough for Nelson to hear. 'You have an officer in place? And "The Saucy Sailor"? Secured. Well done. I'll head down first thing.'

Nelson's face had turned a ghastly puce. 'You've boarded my *yacht*?'

'Not yet, but I intend to once I have my warrant. Until then the boat is off limits. To everyone. I assume that's where your laptop is?'

Nelson's shocked expression confirmed this to be the case.

'I have friends in high places, Detective Inspector, and I intend reporting you for harassment.'

'To your golfing partner, no doubt?'

'Lord Dalrymple also plays golf with your Superintendent,' Nelson said grandly.

Bill shook his head. 'What is it about men and balls?'

* * *

Once inside the car, Bill allowed himself a brief moment to enjoy his victory before he phoned home to apologise for missing his tea again.

'You sound pleased,' Margaret said. 'A breakthrough?'

Bill had to admit it was less than that. 'A small step forward.'

'Better that than a step back.'

As he turned on the ignition, his mobile rang again. Bill thought about letting it go, then saw the caller's name.

'Rhona? I'm just on my way home.'

'Then I'm glad I caught you.'

'What's up?'

'I've just been at Peterssons' flat. His grown-up daughter's there. She arrived unexpectedly, which he wasn't pleased about. He booked her on a plane to London tonight, then on to Switzerland. He asked her to open the door to no one but me.'

Bill, exhaled heavily. 'His daughter? So that's who he was talking about. Is there a mother?'

'She died in a car accident two years ago in Prague.' Rhona paused significantly. 'Brynja said, "The police *told us* a lorry skidded and hit her car," as though it might not be true.'

'You don't think Petersson suspects she was killed on purpose?'

'According to Brynja he's been paranoid about her safety ever since. He also left a message with Brynja for me – apparently William McCartney is alive and coming home soon.'

'He's located McNab?' said Bill.

'It sounds like it.'

'That's good, isn't it?'

'It is if it's true.'

'Nothing more than that?'

'No. I can't reach him by phone and Brynja doesn't expect him back before she leaves.'

'I've ordered Lang brought in.'

'You had to,' Rhona said.

'Let's hope whatever Petersson's up to, it happens before Kalinin gets wind we're after Lang. Now, on the cinema case, I've just finished talking to the former manager of the charity shop. According to his previous cleaner, he's a porn-film collector. I suspect he's shifted the incriminating stuff to his yacht at Helensburgh. I'll take a look tomorrow. He was dropping a certain name quite heavily when he heard about the warrant to search it.'

'Whose?'

'Lord James Dalrymple. Apparently they're golfing partners.'

'I can't imagine Dalrymple playing golf with anyone outside his social sphere.'

'Maybe they do business together?'

'What, porn business?'

'My thoughts exactly.'

The earlier sense of triumph had gone, replaced by something Bill could only describe as dread. He'd felt futile in the Kalinin case from the beginning. Trying to pursue it alone hadn't made that any better.

Trust me, Slater had said, and for once had looked as

though he meant it. Maybe he should have done just that? What if by interfering he'd made the situation worse for his team? All his instincts told Bill that they were fast approaching the crunch point and he could do nothing to prevent it.

38

Ben sat to one side to let Liam view the screen. 'She used "Bladerunner" and added eighty-two to the end. The year the film was released.'

'No emails have been opened since the night she disappeared,' Liam said quietly.

Ben was opening the two messages, checking them. 'They're just spam.'

'Jude would have deleted those. You know she would.'

As far as Liam was concerned, seeing the unopened messages had just confirmed what he already knew.

'Look, there's one that might be something.' Ben scrolled to an older message from info@reelcinemas.com, one that had been opened.

Thank you for getting in touch about the film you discovered in the Olympia Bridgeton. Happy to meet up and chat about it. What about Tues? Jim

'Did she answer this Jim?' Liam said.

Ben was investigating the sent box.

'Here it is.' Ben read it out. 'Meet you at the Lyceum at six – Jude.'

'She was supposed to meet me at seven,' Liam reminded him.

'So, she planned to fit this in beforehand. Where's the Lyceum?'

Liam's head was spinning. 'I have no idea.'

'No worries.'

Ben brought up a copy of Jude's memory stick. They both scanned the folder names.

Liam spotted it first. 'There it is. The Govan Lyceum. Govan's just across the river from Partick. What do you want to do?'

Ben was thinking. 'We could send Jim an email from Jude, asking him to meet her tonight.'

'But what if he has anything to do with her disappearance?'

'My guess is he'll get back to us, assuming we're the police, if only to appear innocent.'

'OK, let's do it.'

That done, they adjourned to the pub, taking Ben's laptop with them. Liam's state of mind was seesawing between despair that nothing would come of it and fearful anticipation that something might. He was also secretly relieved that their latest lead didn't involve Charlie.

While they drank their pints, Liam told Ben about Aurora's revelation.

Ben looked suitably stunned. 'You said he was a nice old guy.'

'I thought he was,' Liam said.

'What did Jude think?'

'She liked him too.'

'Well then, we don't know what to think, do we? I guess we have no way of knowing if it's relevant yet. Anyway, if we get a response from this Jim, where do you want to meet? Outside the Lyceum?'

'Isn't that too obvious?' Liam said.

'Not if he's innocent. And if he's guilty, he'll want to know if it was the police who sent him the email. Are their IT guys following this up?'

'*I* don't know. I'm not supposed to be involved, remember?' grumbled Liam.

Ben looked thoughtful. 'If we are on the right track, maybe we should let Rhona in on it?'

Liam lifted his pint and took a mouthful, hoping his silence was answer enough.

They were on their second pint when the laptop pinged to indicate incoming mail.

'Bingo.' Ben turned the screen so Liam could read it.
Where and when?

Ben typed a reply: *Tonight Govan Lyceum?*

Seconds later the sender was back: *See you in half an hour.*

'Shit!' Liam hissed.

Ben looked equally rattled.

'What do we do when he turns up?' Liam said.

'We take his photo from a distance, but we don't approach unless agreed.' Ben was already on his feet, downing the remainder of his beer.

Neither of them spoke on their way to the underground at Kelvinbridge. Liam, already regretting their decision, didn't dare voice his concerns. It was as though, having bought into this, there was no going back. They were meddling, he knew that. And maybe they would screw everything up. For Jude, for Rhona, for the police. Sherlock and Watson? What the hell were they thinking? Ben seemed equally preoccupied but also determined.

Well past the evening rush hour, the train was relatively

quiet. By the time it reached Partick, the last stop north of the river, the only people sharing their carriage were a young woman who looked as though she was at the end of a long hard day and an elderly man. Neither paid them any heed.

They emerged from the station to find themselves on a side street yards away from Govan Road.

'We never checked how we get to the Lyceum from here,' Liam said.

'The address is 908 Govan Road.'

'We could set off in the wrong direction.'

'We'll ask someone.' The girl from the train was passing as Ben spoke so he smiled at her and opened his mouth to ask, but she walked straight past. The elderly man appeared behind.

'What is it you want to know, son?'

'Which way do we go for the Govan Lyceum?'

'The Lyceum, eh? Why d'you want to go there? The place's been closed for years.'

'We're meeting someone.'

'Well, you want to walk west. You'll pass Govan Old Parish Church halfway. Now *that* is a famous place. We get a lot of folk coming off the subway looking for the church. Further along is the Lyceum, but as I said, it's all boarded up.' He gave them a studied look. 'Watch yourselves at this time of night, lads. Govan isn't what it used to be.'

'Thanks, we appreciate your help,' Liam said.

The man nodded and walked on.

'So we have to watch our backs as well?' Liam said.

'Calm down, bro. I have eyes in the back of my head.'

The warning proved unnecessary, the main street being pretty well deserted. They passed a smart old pub called The Brechin, with the statutory smoking huddle outside the door. Apart from that and a takeaway place, everything was closed.

They were opposite the Old Parish Church now. It stood tall, its back to the river, at the rear of a shadowy walled graveyard. As they passed, a noisy group of lads approached on that side of the road. They were carrying various bottles and cans, and obviously looking for somewhere to drink them.

Ben upped his pace, Liam following suit, but the boys were too intent on their own plans to notice them. When the gang reached the church gate they turned and headed inside, disappearing into the gloom, whooping and shouting enough to wake the dead.

Seconds later Ben ground to an abrupt halt and Liam collided with him. 'There it is.'

The building on the opposite corner, with its distinctive curved frontage and five tall windows, was easily recognisable as the Lyceum.

'There's no one there,' Liam said.

But Ben had already moved on, taking a left turn up a narrow side street. Liam followed.

'We can watch from here.'

They stood in the darkness of a doorway, sheltering from the rain, Liam conscious that the warmth and light of The Brechin was only yards away. He checked his watch. Forty minutes since they'd sent the email.

'Maybe he won't show,' he said hopefully.

'*They* just have.' Ben eased a shoulder out of the alleyway and used his mobile to take a shot of the two elderly men who now stood in the shelter of the cinema entrance.

'There's two of them.'

'Well, there's two of us,' Ben said. 'And they don't look scary. What d'you say we head across?' He set off without waiting for an answer.

Two virtually identical faces watched their approach with some concern. Liam suddenly realised that they were the ones that probably looked threatening.

Sensing this, Ben called out, 'Hi. Is one of you Jim?'

One of the men stepped forward. 'I'm Jim, this is my brother John.'

'We emailed you about meeting up,' Ben said.

'The message came from Jude Evans,' Jim said puzzled.

'We're friends of hers.'

'Where is Jude?'

'That's what we wanted to talk to you about,' Liam decided to be blunt. 'Jude's gone missing.'

'Missing?' Both men spoke at the same time, looking identically surprised.

'She hasn't been seen since Tuesday.'

'We were supposed to meet her here last Tuesday evening but she never turned up,' said John.

'Why don't we head for the pub,' Liam suggested. 'We can talk there.'

The men glanced at one another, then Jim answered. 'Yes, let's do that.'

They set off across the road in the direction of The Brechin, Ben and Liam following.

'It's like talking to one person,' Ben whispered under his breath.

'That recording Jude made. It sounded just like them.'

'You're right. It did.'

The twins entered as though they were familiar with the place and made their way to the bar.

'Have you got any money?' asked Ben.

Liam fished fruitlessly in his pocket. 'No, but I can use my card.' He turned to the twins. 'The drinks are on us. What can we get for you?'

While Liam and Ben waited at the counter, the twins found an empty table. Liam could see them hunched there, talking together, concerned looks on their faces.

'I don't think they knew about Jude.'

'Or they'd already discussed how they were going to play it,' Ben said.

'But they're harmless.'

'They *look* harmless. That's a different thing, mate.'

Liam paid for the drinks and carried them over. Pints for him and Ben, orange juice for the twins. Once seated, they all formally introduced themselves.

'Now,' Jim said. 'What's this about Jude?'

'She was supposed to meet me at seven last Tuesday after she photographed the Rosevale cinema in Partick. She didn't turn up,' Liam told him.

'We had arranged to meet her at six outside the Lyceum. She didn't show there either. We assumed she would email later to explain.'

'But she didn't?'

'No.'

'Did she have a mobile contact for you?'

They shook their heads in unison. 'We only communicated via the website,' said John.

'And she never got in touch again?' Liam said.

'Not until tonight. And that was you, it turns out.'

'When did she first make contact?'

'About a month ago. She said she was doing a project on old cinemas. My brother and I are former projectionists. We met and she recorded us talking about our work.'

'We heard that,' Ben said. 'It sounded like one person. We didn't realise there were two of you.'

'Did Jude ever mention an old film she'd found?' asked Liam.

'Yes, that was the reason she asked to meet up at the Lyceum,' said Jim.

'Did she tell you anything about the film?'

'Just that she wanted to date it and thought we might be able to help.'

It all fits, Liam thought. These guys are bona fide.

'Do you think this film has something to do with Jude's disappearance?' asked Jim.

'It was stolen from her room, along with her laptop, the night after she disappeared.'

'There is a good market for old films, particularly rare footage. Do you know what the subject was?'

The boys exchanged looks.

'We only saw the first few frames,' Liam explained. 'It was pretty violent gay porn.'

The men's shock was obvious. This wasn't what they'd expected.

'Tell them the rest,' Ben urged him.

'When Jude didn't appear I started to worry that she might be lying hurt in the Rosevale. Next day I went to the shop and asked to look in the cinema. That's when we found the body.' Now the brothers looked utterly astounded. 'You must have heard about it on the news?'

'We don't listen to the news,' Jim said. 'Was this death suspicious?'

'That's just it. The papers are hinting at some sort of sexual ritual like we saw in the film.'

'And you think Jude discovered this body?'

'We don't know for sure. It was hidden behind a wall.'

'Did the police say how long the body has been there?'

'A long time.'

'I think we should talk to the police about this.'

'Why?'

'When we were starting out as projectionists, there were rumours about a private club showing films like the one you describe. A young colleague told us about it.'

'Is this colleague still around?'

'He may be. We haven't seen him in years.'

'It's a possible lead on the film, at least,' Ben said.

'But it doesn't help us to find Jude.'

The four parted company outside the pub, the twins heading westward along Govan Road. Liam had considered asking them not to mention this meeting, but had decided not to. Once the twins talked to the police all of this would come out anyway, including the fact that he and Ben had not heeded Rhona's instructions to stop interfering and leave it to the police.

Both of them were silent during the return journey. Even ebullient Ben was clean out of conversation. They'd reached the end of the road, Liam realised now; there was nowhere else to go in their search for Jude.

39

Rhona locked the car with the remote and contemplated what she might find to eat at home. If her memory served her right, nothing. She swithered between phoning out for a pizza or walking to the nearest takeaway.

She finally settled on checking out the various delivery menus by the phone in the kitchen, although she doubted any of them would offer fresh pasta with black olives and anchovies.

The sound of her key in the lock brought Tom rushing to greet her, winding his way through her legs as she made her way to the kitchen. Rifling through the menus, she finally decided on Chinese. She called and ordered the first item she recognised on the long list, then headed for the shower.

When the delivery boy arrived, she heaped the entire contents of the carton on to a plate and carried it through to the living room, taking her mobile with her. She began her meal but abandoned it as soon as her initial craving was satisfied. Despite the spicy flavours, it tasted nowhere near as good as the fresh pasta of the previous evening. She remembered her conversation with Sean, and resolved to get in touch with Liam again.

Rhona rose and switched on the fire, then fetched the duvet from the bedroom. Bed would be more comfortable, but she might fall into a deep sleep and miss the mobile if it rang.

She did doze, but fitfully, her dreams peppered with vivid disturbing images from the past. In the nightmare she saw herself entering that hideous little room where the rent boy had died, saw his body lying face down on the blood-splattered cover, blond hair masking his face.

Just as before, she reached out and rolled the body back to reveal the boy's mutilated genitals. Then the image blurred and changed, and now the body was dry and blackened, the desiccated face masked by dirty dark blond hair and the remains of the penis shrivelled and torn inside a metal ring.

Rhona woke suddenly and sat upright, her mind racing. A violent sexual death, a leather collar, asphyxiation. Trademarks she recognised from the rent-boy case. They had no way of knowing how long Gavin MacLean, the perpetrator, had been operating by the time they'd caught up with him. Could the body in the cinema be another of his victims, undiscovered for close to a decade?

The more Rhona considered the proposition, the more the similarities with the current case seemed apparent. She couldn't believe she hadn't thought of it before, but it was a depressing truth that she saw so much violence day to day that she preferred to forget the details of each case once it seemed to be over. And now Bill had a possible link between the former manager of the charity shop and Dalrymple, who had been implicated in the rent-boy case but slipped through the net thanks to his connections.

She rose and went to make a pot of coffee. Sleep wasn't a possibility now. Not until she looked over her evidence from the Rosevale and carefully considered her latest leap of deduction.

She finally snatched a couple of hours' sleep before dawn. Her mobile hadn't rung and there had been no texts. *No news is good news*, she thought as she showered and dressed, hoping it was true.

In the cold light of day her musings in the small hours seemed more of a dream than a reality. But the notion still persisted. The timing was right. The method of killing could fit Gavin's profile. But none of that was any use without proof that Gavin MacLean had been in contact with the victim, and that was something only trace evidence could supply.

40

'On what grounds was this warrant issued?' Sutherland said, keeping his tone even.

Bill had expected the summons, but it had arrived quicker than anticipated. Nelson must have been on the phone to his Lordship as soon as Bill had left the previous night.

'Mr Nelson's former cleaner identified film material in his room of a violent and pornographic nature. Mr Nelson had access to the Rosevale cinema around the time the body was put there. His behaviour last night suggested he'd removed anything he thought incriminating in antici-pation of my arrival. I assumed he'd taken it to his yacht and thought it should be searched.'

'As I understand it this cleaner has a grudge against Mr Nelson.'

'Mrs Cochrane *might* be lying, but the easiest way to find out is for us to search the boat, Sir.'

Sutherland conceded this with a grudging tilt of his head.

'Nevertheless Mr Nelson has claimed you are harassing him.'

'If asking pertinent questions in a murder enquiry is harassment, then he's right. I'm harassing him.'

The Super shot Bill a warning glance. 'Has the search begun?'

'They're waiting for me, Sir.'

'I think it would be better if you weren't present.'

'May I ask why, Sir?' Bill said, knowing full well.

'It matters little who searches, but whether they find anything.'

Dismissed, Bill rang DS Clark and told her to get on with it. 'Bring everything back, Sergeant. I don't care if it says Teletubbies on the label.'

Bill sat back in his chair, temporarily satisfied. Nelson might have friends in high places but that didn't mean he was above the law.

The internal phone rang and he picked up. It was the desk sergeant.

'Two men named Jim and John Mulligan want to speak to the person in charge of the Rosevale case.'

'I'll be right down.' Bill allowed himself a smile. Two successes and it wasn't even nine-thirty. What did they say about good luck coming in threes?

Bill observed with interest the two men sitting in front of him. He had met twins before, but was struck by how alike these two elderly men were. The same faces, the same build, slight but wiry. He couldn't tell them apart. They were even dressed the same. And the voices! No wonder he'd thought there was only one man being interviewed on Jude's recorder.

The one who'd identified himself as Jim was the spokesperson, although Bill got the eerie impression they were talking in unison, because Jim's every facial movement was duplicated by his brother.

'We don't watch the news, Detective Inspector. We find it too distressing most of the time. So we had no idea that Jude was missing until her two friends got in touch.'

'Who was that?' Bill said, though he had more than an inkling.

'They said their names were Liam Hope and Ben Howie.'

So Liam hadn't heeded his mother's warning. Bill wasn't unduly surprised. 'And how did they get in touch?'

'They sent an email using Jude's email account, asking to meet at the Govan Lyceum last night.'

'And you thought the email came from Jude?'

'We had no reason not to. Except the last time she made an arrangement to meet us, Jude didn't turn up.'

'And that was when?'

'The night she disappeared,' Jim confirmed. 'The boys mentioned an old film reel that had gone missing from Jude's room. The reason Jude asked to meet us that night was to discuss that film.'

Bill sat up in his chair. This was something he didn't know. 'She told you what was on it?'

'No. She said she was interested in dating it and hoped we might help. The boys told us what was on it.' Jim glanced at his brother who nodded imperceptibly for him to continue. 'Then Liam explained about finding the body in the Rosevale, and we remembered something we thought you ought to know.'

'Go on.'

'Some forty-odd years ago, when we were working as apprentices, there was a private club that showed films like that shot in Glasgow. A colleague of ours was involved as a projectionist. His name was Brian Foster.'

'Are you still in touch?'

'We haven't heard from Brian in twenty years. We don't even know if he's still alive.'

'Do you remember where this club was?'

'We think St Vincent Street, but it'll be long gone by now.'

'Had Jude contacted anyone else about this film?'

'I'm afraid we gave Jude the contact details of a man we bought a sixteen millimetre film from on eBay. He lives in the West End. His name is Nelson. At the time we had no reason to believe he would pose any danger to her.'

'And you do now?'

'He recently offered us some rare sixteen millimetre footage, which we declined because of the content.'

'Which was?'

'He hinted that it was early pornographic material.'

The third piece of luck, Bill decided, had arrived.

41

'OK, so we're a little behind the amateurs, but then again they're only running one show, whereas we're running three for you alone,' Sandy said.

Bill grimaced sympathetically. 'I know, I know.'

'On the Sinclair front, he didn't actually call anyone around the time Dr MacLeod left the hotel.'

'You're sure? She says she saw him.'

'I'm sure. He did, however, send a text fifteen minutes later.'

'Where?'

'A Pay-As-You-Go number. The text just said "Can we meet? Need to speak to you".'

'And?'

'A pick-up was arranged from the hotel at the end of his shift.'

'CCTV?'

'Same problem as last time. Car across the road, can't quite make out the licence plate. R2S are running comparison software to see if we can match the two cars.'

He took a deep breath. 'And now we come to the missing girl. I located the service providers for both her mobile and email. Mobile first: your suspect Jason said she received a text when he was with her. That's not true.'

'What about the text to Liam Hope?'

'It was sent when he said. If she tried before that, she didn't have a signal.' He handed Bill a printout. 'Full details here of all calls for your minions to pore over. R2S are plotting the locations leading to the final blackout.' He paused. 'Now, emails. According to her account she sent one last night to info@reelcinemas.com arranging a meeting in Govan.'

Bill interrupted. 'That was sent by our amateur sleuths.'

Sandy looked impressed. 'So they cracked her password. Nice work. Here's a breakdown of the rest. Nothing since her disappearance apart from that one.'

'Did you spot any communication with someone called Nelson about old films?'

'No, the only email correspondence relating to old film was with reelcinemas.'

'Thanks, Sandy.'

'We aim to please.'

Bill made his way back to the incident room, clutching his printouts. With DS Clark away he would have to delegate the job to someone else. DC Campbell, class clown and expert impersonator, was the lucky man. Bill handed over the printouts and issued his instructions.

'In the absence of my right-hand woman, I'm trusting you, Detective Constable.' Bill turned on his heel and entered his office, shutting the door, conscious of the fact that Campbell could do a perfect impersonation of him, too.

Bill sat at his desk, lost in thought. Hundreds of thousands of people in this city, linked by a complex web of actions and interactions, of lies and truths. He'd learned over time that if you did the ground work and asked the right questions, patterns of human behaviour eventually revealed themselves. All lies were liable to unravel, because life was too complicated to cover all your bases.

As he saw it, all the possible suspects in Jude's disappearance had at some point lied or at least evaded the truth, even Liam. Bill refused to let his mind settle on a prime suspect. If you did that, you evaluated everything from then on in that light, shutting your eyes and ears to other possibilities, while the real culprit might be lurking in the shadows.

The guy who'd called himself Jude's uncle had turned out to be a fellow resident in her last care home. Checked out by Sunderland police, he was deemed not to be a suspect in her disappearance. So that left the people who'd encountered Jude in the days before her disappearance. Liam, Charlie, the girl in the neighbouring room, Jason, Angus, Carol, the twins and Nelson. He was looking forward to interviewing Nelson in the light of the discovery that Jude had in fact been in touch with him. Another lie uncovered.

He was deep in his musings when he heard the door open. Bill swung round, expecting one of his team or even DS Clark back from her trip to Helensburgh. He did not expect to see Geoffrey Slater.

'Can we talk? In private?'

'Of course. Shut the door.'

'I'd prefer to do it away from your room full of blood-hounds baying for my blood.'

It was an apt description of his team. Bill rose. 'Lead the way.'

You could have heard a pin drop as they exited, but when the outer door closed behind them, a clamour erupted. Slater said nothing as they headed outside and over to his car. Harry Black was sitting in the passenger seat, staring straight ahead, his face blank. Slater indicated that Bill should get in the back, then started up the engine.

Bill's initial irritation at being herded into Slater's car was fast being replaced by anger.

'What the hell's going on? You said you wanted to talk.'

Slater drew out into the traffic. 'You need to see something first.'

He drove towards the city centre, crossing the river at Eglinton Street. Above them the giant box girders of the new flyover dominated the skyline. Slater took a left and drew up outside a block of flats encased in scaffolding opposite an entry to the M74 construction site. He turned to face Bill.

'I asked you to trust me. Did you?'

It was a loaded question. Bill had no intention of answering.

'I'm asking you about the Kalinin case,' said Slater, his small eyes narrowing.

'I was taken off that case,' Bill shot back.

'And *did* you come off it?'

'I never give up on one of my own. You should know that.'

'So you ordered Johnny Lang brought in.' Slater's voice was thick with accusation.

'Lang was implicated in the Sinclair killing.'

'His footprint was also identified near McNab's open grave, which could put him in the frame.'

The sick feeling in Bill's stomach was rising, fast. 'I wasn't aware of that.'

'It's your job to be aware of such things,' Slater hissed at him.

Petersson's warning echoed in Bill's head. *He will try to bring you down professionally. A policeman stripped of power. Maybe he's already using Slater to do this.*

'Come on, Slater. What's this really about?'

'Your actions had consequences.'

Slater gestured to Black and they got out of the car. Bill hesitated, his mind racing. What the hell was going on here? The two men crossed the road and entered the construction site. Bill got out and followed, suddenly struck by the silence. Apart from a guard on the gate, the site was completely deserted.

Slater strode on ahead, Black one step behind. They were under one of the huge box girders now. A JCB stood idle, its shovel half full of rubble. Slater stopped in front of the pile it had been shifting.

Bill picked up the stink on approach. He'd met that smell before, and not long ago. Then, it had emanated from a burned-out skip on a municipal dump to the south of the city. The murder that had brought Nikolai Kalinin to his and McNab's attention.

Slater indicated where the pile of rubble had been partially removed to expose a blackened and burnt object. It didn't look like a human being, but judging by the sickening smell it used to be one.

'We received word that someone was being held in one of the flats across the road from here. We believe it was McNab. By the time we got there the place had been emptied.

Someone had taken fright when they heard you were bringing Lang in. This is the result.'

A wave of horror swamped Bill. He forced himself to step closer to the corpse, seeking something, anything that might identify it. The face was unrecognisable, nothing left of the hair. Bodies shrink when incinerated, but he would take a guess that the victim had been taller than Johnny Lang. Which meant it could very well be his sergeant.

Bill rose and faced Slater, furious. 'Why haven't you ordered a scene of crime team here?'

'See what happens when you stick your nose in where it's not wanted?'

'You stupid bastard. This isn't about me. This is about you trying to shift the blame for your cock-up. Again.' Bill stabbed a finger in Black's direction. 'Is this how you go about things down south? Cover your back at every available opportunity?'

A flicker of discomfort crossed Black's face.

Bill turned from them and pulled out his mobile to call for a scene of crime team, his hand shaking.

42

'So you think there's a possibility Rosevale man might be linked to the MacLean murders?' said Chrissy. 'I suppose the timing fits.'

'And the method.'

'Gavin didn't crucify them and wall them up alive.'

'True. But the asphyxiation and mutilation mirror his attacks,' Rhona pointed out.

'And you don't usually get multiple perpetrators operating in the same way in the same city at the same time.'

'There's also the possible link between the manager of the charity shop and Dalrymple.'

'God, how I would love to nail that bastard.'

Rhona felt the same, but said nothing.

'So you want me to take over on the plastic sheeting while you check out your theory?' Chrissy said.

Rhona nodded. 'I've recorded the wire puncture marks and taped inside and outside for fibres.'

'What about the Quaser?'

'It identified blood but no semen on the sheeting. Let's do the superglue trick, see if we can pick up any finger-prints.'

'You think we'll get lucky?'

'Let's hope we do.'

If Gavin MacLean had had anything to do with the

sexual mutilation of the body behind the wall, then he'd left something of himself behind. Taping the body had proved to be virtually impossible without risking it collapsing further. She'd had to rely on careful swabbing, particularly round the mouth where the Quaser had definitely identified semen. A rich source of DNA, it could provide their best hope of identifying the attacker.

Deep in concentration, Rhona didn't initially hear Chrissy calling her to the phone.

'Who is it?'

'Bill.'

Rhona took in Chrissy's anxious face. 'What's wrong?'

'He wouldn't say, but his voice was shaking.' Chrissy looked on the verge of tears. 'Is it McNab?'

Rhona couldn't speak, but she forced herself to walk to the phone, removing her gloves and mask on the way.

'Bill?'

'Rhona. We've found a body.'

'McNab?'

'It's very badly burned and unrecognisable. Slater maintains it might be.'

'Where?'

'On the M74 site close to Eglinton Street.'

'I'm on my way.'

Chrissy didn't give Rhona time to put down the receiver. 'Is it him?'

'The body's badly burned.' Rhona didn't repeat what Bill had said about Slater.

'I'm coming with you.' Chrissy's expression brooked no argument.

* * *

It was a silent journey across town. It's come full circle, Rhona thought. It began with an incinerated corpse in a skip. Maybe that's where it's going to end.

'Are you OK with this?' she asked as Chrissy got out of the car and began to suit up.

Chrissy gave her a steadfast look. 'Are you?'

'Yes.'

Chrissy touched her arm. 'Let's go then.'

As they approached the incident tent and the accompanying huddle of officers, Rhona realised Bill's face was ashen not from shock, but from fury.

'That bastard Slater received a tip-off that McNab was being held in the building across the road. By the time he got his arse down here, the place had been emptied.' Bill eyed Rhona with concern. 'You sure you want to be the ones to do this?'

'We're sure.'

Rhona pulled up her mask, lifted the flap and stepped inside. Arc lights had already been rigged up and she stood for a moment getting used to the glare and the smell. Beyond the stench of burnt flesh she detected the cloying stink of petrol.

The blackened shape was situated near the back of the tent against a pile of rubble. A body set alight tended to writhe about as the flames took hold, collapsing to lie on the ground as it was consumed. The shape of this body suggested a crouching position, chin to knees with the arms behind the back. Rhona's first thought was that the victim had been restrained, tied in that position before being set on fire.

What Bill had said was true; at first glance it was

unrecognisable. Rhona made a swift estimate of the height and build. Definitely taller than Johnny Lang, broader too. If there had been any hair, it had been consumed in the fire. She crouched lower, examining the remains of the mouth, trying to picture McNab's smile and match it to the blackened teeth.

Her best chance was to find a part of the body not completely destroyed by the conflagration. If the victim had been placed here, then set alight, the chances were the stones had protected the rear. Rhona began picking away at the rubble, exposing the hands. They were fastened together with barbed wire, similar to the wire they'd removed from Sinclair's corpse.

Now that the hands were free of the rubble, she could make out a gold ring on the fourth finger of the right one. Did McNab wear a ring? She'd seen his hands often enough and she was trained to be observant. Why the hell couldn't she remember if he wore a ring?

Frantic now, Rhona brushed aside the remaining stones and crumbling concrete and spotted something she did recognise. Encircling the blackened remains of the wrist was a watch. A watch she was sure she'd seen on her bedside table in the flat, its soft quartz tick audible as she'd lain awake in the darkness.

Her anguished, 'Oh God,' brought a similar cry from Chrissy.

'What is it?'

Rhona unclipped the watch and eased it free. She rose, legs shaking, the words forcing their way through her rigid lips. 'It's not McNab.'

'You're sure?'

Rhona held out the watch for Chrissy to view, then turned it over. The inscription on the back read:

Heimsins besti pabbi – pín Brynja

43

'Why wasn't I informed that we'd identified the footprints?'

'You were, Sir. Two days ago. I left the report on your desk.' Janice brushed a pile of papers aside and retrieved the folder.

It was the day he'd been busy with Nelson. He'd hardly been in the office. Bill opened his mouth to remind his DS of that fact, then shut it again. It was not her fault. She had no way of knowing what this information really meant, or that by ordering her to bring in Lang, he had put McNab's life in danger.

'Is there anything else I should know about?'

'The material we collected from the yacht is here.'

'Anything interesting?'

'The films haven't been viewed yet. The photographic books are all gay erotica, pretty widely available.'

'Get the films looked at.'

'Yes, Sir.'

'And Nelson?'

'He's waiting for you in interview room two.'

'The dead man has a daughter,' Bill told her. 'She flew to London late last night, and from there to Switzerland. Her name is Brynja Einarsdóttir, and she'll have to be told once we confirm the body as her father's.' Bill felt sick just saying this. 'See if you can locate her.'

'Yes, Sir.' Janice hesitated. 'You're sure it's not McNab?'

'We'll be sure of nothing until the post mortem, Detective Sergeant,' Bill said sharply, then softened when he saw her stricken expression. 'But what we do know strongly suggests the body is Einar Petersson, an investigative journalist who's been trailing Nikolai Kalinin for some time.' He rose from his desk. 'I'm going to interview Nelson. Meet me down there in five minutes,' he instructed her.

Bill took his coffee with him, aware that the caffeine was the only thing keeping him on his feet. Last night he would have been delighted to take a pot shot at Nelson. Now he couldn't think past what had happened under that flyover.

On Bill's entry to the interview room, Nelson immediately rose to his feet, righteous indignation suffusing his face. 'Now, look—' he began.

Bill held up his hand before the man could let rip.

'Tea or coffee, Mr Nelson?' he enquired politely.

Nelson's thirst must have momentarily won out over his fury, because he snarled, 'Tea, two sugars,' and sat down again.

Bill indicated to the officer on duty outside the door to do the honours, then took a seat opposite. 'DS Clark will be with us shortly.'

'The woman who searched my yacht?'

'And took your dirty books and films away. Quite a collection, I hear?'

'There is nothing illegal in my collection.'

'Lying to the police *is* illegal, Mr Nelson.'

'I have no idea what you're talking about.'

'You said you'd never heard of Jude Evans. In fact, you

implied you didn't even know if Jude was a girl's or a boy's name.'

'I had never heard of this girl before you mentioned her.'

'Yet she was given *your* name by Jim and John Mulligan. She wanted to speak to you about an old film she'd found, one that pandered to your sexual proclivities. Did she get in touch with you?'

Nelson's naturally ruddy face began to drain of colour. It looked as though Bill's stab in the dark might have found its mark.

'I think you knew what that film was, and you wanted it for your collection.'

'That's ridiculous,' Nelson spluttered.

'I also believe you kept your set of keys for the Rosevale, and that you arranged to meet Jude there.'

Nelson sat open mouthed, all his bluster gone, as though a clairvoyant had just recited his life story.

'What about the body behind the wall, Mr Nelson? Trussed up, like the men in your films?'

Nelson, his composure slightly recovered, pressed his lips firmly together. 'I'm not saying anything else until I speak to a lawyer.'

Just then DS Clark walked in with the tea. Bill indicated she should set it down and come out with him.

'He's hiding something. Bring the duty lawyer down. I want to hear what Nelson has to say about that club in St Vincent Street, and who else uses his reel-to-reel service.'

44

Liam rose and showered, aware he'd missed yet another nine o'clock maths lecture. He checked his timetable; nothing now until a physics lab at two, although if he headed to the university right away he might catch someone coming out of maths and cadge a copy of their notes.

He stuffed the relevant books in his backpack and set off up University Avenue towards the main library, changing his mind at the last minute when he spotted Gary from his maths class headed into the Reading Room. He was on his way up the steps when his mobile rang. It was Aurora's name on the screen.

'Hey.'

'Hey, you. How'd it go last night?'

Shit, he'd forgotten he'd even told her they were setting up a meeting. She must have been waiting for him to call.

'I'm sorry. My head's mince. It was two guys, twins. They were very helpful – it turns out Jude had a rendezvous set up with them the same night she missed meeting me. The brothers have gone to talk to the police themselves.'

'Won't that get you into trouble?'

'I don't care any more.'

'Where are you?' Aurora's voice sounded weird.

'Outside the Reading Room. Why? What's up?'

'I'd rather not say on the phone. Can you come here?'

'To your room?'

'No. The Driftwood.'

'Are you OK?' Liam said, unnerved by her tone.

'I'm fine. See you shortly.'

Liam retraced his steps to Gibson Street and half walked, half sprinted towards Charing Cross and the Driftwood again, feeling like a character in one of Ben's online games. Forever running down city streets, endlessly looking for someone he would never find.

Aurora was already in the café hunched over a coffee, her eye on the door, waiting for him. Liam hurried across, pulled out a chair and sat down beside her.

'What is it? What's wrong?'

Her voice cracked as she spoke. 'I know where Jude's laptop is.'

'Where?'

Aurora swallowed hard. 'Charlie has it.'

'Charlie!' Liam lowered his voice as the people at the next table glanced round.

'It's in the boot of his car. He was taking something out and I saw it.'

'How did you know it was Jude's?'

Aurora stared at him, big eyed. 'Her initials are marked on the underside in permanent marker.'

Of course they were. 'Does Charlie know you spotted it?'

'I don't think so,' Aurora said anxiously.

'You're sure, really sure the laptop was Jude's?'

'Yes. I mean, I think so. I only saw it for a second,' she said, suddenly uncertain. 'What are we going to do?'

Liam's mind was racing as he tried to fit this new information into the overall story. Charlie could have just taken his chance and lifted the laptop, knowing the room was empty. But what about the film reel? Had he taken that, too? And if so, why? No matter how he looked at it, Liam found it difficult to picture Charlie as a thief. But then he couldn't picture him as a sexual predator either.

He pulled out his mobile, dialled and composed himself as it rang. He would ask to meet up with Rhona, then run the whole lot past her. Everything. The more he thought about it, the more important it became to unburden himself. When he was diverted to voicemail he left a message asking her to call him back as soon as possible.

'Who's Rhona?' Aurora said when he'd ended the call.

'A forensic expert. And my mother.'

Rhona had supervised the transferral of the remains to the mortuary. Three post mortems in twice as many days. Glasgow was more than living up to its reputation as the crime capital of Scotland.

With a heavy heart, Rhona had to admit to herself that she'd found enough to confirm that the body was Petersson's. Apart from the matter of the watch, she'd cut away enough singed cloth to reveal evidence of the tattoos she'd seen on his upper torso the night he'd shared her bed. Her final corroboration had been the contents of the wallet she'd extracted from a back pocket. Inside was a photo of Brynja as a child with an attractive woman, both of them smiling at the camera.

No wonder Petersson had been worried for his daughter's

safety, and insisted Brynja leave the country almost as soon as she'd arrived.

'I'm going to take a look at the room they were holding McNab in,' she told Chrissy, who was still taking samples from the area where the body had recently been.

'Slater's got a team in there already. He told me I wasn't needed,' Chrissy said.

Rhona didn't care what Slater said. He could hardly order her off the scene of a crime. She crossed the road and lifted the tape strung across the entrance to the flats. On closer inspection it was obvious the job of renovating them had ground to a halt, probably occasioned by the financial downturn. There were dozens of construction sites like this one scattered round the city, waiting for the banks to start lending again.

Rhona made her way to the third floor, the scent of dust and plaster gradually displaced by a stink of human waste and blood. She felt bile rise in her throat as she entered the cordoned-off flat. The smell was nothing new but it was almost impossible to process the knowledge that this time the scent was McNab's.

A chair sat in the centre of the room, a length of barbed wire hanging loose from its back. Below and around on the concrete floor was the smeared evidence of blood, urine and faecal matter. McNab had sat on that chair for days. God knows what he had endured.

Rhona backed away, the image of what might have happened there too powerful to cope with, even for her. The two SOCOs working the scene threw her sympathetic looks from above their masks.

'Is DI Slater about?'

'Next door.'

Rhona pulled herself together. If the Russian's henchmen had already dispensed with McNab they would have left him there to find, just like Petersson. The only reason to move him was if he was still alive. She had to believe that.

Slater and Black were in the neighbouring room, deep in discussion. The look Slater shot her indicated she wasn't welcome.

'We have people working the scene. We don't need you here.'

'Where have they taken him? Do you know?'

Slater eyed her, his malice undisguised. 'We're dealing with this, Dr MacLeod.'

'If they'd executed him, they would have left him there,' she said. 'Is he still alive?'

Slater blanked her, turning his attention back to Black.

'Is he alive?' she shouted this time, her voice echoing shrilly in the empty concrete space.

'We have no idea.'

'Why was Petersson killed?'

Black looked to Slater, who gave a slight nod. 'Because he betrayed them.'

'What do you mean betrayed *them*?'

'You still don't get it, do you?' Slater snapped. 'Petersson was working for the Russian. His job was to establish if McNab was alive and if so, locate his current whereabouts. Petersson figured a live McNab would eventually come sniffing around you, so all *he* had to do was fuck you and then wait.'

Rhona ignored the barb. 'McNab trusted Petersson.'

Slater gave a snort of derision. 'McNab always was a stupid bastard.'

'You believe Petersson gave him up?'

'We know he did.'

'Then why did you say Petersson betrayed *them*?'

Rhona looked from face to face, trying to read their expressions. There was something they weren't telling her. Something important. When it struck her it seemed so obvious.

'Petersson helped McNab escape.' By the glances they exchanged she knew she'd struck home. 'Petersson set him free and paid the price for it.' It made sense. 'That's it? Isn't it?'

Slater turned away, dismissing her. This was all she was going to learn, but it was something.

45

Once outside the building Rhona took out her phone to call Bill and picked up Liam's voicemail. He had something important to tell her about Jude and wanted to meet up as soon as possible. She rang him back.

'Liam? It's Rhona. I'm free today, can you come into town?'

'Whereabouts?'

She described how to get to the Central Café.

'OK. When?'

'I should be finished here shortly. I'll go straight there and wait for you.'

There was a pause. 'You've not found another body?'

'Yes, but it has nothing to do with Jude,' she said firmly. He seemed convinced, and rang off.

Rhona knew she didn't really have the time to deal with Liam's latest theories on Jude's disappearance, but she owed it to him to listen to what he had to say. She made her way back into the construction site.

'Liam wants to meet me, something to do with Jude Evans. Can you get a lift back?'

'No problem. How did it go up there?'

'Slater wasn't very co-operative.'

'Now there's a surprise.' Chrissy gave her a penetrating look. 'Anything you want to tell me that I don't already know?'

'He thinks Petersson was working for Kalinin all along to flush out McNab.'

'Jesus, so that's how they knew where McNab was hiding.'

'We don't know it's true.'

'But if Petersson *was* working for the Russian, why would they kill him?'

'Slater thinks Petersson betrayed them by helping McNab escape.'

Chrissy gave a low whistle. 'Jesus, Mary and Joseph.'

It all made sense when you examined Petersson's behaviour with the benefit of hindsight. His anxiety that Bill not alert Kalinin by pulling in Lang, the message he'd left for her with Brynja.

'His daughter turning up must have really screwed things up,' Chrissy said.

'So he booked her on a plane –'

'– before he made his move,' Chrissy finished. Then she frowned as a seriously worrying thought occurred. 'But that's not the only explanation that fits.'

Rhona thought she knew what Chrissy was about to say, but she didn't want to hear the words.

'If McNab found out that Petersson betrayed him—' Chrissy stuttered to a halt.

Rhona had smelt the hatred, fear and desperation in that room. Hate would have kept McNab alive through the pain and torture. If he got free by himself, wouldn't the man who'd betrayed him have been the first one in his sights?

It hadn't been a wise move to suggest the Central Café, but it was the first place that had sprung to mind. And maybe somewhere deep in her subconscious she'd hoped that if she sat here long enough McNab might turn up like he'd done before.

Rhona checked her mobile one more time. If he was alive and free, surely he would have let her know by now? But that had been his mistake the first time round. The clock on the mobile told her she'd been here twenty minutes. Maybe Liam had had difficulty finding the place?

Just at that moment the door opened and in he came, accompanied by a girl with a cloud of light-brown curly hair. Rhona called his name and he turned and shuffled self-consciously in her direction. Rhona, equally unsure how to play this, stood up to welcome them.

'This is Aurora. She's in the room next to Jude's in halls. Aurora, this is Dr Rhona MacLeod.'

Rhona covered their mutual embarrassment by asking if they wanted coffee. Both asked for lattes, and Rhona went to place the order at the counter. When she returned they'd both taken seats on the opposite side of the table. Aurora was busily unfurling a long scarf and opening her coat.

'It's not Starbucks, but it's warm, the coffee's good and it's close to the High Court,' smiled Rhona.

'It's fine,' Liam said, dismissing her attempts to put them at ease.

An awkward silence followed, broken by Rhona. 'I'm glad you got in touch. I was planning to call you and bring you up to date.'

'You've found something?'

'The police have CCTV footage showing Jude leaving the Rosevale.' Rhona stopped, suddenly realising she couldn't mention Jason.

'Oh,' Liam sounded disappointed. 'Did you pick up where she went after that?'

'There wasn't another sighting on Dumbarton Road, I'm afraid.'

Rhona paused expectantly; Liam had asked for this meeting, so he must have something to say.

The girl put her hand on Liam's arm. 'Maybe I should tell her?'

Liam nodded. 'OK.'

Aurora took a deep breath then began. 'The night after Jude went missing I heard noises next door. I thought it was Jude back. Later on, I remembered I'd heard a man's voice around the same time. I assumed it was Charlie, the warden. He walks the corridors when he's on duty. I never thought any more about it until—'

'Until what?'

'Until my friend Sally told me Charlie had been letting himself into her room with his key, and that's why she'd left halls.

'You've told the police all this?'

'Jude thought Charlie was a good guy. We all did. We found it hard to believe Sally was telling the truth,' Liam said.

Aurora continued, 'Then I saw Jude's laptop in the boot of Charlie's car. I knew it was hers because she marks everything with her initials.'

Rhona nodded. 'We found Jude's recorder in the cinema. It was marked the same way.'

Liam looked shocked. 'You found Jude's recorder in the Rosevale?'

'In the projection room.'

Liam shook his head emphatically. 'There's no way Jude would have left the cinema without checking she had all her equipment.'

'Jude was obsessive about things like that,' Aurora added, equally perturbed.

'But what if it fell out of her pocket?' Rhona suggested.

Liam was adamant. 'You don't understand, Jude had this *thing*. She was forever checking her bag, her pockets. She would have realised the recorder was missing before she got far and gone back for it.'

As far as Rhona was aware, the possibility that the girl had returned to the Rosevale had never been considered. Bill had said Jason had a key. Was that what their conversation had been about on the CCTV? Had Jason arranged to let Jude back in?

Liam was scrutinising her. 'What is it?

'DI Wilson needs to know what you said about the recorder. And about Charlie and Sally. Are you both willing to go down to the station and give a statement?'

Aurora glanced at Liam.

'You'll come with us?' He was trying to disguise the anxiety in his voice.

Rhona nodded. 'I'll call Bill to warn him we're on our way.'

46

Bill wasn't sure how to respond to the two young faces who stared earnestly back at him. The story about Charlie had caught him completely unawares. He had no idea whether the warden had been checked out, but it was something that should have happened. He had a strong feeling that he was losing his grip. Carrying too much information around in his head, absorbing none of it.

What Liam had said about Jude's voice recorder made sense. If Jude had Asperger's, she was obsessed with order and with her belongings. It seemed likely that if she left without her recorder she would have noticed pretty quickly and made an attempt to recover it.

Rhona was sitting quietly beside the pair. She'd insisted on a word alone with Bill before he talked to them, and her revelation about Petersson and the probable reason for his violent death had left Bill stunned. But he had to put that out of his mind, at least until after this interview.

He attempted to gather his thoughts, then asked, 'How did Jude find out about the Rosevale?'

'As far as I know she got all her information from websites,' Liam replied.

'Did she ever mention someone called Jason?'

They looked at one another, then shook their heads.

Bill addressed Liam directly. 'Tell me about the Govan Lyceum.'

'Ben worked out Jude's email password and we saw she'd been in touch with a website called realcinemas. Jude had arranged to meet two men, brothers, from the site last Tuesday night at six o'clock outside the Govan Lyceum, so we got in contact with them. They told us they were coming to speak to you about it.'

Bill was less concerned with Liam's interference than he was with what he and Ben had discovered. To reach Govan, Jude would have had to catch the subway from Partick Cross, a short walk along Dumbarton Road, yet they hadn't located her on CCTV after the Rosevale. Initially, he'd thought she might have turned off the main road, but if she was heading for the subway, that wasn't likely. Which left two possibilities. Either Jude had headed back and been missed by the camera near the Rosevale, or she had met someone, possibly in a car.

'Did Jude ever mention someone called Nelson?'

'Not to me,' Liam said.

'She mentioned Admiral Nelson to me once,' Aurora broke in. 'I thought she was talking about a pub, you know, *the* Admiral Nelson.'

'What exactly did Jude say about Admiral Nelson, and when?' said Bill. The intensity of his voice had unnerved the girl. 'It's OK, Aurora, just take your time and think about it.'

Aurora concentrated, her brow wrinkling. 'She said "Admiral Nelson awaits" or something like that. I'm sorry, I wasn't really listening.'

'*When* did she say this?'

Something was dawning on Aurora. 'Oh, God. It *was* that Tuesday, because I'd just heard about the party the next night. I was thinking about asking Jude along but she didn't like crowds.' The girl looked at him with anguished eyes. 'I should have remembered that sooner.'

'It was a throwaway remark. You weren't to know it was important,' Bill assured her.

Both of them looked exhausted, Liam in particular. The case was taking a heavy toll on Rhona's son. Bill decided it was time to let them take a break.

'I'll get an officer to take you down to the canteen so you can get something to eat. Then you can both go home.'

'What about Charlie?' Aurora said.

'I'll deal with him.'

Liam threw Rhona a questioning glance.

'I'll be in touch,' she assured him.

Bill waited until they'd left with DC Campbell, before telling Rhona, 'We brought in Nelson already. He denies ever having met Jude.'

'Whoever was with her in the projection room left their footprints. We have good casts of those. And didn't Nelson have keys at one time? Someone locked that door after Jude left.'

'Let's imagine Jude did go back and Jason or Nelson let her in. Could she . . . still be in there?'

'You searched the place.'

'The building's been internally re-structured at least four times. Rooms blocked off. Parts boarded up. We could have missed something.'

'The CCTV footage showed Jude walking away.'

'The CCTV camera is in the side street beyond the building. What if she came to the front door?'

'Or she was picked up before she reached the subway.'

A car matching the description of Charlie's was parked in the courtyard behind the halls of residence. Bill told DC Campbell to wait there while he spoke to the warden.

'And try not to look too like a policeman.'

'I'm not that much older than the students, Sir.'

'And you act like one of them most of the time.'

Bill walked round to the front entrance, composing himself before going in. He didn't want Charlie suspicious before they started their chat. His demeanour seemed to work because Charlie greeted him as before with the offer of a cup of tea.

Bill settled himself in the cubicle while Charlie boiled the kettle and put a couple of tea bags into mugs.

'So how's the search going for the lassie?'

Bill shook his head. 'Not so great, Charlie. That's why I'm back.'

'Oh dear.'

'Going over old ground again, in case we missed something.'

Charlie nodded his understanding. 'I wouldn't have your job for all the money in China.' He handed Bill a mug. 'Help yourself to milk and sugar.'

Bill poured in plenty of milk. When he was satisfied with the temperature, he took a sip. 'For years I never got to drink my tea until it was cold. I decided it was easier just to make it that way to start with.'

'Aye, I can see your point.'

'What did you do before this, Charlie?'

'Went into the Forces straight out of school. Then an odd-job man, mainly, which helps in this place. You'd be surprised how many young folk can't change a light bulb or mend a plug.'

They both laughed.

'So, Detective Inspector, how can I help?'

'I understand you weren't on duty the night Jude disappeared.'

'No, I wasn't.'

'Did you know Jude had been visiting old cinemas?'

'Not until I went into her room with Liam.'

'You thought she'd come home Wednesday night?'

'The lassie next door said she'd heard her, so I phoned the laddie and he came round. That's when we found someone had broken in.' Charlie looked personally affronted at this.

'You weren't on duty on Wednesday either?'

'I popped in for a bit.'

'Oh?'

'Left my mobile behind. I'd forget my head these days if it wasn't screwed on.'

'I know the feeling,' Bill sympathised. 'Did you go up to the first landing at any time on Wednesday night?'

Charlie's eyes flickered. 'Not that I recall. Why?'

'One of the students thought they heard you up there.'

'There was a party on. Most of them were drunk.' He shook his head in despair at the antics of the young.

'When did you come back here?'

'I can't remember the exact time. Fell asleep in front of the telly, and when I woke up I remembered the mobile.'

'D'you have far to come?'

'Twenty minutes or so by car. I'm just past Victoria Park.'

Victoria Park lay west of Partick.

'You come along Dumbarton Road?'

'Aye.'

None of the questions posed seemed to perturb Charlie. He was still as open faced and smiling as when Bill had first appeared. Bill decided it was time he stirred up the waters a bit.

'Truth is, Charlie, we've heard an allegation about you from a Sally Murphy, who used to stay here.'

Charlie's forehead creased in consternation. 'What kind of allegation?'

'That you sexually harassed her.'

He looked horrified. 'What? That's nonsense!'

'She says she woke up to find you in her room more than once, after you let yourself in with your pass key.'

'I have to go into rooms now and again. It's part of the job,' Charlie said indignantly. 'But not in the middle of the night, when someone's in bed. I wouldn't do that. She's talking nonsense.'

'She also says you gave her a lift one night, back to halls, and that's when it started.'

Charlie was getting angry now. 'The lying wee besom.'

'So it's a lie?'

'Of course it's a lie.'

'We can clear this up, Charlie, if we take a look at your car.'

'My car? Why?'

'If Sally's lying, we won't find any trace of her in there.'

Charlie was rattled, no doubt about it. But an innocent man would be just as flustered when confronted by an accusation of sexual assault.

'The car's round the back.'

Bill was already on his feet. 'It shouldn't take long.'

Charlie followed him out to the car park where DC Campbell was busy chatting up a pretty girl. He jumped to attention when he saw Bill.

'Open up the boot for us, Charlie.'

'You can take it as it is. I've nothing to hide.'

'Open up.'

Charlie fumbled with the lock, then lifted the lid. Bill eased him aside to take a proper look. 'What's in the bag, Charlie?'

'My laptop.'

Bill slid it out and turned it over. A set of initials, partially scrubbed out, were still legible.

'Who's JE?'

Charlie looked puzzled. 'I don't know. It's second-hand. I bought it on eBay.'

'Know what I think, Charlie? I think this is Jude's laptop. I think you stole it from her room the night after she disappeared.'

Charlie looked surprised and hurt. 'I wouldn't steal from the lassie, Detective. I told you I bought the laptop on eBay. Paid a hundred quid for it.'

'You can prove that?'

'I contacted a bloke who offered it for sale. He brought it here and I paid him. That's all I know.'

Bill softened his tone. 'We have a lot to talk about,

Charlie. Are you willing to come down to the station with me?'

'No problem, Detective Inspector. I want to find the wee lassie as much as you do.'

47

Three men. In three different interview rooms.

Bill decided to start with Jason. According to the duty sergeant the teenager had been informed why he'd been detained, and had had his prints and a DNA swab taken.

'A solicitor?' Bill asked.

'He's spoken to one on the phone.'

Now, sitting in the interview room with Jason, Bill noted the boy's ashen face and trembling hands. The lad looked fit to wet himself, but he was trying to hold it together. Jason's former brush with the law had obviously left its mark.

The record of the alleged offence had made interesting reading. Either the girl had got drunk, agreed to sex then regretted or forgotten that she had, or she'd had it forced upon her but then couldn't face taking the assault charge any further.

'Take off your shoes,' Bill said.

'What?'

'I said take your shoes off.'

Puzzled, Jason bent down and untied the trainers.

'Put them upside down on the table.'

Jason did as he was told.

'Someone was in the projection room with Jude last Tuesday and they left their footprints behind. Our forensic department took casts of those prints.' Bill waved an envelope in front of Jason.

'Are these your footprints, Jason?'

'I told you already. I met her at the side of the building.'

'You said the fire escape before.'

Jason hesitated.

'When she realised she'd dropped her recorder she asked if you could let her back in, didn't she?'

'I—'

'You told her to wait for you round the back. Is Jude still in there somewhere? Did you find some hiding place for her body, or did you take her someplace else?'

If Jason had been scared before, he was terrified now. 'I didn't touch her.'

'Where is she, Jason? Where did you put her?'

Jason was crying.

'All you have to do is tell me the truth. All of it.'

The boy snuffled a bit, rubbing his hands together. 'She forgot her recorder like you said. I told her I could let her in if she came back in twenty minutes. I wanted to be sure everyone was away.'

'And?'

'She never came back.'

'Did you go inside the projection room?'

He shook his head. 'When I told Angus what had happened he said to keep my mouth shut . . . because of the other thing.'

'So who locked the projection-room door?'

'Not me,' said Jason emphatically.

'What about the text you said arrived for Jude? The text that doesn't exist.'

He looked stricken. 'I don't know. I said that to make you think she went away. I'm sorry.'

'If I find out you're still lying to me, Jason.'

'I'm not. Honest, I'm not.'

Next door, neither Nelson nor his lawyer were in the best of moods.

'If you're not planning to charge my client with anything, I suggest it's time you let him go.'

'Fine by me.'

'What?'

'He's free to go.'

'But you've kept him waiting here for four hours.'

'And now he can go. However, I'd like to take his shoe size and examine the soles of his shoes first.'

Nelson looked aghast. 'Why?'

Bill waved the envelope in front of Nelson's face. 'Someone was in the projection room of the Rosevale recently, probably with our missing girl. They left a set of footprints behind, and I'd like to eliminate Mr Nelson.'

'I told you I'd never heard of the girl.'

'And she was never in touch with you about a pornographic film, yes, you said that. However, I have evidence to the contrary. The two men who gave Jude your contact details have told us about the film you offered to sell them.'

Nelson was squirming in his seat, a fact not lost on his lawyer.

'I'm going to ask you once again, Mr Nelson. Did you make contact with Jude Evans?'

'I may have.'

'Did you agree to meet her?'

'OK, I did, but she didn't turn up,' he said defensively.

Bill was getting fed up of hearing the phrase 'she didn't turn up'.

'Where did you agree to meet and when?'

'Last Wednesday.'

'You're sure it was Wednesday?'

'Yes.'

'So you lied before, when you said you'd never heard from her?'

Nelson looked indignant. 'You were very aggressive and I had nothing to do with her disappearance. I wish I'd never agreed to look at her film.'

'I have it on good authority that you arranged to meet Jude last Tuesday.'

That floored Nelson, but not for long. 'Then they got it wrong. It was definitely Wednesday.'

'Where and when?'

'At the Rosevale. Five o'clock.'

'Did you try to contact Jude to find out why she didn't appear?'

Nelson was contemplating another lie, Bill could read it in his face.

'Be careful, Mr Nelson.'

'No. She'd wasted my time and I was annoyed. Then I saw the news item saying she was missing, so there wasn't any point.'

'And you never thought to come forward and help the police with their enquiries?'

'Her disappearance wasn't anything to do with me.'

'OK. Your shoes, please.'

'Really, this is ridiculous.' Nelson bent down and loosened his laces.

'Upside down on the table.'

Bill took his time, even though he could see immediately that these soles weren't the ones imprinted in the dust of the projection room.

Bill finally pushed the shoes back towards Nelson.

'Can I go now?'

'We'll need to take a look at your car.'

'Why on earth . . . ?'

Bill ignored his protest. 'I understand you drove here?'

'Yes.'

'I suggest you take the subway home.'

Two down, one to go. Bill sipped another mug of cold tea, mulling over the stories so far. Jason, he decided, had given a good account of himself, in spite of his obvious fear. R2S were working on the CCTV footage of him with Jude, trying to enhance the sound. With luck Bill might yet hear what their conversation had been about. He also made a mental note to talk to Angus Robertson about giving the police false information. If he was trying to help Jason, he was going the wrong way about it.

As for Nelson, if Aurora's memory served her right then he was lying about the day he'd arranged to meet Jude. But Aurora's evidence wasn't enough. They needed more. A sighting of Nelson's car in the vicinity of the Rosevale on Tuesday would help, some evidence he'd been in the projection room, or, better still, trace evidence of Jude in his car.

One other thing kept niggling at Bill. Aurora had said

Jude used the term *Admiral* Nelson. How had Jude known about the nickname? As far as Bill was aware, it had been coined by Angus. In fact, his recollection was that Angus had been the only one to refer to Nelson in that way, apart from himself. She could have come up with it by herself, but it seemed a coincidence.

Bill did a quick web search to see if there was a pub in Glasgow called the Admiral Nelson. The first to come up had the right name but was in Twickenham, London. There was one called The Admiral in Waterloo Street, Glasgow and it served a burger called the Nelson.

Bill sighed. It was time to have a heart to heart with Charlie. He'd handed the laptop over to Sandy for examination, and an initial check on start-up had shown nothing relating to Jude.

'Whoever took it will have tried wiping everything off,' Sandy had told Bill. 'Give us time, we'll restore what was on it before. I take it forensics has checked for prints, et cetera?'

'It's clean, apart from Charlie.'

Charlie was sitting alone in room four with his own mug of tea, though his was steaming. He looked relaxed and not at all put-out. His demeanour was beginning to grate a bit on Bill – it was possible to be too nice.

'You didn't want to contact a solicitor, I hear?'

'I've done nothing wrong.'

'You realise you're being detained in connection with Jude Evan's disappearance?'

'Yes, although I don't know what that's got to do with the story you told me about Sally Murphy. I take it that was a lie to get me to open the boot?'

Charlie gave Bill a sorrowful look, almost disappointed. It was the sort of look Bill imagined he doled out to the students when they didn't come up to scratch. What if Jude hadn't come up to scratch for some reason or other?

'How did you come by Jude's laptop?'

'I told you I bought the laptop on eBay.'

'When?'

'Two days ago.'

'Who from?'

'Someone called Dave.'

'How was it delivered?'

'He was local, so I told him to bring it to the halls to save on postage.'

'And you didn't think it strange that the initials of the previous owner were the same as Jude's?'

'I never even noticed the initials. They were almost scrubbed out. Anyway, if it was hers what are the chances of me buying it, out of everyone looking on eBay? I picked it because it was a good price, and the seller being based in Glasgow was a bonus.'

Charlie gave Bill a look that suggested he was lacking somewhat in intelligence.

'I'll need a contact for this Dave.'

'I gave him the number of the halls via eBay. He called me.'

It was all too easy. Too pat.

'Well, you can leave us his username on eBay and we'll trace him that way. What about the missing film reel?'

'What about it?'

'You didn't buy that on eBay too?'

'Don't talk daft,' Charlie laughed.

Maybe the day had gone on too long. Maybe he was too tired to do this interview, but Bill had an overwhelming desire to smack Charlie one in the face, thus removing his self-satisfied look, if only momentarily.

He thrust that desire away and tried to be dispassionate. There were things that needed checking. Sally Murphy's story. Charlie's background. The whole eBay transaction. Bill was suddenly struck by how much work was created by other people's lies.

Charlie, unperturbed, took another mouthful of tea.

Bill planned his next move. He could take Charlie's prints and a DNA sample and keep him there for the full six hours. In the interim he might get something on the ownership of the laptop, but it was beyond hope he'd get results on anything else.

'How long have you been at the halls, Charlie?'

'A couple of years.'

'Where were you before?'

'Here and there.'

'Where?'

'All over. You get restless when you've been in the army.'

'I'm going to send in one of my detective constables. I'd like you to give him all the details.'

'Sure thing, Detective Inspector.'

Bill rose. 'Another mug of tea?'

'That'd be great. Thinking's thirsty work.'

Bill left Charlie sitting there, knowing that unless the laptop turned out to be Jude's, he had nothing on him. Sally Murphy hadn't felt compelled to lodge a complaint against the warden up to now. That didn't mean Charlie hadn't sexually harassed her. He could have been assaulting young women all over the country, and if none of them had gone to the police they would never know about it.

Bill couldn't shake off a sense of unease, as though there was a whole road he'd not yet discovered, let alone walked down.

'Sir?' Detective Sergeant Clark was eyeing him from the door of his office.

'What is it, Janice?'

'We've found Dominic McGeehan, Sir, or the man impersonating him.'

48

Rhona left the police station, relieved that Liam had given a good account of himself. Observing her son both in the café and the interview room she'd realised it was pride she was feeling. Until now, guilt had been the only emotion she'd ever experienced when confronted with Liam.

Liam's consistent and continued interference in Jude's case had actually proved useful, what with his discovery about Jude's later meeting at the Govan Lyceum and his revelations about Charlie. He should have followed her instructions and left well alone, but Rhona secretly rejoiced that he hadn't. As, she believed, did Bill.

She turned into the laboratory car park, wondering if Chrissy had returned from the construction site. The thought took her back there, the smell of burnt human flesh still powerful and real. Rhona threw open the car door and took a deep breath, trying to dispel the memory.

Her mobile rang as she locked the car door.

'Where are you?'

'Just outside.'

'Hurry up. Coffee's on. And I bought a packet of caramel wafers.'

The strength of Chrissy's stomach never failed to amaze Rhona. Last time they'd attended a scene like the one this morning, Chrissy's favourite had been Jaffa Cakes.

She'd been pregnant back then and forever hungry. Jaffa Cakes were still occasionally produced, but the favourites now were Tunnocks Caramel Wafers and Teacakes.

Despite everything, Rhona's heart lifted a little as she climbed the stairs. Chrissy sounded as though she had something to impart. Something more substantial than a caramel wafer.

While Chrissy dished out the coffee and biscuits, Rhona brought her up to date on Liam's latest adventures.

'He never gives up, does he?' Chrissy said with a degree of admiration. 'Even when he's told to. Who does that remind you of?'

When Rhona didn't respond, Chrissy popped the remaining half inch of her wafer into her mouth and chewed it before saying, 'OK. Here's my news. The blue coat retrieved from the Govanhill Picture House didn't belong to Jude. At least, it didn't match the DNA we extracted from her toothbrush.'

'They've completed the search of the Govanhill?'

'Yes.'

'And the Olympia?'

'Nothing there of any interest bar a partially smoked cigarette in the projection room where Jude found the film reel. Since Jude doesn't smoke, it might have had something to do with the film being there.'

'Bill thinks Jude may have gone back to the Rosevale to collect her recorder,' Rhona said. 'Either that or she was picked up in a car before she got to Partick Cross.'

'That makes sense.'

Chrissy fell silent although Rhona had a pretty good idea what the next question would be.

She answered it in advance. 'The post mortem's tomorrow morning.'

'You're going?' Chrissy looked perturbed.

'Of course.'

'But—' Chrissy stopped when she saw Rhona's expression.

Rhona drained the remainder of her coffee. 'I'm going to get some work done.'

A couple of hours later, Chrissy called in her goodbyes. 'When are you going home?'

'Soon,' Rhona lied.

'I take it there's no news on McNab?'

Rhona shook her head.

'OK, see you tomorrow.' Despite everything, there was a light note in Chrissy's voice.

Rhona knew why.

'Give baby Michael a kiss from me.'

'Will do.'

Rhona watched as the door closed behind Chrissy, experiencing a brief stab of envy. That's how it could have been, she thought. Had I not given up Liam. Had I not asked Sean to leave.

Later, when Rhona pushed open the flat door, the peace and quiet she had chosen for herself didn't seem quite so welcoming. Stepping into the gloom, she quickly flicked on the light. There was a pile of envelopes on the hall floor. Rhona scooped them up and carried them through to the kitchen, leaving them on the table while she fixed herself a drink.

She reached into the cupboard for the whisky bottle,

recalling the night Liam had turned up and Petersson had insisted on hanging around. He'd been surprised, even delighted, to discover that she had a teenage son. Having met Brynja, Rhona now understood why.

But Petersson was dead. Burned alive. It didn't feel real. She, like Brynja, was still living in a world where Petersson might call or walk in at any time.

Rhona poured a double and added a little water. The first mouthful went down like fire. By the time it reached her stomach, she'd swallowed another. The warmth the whisky brought to her chilled heart and body was temporary, but welcome.

She glanced without interest at the pile of envelopes. Mostly white and official looking, except one. Rhona extracted it. It was a proper letter, but from whom? She turned it over. There was no sender's address on the back.

Rhona tore it open and read the words, hearing Einar's voice as clearly as though he was there in the room with her.

Dear Rhona
By the time this letter arrives a number of things may have happened. I have no way of knowing which one, and can only hope.

First of all I owe you an explanation and an apology. I lied to you. Not about everything. I did believe McNab was alive and wanted to find him. I had to find him, because if I did not, someone I loved would have paid the price for my failure. I had already lost my wife. I could not lose Brynja too. I hope you can understand that.

*So I made contact with you. I knew that Detective
Sergeant McNab and you were close, and I believed
if he contacted anyone it would be you. And we found
him together. How happy you were when that
happened. And all the time I planted the thought that
Detective Inspector Slater might be the one betraying
you both.*

*I gave Kalinin what he wanted. A live McNab. I
knew he wouldn't kill him straight away, because he
told me so. He also told me that should I reveal this
to anyone, then whatever he did to McNab, he would
do to me and, much much worse, to my daughter.*

*So I chose to tell them where McNab was, but then
found myself unable to live with that choice. I decided
to set McNab free and help him go south, to make
sure he gave his evidence. The reason? Unless he did,
I would continue to be Kalinin's pawn and Brynja
could never be safe.*

*I do not know if this plan will work, but I expect
you know by now if it has.*

Tell Brynja I love her.

Einar

Rhona laid the letter down. She retrieved the whisky glass
and cradled it in both hands, too shocked to raise it to
her lips.

She had been right all along. She should never have
trusted him. She should never have slept with him. Einar
Petersson had wormed his way into her life with his lies
and his promises. His sole purpose had been to find
McNab, not for her, but for Kalinin. Anger rose like a

thick wave. When it subsided, she raised the glass to her lips and drank down the remainder of the whisky as though in a toast. But whom was she toasting?

McNab, who, if what Petersson had written was true, had escaped death again? Or Petersson, who had sacrificed himself to make that happen?

She had no idea how long she'd been sitting in the unheated kitchen before the buzzer sounded. Rhona rose stiff with cold and went to answer it. It was Sean.

'Rhona? Can I come up?'

'Why are you here?'

'Bill told me about Petersson.'

Rhona released the catch and walked slowly towards the door. When she opened it, Sean was already there. Rhona looked at him, a little dazed, and he stepped inside, closing the door behind him.

'Are you OK?'

'No,' she said honestly. 'I'm not.'

He wrapped his arms about her. The warmth of his body was a shockwave against her own chilled flesh.

'You're freezing. Why's the heating not on?'

Rhona had no idea. She had no idea about anything.

'Come on.' He led her through to the sitting room and sat her on the sofa. 'I'll bring you the duvet. You need to get warm.'

He lit the gas fire and brought through the coverlet, tucking it about her, then headed for the kitchen. Rhona heard the boiler roar into action as the central heating came on.

Tom suddenly appeared and jumped on her lap. Sensing her distress, he climbed to rub himself against her cheek.

Cocooned in warmth she watched the fire leap and dance and thought of Petersson sitting below the M74, his arms bound by wire, smelling the petrol and knowing what was about to happen.

And in that moment she forgave him the lies and betrayal, because who was to say she wouldn't have done the same to protect someone she loved?

'Here. Drink this.' Sean put a mug in her hand. 'I'm making you something to eat.'

'I'm not hungry.'

Sean shot her a look that brooked no argument.

The liquid was tea, but so heavily sugared as to be unrecognisable. It was the classic drink given to those in shock. Am I in shock, Rhona wondered? I've seen uglier, more violent deaths than Petersson's, and watched McNab apparently bleed to death in my arms.

Time slipped past. It seemed only seconds before Sean reappeared with a plate of food.

'An omelette. Is that OK?'

Rhona took it without demur. When she'd finished it and the tea, she did feel better.

'Thanks.'

Sean produced the letter. 'This was in the kitchen, and I read it. I hope you don't mind.'

She shook her head. 'I have to let Bill know about it.'

'What if I call him?'

Rhona was about to protest then didn't. She'd already told Bill what Slater had said. The letter merely confirmed it.

Sean left the room as he dialled, and Rhona was secretly relieved. She never wanted to hear or read the letter again.

He returned minutes later. 'I spoke to him. He says to get

some sleep. He'll see you tomorrow, if not at the post mortem then at the strategy meeting.' Sean looked concerned. 'Surely you don't have to go to Petersson's post mortem?'

'Of course I do. It's my job,' Rhona said, more sharply than she'd intended. 'Look, if you want to get going, I'm fine now.'

'You're sure?'

'I have work to do before tomorrow.'

'And I have a spot to play at the club.'

They were both lying, but it made things easier.

'Can you let yourself out?'

'Of course.'

Rhona thought momentarily of asking Sean to return the key he still held to the flat, but something stopped her. Sean was the only man she'd ever given a key to, and there might come a time he had to use it.

She heard the front door close and found herself relieved at his departure. It had been kind of him to come, but there was a difference between having a lover and having a friend. Rhona wasn't sure the two roles could be combined in anyone, let alone in Sean Maguire.

49

'You've seen these tattoos on Petersson?' Despite the grim circumstances, Slater couldn't quite hide his prurient glee.

'Yes. They're quite distinctive,' Rhona replied evenly. The tattoos had clinched it for her at the crime scene and it was no different here at post mortem. The watch could have been planted, as could the wallet, but the tattoos were instantly recognisable.

Dr Sissons continued with his examination, either unaware of the undercurrent in his audience, or else refusing to acknowledge it.

'And the burns were definitely the cause of death?' Slater asked.

'There's no evidence at the moment to suggest otherwise,' Sissons said, glancing at Rhona. She saw sympathy in the pathologist's eyes before he resumed his recording.

She turned away from the table. Having said what she'd come to say, Rhona no longer wanted to be in the room with what remained of Einar Petersson.

In the changing area, she de-gowned and began to splash cold water on her face, aware that the scent of scorched flesh permeated every hair of her head and pore of her body. Bill appeared silently beside her to do the same thing.

When they'd finished and made use of the paper towels, Rhona fished out the letter and handed it over. Bill scanned it quickly, having been apprised of its contents by Sean on the phone. He folded it and put it in his pocket.

'Looks like I owe Slater an apology.'

'If we believe what it says.'

'Why shouldn't we?'

'I don't think there was ever a time when Petersson told me the truth.'

Bill put his hand gently on her arm. 'I think this time he did.'

'McNab hasn't been in touch?'

'His best bet is to stay off the radar until he turns up in court.'

'I take it Slater's in charge of all of this?' She motioned towards the mortuary.

'Yes.'

'So you didn't have to be here?'

'Like you, they couldn't keep me away,' Bill said.

'Have you spoken to Charlie?'

'I have and what Aurora said was true. There was a laptop in the boot of his car, marked with the initials JE. I've passed it to IT for examination.'

'What did Charlie have to say about that?'

'He was shocked that I could think for a minute that he would steal from 'the wee lassie'. Told me he'd bought the laptop on eBay.'

'You believe him?'

Bill raised an eyebrow. 'We're looking into it. But even if he did steal the laptop, it doesn't necessarily mean he had anything to do with her disappearance.'

'And Sally Murphy?'

'Charlie genuinely seemed hurt about that. Said it was

a lie, of course. Maintained he was only doing his job. He also realised pretty quickly it was more about Jude than Sally. Told me he would do everything he could to help us find her.'

Rhona noted the tone of Bill's voice. 'You don't believe him?'

Bill shrugged.

'When will you find out if the laptop is Jude's?' she said.

'This morning, I hope.'

'I can see why he might steal the laptop at an opportune moment, but what about the film?' Rhona said.

'I've been thinking about that. Taking the film would make the burglary look as though it was linked to Jude's disappearance, and therefore nothing to do with Charlie.' Bill shook his head. 'Now, if we only had a body.'

'You think there is one?'

'Don't you?'

Bill emerged from the city mortuary to find Slater and Black standing outside. He wondered briefly if they had been waiting for him.

'Seems I owe you an apology.' Bill handed over the letter.

Slater opened and read it. When he'd finished, he glanced at Bill and for a moment Bill imagined he saw real emotion in Slater's eyes.

'And all the time you thought I was responsible for McNab getting shot and for him disappearing again. How does it feel to be so wrong?'

Bill didn't answer. 'What happens now?'

'None of your business, as I keep trying to tell you.'

'Has McNab been in touch?'

Silence.

'Thought not. Petersson might think you're innocent but McNab's not so sure. I take it Kalinin will turn up in court?'

'Two days from now.'

'And you expect McNab to be there?'

'I do.'

'You can expect me too, and Dr MacLeod.'

'Dr MacLeod might be better staying away, seeing how she was fucking one of Kalinin's right-hand men.'

Bill walked away, his hackles up. Christ, how he hated that man.

He made a point of putting Slater out of his head as he made his way to the address given him by DS Clark. Sally Murphy had moved from the halls of residence into a flat just off Alexandra Parade, but it took Bill a good ten minutes after parking the car to locate the flat. It was in a row of fairly dilapidated tenements, which judging by the variety of window dressings was definitely student territory.

Sally answered on the first buzz. 'Come on up, it's the third floor.'

The entry area was clean but badly in need of a paint job. At the foot of the stairs, a child's buggy shared a space with a bunch of interwoven bikes. As he climbed, Bill noted at least four occupants listed on every door.

Sally was waiting at an open door. She ushered Bill into a large hall with multiple rooms leading off. From behind the door of one came the sound of an electric guitar. It wasn't ear-splitting but it was near enough.

'Sorry about that,' Sally apologised. 'Tim has to practise and we're all usually out during the day.'

Bill smiled. 'There's a drum kit in our house. Electronic, but it makes as much noise as the old-fashioned kind.'

Sally led him into the kitchen. 'Can I get you a coffee?'

'Thanks, that would be good.'

Bill glanced about. This, he realised, was the sort of place Lisa would be living in soon. Messy, functional and nothing like Margaret's pristine kitchen at home.

Sally opened the fridge. Inside, each shelf had a label on it, reminding the occupants what was theirs to eat. She extracted a small carton of milk.

'I'm sorry, I don't have any sugar.'

'No problem.'

Sally opened the carton and sniffed the contents. Satisfied it wasn't off, she poured a little into each mug.

As she settled herself opposite him at the table, Bill registered how pretty she was, with dark hair coiled up at the back of her head. There was a smudge on her nose that Bill took for paint.

Bill left his tea to cool. 'So, Charlie—' he began.

She interrupted him. 'A dirty old man.'

'Why?'

'Because he comes into your room when he knows you're in the shower, or in your bed.'

'Everyone seems to like him.'

'That's because he targets one person and is ultra careful with everyone else. When that person gets freaked no one believes them, because Charlie's *such* a good guy. Charlie is a creep. Believe me.'

'What happened exactly?'

'He was really good to me when I first moved in. Behaved like a perfect grandfather. No funny business. Then one night he offered me a lift back to halls. It was late. I was drunk. Charlie wanted more than a thank you for the taxi ride. I refused. Then he starts turning up unannounced in my room.'

'Why didn't you report all this to the authorities?'

'Yeah? Nice old guy accused of assault by drunken art student? I decided it was better to move out.' She paused. 'Then I heard about the girl.'

'Jude Evans.'

'Aurora said she had Asperger's. They don't pick up on social signals, do they? It struck me maybe Charlie was working on her and she didn't even know.'

'Charlie denies you were ever in his car.'

'Never in it? I was sick in that car. That's what stopped him.'

'He didn't rape you?'

'No.'

'Do you want to make a complaint?'

Sally looked worried. 'I'd rather not unless you find out he has something to do with Jude's disappearance. Then I'll stand up in court and say my piece.' Her hand trembled as she raised the mug to her lips.

'If we're going to prove you were in Charlie's car we'll need a mouth swab to identify your DNA. Are you happy to give that?'

She nodded. 'How?'

'Can you go down to the station? I'll warn my sergeant to expect you. Ask for DS Janice Clark and tell her what you told me. For the record.'

Sally seemed unsure.

'It won't go any further unless you agree.'

She showed him out, even more vulnerable than when he'd arrived. Bill understood why. Sally had banished the incident with Charlie to the back of her mind but he'd just brought it all back.

When Bill reached the bottom of the stairs a young woman was struggling to free her bike from the middle of the pile. Bill offered his assistance.

'Thanks. That would be great.'

Bill untangled it for her and she bestowed a big smile on him.

No wonder Charlie loved his job, Bill thought. A fresh batch of females, like this young woman, arriving at the halls every autumn. He could play the role of kindly grandfather and handyman. Always obliging. Even when they were coming home drunk and needing a lift.

But maybe this time the friendly warden had overstepped his mark.

50

Rhona didn't go directly to the lab after the post mortem. The truth was she didn't want to be confined to the car with the aroma of the mortuary still hanging about her. She left her car and walked towards the river, hoping the scent of the water would drive other smells away.

She'd intended asking Bill before he left whether they'd located Brynja in Switzerland. She felt a strong desire to speak to Petersson's daughter, to tell her how sorry she was about her father's death and try to explain what had led to it.

She'd reached the river now, far upstream from where they'd discovered Sinclair's body. Rhona knew she should be back at the lab, studying the plastic sheeting Sinclair had been wrapped in and trying to use the debris it held to pinpoint exactly where Sinclair had been killed. But somehow that didn't seem quite so urgent after what she'd just viewed on the slab.

She stood by the water's edge, the brisk breeze whipping her hair back from her face. When this was over, she decided, she would take a trip to Skye, maybe even visit Raasay again. Breathe fresh air.

Turning abruptly Rhona began her walk back, knowing from past experience that the best thing to do when she felt like this was to work. She quickened her pace, remembering that there might be a result back from SDNA by now. The sample of semen she'd retrieved from the cinema victim had been small and she'd had to multiply it using PCR, but she was hopeful of a possible match with that of Gavin MacLean.

Which brought her thoughts round to Edward. He wouldn't be happy if the MacLean case was reopened, particularly if it involved his benefactor, Lord Dalrymple.

The thought brought a brief smile to Rhona's lips. Maybe she should tell Edward how instrumental their son had been in finding the body in the first place? She could imagine how well that would go down.

At the car now, she unlocked it and slipped inside, switching on the air conditioning instead of the heater so as not to encourage the smell again. As she pulled away from the kerb, she noticed a small black car immediately draw out behind, a male in the driver's seat. The thought crossed her mind that whoever had picked up McNab the first time would be very keen to locate him again. And like Petersson, they might imagine she could help them with that.

The car sat on her tail all the way through the town centre, then she lost it as she approached the university precinct. You're getting paranoid, she told herself as she parked outside the lab, knowing that if she'd paid attention to her paranoia regarding Petersson, things might have turned out differently.

Chrissy wasn't there, but had left a message to say she'd gone with the team to examine two vehicles in connection with Jude's disappearance. She had also left details of her examination of the plastic sheeting. Rhona made herself a coffee and settled down to study them.

The best news was that the cyanoacrylate spray they'd used on the sheeting had produced a fingerprint. A good one. Chrissy was pretty pleased about that. Sinclair had been dragged over rough ground as evidenced by the scuff marks on the plastic and samples of small stones picked up on the way were still being analysed. Chrissy had also located blood spots where the wire had pierced the plastic, possibly where the attacker had cut his finger on the barbs. The polythene sheet itself was black and 500 gauge, part of a builder's roll designed for lifting heavy objects.

'Good work, Chrissy,' Rhona said, reading on.

The wire had been identified as high tensile steel, tradesman Apollo. Used with fencing to provide additional security. Both plastic and wire were probably available near to where McNab had been held, either in that building or across on the M74 site itself.

Rhona left the notes and went to check her inbox.

The reply was there from Dundee. She took a moment to compose herself, then read it. The DNA of the semen sample taken from Dominic McGeehan had found a match with Gavin MacLean, a suspect in the murders of Glasgow University students James Fenton and Peter Graham. Which meant Gavin had been operating for at least three years before they'd caught up with him.

Rhona wondered how many more of his victims were out there, hidden like McGeehan, perhaps never to be discovered.

'The laptop belongs to the missing girl,' Sandy confirmed. 'Someone wiped it clean, or thought they did, but all her

material is here. The emails, files and images. And the film
we found on the memory stick? It's here too, but with
more frames than on the back-up. I've passed a copy to
vice. Plenty of participants in it. They'll be older now but
you might be able to identify some of those taking part.
After all, leopards don't change their spots, do they?' He
handed Bill a DVD. 'I'd have a stiff drink before watching
that. The rest of the material from the hard disk is available for your team to peruse online.'

Bill thanked him, although thanks were barely enough
for what they now had access to. All Jude's correspondence and files leading up to her disappearance, together
with the film Nelson had been so keen to get his hands
on; which begged the question, did Nelson already know
what was on it?

Bill headed back to his office. On the way he handed
over the job of examining the contents of Jude's laptop,
minus the film footage, to his investigation team.

'And I don't want to be disturbed,' he told DS Clark on
his way in, coffee in hand. This development, along with
what Rhona had just called to tell him about Gavin
MacLean, had given him plenty to think about. He laid
the DVD on the desk.

Jude had seen all or most of the content of the film,
that much was obvious. The age of the film, however,
might have led her to believe that a crime, if there was
one, committed in it was past its sell-by date. Bill wondered
how much of the film's content she'd revealed to the
Mulligans, or to Nelson.

According to the twins, Jude had only asked if they
could determine its age for her, which might mean she was

considering going to the police with it. Bill recalled the two elderly men, distressed to hear Jude was missing and obviously keen to help. They'd had no reason to present themselves to him, and had Liam not confessed to his continued involvement their existence might never have been discovered.

Nelson, on the other hand, had done everything in his power to avoid the law, even trying to call in the big guns. Why? Because he had something to do with Jude disappearing that night, or because of the existence of this film?

And then there was Charlie. Did he steal the film along with the laptop, and if so, why?

Bill stood up. He had things to do.

'I'm going down to the Rosevale. I need you to get hold of all the plans of the building from when it was a cinema through to the present day. The place is a warren. I want to know every square inch of it.'

'What about the guy calling himself Dominic McGeehan, Sir?'

Bill had totally forgotten about him.

'You interview him. Take DC Campbell in with you.'

Janice looked pleased.

'He's a good actor, Sergeant. Remember that.'

On his way to the car Bill took a turn past the vehicle bay where the SOCOs were at work on the cars. He spotted Chrissy among the swarm of white bees.

'How's it going?'

'Both men clean their cars pretty thoroughly.'

'Not too well, I hope?'

'Not well enough.'

'Sally Murphy says she was sick in Charlie's car.'

Chrissy smiled. 'Good. Vomit's a hard thing to get rid of, and a rich source of DNA.'

'Anything interesting in Nelson's car?'

'Soil. On the accelerator, brake and clutch pedals and under the mud guard. Mr Nelson's been off road, and recently.'

'Any sign of Jude in the car?'

'We have hairs and some fibres, from inside and the boot.'

'No blood?'

She shook her head. 'Not so far.'

Bill left them to it.

He made for Dumbarton Road, but instead of stopping at the Rosevale, he kept on going. Charlie had given his address as Henrietta Street, just past Victoria Park. The flat was in a row of red sandstone tenements.

Bill turned left into Henrietta Street, then promptly did a three-point turn. He checked his watch, then drove back the way he had come, keeping an eye open for cameras. He didn't spot any until he came to a row of shops. No cameras, but plenty of wooded areas between Charlie's house and the Rosevale.

He reached the cinema in eight minutes and parked in the side street that ran down towards the expressway. Rather than entering by the front, he made for the side entrance. A van was parked there, its back open, two men he recognised as Jimmy Dixon and Robert Hennessey busy unloading a green three-piece suite.

'Is Angus about?'

'Inside,' Jimmy told him.

Bill heard Angus's voice before he spotted him. Authoritative and humorous at the same time. A good bloke and a good foreman. Angus emerged from behind a stack of furniture.

'Inspector Wilson. What's up?'

'Can we talk?'

'Sure.'

'In private?'

'We could go outside, I'm due a smoke.'

Bill waited until Angus had lit up and inhaled.

'You called Mr Nelson "the Admiral". Does anyone else call him that?'

'I'm the only one here who knew him.'

'What about Jason?'

'Why would he know him?'

Bill waited while Angus took another draw.

'How well do you know this building, Angus?'

'Pretty well.'

'What about before it became a charity shop?'

'I used to come here as a kid when it was a cinema. Worked here for a bit at nights when it was a bingo hall. Played snooker here too.'

'So you know it well?'

'Better than most. Why?' Angus threw Bill a wary glance.

'What if I said I thought Jude Evans was still inside this building?'

Angus looked mystified. 'That's impossible. You lot searched the place.'

'Maybe not everywhere.' Bill watched Angus's reaction as he spoke. 'There are only two possibilities as far as I see it. Either Jude came back here, or she was picked up by car between here and the subway. I'm beginning to think she came back and someone let her in.'

'It wasn't Jason,' Angus said swiftly.

'How do you know that?'

'He told you at the station. The lassie asked to get back in, but she didn't turn up.'

Angus took another draw at his cigarette.

'So what did Jason do?'

'Came back in the pub. With me.'

'All night?'

'All night.'

'You lied to me the last time.'

'Aye, because I knew the lad had nothing to do with the lassie disappearing,' he said firmly.

'A team will be here first thing tomorrow to search the building.'

'No problem.'

Bill left Angus and went to talk to Carol. When he told her what he thought, she looked horrified.

'But you searched the place.'

'Maybe not well enough.'

'Do I have to shut the shop?'

'Yes, please. Could you be here at eight tomorrow morning?'

It was a long shot, Bill thought as he got back in the car, but one worth playing. As in a snooker game, if you lined up the balls, you had the chance of hitting them all at once.

51

After calling home to tell Margaret he wasn't sure when he would be back, Bill parked out of sight of the Rosevale. He settled himself in the café across the road where he ordered a pot of tea and one of their giant scones. The sign on the door said they closed at six, which suited him fine. The surveillance team would be in place by then and he could join them. Bill set about his cherry scone with gusto.

At five on the dot Carol came out and stuck a notice on the door, no doubt warning customers that they were shut the following day due to unforeseen circumstances. Then she headed off, accompanied by the girl he'd seen working in the shop with her. One by one the men emerged via the storeroom door and went into the pub.

They were no sooner inside than Bill's phone rang.

'We're in place.'

'I'm on my way.'

He paid his bill and complimented the woman on the scone in particular. She offered him one to take away. 'On the house,' she said and popped it in a bag.

Bill emerged and checked for the car. Campbell and Clark were sitting inside, looking like an ideal couple. Bill told them so when Janice rolled down the window, and she made a face at him.

DC Campbell got into the back, allowing Bill to slip into the space he'd vacated.

'OK, nobody falls asleep. We could be in for a long night.'

Three hours later, Angus and Jason were still in the pub. The other three men had departed by seven, leaving the furniture van parked next to the storeroom door.

As the time went on, no one mentioned food, although DC Campbell's stomach had started to protest loudly. Bill eventually told him to hand the camera to DS Clark and go and get pizza for himself and Janice.

'What about you, Sir?'

'I have something here,' Bill indicated the scone bag.

Campbell wasn't long gone when Angus and Jason emerged from the pub and went round to the side door of the charity shop. Angus pulled up the shutter and the two disappeared inside.

'They've put the lights on,' Janice said.

Bill called Campbell's mobile. 'Stay away until I tell you.'

'But I've got the pizza, Sir.'

'Wait where you are, Constable.'

Angus was coming back out carrying a nest of tables which he loaded into the van. Jason followed with a mirror.

'What are they doing, Sir?'

'Pilfering, most likely. And here comes Jimmy Dixon, back to help.'

Jimmy went inside and he and Jason emerged carrying a green armchair. Angus managed its mate all on his own.

'Is this what you were expecting, Sir?'

'I'm not sure what I was expecting,' Bill answered honestly.

Last came the sofa, which two of the men loaded with some difficulty – clearly it was heavier than it looked. Then Angus handed Jimmy some notes and he headed off.

'Yep, looks like they're stealing furniture, Sir.'

'Or making a late delivery,' replied Bill.

Jason disappeared one more time and emerged with a black backpack, then Angus pulled down the shutter, locked it and got into the driver's seat. The engine started up and the van drew out on to Dumbarton Road.

'We could pull him over. Breathalyse him.'

'Just follow the van, Sergeant, and don't make it too obvious.'

'What about Campbell?'

Bill called his DC's mobile, and Campbell appeared from a side street, balancing the pizza box as he ran. He threw it in the back then slid in as DS Clark took off.

The furniture van stayed on Dumbarton Road for several miles, finally taking a right into a row of houses and drawing up. DS Clark came to an abrupt halt.

'Sorry, Sir.'

'Lights out.'

Bill watched Angus emerge, carrying the backpack. Jason climbed out and the two began a heated argument. Jason tried to leave and Angus pulled him back, thrusting the bag into his arms.

'Let's go.' Bill sprang from the car and walked swiftly towards the pair.

Jason spotted him and looked ready to run, but Angus caught and held him, face grim.

'What's in the bag, Angus?'

'See for yourself.'

Bill took the bag and unzipped it. Inside was a camera, a flash gun and a torch, all marked with fluorescent yellow labels bearing the initials JE. 'I assume this belongs to Jude Evans?'

'Aye, it does.'

Jason looked sick. Angus saw his expression and seemed to take pity on him. 'It's all right, son, it's time they were told.'

'Told what, Angus?'

'What happened the night the lassie disappeared.'

52

'Here we are again, Jason. Pity you didn't tell the truth the first time round.'

Jason didn't lift his head as Bill set the tape running and listed who was present at the interview.

'Right. Now tell me *exactly* what happened last Tuesday night.'

The boy took a deep, quavery breath and began. 'What I told you before was true, up to where you saw me on camera talking to Jude. She said she'd forgotten something and needed back in, but I told her I'd have to ask Angus if it was OK. She said she'd hang around. Angus was playing darts so I waited until he finished his turn. He went and let her in. He was back in five minutes. Maybe an hour later, he told me to go and see why she hadn't come back round. The light was still on in the foyer. I headed upstairs and shouted but there was no answer. So I checked the balcony and the projection room.'

'You had a torch?' Bill said.

Jason looked startled by Bill's interruption. 'No.'

'From what I remember it's pretty dark up there.'

Jason shrugged. 'Your eyes get used to it. Anyway, I only opened the doors and shouted her name. She didn't answer.'

'She never picked up her recorder,' Bill said. 'It was in the projection room. We found it later.'

'So she didn't go up there?'

'Maybe she couldn't?'

'What d'you mean?'

'Maybe she was already dead.'

The colour was draining from Jason's face.

'I swear I never saw her.'

'Where did you find the bag?'

'In the foyer near the basement door.'

'When?'

'Wednesday.'

'You're sure it was Wednesday and not Tuesday?'

'I found it on Wednesday.'

'Why were you in the cinema on Wednesday?'

'I go there sometimes,' he said, eyes down.

'You took a girl?'

'No. I was on my own.'

'If you found the bag on Wednesday, why not give it to the police when they arrived on Thursday?'

'You weren't here because of the lassie. You were here because of the body behind the wall.'

'You were planning to sell the camera?'

Jason looked embarrassed. 'If she didn't come back for it.'

'And you never thought it strange that she didn't? All that expensive equipment?'

'I got scared. I thought you'd blame me for her disappearing like that.'

'So you got Angus to lie for you?'

'Angus knows I never did anything to that lassie.'

Once again Bill started a tape running and recited those present.

'OK, Angus. Tell us what happened last Tuesday night.'

Angus cleared his throat. 'I let the lassie in.'

'Jude Evans?' Bill established.

'Aye, Jude Evans. She'd left her recorder behind and wanted to look for it. We talked as I took her through the shop. She asked if I knew a Mr Nelson, who used to manage the place. I told her I knew an 'Admiral' Nelson and I didn't like him much.'

'What was her reaction to that?'

'She didn't react really. I unlocked the door to the cinema and put the light on in the foyer. I asked where she thought she'd left the recorder and she said she wasn't sure. It could be any of the places she'd taken photographs in. I told her to come to the pub when she was finished and I'd lock up. When she didn't arrive, I sent Jason to check.'

'How long was it before you sent Jason?'

Angus shrugged. 'Couple of pints. It could have been an hour.'

'What did Jason say when he came back?'

'That he shouted on her, but there was no answer. We thought she'd left without telling us. Then I went and locked up.'

'Did you lock the projection-room door?'

Angus shook his head. 'I locked the partition door and the front door.'

'What about the backpack?'

'Jason never mentioned a bag, not then.' Angus was scowling now.

'When did he tell you?'

'Not until tonight. That was what the fight was about.'

'Did he say when he found it?'

'No, but it had to be Tuesday when he went looking for the girl.'

'Jason said it was Wednesday.'

Angus's face went darker still with anger. 'I told him not to go back in there.'

'Because he took girls in?'

'Aye, that. And because it could lose him his job.'

'So you weren't aware he was in the cinema on Wednesday?'

'No.' Angus looked about ready to throttle Jason when they met again.

'You told me you saw Jude with a tall blond boy outside the Rosevale.'

'I just said that to get you off Jason's back.'

'Lying to the police is a criminal offence.'

Angus met Bill's eye levelly. 'I'm telling the truth now, Detective Inspector.'

'When you talked to Jude did she mention how she knew Mr Nelson?'

'She'd found an old film that he was interested in. I told her not to trust him.'

'You didn't see Mr Nelson near the building that night?'

Angus gave him a sharp look. 'You think Nelson might have something to do with the lassie's disappearance?'

'Do you?'

Angus considered this. 'The Admiral had an eye for boys, not girls, but he liked to get his own way. If he didn't, he could turn nasty.'

It was a fair summary of Nelson.

'When you sent Jason to check on Jude, how long exactly was he away?'

'Ten minutes, maybe fifteen. He said he called out for her, then checked the balcony and the projection room just to be sure.'

'Did he take a torch with him?'

Angus looked wary. 'No, why?'

'The balcony and projection room are pretty dark.'

'If she'd been there, she would have answered.'

'Not if she was already dead,' snapped Bill.

Angus reacted as though he'd just been punched. 'You think she was killed in there?'

'She never picked up her recorder. It was in the projection room. She left her bag behind. What do you think?'

'It wasn't Jason. I'd swear to that.'

Bill left Angus writing out his statement and retreated to his office with a coffee, fighting off the desire for sleep. The search of the cinema would begin soon and he needed to be there. In the meantime he considered the two stories. They matched, apart from the day Jason said he found the bag. Had the bag always been sitting in the foyer and he hadn't noticed it on Tuesday? Or was its appearance on Wednesday significant?

Bill opened the file DS Clark had prepared on Jason Donald's previous brush with the law. According to the girl involved, she'd been chatting to Jason in a club. He'd seemed nice. They talked for a while, then he'd offered to get her a cab because she was drunk. She'd agreed and they went outside. It had started to rain, so they took shelter in a doorway. She remembered kissing him and then things got a bit more heated. She thought she said no, but they'd had sex anyway. It sounded like most Saturday nights in the town centre. Drunk girls, barely able to stand. How could they be sure if they'd said yes or no to sex?

A second item of information caught Bill's eye. Jason Donald had been born Jason Robertson. His mother had been fifteen at the time. She later married Kenneth Donald, an army sergeant, who was later killed in Iraq. His mother, unable to cope with the loss of her husband, committed suicide when Jason was sixteen. On her death, Jason had moved in with his uncle, Angus Robertson.

Bill lifted his coffee and went back down to the interview rooms. Neither Jason nor Angus had left yet. Both statements were being reviewed before their dismissal.

Angus looked up as Bill entered.

'What's up?'

'What relation is Jason to you?'

'My sister's wean. That's why I look out for him.'

The lights were on in the charity shop when Bill arrived at just past 8 a.m. Bill knocked and Carol emerged from the back and opened the door.

'Can I go now, or would you rather I stayed?' She looked worried.

'It's better if you leave us to it.'

She handed him a set of keys. 'You'll get these back to me?'

Bill promised he would.

'The one with the red sticker takes you through to the old cinema.' She almost shuddered as she said it.

Bill locked the front door behind her. He didn't want anyone coming in while he was through the back, though he had plenty of time before the search team arrived.

Pulling on a pair of latex gloves and retrieving Jude's camera from the evidence bag, he slipped the labelled key in the lock and opened the partition door. Once in the foyer he set the video to replay and listened as Jude gave the time and place, then her reaction.

Wow. It's much better than I thought it would be. The central island paybox is still intact and the terrazzo pattern's designed to radiate from there.

The camera swept upwards to capture the frieze.

Partick, or Partaig in Gaelic, was where the Highlanders came to settle. Look at that mural. Stags and mountains and lochs. Note to self – create a ghost shot in here. Shadowy people queuing at the box. Poster advertising 'Brigadoon'. Someone looking up, longing on their face for the real thing.

Silence followed as she (and Bill) headed for the main staircase and climbed, the torch bouncing in the darkness.

The projection room is usually above the balcony, but not always.

The video camera showed the narrow door on Bill's right. He pushed it open and entered.

There it is. The telltale sign.

The camera screen focused on the 'No Smoking' warning above the Projection Room door.

They pushed open the second door together. There was a break in the recording then it came back on. Now the projection room was lit up.

And we're in the holy of holies. The projection room, or The Box as it was better known.

The camera swung round, taking in the portholes in the opposite wall.

There was a bang like a door shutting.

OK, I'd prefer the door open, said Jude's voice on the film.

The camera was set down. In its eye Bill caught sight of Jude picking up a brick. She was going to wedge the door open.

The recording resumed. As Bill heard her call out, 'Is anyone there?' the hairs on the back of his neck stood up.

She recorded the battery room. Bill heard her mutter something about a bad smell. There was some scrabbling then Jude was through to the usherettes' room. The camera viewed the brick wall, its owner still muttering something about the smell as she moved towards it. Seconds later it was switched off.

Bill retraced Jude's steps to the emergency exit, exited and shut it behind him. He imagined her getting to the bottom, then realising she'd dropped her recorder. He walked round to where she'd been captured on CCTV talking to Jason, wanting back in.

Bill stood there looking round. Where would Jude go to waste twenty minutes? He glanced across the road where the coffee shop beckoned.

'Back again?' The woman behind the counter gave him a welcoming smile. 'Let me guess, tea and a cherry scone, or would you rather a bacon roll for breakfast?'

'Maybe later.' Bill showed her his ID. She looked rather taken aback.

'Were you working here last Tuesday evening around half five?'

'I work every day except Sunday and we shut at six, but you know that already.'

'Did a young girl come in about then? Five foot two, dark hair, late teens, carrying a black backpack?'

She thought about it. 'There was a girl, yes. Came in, ordered a mug of tea. She didn't stay long though. I went through the back for something. Came back, she was gone.'

'Thanks.'

Bill exited and crossed the street, letting himself in through the front door again. Jude had spotted Angus and come to meet him. He'd let her in, opened the door to the old cinema and put on the foyer light for her.

Bill's mobile rang. It was Rhona.

'DS Clark said you found Jude's bag.'

'I have it here for you. Come to the café across the road from the Rosevale,' Bill said. 'I'll bring you up to date.'

53

Bill finished telling Rhona what he now knew, sighed and took a bite of his third cherry scone in twenty-four hours.

'Well. If Angus is related to Jason, that explains why he didn't tell the truth earlier,' said Rhona.

'Maybe he's still not telling the truth.'

'What about Charlie and Nelson?'

'I have nothing that puts Charlie near the Rosevale that night. As for Nelson, I've detained him once for this, so I can't do it again without new evidence linking him to Jude's disappearance.' Bill wearily ran a hand through his hair. 'As I said, we know Jude got as far as the usherettes' room before the camera was switched off. Why don't you take the bag to the lab? Process it. I want to know whose DNA is on it. As to the cinema, I'll call you if or when we find anything.'

Chrissy was waiting impatiently for Rhona's arrival.

'Come and see this.'

The dismantled wall from the cinema had been reassembled in the lab, each numbered brick placed in its appropriate place.

'I used a fine spray of ninhydrin,' Chrissy said. 'It took a week to develop, but look!' She pointed at brick number one.

Triketohydrindene hydrate on the porous surface had reacted with a latent fingerprint to produce a bluish-purple colour, known as Ruhemann's Purple.

'I did a DNA test on the brick, just in case the ninhydrin didn't work. If we get a match with one of the suspects, then we know who replaced that brick.'

'This is great,' exclaimed Rhona.

'I know.' Modesty wasn't one of Chrissy's attributes. 'So what have you got to tell me?'

Rhona told her the story of Jude's bag.

Chrissy looked sad. 'The bag sort of makes it final, doesn't it?'

'Bill wants to bring Nelson in again but he can't unless we can link him to the cinema, or Jude to his car.'

'On the car front, I have a couple of hairs to compare with the control sample from Jude's hairbrush. I also picked up a few fibres, but we have nothing to compare them to. I've taken an initial look at the soil sample. I'd say organic, so it came from cultivated ground, a field, park or garden. I haven't gone further than that.'

They parted company, Chrissy to continue with her samples and Rhona to examine the bag. Laying its contents on the table, she experienced a similar reaction to Chrissy's; Jude's disappearance had already been upgraded to a murder enquiry, but seeing the girl's precious camera equipment laid out seemed to finally confirm her death.

She would have to tell Liam. It was a job Rhona didn't relish, knowing he was nursing a hope, however slim, that Jude might still be alive.

She checked off the contents against the attached list, then began a closer examination, carefully dusting the

exterior of the camera equipment for prints before down-
loading the stored video and stills on to her laptop and
watching the video.

Rhona was just about to start work on the bag itself
when Bill called.

'Can you come down?'

'You've found a body?'

'No, but the dog's picked up on something.'

A crowd of onlookers had gathered outside the charity
shop, no doubt shortly to be followed by a news crew.
Rhona thought of calling Liam to warn him in case the
increased police activity hit the TV screens, then decided
to wait until she had something to warn him about.

Bill filled her in as she suited up.

'Roy compared the plans and came up with spaces
between refurbishments. We checked them all, with no
luck. Then we moved to the basement. There was a room
there the dog was particularly interested in. We pulled
away a set of shelves and found an old cupboard behind.
When we opened the door, the dog went mad.'

They entered the old cinema and crossed the foyer to a
doorway. Beyond, a set of concrete steps led downwards.
At the foot, the smell of damp and mould grew stronger.

'The basement isn't used for storage. Too damp, apparently. We checked down here the first time, but had no
idea there was a door behind the shelves.'

Bill led Rhona to a room at the end of a long narrow
corridor, where a shelving unit had been pulled aside to
expose a hidden cupboard. The cupboard was empty.

The scent of decay was stronger here, but more complex,

clearly caused by more than just mould. Rhona approached the cupboard, crouching for a better view of the floor. As a body began its decomposition it seeped liquids, some of which, she suspected, were present on the floor.

'What do you think?'

'I think the dog was right,' Rhona said.

Bill left Rhona to process the scene while he went back to the foyer, deep in thought. In hunting for her voice recorder, Jude had been planning to check everywhere she'd visited. The foyer was the easiest to search because it had light, and his guess was that after checking there methodical Jude would check the usherettes' room first and work outwards. Since she had never located the recorder, he thought she'd been disturbed before having the chance to look around the projection room properly. The question was, who had disturbed her?

She'd indicated to Aurora that she planned to meet Nelson. Would that have been at the Rosevale? And if Nelson had arrived in time to see her go inside, would he have followed?

According to Angus, Jason had gone to check on Jude an hour after Angus had let her in – plenty of time for Nelson to encounter Jude, kill her and hide the body.

If Nelson *had* killed her, he must have hidden the body in the cupboard planning to dispose of it later. As he had keys to the building, that wouldn't have been a problem. But why would he leave the bag in the foyer?

Bill left the old cinema and stood for a moment on the silent shop floor, before heading for the storeroom. Jason had said he'd stored the backpack in his locker. Bill went into what looked like a cloakroom. There were overalls on wall hooks and half a dozen named lockers. Bill opened Jason's; it contained a sweater, a pair of dirty jeans and a can of Irn Bru. He didn't touch anything, intending to have Rhona or a SOCO take a closer look.

He walked through the piled-up furniture, including three suites and two large wardrobes, recalling the men loading the heavy sofa into the van the previous night. He'd set up the surveillance in the hope that Angus or Jason would react to his threat to search the building again, and it had succeeded up to a point. He had Jude's bag, but not her body. The van had been searched and the furniture checked out; the sofa was a sofa and nothing more, although when he'd watched the men struggle to load it in the van he'd thought briefly there might be a body concealed inside.

Bill abandoned the storeroom and went to check on Rhona. A team of SOCOs had arrived, so Bill dispatched one of them to check out Jason's locker.

'I've taken samples from the cupboard,' Rhona told him. 'We should be able to establish quite quickly whether the missing body was Jude's.'

'Can you tell when it was removed?'

'It's possible I could give an estimate, once I analyse the chemical make-up of the leakage. I have to go, I'm afraid, but the SOCOs will do the rest.'

'Did you get a chance to look at the bag?'

'I listened to the recording and watched the video.' Rhona's voice faltered. 'I need to speak to Liam before this hits the news.'

'I agree. It's better if he hears it from you.'

54

When she rang Liam's mobile he picked up straight away.

'You've found her?' he asked, his voice high and thin.

'No. But we've found something. Can we meet so I can tell you about it?'

There was a moment's silence. 'Can you come by the flat?'

The police had set up a wider cordon round the charity shop in an effort to allow access for crime-scene personnel without them having to push through the curious throng of onlookers. Rhona escaped the mêlée and headed for her car; the sooner she reached Liam, the better. Bill was going to have to give a statement soon and she wanted to pre-empt that.

Rhona composed herself as she climbed the stairs. She certainly hadn't envisaged visiting her son's flat for the first time carrying news like this.

Liam had the door open and was waiting for her.

'It's bad, isn't it?' he blurted.

'It's not good.'

He led her through an untidy hall and into a good-sized bedroom, then shut the door behind them.

'Well?' he said.

Rhona's heart went out to him. 'Sit down first.'

He took a seat at the computer.

'We searched the Rosevale with a dog this morning, one

trained to find human remains. We didn't find a body, but we did find evidence to suggest there had been one hidden in the basement. We also found Jude's bag with her camera equipment.'

Liam had clearly been expecting the worst, but the news still hit him hard.

'Jude was killed in the Rosevale?'

'We think so, yes.'

'But you said she left there. You saw her on CCTV?'

'She went back for her recorder, just like you said she would.'

Liam was absorbing this, his face strained and white. Rhona wanted to embrace him, but knew that wasn't possible. Liam wasn't a child and she wasn't really his mother, not in the ways that really counted. She wondered whether he had spoken to his adoptive parents about what he had been through recently. She hoped so.

'I'm sorry, Liam.'

'What happened to her body?'

'We don't know yet.'

'Will you find it?'

'I hope so.'

He stood up and began to pace. 'I should have gone there sooner. I should have looked harder.'

'This isn't your fault. You searched for Jude. You wouldn't give up even when I told you to.'

'It didn't make any difference, did it?' he snapped at her. 'Nothing made any difference.'

'You tried. That's what matters.'

He shook his head as though dispensing with her platitudes and made for the door. 'I'll have to tell Ben. And Aurora.' He looked sick at the prospect.

'I could speak to Ben if you like?'

'No,' he said, sharply. 'I'll do it myself.'

Rhona stood up. She could tell he just wanted her to leave.

'It'll probably be on the news later,' she warned him.

Liam said nothing as he escorted her to the front door. As she was leaving, Rhona caught a glimpse of Ben waiting for the bad news in the doorway of his room.

55

Carol Miller didn't look surprised to see Bill.

'You've brought the keys?'

'I'll have to hang on to them a bit longer, I'm afraid.'

'You found something?'

'Yes.'

'What?'

'Can I come in?'

Carol fought to regain her composure. 'Of course. Go into the lounge.' She pointed ahead to the left. 'Can I make you some tea?'

'No thanks. I won't stay long.'

Bill entered a bright but small sitting room where a three-piece suite took up most of the floor space. It was an old-fashioned model but looked comfortable. Carol caught his glance. 'I paid for it. The going rate. Most of the workers have bought an item of furniture from the shop. It's a perk of the job. So, what did you find?' She seemed to be bracing herself for his reply.

'A dog trained to find dead bodies indicated that one had been in the basement.'

'But you already checked down there, didn't you?'

'There was a cupboard hidden behind some shelving.'

'You think it was the missing girl?'

'It seems likely.'

'My God.' She shook her head in disbelief. 'I should never have let her go in there.'

'Can you tell me who holds the keys to the furniture van?'

His question had startled her. 'There are two sets. One stays in the storeroom. Jimmy has the other set during the day, because he does most of the collections. He usually parks the van at the side door and leaves his keys with the other set.'

'So someone could have borrowed the van?'

'I suppose so.'

'Is the van always parked up outside?'

'Occasionally Jimmy takes it home if he has an early collection.'

'Do you have a note of when that happens?'

'No. That's Angus's department.'

'What happens to the furniture you can't sell?'

'We give some bits to homeless charities. If it's in poor condition we take it to the dump.'

'How often do you use the dump?'

'Once a week on average.'

Carol was working out what was behind all the questions. 'You don't think someone from the shop was involved in this, do you?'

'Someone locked the door to the projection room. I'd like to know who that was.'

Carol shook her head in bafflement. 'I have no idea, Detective Inspector.'

Bill left her then, feeling troubled. He'd planted a seed of suspicion in Carol's head about her staff and she wasn't happy about it. Bill knew the feeling well.

Suspicion was the only thing occupying his own mind at the moment.

He got into the car, although he was really too tired to drive, or to think clearly. He called DS Clark and told her he was headed home to catch up on some sleep.

'But if anything comes up, I want to know about it. Right away, please. Got that?'

Bill opened the front door to a silent house and realised both Margaret and the kids would be at school. He climbed the stairs wearily and lay down on top of the bed, his mobile close by where he would hear it if it rang.

56

Rhona eased her mask out a little in order to get a better sense of the smell emanating from the base of the black canvas bag. If what she suspected was true, the bag had been in close proximity to the liquid she'd sampled in the cupboard.

Decomposition would have begun minutes after Jude's death. Soon after that enzymes would have begun to dissolve her cells from the inside out, causing them to rupture and release nutrient-rich fluids, blistering the skin. Hence the seepage.

Rhona doubted whether Jude had lain in the cupboard for long after the initial stage. Even if the corpse was wrapped, putrefaction would have left more of an impact in that enclosed space. Someone, she would guess, had shifted the body as soon as possible and certainly within forty-eight hours.

It followed that Jason had lied about the backpack. It couldn't have picked up a deposit such as this from the foyer or the locker. It had to have been in contact with the body or hidden in the cupboard.

Bill's voice was bleary when he finally answered his mobile.

'Did I wake you?' said Rhona apologetically.

'No problem. What is it?'

'The same fluid was on the bag as in the cupboard.'

'So Jason was lying about where he found the bag?'

'It looks like it.'

Bill made an exasperated noise. 'I've had it with that pair.'

'You think they're both involved?'

'I think Angus has been covering for him all along.'

Bill had a quick shower and fixed himself a sandwich, then wrote a note for Margaret and left it on the kitchen table.

He'd already called DS Clark and asked her to organise the arrest warrants, one for Jason and one for Angus. Gradually everything was coming into focus. The way Angus had avoided admitting his connection to Jason, although they lived in the same house. The changing stories, always, Bill suspected, concocted by Angus. Angus's blatant admission that he looked out for Jason, even to the point of lying for him.

Bill drew up in front of the semi-detached house from the previous night. There was no van there now, but the sitting-room light was on, as was a light in an upper room. Bill walked up the path and rang the doorbell. It was Angus who answered.

'DI Wilson.'

'Can I come in?'

'Of course.'

Angus led him into the sitting room. Bill was reminded of Carol's house. This time the suite was leather and still too big for the room. Angus waved him to a seat.

'What's up now?'

Bill decided to be blunt. 'A forensic examination has shown Jude's bag was in contact with a dead body, probably hers.'

'What?' Angus looked bewildered. 'I don't understand. Jason said he found it in the foyer.'

'I know. I have to ask you, Angus. Did you help Jason remove Jude's body from the cinema?'

Angus looked at him in horror. 'You really believe he harmed that lassie?'

'It looks that way.'

Angus buried his head in his hands. When he emerged, he looked a broken man.

'I thought he was OK. After the last time, he promised he would . . .' He stuttered to a halt. When he spoke again, his voice was almost too low for Bill to hear. 'Jason asked for the van keys last Wednesday night. When I asked why, he said a mate had bought a stereo from the shop. He wanted to deliver it himself. I gave him the keys.' The pain of what he was saying showed on Angus's face.

'Is Jason here?'

'Upstairs.'

When he appeared Jason looked flushed, like an embarrassed teenager called to face his elders. Bill told him to sit down.

'Where did you find the bag, Jason?'

He looked surprised. 'I told you. In the foyer.'

'Tell the truth now, boy,' Angus ordered, sharply.

'It *is* the truth.' Jason's eyes darted from Angus to Bill and back again.

'The bag has been in contact with a dead body,' Bill said. 'Jude's.'

'What? Jason shook his head wildly. 'No way! It was sitting in the foyer. Abi saw it first—' he stopped dead.

'Abi?' Bill said.

Jason visibly cringed under Angus's furious glare.

'The wee lassie from the coffee shop? Jesus, boy, she's only thirteen.'

'She's fourteen and we didn't do anything. I just took her in to show her the balcony.'

'You were with a girl?' Bill said.

Jason nodded. 'It was Abi who noticed the bag first.'

'Where was the bag exactly?'

'At the door to the basement. I had a look inside and saw the camera. I told Abi a girl had been there photographing the cinema and she must have forgotten it.'

'You never saw this bag on Tuesday night?'

Jason shook his head.

'Why didn't you tell me this before, Jason?'

'Why d'you think?' Jason looked at Angus.

'What about the van?' Bill said.

'What about it?'

'You borrowed it on Wednesday night. Why?'

Jason shrugged as though giving up on the fight. 'I took Abi out for a run.'

'What?' Angus exploded from the sidelines. 'You said—'

'We only went as far as Victoria Park. Parked up and listened to Radio One.'

'And Abi will vouch for that?'

'I told her not to say anything.'

'I'll need Abi's address,' Bill said.

'Her mother runs the coffee place across the road from the shop,' Angus told him. 'Her name's Joanne Fisher.'

57

Bill pushed open the coffee shop door.

'Back again?' Joanne flashed him a smile. 'The usual?'

'Just tea. Can you spare a few minutes to talk to me?'

'OK.' She looked intrigued. 'I'll tell Abi to keep an eye on the counter.' She disappeared into the back and re-emerged with a young girl in tow. Dressed in school uniform, she looked younger than fourteen, despite the make-up. A grumpy look on her face, she settled herself on a stool and produced a magazine, which she proceeded to flick through.

Bill wondered how he was going to play this. He hadn't expected Abi to be there, although it might prove easier in the long run.

Joanne brought his order to the table along with a cup for herself.

'Right. How can I help?'

'I wondered if you knew Jason Donald. The lad that works across in the storeroom of the charity shop?'

Joanne's eyes flicked between Bill and her daughter. 'Why d'you want to know?'

'Jason says he's been seeing your daughter, Abi. I wondered if that was true?'

Joanne was silent for a moment. 'He's too old for her. She's only just turned fourteen.'

'So she knows him?'

Joanne nodded.

'Could I speak to Abi?'

She looked guarded. 'I don't know about that.'

'It's important, or I wouldn't ask.'

Joanne crossed to the counter and spoke quietly to Abi, who shot Bill a frightened look. Her mother brought her across and they both sat down at the table.

'Abi, I'm Bill Wilson. I'm trying to find out what happened to a girl a little older than you who disappeared from the cinema across the road last Tuesday night. You heard about that?'

She nodded.

'And you know Jason Donald?'

Abi tried to avoid her mother's eye.

'He works across in the storeroom.'

'You're friends?'

She considered whether she could admit that much. 'I know him,' she conceded.

'Have you ever gone into the old cinema building with him?'

'No!' She sounded shocked, but she could be a good actress.

'So you weren't in the cinema with him last Wednesday night?'

Abi shook her head vehemently.

'Did you go out in the van for a run with him on the same night?'

'No!'

'Then Jason is lying?'

Now she looked unsure.

'Because he said you did and he told you not to tell anyone.'

Joanne intervened. 'I want you to tell the Detective Inspector the truth, Abi. I won't be mad at you.'

Abi didn't look convinced.

'But I *will* be mad if you lie,' Joanne continued sternly.

Abi shrugged. 'I wanted to see the old cinema. Jason took me in.'

'And?'

'You want to know about the bag, don't you?'

'What bag?' said her mother.

Abi looked uncertain again, then made up her mind. 'There was a backpack with camera stuff in it lying in the foyer.'

'Did Jason say anything about the bag?'

'He thought it belonged to the girl who'd been there taking photos. He said she'd come back for it.'

'Then what happened?'

'He showed me the old balcony,' she flushed, 'then we went in the van to Victoria Park and listened to Radio One. Then I came home.'

Joanne Fisher looked at Bill. 'Is that what you wanted to know?'

'It is.'

Joanne took her daughter's hand and squeezed it.

58

'His name is actually Philip Matheson,' said Janice. 'He maintains he never knew Dominic McGeehan, just stole his identity. He was in debt, a lot of it. Started running it up when he was a student, and added some more via gambling as he tried to repay the original sum. Eighty grand in total. It was easier to leave that behind.'

'And his story checks out?'

'It does, Sir.'

'OK, back to Nelson. What about the material you took from his yacht?'

'The team are still working through it, but the opinion is we can charge him under Section 34.'

It was something, but not yet enough for Bill. 'And no sign of the reel of film?'

'No.'

'I want Nelson brought back in and detained on suspicion of being in possession of extreme pornography.' Bill rose. 'I'm going to speak to the Super.'

'You're confident that the material viewed can be prosecuted under Section 34?'

'A number of the moving images realistically depict an act which takes or threatens a person's life. Even if the person consented—'

The Super cut him off. 'I don't need to be reminded what Section 34 says.'

'There's more than just that, Sir. Nelson has a library of extreme images. He used to manage the charity shop and had access to the old cinema around the time of the killing. Dr MacLeod has identified Gavin Maclean's DNA on the corpse. I believe there is a strong possibility that MacLean and Nelson were known to one another.'

'What has that to do with the missing girl?'

'The film Jude Evans discovered in the Olympia was in a similar vein to Nelson's material. On the night she disappeared, Jude had arranged to meet Nelson about that film.'

'This will reopen the MacLean case?'

'Gavin MacLean's semen was on the cinema victim.'

Sutherland made an exasperated noise.

'I sincerely hope you're not going to hound members of the public who have already been cleared in the MacLean case?'

'Not unless their image appears in any of the captured material, Sir.'

'I want any such evidence run past me before you act on it, Detective Inspector.'

'Of course, Sir.'

Bill left then, thinking to himself that if Dalrymple was identified as an onlooker or participant in any of the material taken from Nelson's library – or for that matter in the older film – he would take great delight in going straight to Sutherland to tell him.

'Nelson's here, Sir.'

'Any word from the lab on his car?'

DS Clark shook her head. 'Not yet. Shall I give them a call?'

'Get Campbell to do that. Tell him to break in on us if we get a result. You come with me.'

While Bill waited outside the interview room for Janice to catch him up, he observed the suspect through the glass. Nelson already had a lawyer with him, and judging by the smart cut of his suit, an expensive one.

Clark arrived. 'Dr MacLeod will get a message to us as soon as they have anything.'

Bill had to be content with that.

They entered and took seats opposite Nelson. Bill's first thought was that the old bugger looked pleased with himself.

Bill started the ball rolling. 'Are you aware of Section 34?' When Nelson didn't reply, Bill quoted him its contents and said, 'It is under this section that we plan to charge you.'

Nelson didn't look perturbed; in fact, Bill could have sworn he made out a smothered smile.

'No comment.'

Bill felt his hackles rise. He would be lucky to get anything out of Nelson, especially with his lawyer present to tell him when to keep quiet. Bill longed for the day, only just recently, when he could have had Nelson all to himself for six hours.

'Where were you last Tuesday evening?'

'At home.'

'Can anyone vouch for that?'

'I live alone, as you well know, Inspector.'

'So you didn't arrange to meet Jude Evans about an old film reel?'

'I already told you, our arrangement was for Wednesday evening at six o'clock.'

'Where?'

'At the Rosevale on Dumbarton Road.'

'But she didn't turn up?'

'That's right.'

'You waited for her? Where?'

'On the side street.'

'Was the shop's van parked there?'

'I don't know. Yes, I think so.'

'How long did you wait?'

'Twenty minutes.'

'There's a CCTV camera nearby, so we should be able to check that.'

Nelson's confident expression slipped a little.

'Your car had a lot of loose soil on the pedals and the mudguards. Care to tell me why?'

'It's muddy down where the yacht's moored.'

'The soil came from there?'

'Yes.'

'Soil is unique to location. So we'll be checking that too.'

The mask of confidence slipped some more. Nelson looked to his lawyer, who shook his head.

'As I understand it, Jude was taking photographs of derelict Glasgow cinemas for her Art School project. In the Olympia Bridgeton she found an old film reel. She contacted people online to try to find out more about the film, and was given your name. You were keen to see the film. Am I right so far?'

Nelson nodded reluctantly.

'For the benefit of the tape, Mr Nelson has nodded. Jude arrived at the Rosevale at four thirty on Tuesday evening. She re-emerged around five thirty only to discover she'd left her recorder inside. The storeman let her back in to look for it.'

Nelson sat back, looking bored.

'When she hadn't reappeared an hour later, Jason Donald was sent to check on her. Both men believed she'd left, and Angus locked up.'

'If you say so, Inspector. As I say, I wasn't there.'

'Do you have a set of keys for the charity shop?'

'I do not,' Nelson said firmly.

'And you weren't in the Rosevale cinema on Tuesday night?'

'Most definitely not. I never went into the old cinema, even when I worked in the shop.' Nelson seemed adamant.

'What about the basement?'

'What about it?'

'Were you ever in the basement of the old cinema?'

'No. Why would I be?'

'Did you ever meet Jude Evans?'

'No.'

'She did not give you the film reel?'

'I never met her, I told you.'

'When you heard she'd gone missing, why didn't you come forward?'

'It wasn't my business. I didn't know the girl.'

The lawyer intervened. 'Can we get to the reason my client was brought here? The material removed from his yacht.'

'Did you know what Jude's film reel contained, Mr Nelson?'

'No.'

'Jude didn't describe what was on it?'

'She just said it was old and where she'd found it.'

'Are you familiar with the Olympia Bridgeton?'

'In its heyday, yes.'

'Did you know the projectionist there, a man called Brian Foster?'

Nelson visibly started, something noted by his lawyer, who quickly intervened.

'I still don't see what this has to do with the material on my client's yacht?'

Bill ignored the interruption and continued. 'Many years ago Brian Foster was also the projectionist at a private club on St Vincent Street which showed violent pornographic films, shot locally. I think you suspected the film Jude found was one of those.'

Nelson squirmed in his seat. Clearly he did not want to hear this.

'When Jude discovered what the film depicted, she decided to give it to us rather than you. You weren't happy about that, were you?'

Nelson opened his mouth, then shut it again as his lawyer touched his arm.

'One more thing before we take a break. Does the name Gavin MacLean mean anything to you?'

59

'They're exactly the same.'

Chrissy moved from her microscope to Rhona's and back again to check.

'It's marine-grade dyed acrylic,' Rhona told her. 'UV-, water- and mildew-resistant. Used for awnings, outdoor furniture and boat tops. He wrapped the body in it.'

A single fibre had been retrieved by Rhona from the basement cupboard, and Chrissy had found hers in the boot of Nelson's car.

'Plus leakage evidence from Jude's body in both places. But that's not all,' Chrissy said triumphantly, producing an AFR report. 'We have a match on the fingerprint I retrieved from the brick and, even better, a DNA result. Both belong to Nelson. Which means we could have him for more than just Jude.'

'That just leaves Charlie.'

'No sign of Jude in his car. But the vomit is there, and it matches Sally Murphy's DNA sample.'

Under new arrangements, provided Nelson had access to a lawyer, Bill could keep him there for twelve hours rather than six. But he would have to make up his mind soon what he planned to charge Nelson with.

He was on safe ground with Section 34, but Bill wanted

him for more than just that. Nelson had been furious when he'd brought up the subject of Brian Foster. It had been a shot in the dark but it had paid off.

That's why Nelson had been so keen to get that film; he knew if Jude found it in the Olympia, the chances were it was one from back then.

Bill tried to picture what had happened that night. Had Jude angered Nelson by refusing to hand over the film? Or had he killed her because she told him she knew what was on it and intended giving it to the police?

'Sir, Dr MacLeod is on the phone in the incident room. She says it's urgent.'

Bill listened to Rhona's explanation of the trace evidence collected from the cinema and from Nelson's car without interrupting, then said, 'Nelson insists he was never inside the cinema.'

'His print and DNA are both on the loose brick taken from the wall in the projection suite.'

'Nelson replaced that brick?'

'That's my guess, yes.'

Everything began to fall into place. Nelson arriving at the cinema, finding Jude in the usherettes' room; maybe she'd mentioned the smell or had been trying to extract the brick.

Nelson had been expecting to collect the film reel from her, but had suddenly found himself with a much bigger problem. Once Jude made up her mind to do something, she did it, and Nelson got aggressive when he didn't get his own way. The result that night had been the violent murder of a young girl.

There was still something he needed to check.

'What about the bag? Is he on that?' Bill said.

'He is, and so is Jason.'

Nelson *had* been at the Rosevale on Wednesday night, just as he'd said. But he'd been there to remove Jude's body, not to meet her for the first time.

Unfortunately for Nelson, Jason had chosen the same night to bring Abi in for a session on the loveseats. Nelson must have heard them and fled, leaving the bag behind – just as Jason had described.

Bill thanked Rhona and put the phone down. Around him the incident room waited in silence. Bill was sure the expression on his face told them all they needed to know, but he said it anyway: 'We have him.'

60

'There's no record of the laptop being advertised on eBay,' DS Clark told Bill. 'Charlie's lying about that.'

'Surely he would have known we would check?'

'Most people have no idea how eBay works unless they've used it themselves. Probably he just said it because he couldn't think of anything else at that moment. A few years ago, he would have said a car-boot sale.'

'He took the laptop from her room and tried to scrub out the initials.'

'Looks like it, Sir.'

'Chances are he took the reel of film, then.'

'Stealing the film would make it look less like an inside job,' agreed Janice.

'And it would also link the robbery to Jude's disappearance.'

Charlie might not be up to date on eBay transactions but he had a devious enough mind.

'I think I'll have another wee word with our friendly warden.'

Charlie was busy talking to a female student, as attentive and grandfatherly as ever. When he spotted Bill he smiled and said goodbye to her.

'OK,' said Charlie as he settled himself into a chair. 'What can I do you for this time, DI Wilson?'

'I've come for the film.'

Charlie looked startled. 'I don't have any film.'

'I think you do. I think you took it along with the laptop.'

'I wouldn't—'

'There's no record of the laptop sale on eBay.'

Charlie shrugged. 'I should have said I bought it at the Barras.'

'Jude's dead, Charlie. We're certain of that now.'

'I'm sorry to hear that, son.'

'You don't sound surprised?'

'A lassie disappears. The police get involved. It doesn't look good.' He shook his head sadly.

'I talked to Sally Murphy,' Bill continued.

'What's she been saying now?'

'That you gave her a lift, then jumped on her.'

Charlie huffed in disbelief. 'These lassies, drinking too much, taking drugs. They don't know what they're doing half the time.'

'So you never gave Sally a lift?'

'That's right.'

'Vomit's a hard thing to get rid of, even for a man who cleans his car as well as you do.'

There was a long silence. Charlie looked more thoughtful than worried.

'So what happens now, Detective Inspector?'

'You give me the film.'

'Or?'

'Sally's in two minds about taking you to court, but she's

concerned about you working here and using your keys to let yourself into other girls' rooms.'

Charlie sat bolt upright. 'You're threatening my job?'

'Oh, you're *leaving* your job. Question is: do you leave quietly, or do I charge you with sexual assault?'

'And this all depends on you locating this film?'

Bill nodded slowly.

Charlie shrugged. 'Funny what you find lying around.' He opened a drawer and took out a reel of film. 'Is this what you're looking for?'

Bill took it and rose. 'I suggest you have your resignation ready, Charlie. One more thing. We have your DNA on the database now. So any complaints from the girls . . .'

'The DNA sample won't stay on there if I'm not charged with anything. You know that as well as I do.'

'Oh, you'll be charged. For stealing a laptop and film reel from the room of a student in the Hall of Residence, while working here as a warden.'

Charlie met his gaze steadily. 'Can I have my car back now, DI Wilson?'

Bill called Liam's mobile from outside the building. It went to voicemail, but as soon as Bill hung up after leaving his message Liam called back.

'Who is this?' he said.

'Liam, it's Detective Inspector Wilson.'

There was a short silence. 'I know about Jude. Rhona told me.'

'Where are you?'

'At my flat.'

'Can you meet me, perhaps at your nearest pub? Aurora and Ben too, if you can reach them.'

Liam considered this. 'It's the Stravaigin, on Gibson Street.'

'I'll be there, waiting for you.'

Gibson Street had changed a lot in the last ten years. If Lisa had chosen Glasgow University she might have been living in a flat near here, Bill thought as he parked the car. But she had wanted to go further afield. Away from her dad and his fussing, no doubt. It could be worse, though – his daughter could have headed north to Aberdeen, or to one of the southern universities. At least Edinburgh was only an hour away.

He located the Stravaigin and ordered a pint of shandy, choosing to sit upstairs where it was quiet. While he waited, he worked out what he wanted to say to the three young people.

Thank you. That was it, really. Thank you for not giving up. And sorry that you couldn't save her. It wasn't much, but it needed to be said.

They arrived soon after, clutching their drinks as they climbed the narrow staircase. Liam had to duck to avoid a cross beam as he headed towards the corner table Bill had chosen. Rhona's son was as tall as his father, thought Bill, but he didn't have Edward's temperament, that was for sure.

Bill stood and offered his hand to each of them in turn. The solemn gesture surprised them, but he didn't think it caused embarrassment. Bill waited until they were settled before speaking.

'We've charged someone with Jude's murder.'

'Who?' said Liam.

'A man called Nelson.'

'The one Jude was going to meet about the film?' Aurora said.

'Yes, you remembering about Nelson really helped.' He turned to Ben and Liam. 'The Mulligan twins led us to Nelson too, and even further. We believe Nelson also knows something about the body in the projection room.'

'Wow!' Ben looked stunned.

'I wanted to thank you all. For Jude's sake.'

Liam looked down, emotion contorting his face. Aurora slipped her hand over his.

'What about her body?' he asked, his voice choked.

'We haven't located it yet. We believe he may have dumped it at sea.'

'So it might never turn up?'

'In my experience the sea gives things back eventually.' Bill knew it was a platitude, but it was also the truth.

'I spoke to the Art School,' Aurora told them. 'They're going to put on a special exhibition of Jude's "Cinema City" project.'

'I'll look forward to that,' said Bill warmly. 'I ought to warn you that you'll all have to give statements, and appear as witnesses in court.'

If he'd been concerned that they might take fright at this, he was pleasantly surprised; they all nodded eagerly, seeming almost pleased at the prospect.

'Your role in apprehending Nelson has been invaluable, and I wanted you to know that,' he told them.

*   *   *

Later, arriving at home, Bill slipped his key in the lock. From within he could hear the voices of those he loved, alive and well. He closed his eyes and said a brief prayer of thanks before opening the door.

61

Rhona hesitated on the steps of the Jazz Club. She would rather have celebrated their success with Bill and his team in the pub as usual, but Bill had chosen to go home.

'If I don't, Margaret will forget who I am. I'd take Chrissy up on her offer. Go to the Jazz Club.' He'd given Rhona a look she couldn't quite read.

Chrissy would be in there now, waiting, and it wasn't much to ask. Chrissy was more than just an excellent forensic assistant. She was a very good friend.

Rhona headed downstairs, making a mental note not to drink too much this time, and not to succumb to any sweet talking from Sean Maguire.

She was surprised to find the place buzzing until she realised it was Friday night; a time when sensible people forgot about work and got down to the business of enjoying themselves. That was something she'd almost forgotten how to do.

'Hey,' said Chrissy.

'Hey yourself.'

'Thought you might chicken out. There's a special bottle of wine set aside in anticipation of your arrival.' Chrissy grinned, delighted. 'Courtesy of the management.'

'Red, no doubt?'

'No. White.'

Now there was a surprise.

The chilled bottle appeared, was opened and a glass poured for her. Rhona took a sip. It was good.

'Sean and Sam are about to take to the stage,' Chrissy told her.

That's good too, Rhona thought. Better on stage, than here with me.

Chrissy was still beaming at her.

'What?'

She shook her head and pressed her lips together.

'What is it?'

'I'm not allowed to say.'

'Someone told you a secret and expected you to keep it?'

'Just drink your wine, sit back and enjoy the music.'

The crowd erupted in applause as Sean and Sam stepped on stage. Sean looked over at the bar, spotting her and smiling when she raised her glass to him. Sam began his introduction and the crowd fell silent. Rhona recognised the tune almost immediately; it was 'Misty', one of her favourites. Sean had often played it to her.

OK, she thought, I'm being set up for something here.

They played four more. Jazzy but tuneful, although she couldn't have put a name to them. When the applause died down on the last one, the two men left the stage. Rhona had assumed Sean would come over to talk to her and was surprised when he didn't.

Sam greeted her affectionately and accepted her praise for his playing with his usual modesty.

'He plays "Misty" at home,' Chrissy told her. 'It puts Michael to sleep.'

Maybe the track hadn't been meant for her after all. Rhona was surprised to find herself disappointed.

'Sean wants a word. In private,' Sam said, suddenly serious.

Rhona looked over at Chrissy and arched an eyebrow.

'Is this the surprise?' she said when Chrissy wasn't forthcoming.

'You could call it that.'

Curiosity got the better of her. Rhona finished what was left in her glass and set it on the counter before heading over to Sean's office and pushing open the door. A small desk light was on, but apart from that the room was in shadow. Rhona reached for the main light switch.

'Better not, or I'll have to put on my sunglasses – I've not seen daylight for a while.'

Rhona's heart jumped into her mouth as McNab stepped out of the shadows. Behind him she could make out a camp bed, and suddenly she realised what this was all about.

'How long have you been here?'

'Since Petersson let me go.'

He came a little closer, but she still couldn't make out his face.

'Sean let me stay. No questions asked.'

'I would never have thought to look for you here.'

'Me neither.'

His face looked as though it had been stepped on hard and frequently. He raised his hand as though to shield her from it, and she saw that three of his fingers were in splints.

'You're back to being ginger,' she said, because she couldn't bear to mention the injuries.

'Red's all the rage,' he joked. Seeing her concern, he waved his left hand. The fingers were dark with bruising but they hadn't been broken. 'I can still beat you at snooker.'

'What about poker?'

'I think I'll give poker a miss for a while.'

There was so much to ask, but Rhona knew he didn't want her to.

'So what happens now?'

'You go out there and enjoy your night. I head south. We meet in court as promised.'

Rhona wondered how he was getting to London, but it was best for him if nobody knew. Was he going to be safe?

'Petersson had a daughter,' she began. 'That's why—'

'It's OK. I know.'

She reached up and touched his cheek.

'He's a good guy, your Sean.'

'He's not *my* Sean,' she corrected him.

He smiled. 'Rhona MacLeod doesn't belong to anyone but herself.'

'Just like Detective Sergeant Michael Joseph McNab.'

She walked back to the bar where Sean was waiting. He handed her her topped-up glass.

'OK?'

'Better than OK.'

62

Sandy looked pleased with himself as he ran Bill through his findings.

'I isolated eight individual facial images. With a little help from an ageing programme, I came up with six matches on the sex offenders' database. Three had convictions for paedophile activity and the others were picked up for various sexual offences including male rape. The other two we're checking against the names you gave us.'

Bill nodded and motioned for him to continue.

'Location was also interesting. I compared the background to the images you supplied me from the MacLean case. I would swear it's the same room. Digitally converted, the wallpaper and curtains on the four-poster bed look the same.'

'In which film?'

'The old reel the girl found.'

'But it's in black and white?'

'Yeah, but the patterns are very distinctive. Add appropriate colour to the digital representation and it's the same place. There's other things too. Cornices, for example. Intricate and easily distinguishable one from the other. This one has a coat of arms woven into the pattern. Before digital photography it would have been impossible to blow it up enough to see that. Not any more.'

'You're saying shots in the Olympia film were taken in that room?'

'I am. There's other material too. Photographs from Nelson's collection, and another film, all shot in the same room. I take it you know where this room is?'

'I do.'

'Then someone died in that room.'

Bill had watched the film, or the digital version of it. He'd chosen to do it in the company of his team, as he wanted them to know just what they were dealing with. One guy had had to leave the room. DS Clark had soldiered on, but it hadn't been easy for any of them.

He'd got nothing further from Nelson. The mere mention of Gavin MacLean had shut him up, and this time Lord Dalrymple's name was met with a blank expression. Bill suspected Nelson's representation was being paid for by Dalrymple; he'd tried finding out but had met with another brick wall.

With forensic help Bill could place Nelson in the projection room of the Rosevale, but he couldn't prove Nelson knew anything about the body behind the wall; that crime would be laid at Gavin MacLean's door. But this? This was powerful material leading straight back to Dalrymple. Bill looked forward to seeing how Dalrymple would wriggle out of this one.

Sutherland had asked to be informed of any further developments in the MacLean case. Bill thought it was time he was told exactly what they'd found.

*   *   *

'This film is how many years old?'

'We don't know exactly, but—' Before he could give an estimate, Sutherland interrupted him.

'This is a very serious accusation you're making.'

'A girl died trying to bring this film to our attention, Sir.'

'We're not discussing Jude Evans' murder at the moment.'

Bill bit his tongue.

'If we intend to progress this, you must have ample proof for a conviction before the procurator fiscal's office will entertain it. I take it we haven't identified the victim in the film?'

'No, but we have identified members of the audience.'

'You intend charging them?'

'And the owner of the premises being used, Sir.'

'We've tried that before, Inspector. It didn't work.'

'It should have.'

Sutherland ignored him. 'Have you located this Brian Foster?'

'He died three years ago.'

'That's unfortunate.'

Sutherland actually sounded as though he meant it. Bill was nonplussed for a moment. He'd assumed Sutherland would do everything in his power to thwart any action against Dalrymple. Maybe he'd been wrong?

Sutherland moved to the window, his back to Bill. 'Contrary to what Mr Nelson may have said, I do not play golf with him. Neither do I spend any time in Lord Dalrymple's company that I can possibly avoid.'

Bill was taken aback by this sudden declaration and had

no idea how to respond. If it wasn't true, it meant the Super was already distancing himself from trouble.

'I'd go for Section 34 on this one, Detective Inspector. You're more likely to get a conviction.'

His superior officer was right, but it still stuck in Bill's craw.

As he made to leave, Sutherland called him back.

'What was the name of the newspaper man who blew the lid on the MacLean story the first time round?'

'Jim Connelly, Sir.'

'Better make sure no one talks to him about this.'

Was that a suggestion or a warning, Bill wondered as he made his way back to his office. If he'd read the interview correctly, Sutherland wanted Dalrymple charged under Section 34. And he didn't mind Jim Connelly finding out about it.

63

Bill handed Rhona her ticket and they passed through the turnstile.

'First class?' she said, impressed.

'Courtesy of the Met. It was the least they could do.'

'We're not sharing a coach with Slater, I hope?'

'He and Black have already given evidence.'

They found their seats and settled in. They hadn't seen each other since before she'd been to the Jazz Club. Only now did Rhona appreciate why Bill had worked so hard to get her there.

'When did you find out where McNab was?'

'About the same time as Chrissy, and an hour before you,' he told her.

'Sean came to see me the night we found Petersson. It must have been hard for him not to tell me then.'

'He was right not to.'

Rhona thought back to the care Sean had lavished on her that night and felt bad about how abrupt she'd been with him.

'What's happening about Petersson's murder?'

'That's Slater's department. As are Brogan's and Sinclair's. Slater thinks Lang has left Glasgow for London, but chances are he'll find him floating in the Thames soon too.'

The trolley came by and Bill ordered them drinks.

'Is this on the Met too?' she asked.

'No. This is on me.'

He produced an early edition of the *Evening Post* and pushed it towards her over the table.

'Something to toast Jim Connelly with.'

The front page headline read:

SNUFF MOVIE SHOT IN STATELY PILE

64

There were no shadows here to hide in.

Every swelling, bruise and cut were in full view. McNab kept his dark glasses on until he reached the witness box, then removed them, visibly shrinking from the brightness of the light. His eyes looked as though someone had tried to scoop them from their sockets.

Someone had.

McNab glanced up at the front row of the public gallery and raised his hand in a fist when he spotted her and Bill.

It took all Rhona's willpower not to give a cheer in return.

THE GLASGOW EVENING POST
Reporter: Jim Connelly

BACK FROM THE DEAD

The trial of Russian businessman Nikolai Kalinin took an astonishing turn today when a Scottish CID officer, Detective Sergeant Michael McNab, literally 'came back from the dead' to appear as chief witness for the prosecution. The officer had been gunned down earlier this year by person or persons unknown outside a poker club in Glasgow in a seeming effort to prevent him giving evidence. The Metropolitan Police subsequently kept his survival a secret to protect him. The witness appeared with severe facial injuries, said to be the result of yet another attempt on his life.

MUMMY'S TOMB SHOCK AT CINEMA

The discovery of mummified remains in the projection room of the Rosevale, once one of Glasgow's largest cinemas, reads like the script of a Hollywood film. The man's death has been linked to an earlier case where three young Glasgow males were mutilated and murdered in sexually motivated crimes by Gavin MacLean. MacLean had been an IT specialist at the time working for Strathclyde Police Force. He died before being brought to court.

FACEBOOK FRIENDS OUTFOX FORCE

Over 200,000 people go missing every year in the UK, but when Glasgow art student Jude Evans disappeared while photographing the Rosevale Cinema, her friends refused to give up the search for her. Although Jude's remains have not yet been found, due to the determined efforts of Liam Hope, Aurora Sermannis and Ben Howie, one Albert Nelson has been charged with her murder.

An exhibition of Jude's work entitled 'Glasgow – Cinema City' is to go on show shortly. The principal of Glasgow School of Art said, 'Jude's insertion of ghostlike figures into the stunning interiors of these derelict picture palaces gives a sense of just how important "going to the pictures" was to the people of Glasgow. This show will be a fitting tribute to her great talent.'

THE FALL OF THE HOUSE OF DALRYMPLE

The discovery, in a derelict Glasgow cinema, of an old film reel depicting sexual sadism has led to the unearthing of a library of similar images, all shot here in Cinema City over a period of fifty years or more.

Embroiled in this story is the wealthy and influential Lord James Dalrymple. A former rent boy named Neil MacGregor has come forward with evidence linking these films with both the Gavin MacLean case and the ancestral seat of the Dalrymples. Lord Dalrymple yesterday declined to comment, but calls are already being made to strip him of his title.